THE HUNTER & THE HEIRESS

CLAIRE DELACROIX

DEBORAH A. COOKE

The Hunter & the Heiress
By Claire Delacroix

Cover by Teresa Spreckelmeyer of The Midnight Muse Designs

❀ Created with Vellum

MORE BOOKS BY CLAIRE DELACROIX

UNICORN BRIDE

PEARL BEYOND PRICE

Rogues & Angels

ONE KNIGHT ENCHANTED

ONE KNIGHT'S RETURN

Time Travel Romances

ONCE UPON A KISS

THE LAST HIGHLANDER

THE MOONSTONE

LOVE POTION #9

The Bride Quest

THE PRINCESS

THE DAMSEL

THE HEIRESS

THE COUNTESS

THE BEAUTY

THE TEMPTRESS

The Rogues of Ravensmuir

THE ROGUE

THE SCOUNDREL

THE WARRIOR

The Jewels of Kinfairlie

THE BEAUTY BRIDE

THE ROSE RED BRIDE

THE SNOW WHITE BRIDE

The Ballad of Rosamunde

The True Love Brides

THE RENEGADE'S HEART

THE HIGHLANDER'S CURSE

THE FROST MAIDEN'S KISS

THE WARRIOR'S PRIZE

The Brides of Inverfyre

THE MERCENARY'S BRIDE

THE RUNAWAY BRIDE

The Champions of St. Euphemia

THE CRUSADER'S BRIDE

THE CRUSADER'S HEART

THE CRUSADER'S KISS

THE CRUSADER'S VOW

THE CRUSADER'S HANDFAST

The Brides of North Barrows

Something Wicked This Way Comes

A Duke By Any Other Name

A Baron for All Seasons

A Most Inconvenient Earl

Blood Brothers

THE WOLF & THE WITCH

THE HUNTER & THE HEIRESS

Short Stories and Novellas

An Elegy for Melusine

BLOOD BROTHERS

A MEDIEVAL SCOTTISH ROMANCE SERIES

The three sons of a notorious mercenary should never have met...but now that they are sworn allies, the Scottish Borders will never be the same...

1. **The Wolf & the Witch**
(Maximilian and Alys)

2. **The Hunter & the Heiress**
(Amaury and Elizabeth)

3. **The Dragon & the Damsel**
(Rafael and Ceara)

4. **The Scot & the Sorceress**
(Murdoch and Nyssa)

~

THE HUNTER & THE HEIRESS

DEAR READER

The Hunter & the Heiress is the second book in my *Blood Brothers* series of medieval romances, in which the heroes are all sons of a notorious mercenary. **The Wolf & the Witch**, book one in the series, is Maximilian de Vries' story—the oldest of the sons, Maximilian was the most likely to be his father's heir. When he is not, he returns to Scotland to a holding called Kilderrick that he seized in his father's name years before. Once he learns that the daughter of the house survived that attack and lives in the forest with a group of women believed to be witches, Maximilian—also known as the Silver Wolf—is convinced they should wed. Alys, who blames this mercenary for the loss of so much, disagrees and their battle of wills ensues.

When I first planned the *Blood Brothers* series, I didn't include the story of Amaury, the son who is astonished to learn of his parentage at the mercenary's funeral. Raised in privilege, Amaury is a knight and utterly unlike his mercenary half-brothers. When his inheritance is swept away from him, though, he has more in common with Maximilian than he would prefer and joins the company destined for Scotland. He becomes the hunter for Kilderrick, ensuring that the ever-growing company has enough to eat, but knows he didn't train for years to become a knight only to serve as a huntsman. His one consolation is the sight of a noblewoman who lives with the women in the woods. Amaury recognizes Elizabeth as someone from the world he misses. He also is struck by her beauty. With one glimpse, he surrenders his heart, and when Elizabeth is abducted, Amaury knows it is his knightly duty to rescue this damsel in distress.

The Hunter & the Heiress begins with that pursuit and rescue. This story was great fun to write because Amaury and Elizabeth's perspectives seem to be completely at odds. Amaury insists upon the merit of logic, particularly when it comes to marriage, and is much concerned with responsibility. He is convinced that Elizabeth's uncle must have made a good match for her and insists that she fulfill that pledge to her betrothed. Elizabeth trusts her instincts and is mightily annoyed by this inscrutable knight who will compel her to act against her own desires in the name of duty. Amaury recognizes quickly that Elizabeth holds love in high esteem, and concludes that he must hide his own feelings from her. He is determined to protect her and deliver her to safety, but cannot offer more: without a holding or an income, he believes he can't take a wife. Their battle of wills is entirely different from that of Maximilian and Alys, as Elizabeth tries to find the heart in her defender who is seemingly wrought of stone. Elizabeth has endured a great deal and distrusts men, but since Amaury apparently has no desire for her and is entirely principled, she trusts him—that allows her to heal and regain her confidence. I loved watching her blossom from a fearful maiden to a woman unafraid to speak her mind, and to see Amaury fall more deeply in love as she challenged each and every one of his convictions of how women should be. I hope you find their romance as potent as I do.

The Hunter & the Heiress, like **The Wolf & the Witch**, is available in ebook, trade paperback and a hardcover collectors' edition. As I write this, the audiobook is being recorded by Tim Campbell and I know he'll deliver another wonderful performance. Next in the series will be Rafael's book, **The Dragon & the Damsel**, coming this fall. Rafael is a mercenary who specializes in Greek fire, a weapon mentioned often in medieval treatises and feared mightily. Its formulation was a closely guarded secret, and scholars still aren't certain what it contained. I always like heroes who have secrets, and this is only one of Rafael's. He has already crossed swords with Ceara, another of the women who took shelter with Alys, and Ceara was triumphant. Rafael isn't the kind of man who forgets either a slight or an intriguing and beautiful woman. Ceara certainly isn't interested in being claimed or tamed. You'll get a glimpse of Ceara at the end of this book and the past she has left behind. I'm looking forward to writing their story. Pre-orders are available at some portals for Rafael's book—you'll find links at the end of this book or on the landing page of my website for **The Dragon & the Damsel**. The fourth book in the series will be **The Scot & the Sorceress**, Murdoch and Nyssa's story, but I'll tell you more about that next time.

You can, as always, find additional resources on my website. There is a list of characters in the series, which is updated after each book. I have a Pinterest page for the series—there's a link on the ***Blood Brothers tab*** on my website—which is a work-in-progress and will give you a glimpse of my inspiration. There are also a number of blog posts, linked on each book's landing page, about my research for the series.

And of course, you can sign up for my medieval romance newsletter, ***Knights & Rogues***, to receive an alert when I have a new release, and to hear my news as well as any special offers or sales. There's a link on my website under the *Newsletter* tab. You can also follow me at many portals—those links are on the **About Claire** page.

Until next time, I hope you have plenty of good books to read.

All my best

Claire

http://delacroix.net

CHAPTER 1

Annandale, Scotland—November 26, 1375.

Captive, again.

It was thoroughly vexing.

To Elizabeth's thinking, she had endured more than her share of men and their earthly demands. If this grim pair of warriors, who had seized her from Kilderrick against her will, believed that she would cede readily to any demands, she would compel them to reconsider the matter. She would take a lesson from Alys Armstrong, who had granted her shelter for the better part of a year, and surrender only what she wished to give.

These two would have nothing, even if the price of defiance was her life.

Enough.

Elizabeth ached from head to toe; she was soaked to the skin, chilled to her marrow, hungry and uncomfortable. Only anger—and the inspiration of Alys—kept her from yielding to the temptation of closing her eyes and never opening them again. Once, she would have ceased to fight, but no longer.

Not long ago, she had been weak, but Alys had fought back and earned an enviable love, as well as a devoted husband. That was more than sufficient inspiration to make a change.

Fortune's smile, it was clear, had to be earned.

It had been almost a year since Elizabeth had fled Beaupoint, her beloved childhood home. Upon her father's death, her uncle had claimed the holding and Elizabeth's fate had changed. Uncle James had made an agreement for Elizabeth to be wed to Calum Moffatt—against her own desires. Her uncle refused to break the agreement despite her protest, so Elizabeth had fled Beaupoint. She had thought to make a protest, to take refuge in the next town, but she had erred. Elizabeth had been seized by reivers, and ultimately saved by Alys, only to live in the forest without comforts. Now, she was seized again, but no longer meek or accepting of her fate.

One lesson she had taken in this past year was that men had little in common with the honorable knights in the troubadours' tales—well, save for one. Her heart warmed in memory of Amaury de Vries, the handsome warrior who had arrived at Kilderrick with the *Loup Argent*. He had brought her a hot meal after she had sheltered his lost peregrine falcon. Later, he had carried her to safety when she had fallen in the forest. She had been afraid of his expectations, but he had treated her with courtesy. Was he different or had he been biding his time? It mattered little, for she was unlikely to ever see him again.

In hindsight, Elizabeth regretted never speaking to him, not even when he had sat vigil outside her hut at Kilderrick. She would never forget his silhouette as he guarded the door, silent and as likely to move as a great rock.

Had he guessed that she found his presence reassuring?

Given a second chance, she would do better, she vowed. She would be bold and speak to him. But that eventuality seemed unlikely in this moment. She might not have much of a future at all, unless she could escape her captors. Elizabeth had nothing left to lose, which bolstered her determination to fight.

These two scoundrels were dirtier than most of the men she had encountered in the past year, which said little good in their favor. They were roughly dressed, unshaven and crude in their habits. If one of them spat again, she might find a way to kick him. Their speech was rude and foul, though Elizabeth pretended she could not understand their Gaelic. She had overheard their plan, though. They meant to deliver her to Caerlaverock and collect the bounty Calum Moffatt offered for the return of his betrothed.

Thus far, avarice had kept any lust in check. She did not expect that situation to last, even in her current sorry state. Such men could not be particular about female companionship.

Elizabeth was slung over a pony's back, ankles bound together with rough rope, hands tied behind her own back, gagged to silence with her hair falling loose to obscure her view.

She would be delivered like a filthy sack of grain.

She wondered whether that would influence Calum's interest in the match.

Of course, all was about Beaupoint. What a marvel it would be for someone to have interest in her for her own self, but Elizabeth would not hold her breath waiting for that moment.

It had begun to rain just after they had left Kilderrick. As the evening fell and the skies darkened, the rain became colder. The onslaught was turning to sleet, tinkling in the trees, drumming against Elizabeth's wet back. One man rode with her, the weight of his massive hand upon her back to steady her. The other rode his pony close enough that her head bumped the beast's flank on occasion, though neither captor noticed.

The ponies were as dirty as their riders, their flanks caked with mud, their manes and tails tangled. Doubtless there were vermin living in their fur, for they were not well tended at all. She could feel the bones of this one's spine, rubbing against her own ribs, for her captor rode without a saddle.

They were barbarians.

She recalled Amaury's destrier, a chestnut stallion with a white star on his brow, and even the memory lifted her heart. The horse had been brushed to a gleam even when the knight rode to hunt, glossy with good health. *There* was a horse. He was pampered and fed well, brushed down and tended like the prize he was.

She remembered her first sight of Amaury in Kilderrick's autumn sunlight, his falcon on his fist, the reins in his other hand, his every move filled with purpose. He had been garbed simply, in dark clothes with a chain mail hauberk and boots, but only a knight could possess a horse of such splendor—his spurs revealed the truth. The mercenaries might steal such a horse, but they would never ride to hunt as Amaury did. The sight had reminded Elizabeth of former days, of her lost life and sacrificed dreams, and she had felt an odd kinship with the handsome stranger—before fear had made her flee.

She would be timid no longer.

Her captors began to argue about the best route to Caerlaverock while she had a wondrous view of the muddy path. If her belly had not been so empty, she might have been ill from the motion. Hunger, in this case, was a blessing.

"I told you we should have taken the larger road," said the one riding behind her. He was blond and the other was dark, but there was little other difference in their appearance. They both had bushy dark beards. "'Tis more direct and thus quicker than following the coast. We should have been within sight of the keep by now, instead of miles away and deep in mud. We might be by the fire, our reward in our purses and ale in our cups, instead of riding ever onward in rain and darkness."

The ponies' hooves made a sucking sound in the mud and Elizabeth could smell the familiar salt-tinged breeze from the firth. Beloved Beaupoint, on the opposite side of the firth, could have been as distant as Jerusalem itself.

"Oh, aye, and there would not have been a soul on that busy thoroughfare who would have questioned the woman's presence? Not a one who would ask why we carried a bound noblewoman as our captive?" His companion was sarcastic. Elizabeth had already noticed that he believed himself to be the clever one.

"No one would know she was nobly born. We could say she was a runaway slave."

"With golden embroidery upon the hem of her dress," scoffed the other.

"It could have been a cast-off from a former mistress. Or stolen. 'Tis so dirty and worn that no one would take note of it."

"You have less respect for keen eyes than I do," said the companion. "We should have found ourselves before a sheriff by now, if not in some laird's dungeon, obliged to give an accounting of the situation. You may be sure that she, given the chance to speak, would spin a tale that made us villains in truth."

"We are scarcely innocent," ceded the first after a moment's pause. "We did steal her from Kilderrick."

"We are *collecting* her," corrected the second, his tone stern. "We are delivering her to her nuptials, that she might fulfil her guardian's pledge and wed Calum Moffatt. Collecting a bounty is honest labor and marriage agreements are binding upon all parties. If she is in discomfort, it is her own fault for trying to evade her duty."

Elizabeth narrowed her eyes in annoyance. She tired of talk of duty, to be sure. Men were vermin, all of them. They took what they desired, forced their decisions upon all, then blamed women for the result.

"How did she come to be in Kilderrick?" mused the first. "That is a long way from her uncle's holding. Beaupoint is west of Carlisle, across the firth."

"And therein lies its value. Whoever holds Beaupoint can watch traffic on the water. Perhaps they mean to take a toll from those who would use the old weths." The one who thought himself clever chuckled. "The Moffatts are no fools, to be sure. Calum would advance their fortunes with such a match, building their influence."

"I do not understand."

"Because you know naught of English politics. The old Lord de Beaupoint was Warden of the West March on their side of the border. It is a position of power and influence, but also one that would offer many opportunities for a reiving family like the Moffatts."

"What manner of opportunities?"

"Sanctuary, if naught else."

"But how did she come to be at Kilderrick?"

"Perhaps she stole a horse," said the other with impatience. "Perhaps she had another aid her escape. It matters little. What is of import is that we have her and we will collect the bounty. It will see us settled for the rest of our days and nights."

The first one laughed. "Aye! I will claim that hut on Islay and take the MacGregor's lass to wife..."

"You should be so lucky for her to accept you," the other retorted, pulling his pony to a halt. "Is this not the River Annan?" His companion stopped beside him and Elizabeth could see water flowing around the ponies' hooves. Drops fell into the darkness in a steady pattern. The tide was in, by the depth of the water.

"Aye, it must be, though I have not crossed it so close to the firth before." The first man, whose hand still rested on Elizabeth's back, sighed. "You are one to risk the water at high tide, given your family's fondness for swimming." He said this as if it was an incomprehensible habit. "But I have not the taste for it in the dark. There is nary a slice of moon this night!"

"There are clouds," the other noted with disdain. "No moon shines through clouds so thick as these."

"There are times when the moon does shine through the clouds..."

"But the darkness aided our escape," said the other. "And that cannot be worthy of objection."

"Aye, there is that."

"And better yet, if this is the Annan, then the old keep is upstream and abandoned. We might take shelter there and arrive at Caerlaverock at first light." Of course, that one knew more. Elizabeth fancied that he believed he knew all.

"There is an old keep?" asked the other.

Even Elizabeth felt a tweak of interest at even the possibility of dry shelter. Could these two kindle a fire?

Would she be able to escape them?

Or would they assault her? She halfway wished they would ride on, but no one—as usual—asked for her view.

"The de Brus family built it years past. My father used to talk of it. They built it tall and fine, a motte-and-bailey, but the river changed course and it flooded. They built Lochmaben further upriver instead. Come along. It cannot be far, for they used to defend the river near the firth." He, of course, knew the entire history of Annan and began to recount it. He turned his pony and rode to the right as he talked, Elizabeth's captor following.

They had not ridden a dozen steps when a bird called in the forest behind them. Elizabeth's heart stopped at the familiarity of the cry.

It was a falcon. She knew it well.

Just as she knew no falcons would breed in this lowland. There was no keep for miles, and no cause for a nobleman to hunt at this hour in such foul weather.

Hope made her heart skip a beat.

Her captor halted his pony and glanced back. "What was that?" he whispered.

"A bird," said the other with disdain. "Have you lost your wits in the dark?"

"It sounded fearsome."

The other scoffed, drawing further ahead of them. "A thrush cannot sound fierce."

"It could have been a crow," said the first, touching his heels to his pony's side so that he rode alongside his companion. They both quickened the pace of their mounts. "Or a raven come to tear our innards or peck out our eyes."

"A thrush," insisted the other, his tone dismissive even as he urged his pony onward.

But it was not a thrush, Elizabeth knew. Neither was it a crow or a raven. That had been the cry of a peregrine falcon. And the sole man she knew in the vicinity who rode with a hunting falcon was Amaury de Vries.

Could he be riding to her aid, following the villains, like the hero in a tale? Could he be a knight in the trade of aiding damsels in distress?

Or would he seek a reward of his own for doing her such service?

AMAURY RODE relentlessly in pursuit of the fiends who had captured the lady who held his heart. He did not know this land and he did not comprehend the native tongue, but he no longer cared. Indeed, the abduction of Elizabeth d'Acron was a gift in an odd way: it gave him a quest. He could not stand back and let her be stolen and possibly abused, especially given his conviction that she had endured much already.

And that gave him purpose. Every champion in every tale had a quest and Amaury would not fail in the completion of this one.

Even better, his noble quest took him from beneath Maximilian's thumb.

Amaury had ridden to Scotland in partnership with his half-brother, but not out of any true desire to do as much. He had never wished to ally himself with mercenaries and less ambition to abide in this hostile northern land. But, abruptly disavowed by the man he had believed to be his father, left with only his steed, his dogs, his hawk and the garb upon his back, Amaury had not known what to do. No holding, no coin and no alliance meant he had no means to survive.

Save following his half-brother, Maximilian.

He had let emotion guide his choice, momentarily forgetting to let duty and honor be his guide. He had impulsively accepted Maximilian's suggestion, shaken by Gaston's betrayal.

He knew now that he should have ridden to his uncle's abode, Château d'Evroi, and pledged himself to that man's service.

Just as Uncle Raymond always insisted, emotion led a man astray.

Amaury would never forget that again.

Of course, it had been a negotiation with Maximilian. For a mercenary like *the Loup Argent*, no agreement was about honor or justice, or even familial loyalty: it was solely about the exchange of advantage. Amaury was a competent hunter and that meant he was useful to Maximilian's party. Every company had to eat and Maximilian had—as ever—strategic reasons for making the offer.

But Amaury had not trained for a decade to earn his spurs then spent fifteen years winning tournaments to become a huntsman, providing for the table of Maximilian's remote Scottish abode. He tired of owing all to his half-brother—and he knew that a lifetime of service would not set him free from this bond.

Amaury had resolved to leave before the maiden had been abducted. The rescue of Elizabeth gave him the opportunity to leave Kilderrick as well as to fulfill a knightly duty—and no one knew yet that he had no intention of going back.

The unfortunate fact was that he and Oliver, the squire granted to his service by Maximilian, were hours behind the lady and her captors. Amaury knew they might fail. He could arrive too late.

He might already be too late.

He had to succeed for the sake of the maiden who had snared his heart with a glance. Elizabeth was so lovely, so undefended, so very gentle. In another time or place, he might have offered for her hand himself, but Amaury understood his lack of prospects all too well.

Even destitute, she deserved better than he could offer—but he could nobly serve her and ensure her welfare. That was a knight's choice.

He gave Zephyr his spurs, oblivious to the cold slant of rain or the mud splashing under the stallion's hooves. His dogs ran alongside him, Grise and Noisette on his left and Bête on his right, tongues lolling as they kept the pace. Persephone perched on his fist, hooded, her jesses tight in his grip. Oliver rode behind Amaury on one palfrey, leading two more with Amaury's considerable baggage. The rain pounded down upon them, soaking them all, as they rode in grim silence.

Darkness had fallen by the time Amaury found the trail.

He had guessed the captors would take the coastal road, for it was less traveled, and he nodded with satisfaction at the hoofprints in the mud that proved him right.

"Is it them?" Oliver asked.

Amaury nodded. "Not far ahead, by all appearances." The imprint was so clear in the mud that he knew a pony had stood in that spot recently. He listened but could discern no sound. He could not see them either no matter how intently he peered into the shadows.

"Then we have caught up," the boy said. "How? They were far ahead of us."

His suspicion was not undeserved.

"Their ponies might be slow."

The squire nodded, his gaze flicking. He had hunted with Amaury at Kilderrick and was keenly observant. "I do not hear them," he confessed.

"Nor do I, yet they cannot be far." Amaury considered his surroundings. The lady's captors had halted, it appeared, before a river that wound down to the firth. Evidently, they had considered their options, for the ponies overstepped their tracks, as if held in one place for a while. They had to have debated their course. By all accounts, Caerlaverock lay ahead, further west along the coast of the firth. What was located upstream, on this river? Amaury could not see a glimmer of light.

"Why halt here at all?" Oliver asked.

"'Twas an odd choice," Amaury said, surveying the river. "They could have readily forded the river here." He turned back to the boy. "Were we not told that Caerlaverock was close to the water as well?"

Oliver nodded. "Perhaps they sought shelter."

That offered little good for the lady's prospects, unless there was a town or a tavern—but that would make it harder to aid her escape. The tracks from the ponies led to the right, following the riverbank as it rose to the north.

Amaury set the dogs upon the trail and it took Bête only a moment to find the scent. The big black dog trotted back and forth, nose to the ground, tail wagging in the excitement of the hunt. He was the largest of Amaury's dogs and the best tracker. When Bête disappeared into the shadows on the right, Noisette was close behind him. She was a sleek brown female of sweet disposition and the youngest of the three. Grise trotted alongside Zephyr, her long grey fur so wet that it was slick to her body, alert as ever. She spared Amaury a glance, her bushy eyebrows so expressive that he almost could guess her thoughts.

Aye, a fire and a bowl of stew would be most welcome, but Amaury knew they were unlikely to find either soon.

What if he succeeded in this quest? He might be spared a coin for finding the lady. He might find another mission thereafter, earning his way back to France by following the principles he admired instead of those of a mercenary pursuing only his own advantage. But in the rain and darkness, the world he knew seemed very far away.

They followed the tracks in silence, Bête cantering in front, Oliver behind. The dog stopped suddenly, growling as the hair bristled on his neck, and Amaury slowed his horse.

Ahead of them, on a mount, was what looked like a ruin. Even in the poor light, he could see that it was large, with considerable earthworks and a moat both broad and deep. Amaury had a moment to wonder how they would enter a fortress and what tale they might tell before he realized that the palisades were broken or missing around the bailey. The design was that of a motte-and-bailey: there must have once been a central mound with a palisade around it, then a bailey, also fenced, surrounding that. The moats were deep on the eastern side, evidence of the earth that had been moved to build the mounds, but the barriers had vanished on the river side, on the left.

Was it abandoned?

Amaury might have thought that the villains had ridden onward, but he smelled the sharp tang of smoke.

Someone strove to light a fire within the ruins of the motte.

The possibility of success rose slightly.

He exchanged a glance with Oliver, who shrugged. The boy did not know the land either or evidently the name of this place. A motte-and-bailey was usually built with just one entry since it was a defensive structure. Amaury could only hope this one followed the usual plan. He motioned to Oliver to remain behind him and called back the dogs with a murmured command.

The party rode silently and slowly into the old bailey, peering into the shadows lest there be opposition. There was none. The wooden palisade remained only on the right side, and even there, it was broken down in some places with entire sections missing. On the left, there was no barricade, only a cliff and the sound of the river. The ground was broken, as if the protective wall had been washed away by a flood.

What had happened to the occupants? Amaury saw no signs of fire, no stains from copious blood.

The bailey was simply empty.

It must once have been round and of goodly size, with palisades all around it, that moat dug deep to encircle it. It would have had a pleasing symmetry and been imposing upon the bank. But the river had stolen the western side of it. The people and the laird who had built it must have moved elsewhere, taking what they could.

It was eerie to ride down what had once been the road from the gate of the bailey to the gate of the keep on the mound. The horses' footfalls seemed unnaturally loud, though the sound of the rain hid any evidence of their arrival from another. Amaury glimpsed hearthstones and thatched pallets within the shadows of the huts that remained. He heard the scuttle of small wild creatures, roused by the presence of the dogs, but rode steadily toward the motte.

When they approached the steep path to the motte, Amaury spied a thin ribbon of smoke rising ahead. He heard the guttural laughter of two men and knew he had found his prey.

There was a larger hut to one side of what had been a road and it was in better condition than most. Amaury rode into it, struck by the size of the portal, then the smell of ash and iron told him that it must have been the smithy. The dogs circled and sat at his gesture, Bête quivering to continue the pursuit, Grise less enthusiastic but attentive. Noisette sat for only a moment, then curled up in a ball in a corner, eyes open. Amaury knew she would leap to her feet at his gesture, should he give it.

"You will remain here while I see what transpires." Amaury dismounted and surrendered the hawk to Oliver, who took her on his fist. The boy brushed the rain from Persephone's feathers and found her a perch where she shook. Then he tethered the reins of Zephyr, rubbed the stallion's nose that he might be silent, and waited in the shadows, as diligent and attentive as any squire Amaury had known.

In the darkness, preparing to confront two villains who were likely inclined to violence, Amaury regretted the gaps in his knowledge.

"Remind me of all we know," he invited Oliver in an undertone.

The boy folded his hands behind his back, as if reciting a lesson, but kept his voice to a murmur. "The lady is Elizabeth d'Acron. The king said she fled an arranged marriage with Calum Moffatt, a match made after her father's demise by his brother and heir. The king said also that the lady had been raised at Beaupoint, on the south coast of the firth. Calum has offered a reward for the delivery of his betrothed to Caerlaverock."

Amaury nodded, for this was what he recalled as well. The lady was English and noble, thus the arrangement of her marriage. "Is Calum the lord of this Caerlaverock?"

Oliver frowned. The boy was tall and slender, having seen perhaps sixteen summers. He had ridden with Maximilian in the Compagnie Rouge and obviously had earned Maximilian's respect, for he had been included in the smaller group headed for Scotland. Most of the Compagnie Rouge had remained on the continent. "No one said as much, sir."

"Nay. No one did. And that tempts me to believe he is not." It also revealed that Beaupoint could not be a rich holding or of much value in itself. If the lady was an heiress, it was not to great riches. "Why then has he a desire for a noble bride? Was his lineage her objection to the match?"

Oliver shrugged. "Then why would her guardian have arranged it? The man must have some asset."

"One she does not see."

"Perhaps she wished to choose a husband for herself."

"Perhaps. I doubt as much." Amaury was dismissive of this. "Noble women wed whomever they are told to wed, at least the first time. There must be some detail about Calum Moffatt, one that her guardian thought irrelevant but which changed all for the lady."

"Perhaps he is unattractive or aged."

This time, Amaury shrugged. It was possible, but seemed a feeble reason to flee the luxuries of her father's home and live in the forests of Kilderrick, without any comforts at all. He had noticed that the lady's clothing had once been fine. He reviewed the exchange with the king and did not think that man took this Calum's side in the matter either. The king would not have directed Amaury to Caerlaverock if so. It must be a matter of politics and alliances, another matter about which he knew little. "Perhaps she has no legacy herself and the match was made where it could be."

Oliver nodded agreement.

"What do we know of her captors?"

"Precious little," the boy replied. "They are two, having arrived in Kilderrick in the company of Godfroy Macdonald. They abandoned his cause when they seized the lady."

"Tempted by the reward promised by Calum Moffatt," Amaury murmured. "That is simple enough."

Oliver cleared his throat. "May I ask your intention, sir?"

"To rescue the lady, of course."

"And after that, sir?"

Amaury turned to confront the squire. Oliver had straight brown hair that hung to his collar and eyes of such a clear hue of green that they seemed to glow. Amaury always felt that the boy's gaze was uncanny, as if he could read the thoughts of others. He also found the boy more outspoken than squires previously of his acquaintance—in another time and place, he might have called it insolent. No doubt the boy had learned this attitude in Maximilian's service, where rules were more lax than a noble court.

"Why?" he asked, his tone discouraging a confession.

Oliver was not daunted. He surveyed the palfreys loaded with baggage. "You have brought all you possess, sir. All your baggage. All your hounds. All your armor. Even the peregrine, though it is not good for such a creature to be abroad in such weather when there is no promise of shelter and warmth ahead." He confronted Amaury, fairly challenging him. "I suspect you did not leave so much as a pin behind at Kilderrick."

In truth, Amaury had not. "And so?" he invited, wondering how much the boy would say.

"I fear that you do not intend to return there, even in triumph."

"There would be no triumph in returning to Kilderrick. There I am no more than a huntsman obliged to serve the *Loup Argent*."

Oliver held Amaury's gaze steadily. "Where, then?"

Amaury glanced toward the shelter. "'Tis not the time for such discussion."

"On the contrary, 'tis an ideal time for such discussion," the squire countered with the audacity that still caught Amaury unawares. He was accustomed to squires being silent and obedient. "I am pledged to the service of the *Loup Argent*," Oliver continued. "Thus, while I am assigned to serve you on this quest, my fate is not yours to determine. Further, it would be a wise strategy for you to ensure that I will defend your back."

"What else would you do?" Amaury asked, startled by this blunt discussion.

"I might return to Kilderrick as soon as your attention is diverted, of course. I might return the palfreys to my commander and tell him you had ridden onward." The boy held Amaury's gaze in challenge.

"I would call that disloyalty and a betrayal."

Oliver smiled, something in his expression reminding Amaury of Maximilian. "Another might call it prudent," he said without remorse. "Unless I know your plan and find it compelling, I cannot pledge that I will remain and aid in it." He bowed his head slightly, aware that he had been sufficiently outspoken to astonish Amaury. "Sir."

Amaury felt a surge of irritation that he was to be reminded in this moment that he did not even have a squire and that this one could desert him by choice at any moment. He reminded himself that emotion was no good master.

What inducement could he offer for Oliver to stay?

He could reply to the boy's question and not much else.

"I mean to rescue the lady," he repeated tightly.

"And then?"

"I will escort her to Caerlaverock that she might wed her betrothed as promised."

"And then?"

Amaury felt that his own plan sounded foolish when uttered aloud. "And then I will find another quest and another, until I earn sufficient coin to pay my passage back to France."

The boy's brows rose. "I thought you meant to claim the lady yourself."

"I have nothing to offer a lady of good birth." *Yet,* Amaury amended silently. He had need of an heiress, even if he did find Elizabeth most alluring. His situation demanded practicality, much as he might have wished otherwise. "She should wed this Calum Moffatt, as was arranged. It is her duty."

"Your admiration was undisguised."

"Marriage is not a matter of sentiment," Amaury chided. "And I would not dishonor the lady with any other suggestion."

Oliver nodded slowly. "And me?"

"You may do as you wish. I have need of at least one squire, but will find another if you prefer Kilderrick's charms." He doubted he would find another squire in these parts, but he would not owe more to Maximilian than he already did. He would manage somehow. "I would ask you to remain with me until this lady is safe, if that is not too much of a request." Oliver said nothing at all. "I intended to discuss this with you after the lady's safety was assured. I assumed you would not ride this far without witnessing the resolution of the tale."

"Indeed, sir, I would not. I do, however, prefer to have matters clear." He had learned that from Maximilian, as well.

"And once the lady's welfare is assured?"

"I will return to Kilderrick, sir. I have no inclination to return to France, ever."

Amaury wondered at the boy's conviction but his steady gaze did not invite more questions. Truly, being raised by mercenaries had left Oliver without social graces that Amaury understood—and the boy's choices, once their ways parted, were scarcely his concern. "You may leave now, if that suits you better."

"Nay, sir. I will linger as the *Loup Argent* would expect as much." Oliver inclined his head slightly, even Amaury was a little galled that his brother's expectation would trump his own, even at such a distance. "I have your falcon, sir, and will protect your possessions." His hand dropped to the dagger on his belt. "And I will guard your back."

For the moment. That implication was clear.

They tethered the palfreys in the shelter, working swiftly together as if they were comrades rather than knight and squire. If Amaury had stood aside, as once had been his habit, the tasks would have taken too long, and the lady's welfare was tantamount.

Amaury took his crossbow and a fistful of bolts, loading one. He commanded the dogs to remain where they were and they settled in place, though Bête's nose still quivered.

Then he left the smithy, climbing the muddy trail to the gates to the motte, aware of the weight of Oliver's gaze. He glanced back once, verifying that his small company remained hidden from view. All he could see was the gleam of Bête's eyes in the darkness, but it could have been a wolf taking shelter from the elements.

Another wolf howled in the distance as if to reinforce that thought.

There had been plenty of them near Kilderrick and that holding was not so distant as that. It was a savage land, to be sure.

It was no place for him. The sooner he completed this quest, the sooner he could take another—and the sooner he would return to familiarity.

This night, he would hunt.

CHAPTER 2

Two men argued in the darkness ahead, though Amaury could not understand their words. The rain slanted down, making the climb to the motte most slippery. It also disguised small sounds. He reached the summit, hiding in the shadows on the right beside the remnant of the wooden palisade. On the left, the motte was undefended, with the lip of a cliff overhanging the flowing water.

There was one decrepit structure ahead on the far side of the clearing, a fire burning fitfully before it. The shadows within were impenetrable, making him fear for the lady's situation. The two captors were silhouetted before the fire, and it was clear they disputed some matter. Their agitated conversation covered any slight sound of approach, but Amaury moved slowly all the same. He eased into the shadows on the inside of the palisade, taking advantage of their inattention to move closer.

Two ponies were tethered partway along the palisade, their pale rumps gleaming in the darkness. They had been left in the rain, which was no kindness to a creature. That also meant they could likely be encouraged to flee. Amaury eased behind them, stroking the side of the closest one to soothe it. The creature blew out its lips and nickered, but did not shy. Amaury crouched behind the ponies to watch the men.

The pair of warriors were burly, dressed like those who had accompanied Godfrey in furs and boiled leather. Their beards and hair were long—one was dark and one fair—and they were of formidable size. Each had multiple knives on his belt. They stood before their fire warming their hands, claiming all the heat it generated as they bickered.

Amaury could guess the subject of their dispute, but he could not see the lady.

Surely, they had not killed her or cast her over the cliff? Nay, nay, she was worth more to them alive than dead. But still, once he had the thought, Amaury could not readily dismiss it—or the uneasiness it fed within him.

The fair man poked the other with a heavy hand, then pointed back into the shadows of the structure. The dark-haired man shook his head, his voice rising as he made his point. He also gestured toward the shelter. Amaury peered into the shadows there, wondering whether he discerned any movement. The lady had to be there. There was no other place she might be hidden.

And they argued about...what? Her fate? Her location? Who would savor her first? Curse his inability to understand them!

They raised their voices yet more in annoyance with each other.

Whatever the root of their dispute, Amaury had to believe that one or both of the captors had realized that all the coin would be better than half of it.

Could he feed their inevitable distrust of each other?

If so, the odds of his triumph would be vastly improved, but without speaking their tongue, that was unlikely.

Nay, he would simply have to eliminate them, one at a time.

He watched closely, his bow at the ready, awaiting his opportunity.

THE ROPE finally began to fray.

Elizabeth sat against the outer wall of the wooden shelter where she had been dropped, grateful to be both off the pony and out of the rain. She was yet more relieved to have spotted a sharp stone and managed to move so it was hidden behind her. She braced it against the wall and sawed the rope that bound her wrists against it as hard as she could without revealing what she did. Her cold hands were numb but she dared not stop.

She had to have been wrong about the falcon, for no one followed them into the ruined keep. She had only herself to rely upon, so she had to work her hands free. The rope was thick and the knot tight, but she persisted.

Her two captors had lit a fire and now argued beside it. The fair one had not wanted to stop at all, but the dark-haired one had been adamant. It seemed he had ideas about her that the first did not find acceptable.

"She must be a maiden when delivered," insisted the fair one who had ridden with her. "Lest the bounty be sacrificed."

"Who would know?" demanded his companion.

"She would tell."

"And who would believe her? They already know that she fled the match. She is scarcely a willing bride and might seize on any excuse." The dark-haired one cast a glance over his shoulder toward Elizabeth, one so lustful that her heart skipped a beat. She froze, then when he smiled and turned back to his companion, she rubbed the rope against the stone with greater vigor.

She might not be able to escape, but she had to be able to fight back. Desperation gave her strength.

"I think it a bad idea."

"I do not care." The dark-haired one gave the other a prod in the shoulder. "I will take what I desire and you will follow. No one will know the difference."

"I think it folly," insisted the fair-haired one.

"Because you are a coward," charged the other with disdain. He turned toward Elizabeth then, ogling her, and missed the flash of anger in the eyes of his companion.

"You will cost us all!"

"And you will deny us a ride," the dark-haired one had time to say before his companion seized his shoulder. He was spun around, his fair-haired warrior's fist collided with his nose, and he staggered backward in shock.

The pair froze, staring at each other. The dark-haired one raised a hand to his face in apparent disbelief and Elizabeth saw the blood on his hand.

"You struck me," he said in astonishment.

"I defend my earnings," insisted the first, and the second dove at him with a snarl.

Elizabeth sawed the rope against the stone furiously. She felt one ply snap, then the rock must have cut her skin, for her hand was slick with blood. She glanced over her shoulder in terror, fighting against her bonds with all her might.

A second ply of the rope snapped.

The two men grappled with each other, battling for supremacy. Blows were landed and there were grunts as they scuffled back and forth across the motte. Both had bloody noses now, and one had a cut lip. Elizabeth worked the rope against the stone in a frenzy, no longer concerned about them realizing what she did. They were fully occupied with each other.

The third ply broke and she looked up, fearful they would discern the truth. The dark-haired one punched the fair one in the gut, then in the face, and his opponent doubled over before he fell hard to the ground. There was no other sound than the tinkle of the icy rain and the dark-haired one's heavy breathing. He kicked his companion and spat upon him, then wiped the blood from his face as he turned that simmering glance upon Elizabeth again.

Her blood ran cold.

She knew that expression all too well.

"To the winner go the spoils," he growled, smiling slightly as he surveyed her. Elizabeth's heart leapt in her chest, then raced with terror. She gripped the stone, determined to do him damage before he made any claim. "Aye, you can scarce wait," he murmured with what he obviously thought was a beguiling expression. "'Twill be worth the small delay, I promise you, wench."

Instead of approaching her, he headed for the cliff overlooking the river and endless darkness. Elizabeth could hear the flowing water, and judging from their climb to the motte, it had to be quite a drop from the cliff. What was he doing?

When she saw the spray of urine, Elizabeth knew.

She did not have much time.

While his attention was diverted, she managed to unknot the rope binding her ankles together, though her fingers were cursed cold. She hid her feet beneath her skirts and kept her hands behind her back, holding fast to that stone as she resumed her pose. It was too far to run across the motte and escape him, and she was not certain she could trust her feet to carry her. Surprise would have to suffice. She yearned to spit out the dirty cloth that gagged her to silence, but that would reveal that she was free.

She had to endure it, just a few moments longer.

Her captor wiped his hands on his breeches, taking his time, perhaps savoring the prospect of pleasure ahead.

Elizabeth would have to strike him down. She would have to await her moment and land a lethal blow. She would have only one chance and she had to make it count.

Her breath was coming quickly when the dark-haired man turned to face her. He smiled and started toward her with resolve.

Then, against every expectation, there was a clear whistle. Her captor glanced toward the ponies, who surely could not whistle. Elizabeth jumped along with her captor when he was struck in the throat by the bolt of a crossbow. The force of the blow sent him staggering backward.

In that same moment, the ponies nickered and scattered, fleeing toward the gates.

A man was revealed, one who had been hidden in the shadows behind the beasts, his expression so grim that he might have been an avenging angel.

Amaury de Vries.

The half-brother of the mercenary Maximilian.

Elizabeth wanted to shout for joy.

But he had changed. There was no kindness in the knight's expression this time, no protectiveness or hint of noble intention. His features might have been set in stone and he moved with a grim purpose that she did not recall. Given his demeanor, Elizabeth was not certain she should be relieved by his presence. His hair was wet and looked darker than the deep golden brown she knew it to be. Still, he was the most handsome man she had ever seen. He carried a crossbow and leisurely loaded it with another bolt as she watched.

Did he mean to kill her?

Meanwhile, blood flowed from the throat of the dark-haired captor as he tried to grasp the bolt embedded there. The bolt was slick with dark blood and he was staggering as he struggled to remain on his feet. He pointed at Amaury and made a horrible gurgling sound, then retreated one step too many. His expression turned to alarm when his foot found no purchase, then he vanished over the lip of the cliff.

There was a splash far below.

Amaury strode toward the place from which the man had fallen. He scuffed his boot in the dark stain from the spilled blood, then peered down at the water. When he turned, his brow was darker.

Why? Had he not expected the man to die? Was that his opinion of the man who would have attacked her? Or did he think the fight had been disappointing? Elizabeth could not say.

She would have liked to have seen relief light his eyes, but he spared a glance toward the gate. Who did he await? Did he ride alone or with another? Where was his destrier? Elizabeth could not believe he would have left it tethered and alone.

Then the fair-haired assailant stirred. Elizabeth caught her breath as he rolled over, proving that he had been watching the knight, and saw his knife flash in his hand. Amaury pivoted, perhaps hearing the small involuntary sound she had made, and immediately loosed a bolt. His aim was as true as before. The knife fell to the ground from the man's hand and he fell backward with a grunt as the crossbow bolt buried itself in his chest.

Impassive, Amaury strode toward his victim. Elizabeth tried to ease backward, but her back was against the wall. She was cornered. The knight slung the crossbow over his shoulder, taking his time, then picked up the fallen knife. His fleeting expression of disgust revealed his opinion of the blade, then he cast it aside. He pulled his own dagger as the fair-haired captor made helpless sounds, then efficiently finished what he had begun.

Still he showed no emotion, neither remorse nor relief. He was a hunter. It did not matter what or who was his prey. He made a plan and executed it with impressive accuracy.

Elizabeth was certain he would hear the thunder of her heart. She shivered when he glanced toward her, fearing his plan for her.

Though the second captor was motionless, Elizabeth was far from certain that she was safe. This knight had been kind to her at Kilderrick, but that might have been a ruse. Had she been his captive at Kilderrick or Maximilian's? She doubted it would have mattered in the end.

Men all demanded the same price.

Alone in this place, this man would take his due of her.

He must have followed their party for a reason, after all.

This was no troubadour's tale.

But he could be surprised, as well.

Elizabeth gripped the stone behind her back, maintaining the illusion that she was still captive. Amaury pulled something from the corpse and wiped it on that man's garments. She realized it was the bolt from his crossbow when he tucked it into his purse with care. Then he hauled the corpse to the cliff and cast the villain after his companion.

He nodded with satisfaction at the resulting splash, then turned again to Elizabeth.

She could not take a breath as he approached her with steady footfalls, his gaze locked upon her, his mouth drawn to a relentless line. He looked wet and tired and utterly without emotion. This was the moment of reckoning. He might have been stalking her. Elizabeth was keenly aware of how much bigger he was and how much more powerful—just as she was resolved to never be abused without a fight again.

She would mar his handsome face before she surrendered to his demands.

Amaury squatted down beside her in silence as she watched him warily. He was too far away for her to strike and she had to believe that was no accident.

She had to wait.

His eyes were so very blue, and he was more alluring than a man had any right to be. Her heart fluttered at his proximity and the intensity of his regard and she dropped her own gaze as if modest. In truth, she did not want him to guess her desperation. His good looks tempted her to dismiss her suspicions, but a handsome face could readily disguise a dark intent. She reminded herself of his half-brother's reputation, for the *Loup Argent* was known far and wide as a ruthless mercenary. They were kin. They had to have traits in common. They were warriors both and she had just witnessed how readily Amaury could end a life. She braced herself to make her one chance count.

Her heart fluttered like a caged bird and she had never been so afraid before.

"They will not do you injury again," he said in Norman French, his voice deeper and more reassuring than she had expected it to be. "I pledge it to you." Her grip faltered that he would promise her such a thing and she wanted to believe him—but it could be a ploy to disarm her.

She would not cede willingly to any man.

When she made no sign that she understood, Amaury reached for the rough cloth that had been used to gag her. "How badly are you hurt?" he asked, his gaze flicking over her wet kirtle. "When did you last eat?" Though he asked such questions, his tone was not filled with concern. He simply sought information from her, perhaps the better to pursue his own course.

Elizabeth struck while his attention was diverted, driving the sharp edge of the stone against him. She aimed for his throat, the bit of skin unprotected by the coif that had fallen around his neck. But he moved in the last moment and the stone collided with his shoulder, striking his tabard and halted by the chain mail hauberk beneath.

The blow was wasted.

Elizabeth saw his eyes flash as his hand moved like lightning, seizing her wrist so that she was compelled to drop the stone. His hand was warm, his grip firm. She struggled against him even as she spat out the gag, and tried to strike him with her other hand. She would have clawed out his eyes or scratched his face, but he caught that wrist easily and stood, drawing her to her feet and holding her captive before him. He did not hurt her but she was helpless—by his design.

To her surprise, he did not press his advantage, merely stood, holding her, and waited. The rain drummed on the roof overhead. The shadows claimed one side of his face, but she could not look away from the bright gleam of his eyes.

The corner of his mouth twitched, as if he would smile, but his gaze remained cool and that smile never appeared. Elizabeth was infuriated at even the hint that he thought her defense amusing. "You have a curious way of expressing gratitude," he noted and she aimed a kick at his groin. He stepped out of range and she twisted in his grip, helpless and frustrated.

Vermin. They were all vermin.

"You will not possess me easily," Elizabeth vowed. "I will fight you to the last." She tried to kick him again but Amaury guessed her intention. He swung her into the air as if she had no weight at all, spinning her around so she ended up captive against him. Her back was against his chest, his arms locked around her and holding her arms at her sides, her legs trapped between his. She seethed with fury even as she bucked against him. He was as immovable as a tower of stone.

"I like my women willing," he murmured in her ear, his breath launching an army of shivers over her flesh. Again, she was tempted to believe him and again, she called herself a fool.

"I wager you like them any way at all."

He scoffed, a mere breath of sound. "After a month in these lands, you might be right."

His jest, if it was one, did nothing to reassure Elizabeth.

"Wretch!" She twisted against him, flailing in her effort to free herself, but made no progress at all. She was aware that her buttocks were rubbing against him, but thought only of escape until he spoke.

"Did you fight him thus? Is that what put seduction in his thoughts?" he asked and Elizabeth froze.

"I did *not* tempt him," she retorted.

He spoke evenly, his tone reasonable, as if his conclusion could not be doubted. "'Tis clear that you did, whether you meant to do as much or not."

Infuriating man. She gritted her teeth. "The situation is not my fault."

"Nay, it is not, but you may have made it worse with your choices."

He spoke as if he argued with a child, and Elizabeth was outraged anew.

How dare he?

She drove her heel into his knee and was pleased by his resulting grunt. "Let me go!"

To Elizabeth's astonishment, Amaury did just that, and released her so quickly that she stumbled. Her feet were cold and numb, but she managed to gain her balance and flatten herself against the wall. She spun as she straightened to her full height, facing him, wary and ready to fight. He towered over her, though she was not short, and had to weigh twice what she did. She would not even consider how much stronger he was than she, or that he was defended by a mail hauberk and she wore only a wet kirtle.

Amaury bent and picked up her stone, considered it, then with a flick of the wrist, he threw it into the river. The distance was considerable, but he made the throw look effortless, and Elizabeth resented even this sign of his prowess.

Then he folded his arms across his chest to consider her, still impassive. God in heaven, he had the face of an angel. Even the shadows could not hide that. "Is this how you thank those who come to your aid?"

"Aye, when I do not know their price."

His eyes narrowed slightly but that was the sole sign that he might be insulted. "I have no price."

"All assistance comes at a price," she said bitterly. The fair-haired captor's knife was still on the ground in the rain, its blade glinting. Elizabeth shivered then eased away from the wall, as if she headed for the fire. "*All* men desire a reward for their efforts and most demand the same one."

Amaury watched her so intently that she could not guess his thoughts. "Then these are not the first to so threaten you?" he asked. "Am I right that you have been abused in the past?" He had a curious way of asking a question, as if he already knew the answer and simply requested confirmation. It was an irksome trait, implying a confidence that he already knew all. She was tempted to deny his suspicions, simply to see whether he would accept her word over his own convictions.

Elizabeth doubted he would. "What difference?" she demanded.

"It would explain your fearfulness at Kilderrick."

"Why would you care?"

He lifted a brow. "I simply seek to know all of the facts."

Elizabeth refused to think him noble or honorable. She would be certain of his intentions first. "I am a woman undefended. I am ready prey for any villain."

"Not so ready as that," he noted, touching the scuff on his tabard from the stone.

Elizabeth did not wait to be flattered upon her tactics. She dove for the knife in the muddy motte. Amaury was upon her with three steps, but she already had the weapon in her hand. She spun, striving to injure him with the knife while she could.

She had no real chance. He hooked a foot around her ankles, tripping her then catching her again before she could fall to the ground. She landed atop him, in his arms, which was the last place she desired to be. When she struggled against his grip, the pair of them rolled together on the ground. She strove to do him injury, but his hand had already locked around her wrists and she could not. Elizabeth fought him with all her might, but he divested her of the knife so readily that she might have wept.

Once again, she found herself defeated and powerless, at the mercy of a man. Once again, her hands were held captive and a man's weight pinned her in place. She was on her back and Amaury was atop her, that perceptive gaze too close to be evaded.

How could his eyes be so very blue?

She turned her head away, her breath catching in fear. Would it end like this? In the rain and the mud, him atop her and taking what he desired? And then what? Would he use the knife to end her life? Elizabeth could not bear to think of it.

"If you fight someone larger and stronger and intend to win," Amaury chided gently. "You must use your wits. Subterfuge and surprise are your allies."

Elizabeth blinked. He had not moved. He had not touched her face or her breasts, much less eased between her legs. She realized belatedly that he braced his weight above her and only trapped her in place instead of crushing her. That cold rain slanted down upon them and the ground beneath her was wretchedly muddy and cold. His mail radiated a chill, too.

She cast him a glare, but her fury did not have the impact she had hoped.

"This situation is somewhat less than ideal," he noted, his tone as calm as ever. "I, for one, would take advantage of the shelter and the fire, even savor a warm meal after this day's ride." Her belly growled, as if to agree, and she thought again that he almost smiled. He still looked resolute and formidable. "Pledge that you will not attack me and I will see to your protection this night."

"And if I refuse?"

"We can remain thus for the night." He yawned, so reveling in his power over her that she wished again to do him injury. "I might even manage to sleep with such a sweet cushion beneath me."

Elizabeth weighed the merit of spitting at him, but he was above her and any missile would likely end up on her own face. "At what price?"

He considered her and his expression was so intent that she wondered how much he discerned of her thoughts. "I suppose you would decline to grant a kiss."

A kiss? It was a ploy that he might take what he desired of her, and blame her for encouraging him.

Blackguard.

"I do decline," she said, even as her gaze fell to his lips, seeming of its own accord.

She feared for a moment that he might simply take his due. "Then I will have to settle for a tale," he said readily, to Elizabeth's astonishment.

She eyed him, but he appeared to be most serious. "You mock me," she charged, even as she wondered.

Amaury shook his head. "Not I. I love a tale better than most things."

"Even more than a kiss?"

"More than one given unwillingly, to be sure," he said, confusing her anew. "But truly, if ever there was a night to sit by the fire and hear a tale, this must be it."

Elizabeth did not believe him but she had no desire to remain in the cold mud. Still, she tried to divine the trick. "Any particular tale?"

"You might tell me yours," Amaury invited. His voice dropped. "Or you might tell me what you know of Calum Moffatt and Caerlaverock."

"Why?"

"Because your tale is entwined with his, but you did not wish it to be." He lifted a brow. "There is a story in that, to be sure."

Aye, there was. Elizabeth was not certain she wished to share it, though as prices went, his was a low one. But he served the *Loup Argent*, even against his will—would he take her back to Kilderrick if she confided in him? Elizabeth could only hope as much.

"Agreed," she said, bracing herself for his reaction for she was still uncertain what to expect. He might steal his kiss when she eased her guard. He might make his claim when she could not fend him off. He might assault her in her sleep—if she was fool enough to doze. A thousand dire possibilities flooded her thoughts, but not a one of them was right.

For Amaury rose immediately to his feet, offering his hand to her as if she were a grand lady at a king's court. He whistled inexplicably as he raised her out of the mud. Elizabeth looked but no one seemed to respond to his summons, if that was what it had been. He escorted her to the shelter of the ruined structure, then swept off his dark cloak and offered it to her. His tabard was the dark and unadorned one she recalled, his garb simple but well made.

"I would suggest you let your garments dry for the morrow," he said when she did not take the cloak. "They can be hung from the rafters here and you may wear this for the night."

The cloak was lined with thick fur, perhaps miniver, and it was warm from the heat of his body. The wool was thick and damp but not soaked through. Elizabeth accepted it, unable to keep herself from gathering it close for she was so very cold. Indeed, her fingers slid into the fur seemingly of their own volition. The weight and texture of the cloak reminded her keenly of the luxuries she had abandoned and she stroked the fur without meaning to do as much. She flushed at just the thought of that softness against her bare skin.

She was startled to realize that Amaury's gaze was locked upon her, his expression as watchful as that of his hawk, and then she guessed his nefarious scheme. "And if I disrobe like a harlot, then any result would be by my invitation?"

He looked so startled that she felt unkind. "I think of your comfort and no more," he said stiffly. His gaze hardened. "I gave you my word and that is no small thing. There is a clean chemise in my baggage that you may borrow if you prefer and I pledge again that no man will touch you this night."

He pivoted then, before Elizabeth could decide whether to apologize.

What a vexing man. He was as inscrutable as a statue, yet took offense that she did not immediately trust him. He asked for a kiss but would settle for a tale. She did not know what to make of him.

She dared not be lulled into trusting him.

She saw that a small party had appeared at the gates to the motte. Oliver, the squire from Kilderrick, led Amaury's destrier and three palfreys, and such was Elizabeth's state that she was relieved to see another familiar face. The squire carried Amaury's hawk upon his fist—which meant she *had* heard a falcon—and the entire party were wet. The horses had their ears folded back though they trudged onward with forbearance. The two ponies followed behind the larger horses, reins trailing, obviously hoping they might be tended and fed.

Or perhaps they thought it safer to be with the knight than face the wolves.

Amaury's attention was fixed upon them.

This was her chance.

AMAURY KNEW the lady's intent before he turned his back upon her. There was a new fire in her dark eyes, one he had not seen before, and he knew she had not truly yielded to him. She feared men, therefore she feared him. His impression at Kilderrick had been correct and she had been abused in the past. He did not like that she included him in the company of villains, but he could not blame her for such a conclusion.

The difference was that she was prepared to fight, and he could only salute that impulse. Indeed, he wished to encourage it somehow.

He heard her step behind him, the barest sound in the mud. He braced himself for her assault, all the while pretending he was unaware of what she did.

She sprang upon him from behind, seizing his dagger from its scabbard with impressive agility.

"A bold play," Amaury murmured. He spun and seized her wrist so that she could not turn his own blade against him. Her eyes flashed and she would have struck him with the other hand, but he caught that wrist, then held them both together. She struggled and fumed as he held her captive with one hand, plucking his dagger from her grip and replacing it in the scabbard.

"Wretch," she spat.

"*That* was not using your wits," he felt compelled to observe.

Her eyes blazed and her full lips tightened. She could not know how alluring she was. He had been struck by her beauty before, her long auburn hair, her sleek curves and her lovely face, but now her vitality dazzled him. Her hair was unbound and hung in dark gleaming waves to her waist, while her wet kirtle revealed the splendor of her curves. How curious that he had always thought women should be demure and biddable, but this one's fury stirred his very soul.

"I take advantage of your weakness," she countered hotly.

"You were predictable," he insisted. "Of course, you had not surrendered. Of course, you would attack me once I averted my gaze. I anticipated you, and that is the most fatal error of all."

"Fiend and rogue," she muttered. "Scoundrel."

"You will never succeed if you act in passion," he informed her. He tired of battling her in the cold rain, but he would do so as long as necessary. Her strength showed no signs of fading, a sure sign that it was fueled by both anger and fear. And he could not fault her for being uncertain of his intentions.

"I feel no passion," she insisted even as her cheeks blazed with color.

"Fury, then. Anger is a false leader. It encourages haste and thus error." He shook his head. "My uncle taught me thus when he trained me for my spurs. You must be calm when you fight and ensure that your thoughts are clear. Anger clouds them and influences results. It encourages one to take risks that are not likely to yield results."

She eyed him, her gaze simmering. "But passion makes all worthwhile."

Amaury shook his head. "Emotion is an unreliable master." He would never forget this again.

"Does injustice not make you angry?" she demanded. "Is it not passion that makes one seek vengeance and retribution?"

"Of course, but retaliation should be delivered with cold deliberation. It should be planned and meticulously executed."

"There is the thinking of a villain."

"Or a hunter," he said, holding her gaze. She considered him as if unable to look away. Amaury did not even wish to blink and miss a glimpse of her. "Even a knight."

Her eyes narrowed before she fought his grip again. "Release me," she demanded and Amaury immediately did as much. She staggered backward in surprise, nearly losing her balance. "You mock me!" she said, but it was embarrassment speaking and Amaury knew it.

"I endeavor to teach you. What did I do the last time I held you captive, but moments ago?"

"You abruptly released me."

He raised a finger. "At your request. And so you should have anticipated that I might do the same again. It is only logical."

She might have ground her teeth. Certainly, the fire in her eyes would have set any dry tinder alight. "Who can guess the intention of a man bent on abuse?"

"But I am not bent on abuse," he countered, his tone deliberately calm. "Even if I was, I might be predictable. Abandon your anger and make a plan."

Amaury did not doubt that hers would be a scheme to do him injury and thus escape.

In truth, he was intrigued to learn what she might do.

"Is all well, sir?" Oliver called.

Elizabeth turned her back as the squire drew closer. She hastened to pick up Amaury's cloak and drew it over her shoulders, holding it closed as she glared back at him. "Now there are two of you," she whispered. "I know what to expect."

A fierce desire rose within Amaury to see this lady avenged. Who had touched her against her will? He would demand a reckoning from that man's hide without hesitation.

Better, he would give her the confidence to influence her own fate.

"Do you truly wish to know how to defend yourself with a knife?" he asked, knowing she would glare at him.

"What if I do?"

"Then I will teach you."

Her suspicion was undiminished. "And what will I owe you for that?"

"Perhaps another boon." Amaury dared to tease her, wanting to see her reaction. She was lovely, to be sure, but it was her passion that made her a rare beauty. He would never have his fill of the sight of her.

Her cheeks blazed red as she shook a finger at him. "Aye, and you will blame me for seducing you or offering myself to you. I decline if that is your price…"

Enough.

"I never take what is not freely granted," Amaury said firmly, interrupting her. He knew his ferocity must have shown, for her eyes widened slightly in surprise. "I accept only what a lady offers, no more and often much less. You forget that I vowed to defend those weaker than myself when I earned my spurs."

"I did not forget what I never knew," she replied hotly.

Amaury looked pointedly at his spurs, the mark of his knightly vows and of universal meaning. She set her lips tightly, but did not cede.

He turned to Oliver then, pointing beneath the tumbled shelter and sharing his plan. "The horses can be tethered there, out of the rain, the luggage piled against the wall," he instructed the boy, granting the lady a moment to gain command of her emotions. "I would ask you to brush them all down."

"Aye, sir." If nothing else, Oliver was efficient.

"It is sufficiently dry here for a fire and I can use some wood from the end of the ruined structure. Since the lady will desire some privacy this night, we can hang Zephyr's caparisons from the rafters." Well aware that Elizabeth listened to him, Amaury pretended to be oblivious to her. He checked the strength of those beams and was glad to find they had not rotted. "Have you any other suggestions?"

"Meat, sir," the boy said immediately. "I can put a pot in the rain for water and then heat it, but meat would make a welcome soup after this day."

Again, the hunt. Amaury did not mind on this night, though. He was hungry himself. "You speak aright. I will see that all is settled here first."

"Aye, sir."

Amaury turned to see that the lady's anger had faded, making her uncertainty clear. She looked smaller and more vulnerable than he knew her to be, her hair wet and her eyes wide. She was pale and he wondered when last she had eaten, for she had not answered his query.

Amaury was not truly surprised that she bent to pick up another stone as he watched and clutched it beneath the robe. She was not defeated then, and he was glad.

"You lie to me," she said.

"Never."

She shook her head with disgust. "Why tell me that you never take more than is offered? Do you think you will dismiss my fears so readily as that? I know what will happen this night!"

"Aye, so do I," Amaury said, speaking crisply so there could be no doubt. "We will set camp. Oliver will tend the horses. You will bathe, if you so desire, and change your garb while I hunt." She made a skeptical sound that he ignored. "When I return, I will teach you more of fighting with a knife, you will surrender the tale you owe me as a boon while our meal cooks, then we will eat and we will sleep. That is what will happen this night." He pivoted and removed his saddle from Zephyr, his movements quick.

"You leave out the part of the tale that concerns me most."

"I omit no part of the tale." Amaury spun to give her a steady look. "I swear it to you, upon my word of honor."

Doubt warred with fear in her eyes but she lifted her chin to challenge him. "Why should I believe you are different?" she demanded and Amaury's restraint snapped.

He knew his anger showed but no longer cared. "Because my blood father took what was not his to claim," he said, biting off the words. "It was his trade as a mercenary and his habit in the conquest of women. My own mother was not willing, she was betrothed to another, and it did not matter to him." He raised his hands as she stared at him. "You see before you the result of that encounter. I will never *ever* be of his ilk." He spoke with heat and he knew it, but Amaury could not quell his hatred of Jean le Beau.

He returned his attention to his destrier, striving to control his anger. He was keenly aware that the lady watched him still and did not doubt her gaze was assessing.

Moments later, she cleared her throat and he heard her footfall as she approached. "Do you ride to France?" she asked.

"Not yet." He flicked a glance her way and she recoiled, taking a step back. He felt churlish that he had frightened her, however inadvertently, and tempered his tone. "I rode in pursuit of a lady taken captive."

"Why? Were you so commanded? And if so, by whom?"

"I took the quest of my own volition, in the interest of honor and duty."

"Why?" Her skepticism was clear in her dark eyes.

"Because that is what a knight should do," he said, speaking with precision. "I took a vow to defend those less powerful than myself and it is a pledge I will never forget."

She nodded then and dropped her gaze. "Is that why you say you will teach me to fight?" There was a promise of trust in her tone, a hint that he made progress, and Amaury welcomed the change.

"Nay. I will teach you to fight because you asked. A knight always serves a lady's bidding."

She looked at him then, her eyes wide with surprise and her lips slightly parted. It made Amaury ache that she had been so abused that she no longer believed any man could treat her well, but he held her gaze steadily. If he could have willed her to believe him, he would have done it. "I will never injure you," he said softly but with resolve.

"But you intend to leave me alone now," she said, her gaze flicking to Oliver.

"Only for a short time." No sooner had Amaury uttered the words than he realized that the outcome she dreaded often did not take long. He did not want her to feel unsafe in his absence.

There was but one thing he could do.

On impulse, he removed his dagger and presented the hilt to her.

CHAPTER 3

"Take it," Amaury said when Elizabeth did not move to accept the blade. She feared a trick, for his dagger was fine. He could not be truly surrendering such an expensive weapon to her. How could he trust that she would not use it against him? She had already tried to injure him—and she might succeed if he slept in her presence.

In her heart, she wondered whether she could strike that blow.

"Put it in your garter and I will show you upon my return how best to wield it." Amaury was as impassive as ever. How Elizabeth wished she knew the truth of his thoughts. "You will find it more effective than a stone." There was a gleam in his eyes, as if he teased her, but his mouth remained a taut line.

Elizabeth was tempted to believe him. But a few moment's conversation and her resolve melted away. If the man ever smiled outright, she would be lost for certain.

Cautiously, she took a step closer and accepted the blade. She studied it, still warm from his grasp, as much to evade his gaze as anything else. She felt laid bare to him, her intentions as clear to him as if she declared them outright. At the same time, she could not guess at his. It was a most troubling situation.

At the same time, she could not ignore how handsome he was, and the fact that he had been kind to her, more than once. To stand so close to him made her heart race and her breath catch; his stillness made her feel more unsettled. Her stomach churned beneath his scrutiny and she felt as if she had run all the way from Kilderrick.

Yet he did not try to seize the blade back or use it against her.

Amaury held his ground.

He kept his word.

She flicked a glance to his eyes, leery of her dawning trust, and he nodded once, then turned to check upon Oliver's progress. She studied him while his attention was diverted, liking his decisiveness.

Indeed, she yearned to touch him, an inclination both new and terrifying. Hers was a reaction other than fear, and a sensation she had seldom experienced in a man's presence.

She felt safe, as she had with her father, but it was more thrilling that the confidence she had felt at Beaupoint before her father's death. It made no sense to feel thus with a warrior in a ruined keep at night, one who had proven repeatedly that he could overcome her by force if he so chose, but she could not dismiss this unexpected trust.

He pledged that he would not injure her.

And she believed him. Elizabeth could not ignore her reaction to that, either.

His suggestion of a kiss as a boon had been lightly made, as if he had known she would not accept such terms. And that made her wonder. What would it be like to kiss such a man? What would it be like to feel his lips against hers? She had never been kissed in passion or given such a caress herself, but the prospect was oddly enticing.

Would she be disappointed? Elizabeth did not know. She could not guess. There was but one way to know and she would not invite it.

She studied the dagger instead. It was a fearsome and beautiful weapon. The hilt was elaborate, twisted like a length of rope, embossed with a shield graced by a griffin rampant. The pommel was an orb of red stone, held by what appeared to be four sharp talons. The blade was wickedly sharp and gleamed with purpose.

There was no doubt that she had insulted him with her doubt, but he had given her this gift when he could have taken a reckoning from her.

He had armed her, which made her heart glow with something she could not name.

By the time she had admired the weapon, Amaury had returned to stand before her. He removed the scabbard from his belt and presented it to her. She took it, lost for words, but he did not seem to expect any. He turned away again, lifting a saddlebag from a palfrey and making a jest with Oliver.

Elizabeth gripped the sheathed blade as she watched. Knight and squire worked together in comparative silence. There was only the sound of the rain falling steadily on the roof. A pot and a bowl were set in the rain to catch water. The fire was coaxed to a blaze; the horses were fed, watered, and brushed. In the quiet, Elizabeth felt the weight of her exhaustion.

At a gesture from Amaury, Oliver brought her a chemise of fine linen. He bowed before her, presenting it on both hands. "My lady," he said.

She pushed the scabbard into her belt so she could accept the chemise. The linen was so clean and smooth that she could not help but stroke the cloth. Tears of gratitude pricked her eyes. The boy bowed again, then turned to place a bowl of water over the fire. He provided her with a rough cloth and a comb, then apologized politely for the lack of soap. Then he returned to the baggage, so busily making preparations for the night that Elizabeth knew he had no interest in her or her charms.

He did not seem to recall that she, Ceara and Nyssa had taken him captive at Kilderrick, or at least he did not hold that against her. She was sure that there was yet a bit of woad in his hair, a remnant of the dye they had rubbed all over his skin before releasing him. He had not been harmed but he had been tricked.

Kilderrick seemed in this moment to be very distant and she could not wait to return there again.

The caparisons were hung from the rafters, dividing the space with white cloth bordered in deepest blue. The griffin rampant was upon each quarter of the trapper for the horse, so richly embroidered that Elizabeth could not doubt Amaury's knightly status. Used thus, they shielded her from even the most casual glance of the squire. The fire snapped and crackled before her, casting a welcome warmth into her little haven.

She would be able to wash in hot water and don a clean chemise. Once that would have been routine—now it was a gift beyond all expectation.

Once all was to his satisfaction, Amaury took his crossbow and strode into the night without a backward glance. The three dogs darted after him, but he gave a command to the grey one and the brown, taking only the large black beast with him. Those two smaller dogs returned to Elizabeth, one seating on each side of her as if guarding her, both staring after the knight with longing. She dared to pat the head of the taller of the two, a grey dog with long hair and bushy eyebrows. It leaned against her leg, watching the knight depart so fixedly that she knew he treated creatures well.

A dog's loyalty could not be bought, her father had always said.

He had also said that the merit of a man who was good to his hounds and his horse could not be doubted.

God in heaven, how she missed him and his good counsel.

Elizabeth patted the dog, considered the obvious good health of both destrier and falcon, and reviewed Amaury's deeds thus far. If he had a dire plan for her, he was leisurely about its pursuit.

Did he give her the opportunity to disrobe and wash so that he would find it more pleasing to possess her? That was Elizabeth's first suspicion, but she had more than a few doubts. If that had been his intention, the deed could have been done already. There was no reason for him to give her a weapon, much less to promise to teach her to use it.

Was that true about his father? She saw no reason to doubt him, especially since he had spoken with such heat. But if Jean le Beau was his father, then how had he become a knight? Why was he not a mercenary, like Maximilian, the *Loup Argent*?

Elizabeth was surprised by how much she wished to know.

Oliver continued his labor, brushing the horses and murmuring to them. The palfreys nickered. The brown dog curled up in a ball and fell asleep. The grey sat vigilant beside her. The peregrine murmured away to herself on her perch, all familiar and reassuring sounds. The rain fell but no threat assaulted Elizabeth.

In the end, the temptation of the hot water and clean chemise was too much to ignore. She disrobed beneath the cloak, alert for a move from Oliver. He began to whistle as he worked, giving her a clear notion of his location.

The water was hot and the cloth clean, the cloak soft and heavy and warm. It was not as good as a bath, but the change was welcome, indeed.

By the time she had donned Amaury's chemise—which hung to her knees and enveloped her in smooth linen—and wrapped herself in the cloak again, Elizabeth felt almost civilized. She put her boots near the fire and hung her garments from the rafters to dry. She sat before the fire to comb her hair and the dogs nestled against her, one on each side, so vigilant that she surrendered the last of her fear.

It was enough to remind her that she was very hungry.

AMAURY DISLIKED that Elizabeth was so terrified of men. Though she had fled from him once at Kilderrick, he had thought her frightened of Bête. On this night, her terror had been tangible and it had been of him. She was not a fool, so her reaction had been learned. Why were there so many men intent on claiming what was not theirs to possess? Fury lent speed to his steps before he compelled himself to halt.

He could not change the past, no matter how the injustice of it troubled him. He might be able to influence her future by teaching her how to defend herself, at least a little. Sadly, that service was the sum of what he could offer her.

He would not consider what had been done to so fill her eyes with fear.

Anger would only ensure that he was unsuccessful at the hunt.

They three had to eat so he needed to calm himself.

Amaury stood in the gorse and breathed deeply, willing his anger to diminish and feeling his senses sharpen as it did. Bête sat down beside him, alert as ever. Amaury refused to think of the bolt he had lost this night—though he regretted it, the sacrifice had been well worth the price. Somewhere in this rough land, he might find a smith who could fashion bolts for his crossbow before he had none at all.

For the moment, he would retrieve each one he could.

As was Amaury's habit when he hunted, he stilled his thoughts and considered what would be the best prey. He did not know how it worked, but when he decided, creatures of that kind inevitably revealed themselves in short order. He knew from Kilderrick that the forests of Scotland were thick with wild creatures, which was a blessing on a night such as this.

A stag or a hart was too big to cook with speed, and would provide too much food for three, even with the dogs. 'Twould be wasteful to take one on this night. Grouse were too small and he would need too many of them for a meal that would satisfy. They also were active at night, thus harder to capture.

Hares would be ideal. They were abundant in these parts and sufficiently small that they would cook quickly. They also froze in place when they perceived that they were pursued, and such stillness ensured a perfect target.

They could have a stew, thick with meat but thin of sauce, within hours.

Amaury stood in the forest, his crossbow loaded, as the rain soaked through his tabard. He thought of hares, large hares in abundance, filling the thickets on all sides. He pondered those hares, he envisioned them, and soon, he heard them rustling in the undergrowth. He nodded to Bête and the dog sprang into action, flushing their prey so the hunt was on.

ELIZABETH MUST HAVE DOZED before the fire's warmth for she was startled to wakefulness when the two dogs suddenly abandoned her. She was relieved to see Amaury striding across the motte, the black dog beside him, and the other two raced to greet him. They cavorted around him with obvious delight, barking and wagging. Their enthusiasm at his return was so evident that Elizabeth could not stop herself from smiling. It was also in marked contrast to Amaury's own expression. He was as impassive and inscrutable as before.

This did not trouble the dogs, evidently.

The rain had halted for the moment, but it was still cold and damp. Amaury glanced her way then spoke quietly to Oliver before crouching on the cliff to clean his kill. Oliver set a large pot on the fire, then retrieved a bowl and went to Amaury, evidently as instructed. The boy had set another pot out in the rain earlier and it was half full of water. Elizabeth saw that Amaury had several rabbits and her empty stomach growled. If he meant to lull her into complacency with small luxuries, his scheme had a chance of success.

She sat straighter and steeled herself against this man's allure.

Meanwhile, the dogs circled him in anticipation, barking as they were tossed scraps of raw meat. The peregrine called from her makeshift perch under the shelter, as if she did not wish to be forgotten. Elizabeth suspected the bird smelled the blood. When Oliver added the meat to the pot on the fire, browning it, Amaury took something to the peregrine. Elizabeth guessed it was liver. He sang the falcon's feeding song as he approached the perch, the one she remembered from Kilderrick, and the bird's anticipation was evident.

Elizabeth had to admire how he tended to all those reliant upon him and his protection. The falcon snatched hungrily at the meat as Amaury sang to it, the sight and sound taking Elizabeth back to days spent hunting with her father.

She wondered how well her Uncle James cared for the falcons. She was not sure her uncle rode to hunt. There had been two peregrines at Beaupoint, beautiful and powerful birds, and she vividly remembered the day she had first been allowed to hunt with one. Her mare, too, had been left behind when she fled, along with all her kirtles and other clothing. She had taken her gems, but they had been seized from her quickly enough. It was impossible to believe that once she had lived in such splendor, no less that she had not appreciated her own good fortune until it was gone.

Indeed, she had not been so idle as she was this night since those days. Living at Kilderrick had taught her that every soul had to contribute for the good of all.

"What should I do to assist?" she asked Oliver who glanced up with surprise.

"Nothing, my lady," the boy said, adding water to the browned meat. Though the soup would be simple, the scent was almost enough to drive Elizabeth mad with hunger.

Amaury cast the waste into the river even as the dogs watched, then turned toward the fire. Elizabeth's mouth went dry as he drew near and her grip tightened upon the knife. Now that all his labor was complete, she would learn the worst of his intentions.

He shed his plain dark tabard when he approached the fire, which made her heart leap with fear. Oliver moved to untie the lace at the back of his hauberk. He bent over so his hauberk dropped over his shoulders and caught it before it landed upon the ground. He cast it to Oliver who carried it away. Amaury was already removing his stained chemise. Elizabeth glanced away from the sight of his bronzed skin, a reminder that he was not of these lands, and tried to contain her fear that he meant to have his due.

She was aware of him halting on the other side of the fire. She felt his scrutiny as surely as a touch and she could not draw a breath. Her grip on the dagger was tight. Why would he grant her a weapon? Because he had shown that he could readily divest her of it. 'Twas all a scheme to remind her of her weakness, no doubt, to ensure she was aware of her vulnerability. Aye, men were all vermin, though their methods of torment might vary.

To her surprise, he did not come closer. Elizabeth looked up through her lashes at the sound of splashing water.

He washed.

Oliver had brought a bowl of hot water and a cloth similar to the one she had used. Amaury had washed his hands by the time she looked up and he rubbed the cloth over his face, his closed eyes granting her a chance to survey him. The sight of his muscled strength was scarcely reassuring and she averted her gaze again.

Such a handsome man was undoubtedly vain. He wished her to admire him. Perhaps he believed that would diminish her resistance. Perhaps he thought to gain with charm what others had taken by force, but Elizabeth would not comply. She would not look upon him.

Instead, she stared down at her lap, turning the dagger in her hand beneath the cloak. Amaury was utterly at ease, washing as if he was alone in a bath house. He turned and Elizabeth risked a glance across the fire. Oliver washed Amaury's back, as dutiful an attendant as any could desire. The man's back rippled with muscle, gleaming in the firelight, and Elizabeth's mouth went dry before she dropped her gaze again. Amaury accepted a clean chemise from Oliver with a sigh of contentment.

When he pulled his chemise back over his head, leaving it untied and untucked. Elizabeth expected him to approach her. When he did not, she stole a glance at him. He was watching her from across the fire, his eyes as dark as indigo. The firelight flattered him, drawing out the dark gold in his hair, gilding his tanned skin, making him look even more vital and male than he had before. She felt a flutter of something in her belly, something that was more pleasant than fear, but dared not trust it. It was because he was half-disrobed that she was so affected, Elizabeth guessed.

She told herself it was trepidation but did not believe as much herself.

He shoved his fingers through his hair, then fixed her with a look. "Do you feel better?"

Though she had not anticipated that he would ask as much, Elizabeth could neither lie nor forget her manners. "Much better. I thank you." She braced herself for some request that she show her appreciation by offering herself to him, but Amaury remained on the opposite side of the fire.

Indeed, he seemed to be disinterested in her person.

"Will you surrender your tale while our meal cooks? It will be a thin stew, but we must make do."

"It is said that hunger is the best sauce," Elizabeth contributed without meaning to speak at all.

He nodded. "If I have learned nothing else in this land, I have learned that." He rubbed the ear of the enormous black dog as she watched. The grey one returned to her side while the smaller brown dog leaned against Amaury's leg. "You have won Grise's approval, I see," he said, nodding toward the grey dog. "You should know that she is most discerning."

The dog made a growling rumble in her throat, as if she would comment upon his praise. Elizabeth wondered whether he simply intended to set her at ease with such comments.

"And talkative," he noted. "Grise always has an opinion to share."

The dog yawned noisily, then tipped her head back to consider Elizabeth. Her dark eyes seemed to be filled with understanding and Elizabeth could not resist the urge to pat her again. Grise grumbled in contentment and nestled against her, claiming the hem of the cloak as her bed. Elizabeth had a sudden recollection of a great silver wolfhound following her as a child. That dog's name had been Grendel and he had bared his teeth to any who approached the daughter of the house.

She had not thought of dear Grendel in years. He was laid to rest at Beaupoint along with generations of her kin. She wondered whether she would ever be home again but knew the price was not worth the reward. She patted Grise, whose wiry fur was showing all the myriad shades of silver and grey she recalled from Grendal's coat and blinked back a few tears before scolding herself.

She had to recall her situation. She had to remain alert for an assault. She straightened and eyed Amaury, holding the dagger tightly again.

Why *had* he given it to her?

"I have been remiss, my lady. We have not made all the introductions," Amaury continued, making her wonder if he had noticed her reaction. "This is Bête, aptly named for his size and vigor." He rubbed the black dog's chin and the dog stared at him adoringly. "He tracks most well."

"He terrified me that day at Kilderrick." Elizabeth could easily recall that dog closing fast behind her, never mind the fearsome sight of his teeth.

"You did not know that he awaits my command to attack."

"I did not know you had not given it already."

Amaury looked startled. "I would not set him upon a lady."

"How could I have known that?"

He eyed her. "How could you have feared such a thing?" he asked softly, then frowned and shook his head before continuing. "Regardless of my command, he would never have done you injury. He is a gentle giant and can easily be cajoled with an ear rub or a morsel from the table. That day, I bade him follow you, no more and no less."

"Why?"

He looked up, meeting her gaze. "Because I wished to find you."

Elizabeth shivered at that. "You stalked me, like a hart."

His eyes narrowed. "You are determined to believe my intentions wicked."

"'Tis a lesson learned."

"But not with me."

It was true enough. This particular man had always treated her with courtesy and consideration. Was it simply a question of opportunity? Elizabeth wished she knew.

"I used what means I had to find you, that I might thank you for sheltering Persephone," he continued mildly.

"With the roast partridge." Elizabeth readily recalled the night that Amaury had brought roast meat to her and her companions. She also recalled how hungry they had been, and their trepidation of lighting a fire that night. No meal had ever tasted better, in her estimation.

And she had thought well of him then, secure in the company of the other women and him at a distance. She flicked a glance at him, wondering.

"Maximilian would have cast me out if he had known," Amaury said, his tone wry.

Elizabeth was surprised by this confession. "Why?"

"Oh, there was a ruckus about the missing partridge, to be sure. I had to say that there had been one less than was truly the case, but the cook, Denis, would not surrender the point." He shook his head.

He had lied to the *Loup Argent* to see her fed?

"I *knew* it," Oliver said with heat and the knight glanced up.

"Is it not worth a small deception to see a lady rewarded for her kindness?" Amaury held her gaze as if he would persuade her to believe him, then turned his attention back to the dog.

Would a man of honor, as he proclaimed himself to be, tell such a falsehood, even for good reason? Or was this a hint that he had more in common with his brother? The *Loup Argent* was not a man to defy. The prospect made Elizabeth question her doubts of him.

Again.

How she wished it could be morning, that she could be back at Kilderrick to consider the puzzle of Amaury's nature and intentions in safety.

Amaury rubbed Bête's ear and the black tail thumped lazily against the ground. "And this is Noisette." He turned to the brown dog, who was sleek and smaller. She had curled into a ball beside him, but her eyes were open and she seemed most alert. "She is the youngest and the fastest." He rubbed her ears and she nuzzled his hand before nestling into her place again. "Of course, you remember Oliver, and you know Persephone well."

Elizabeth nodded and swallowed. "Aye."

"She is indebted to your kindness, as am I. The destrier is Zephyr." That creature stomped a foot and shook his head. "Are the palfreys named, Oliver? I confess I do not know."

Elizabeth felt a surge of annoyance that his truth had been revealed. How could he not have seen them named? Were the mares who carried his baggage so beneath his attention as that?

The boy gave him a look that showed he shared her view. "The *Loup Argent* sees all the horses named," he said, his admiration of the mercenary clear in his tone. He gestured to each palfrey in turn. "This is Flora." The chestnut palfrey with white socks swung her tail at the sound of her name. "And Esther." This chestnut mare had a star upon her brow. "And Ghita." The dapple with a dark mane and tail tossed her head before she nickered.

"It seems they like to be acknowledged," Elizabeth could not keep from noting.

"Indeed, it does." Amaury seemed about to say more but decided against it, fixing her instead with a look. "Will you begin your tale?"

"I do not know what to say." She fingered the dagger, hidden beneath her robe—his robe—and told herself she would find a way to use it, if necessary. She would not relinquish her wariness, no matter how he strove to put her at ease.

"Then let me be of assistance, my lady." Amaury looked down at the fire and she could not guess his thoughts. His expression was so composed. Was it possible he had no feelings at all? Was there a stone lodged where his heart should be?

"Your marriage was arranged to a man named Calum Moffatt," he said finally. "And you fled this match." He looked up suddenly, his eyes such a vivid blue that she was startled. "Will you tell me why?"

Elizabeth was taken aback by his curiosity and uttered the truth before she thought twice. "I did not like him."

He seemed to be puzzled. "Of what import is that?"

"It is of tremendous import, for I was to put my hand in his!"

"What did he say to so offend you?"

"I knew before he uttered a word." Elizabeth could not doubt the force of her reaction. It had been fierce and immediate, as well as undeniable.

"What whimsy," Amaury said under his breath and Elizabeth's temper flared.

"Do you not think a maiden should have some choice in the matter of her marriage?"

"I think a maiden may have little understanding of greater concerns, and that it is her duty to wed as her father dictates." He spoke calmly, as if there could be no question that he was right.

"Greater concerns," Elizabeth echoed. "Like what?"

"A man's reputation, the measure of his wealth, his nature and his connections." Amaury raised a hand to add to his list. "The location of his holding, if he has one, and how the alliance between husband and wife will influence alliances surrounding them. There are many considerations." He slanted a glance her way. "Doubtless there were months spent upon arranging the connection and ensuring that it was a good one." He shook his head. "But you knew with a mere glance that Calum Moffatt should not be your spouse. Many would pay good coin for such perceptiveness."

Oliver chuckled.

"It is not a jest," Elizabeth said, bristling. "I would be alone, without so much as a maid I might rely upon to take my side. It is no small thing to put oneself in a man's power, and I *did not like him.*"

"Why?"

"What does it matter? I knew I could not wed him."

"With a single glance," he said, shaking his head. "Is he old?"

"Of an age with you, I would wager."

"Not so old as that, then. Disfigured?"

She shook her head.

"And what happened after you expressed your dislike?"

"Nothing," Elizabeth said bitterly. "My father would have heeded my reaction, but my uncle did not. He insisted the match be made as agreed." She took a breath when Amaury waited for her to continue. "I fled and all went awry. I surely did not intend to spend most of a year living in Kilderrick's forest."

"What did you intend?" He asked as if he could not understand her reaction. Was passion and intuition so alien to him as that?

"To object. No more and no less." Her choice sounded foolish even to Elizabeth's own ears and a part of her marveled at how much she had learned in less than a year. "When my uncle dismissed my concerns, I fled in the night. I meant to flee only to the next village, to feed his concern for my welfare, and then return in a day or two." She felt her lips tighten. "Matters did not transpire as I had hoped."

Amaury's brows rose. "But you left your home with companions to defend you?"

"No, not one."

"Alone? At night?"

"Aye."

He shook his head, his view of her impulsive choice clear. "And the result surprised you. How sheltered an upbringing did you have?"

"There were reivers! I could not have known that they were abroad that night."

He shrugged, unwilling to cede even that much.

She set her lips, too aware of their solitude and the press of darkness to recall that first night. "I was robbed of my gems and endured much. I will not speak further of it. Eventually, I arrived at Kilderrick in that company of reivers. Alys and her comrades attacked their party."

"Much as they attacked ours when we arrived at Kilderrick."

Elizabeth nodded. "And I was freed from my captors as a result. I chose to remain there with Alys."

It was a succinct summary, though omitted the worst detail. They sat in silence for a long moment.

"Why did you stay at Kilderrick?"

"I had no other place to go."

"You could have returned to Beaupoint. Your uncle would surely have welcomed you."

"And seen me wed against my will!"

"But that hut was short of luxuries. There must have been times you did not eat well or were cold."

"What of it? It became home." By the next night, Elizabeth hoped, she would be back in the hut she now shared with Eudaline at Kilderrick. That cottage was far more comfortable and she yearned for it, even in its simplicity. She might even have a chamber in Kilderrick's hall by the Yule.

Amaury, though, impaled her with a very intent look. "Surely, comfort, security and affluence are worth a marriage, even to a man you would not choose for yourself?"

"Surely not! A lady should have the choice of her spouse..."

"So she can wed for love instead of duty?" Amaury demanded, interrupting her. His tone turned hard. "Duty steers true, for it is rational and considered. Passion is no basis for a nuptial match, save perhaps for those of peasants. Your choice was foolish and you are fortunate that you did not pay a higher price for it."

Elizabeth gasped. "How dare you say as much?"

"I remind you only of the truth, which you must surely know. Not every woman survives an assault by mercenaries or reivers."

Elizabeth bit back her response, hating that he was right.

"You are vexed with me," he said, as calm as ever. "But I suggest that the main reason you disliked your intended was that you did not choose him yourself. Indeed, you knew little else of him when you decided that he would not suffice."

"You know nothing of my thoughts."

"But I can guess. I witnessed the arguments between my cousin

Felicia and my uncle, her father, when I trained for my spurs in his abode."

Elizabeth found herself listening, for she was curious to know more of him and his life before Kilderrick.

"She, like you, believed life should resemble a troubadour's tale, filled with pageantry, love and good fortune. My uncle arranged a match for her with a wealthy duke some thirty years her senior." Amaury gave Elizabeth a stern look. "It was a good match, skillfully negotiated. My uncle gained considerable advantage, due to my cousin's beauty." He shook his head then. "But she was furious and refused to accept the man."

"She won her way and endured a dire fate?" Elizabeth guessed, believing there had to be a moral to this tale and not one she would like.

He smiled so quickly that Elizabeth barely had a glimpse of his expression. Even so, the sight made her catch her breath. It should not be possible for a man to be so finely wrought.

"No, no. My uncle would not bend. The match was good in all ways, so he insisted." He rose to stir the soup and Elizabeth wished she could have seen his expression. "Never would I have believed that a fair maiden could rage so furiously as my cousin did."

"She did *not* wed the old duke. She could not have done so. If your uncle held her in esteem, he could not have compelled her to make the match." Elizabeth was horrified by the possibility.

Amaury looked up to meet her gaze with that maddening confidence and nodded, as if no other outcome was possible. "She did."

"And she died miserable, thanks to the men who made her choices for her."

"And by the time of her first son's birth, Felicia adored her husband."

"That cannot be so."

"It is. I pledge it to you."

"They cannot still be so happily wed."

"It has been fifteen years. They have five sons and a daughter and my cousin is radiantly happy. Her beauty is ten times what it was when she was a maiden. My uncle said she could choose for herself the second time, but she is resolute that she will love her duke and no other, for all time."

Elizabeth stared at him, realizing his implication. "You think I will change my thinking once I am wed."

"I think many a good match begins with doubts from one party or both." He spoke in measured tones, so reasonable that Elizabeth wondered whether any incident could spark his temper or persuade him to raise his voice. "I think good will on both sides puts such doubts in the past."

"Then you would agree with my uncle." She could not keep the bitterness from her tone. "You would not insist as much if the match was yours."

"Because it is not thus in all the tales?" He scoffed at that. "Surely you have learned that most of us do not reside in tales. If we did, you would have found a champion in the woods and lost your heart to him at a glance, and I would have found an heiress who was immediately enthralled by me. Whimsy, all of it." Amaury shook his head, oblivious to Elizabeth's astonishment. He sought an heiress? Why? He continued with resolve. "Nay, a plan based on reason is best when it comes to marriage, as in all other matters."

Suddenly, Elizabeth had a terrible feeling of premonition. He had chosen a path, without consulting her, and she suspected she would not like it. She had assumed they returned to Kilderrick, but Amaury could only be arguing in favor of her match with Calum for one reason.

He meant to claim the bounty himself.

"We are not returning to Kilderrick, are we?" she asked in a whisper.

Amaury looked up. "Why would we?"

"Because you abide with the *Loup Argent* and he makes his home there. Because you rode in pursuit of me from Kilderrick." Elizabeth heard her voice rise as the knight simply returned her regard, as if she spoke nonsense. He was utterly unmoved by her argument, which could only mean that he did not agree and was not swayed. Still, she could not stop herself from adding more. "Because Oliver is the *Loup Argent*'s squire. Because my friend, Alys, is his wife and she knows I will not wed against my will." She took a shaking breath and cited her final reason, hoping it would persuade him. "Because I wish to return to Kilderrick and a knight serves a lady's will, I am given to understand."

"Not in this case," Amaury said so readily that she yearned to do him injury. "A knight also upholds duty and honor. You are pledged to wed Calum Moffatt, and I shall escort you to Caerlaverock to do as much. Your uncle's agreement must be honored. You must see as much, my lady," he chided. "You have only delayed the inevitable."

She gaped at him, astonished that he could be so cruel.

And he did not care. He inclined his head to her as he rose to his feet. "You will see that your uncle was right, in time. I am certain of it." Then he turned, calling to Oliver for bowls and spoons.

Nay! Elizabeth could not be compelled to wed against her will after all she had endured!

CHAPTER 4

The lady would run, again, and no good would come of it.

Truly, whimsy and impulse were poor masters. She chose on the basis of impulse alone, and it could only lead her into peril. The sooner she arrived at Caerlaverock and wed her betrothed, the better.

The sooner she had a babe in her belly, the better, though that was not Amaury's responsibility. He had to proceed with caution and ensure she never guessed the depth of his admiration for her. Oh, he would cherish such a lady as his wife, but what folly any match between them would be! Passion would not keep them fed or warm, though he feared the lady would not agree with his assessment.

She must never guess of his regard.

Amaury turned away, hiding his thoughts. Elizabeth was as passionate and resolute as his cousin had been—and he knew, as his uncle had, that if she granted the arrangement a chance, all would be well. He recalled Felicia's fury, the breaking of crockery and the shouting, followed by her rapturous happiness, and knew he was right.

He was fortunate that her eyes so clearly revealed her thoughts. They shone with such defiance that he could not have believed for a moment that he had changed her thinking.

He would not be able to sleep this night, for he would have to keep a vigilant watch over her, for her own protection. 'Twas almost enough to make him wish for some of Eudaline's poppy powder that she might be compelled to sleep as Alys once had been. But Amaury did not have any, which meant he had to use his own wits against hers.

Elizabeth was not simple, but she was stubborn. As much as he could appreciate her tenacity in clinging to her view, he would have expected the past year to have softened her resolve. Clearly, he erred in that.

They ate in silence, the lady casting poisonous glances his way as if he was the villain to blame for her situation. Amaury pretended he did not notice. When the soup was gone and the bowls washed, Oliver went to bed down near the horses. Amaury wrapped himself in his great cloak and settled against the back wall of the remaining structure. Away from the fire, there was less chance of the heat lulling him to sleep. It was no small advantage that the lady was silhouetted by the dying flames of the fire. Bête flung himself down beside Amaury and fell asleep, content.

Amaury feigned sleep, knowing Elizabeth did the same.

Would she simply flee? Would she take a palfrey? Or would she drive his own dagger into his heart before she abandoned him? The possibility was intriguing. If she could have struck him down with a glance, she would have done as much this night, for certain.

How could Calum not be enchanted by his bride? How could any man fail to do whatever was necessary to make Elizabeth smile, to prompt her joy, to make her happy? Amaury had no doubt all would come aright.

He was beguiled by her magnificent eyes, how they lit with joy or flashed with anger, revealing the nuances of her reactions. He thought of the sweet curve of her lips and yearned for more than he should. He wondered when he would have the right to touch a lady again.

An heiress would be ideal. Perhaps he could reach France by spring, when the tournaments would begin again. He could enter the lists again and battle at tournament to attract the attention of the heiress he needed.

How did Sylvia fare in these times? It was true that he had not welcomed her attentions more than was polite and Amaury appreciated the irony that if he had wed Sylvia five years before, he would not be in his current situation.

He would never confess as much to Elizabeth, but he, too, had dreamed of a match founded upon love and not advantage—in the foolhardy days of his youth.

If he had slept, he would have dreamed of the lists and the pageantry, the attention of ladies and the prospect of heiresses, but Amaury remained awake.

The fire burned down to embers and the skies cleared overhead, revealing the stars. Oliver began to snore softly, as did one of the dogs. Noisette had a dream, her feet twitching as she chased some creature or other.

It was not long before Elizabeth stirred. Amaury remained motionless, breathing slowly and deeply, letting her confidence build. He heard her pull on her boots and opened his eyes the barest increment to watch her. He saw her admonish Grise to remain silent with a touch and heard the rustle of his own cloak as she got to her feet. He felt the weight of her gaze as she rounded the embers of the fire to look back at him. He breathed steadily, waiting for her to be reassured, then she pivoted to flee.

"Have you learned nothing at all?" he asked quietly and she jumped in astonishment, spinning to glare at him. "There is little point in granting you advice if you will not take it."

Of course, he was awake.

Confident, taciturn, infuriating man.

Of course, he foiled her plan to escape. Elizabeth should have guessed that he would remain awake at all costs, simply to ensure that she did her duty by her uncle's pledge.

Duty. The very word made her want to spit.

And he insisted that he came to her rescue. Hardly that! Indeed, it seemed she had jumped from the fat to the fire. Amaury was not intent upon sampling her charms, but still he would dictate what she might do or not do, still he would see her pledged to a match she did not desire.

Men.

How she loathed them all.

"You!" she whispered with heat.

"Who else?" He was maddeningly calm.

"You would trick me," she said through clenched teeth.

Amaury rose to his feet and strolled toward her, like a lion approaching its cornered prey. She hated how a part of her admired his power and grace. If she used the knife, he would take it from her. She doubted that he would ever teach her to use it. Its surrender had been a ruse to win her confidence, no more and no less. He would simply repossess it in the morning.

She should have kicked him harder when she had the chance.

"You are the deceptive one, my lady, to be sure." He stepped into the glow cast by the last embers, and the golden light made him look only more imposing.

'Twas then she recalled that he no longer wore his hauberk. She might have a chance to strike a single blow that was of import. She gripped the dagger, her hand hidden beneath the cloak.

"That is an unkind charge," she said.

"Do you not mean to flee in the night?"

"I seek the latrine," she lied.

He shook his head. "It is in the other direction and you know that well. You have visited it already."

She exhaled mightily and his eyes glinted. If he laughed at her, she would cut out his heart. "You could take me to Kilderrick."

He shook his head with greater resolve. "I will never return there."

"Why not?"

Again, his voice hardened, and she seized upon this one hint that he revealed some detail of import. "I will not owe one more debt to the *Loup Argent*."

"How is it that you ride with him at all?"

"My tale is not of import."

But Elizabeth thought it was. "Can I not be curious in my turn?" When he did not reply, she continued in a tone that did not hide her vexation. "It is only *sensible* to know some detail of one's companions. Only a *foolish* woman would sleep in the company of strangers."

To her astonishment, Amaury chuckled.

As she had anticipated, his appearance was utterly changed by his smile. He looked less resolute and kinder, as well as infinitely more alluring. Her heart proved its unreliability, leaping at the sight, though the sound of his merriment faded all too soon. His eyes, though, gleamed as he surveyed her. She had seen that he had a dimple, against every expectation. Elizabeth could only stare at him as he closed the distance between them with steady steps. Her mouth went dry when he stopped right before her and that gaze bored into her own.

Her sole salvation was that his smile had vanished so completely it might never have been.

"Well played, my lady," he said, his voice a low rumble that provoked an echo deep inside her. His fingertips brushed her elbow. "I would invite you to return to sleep now, for dawn will come soon."

"Too soon, by my thinking." Elizabeth swirled the cloak about herself and huddled beside the embers, seeking a scheme.

How could she surprise him? It seemed the man was never taken unawares.

Amaury brought more wood and stirred the coals, setting the fire ablaze again, his consideration of her comfort melting a measure of Elizabeth's resentment.

"Where will you go if you do not mean to return to Kilderrick?"

"Back to France," he replied readily, as if the answer was evident.

When he did not continue, she prompted him. "A large territory. You must have a more precise destination."

She earned a look for that. "To my uncle's abode."

"Where you earned your spurs."

He nodded, his gaze fixed on the fire.

'Twas like pulling teeth to draw a tale from this man.

"And then?" Elizabeth prompted.

"I will pledge to his service, if he is agreeable, then likely enter the lists in the spring."

She was horrified. "You will joust?"

"Why should I not?"

"My father said it was reckless and wasteful, that a knight should hone his skills at true battle. You seem neither reckless nor wasteful to me."

He was not apparently insulted. "Yet it is my best chance to secure my future."

"Have you jousted before?"

He met her gaze, as if he could not understand why she doubted it. "I rode to tournament for fifteen years."

Elizabeth could make no sense of his claim. He was a huntsman, who rode with mercenaries. Jousting was a diversion for the sons of wealthy knighted noblemen. It made no sense that he should have such experience yet have been at Kilderrick. 'Twas true he rode a destrier, but she had assumed he was a knight with few prospects or one seeking adventure in Scotland. She could not reconcile the two.

Of course, Amaury did not explain.

Elizabeth waited as long as she could, but in the end, she could not remain silent. "How can this be?" she asked when the fire blazed high again. "It makes little sense that you earned your spurs and were trained for knighthood, yet rode with a company of mercenaries. It makes no sense that you live as a huntsman but have jousted for so many years."

"Nay, it does not," he admitted readily, but again, he did not elaborate.

Was ever there a man more taciturn and irksome?

The fire crackled and Elizabeth waited for either a tale or an opportunity. As the moments passed in silence, she feared she would have neither soon. "I spit upon duty," she whispered to herself and was surprised by Amaury's quick glance.

"You will be reconciled," he said with that annoying conviction.

"No doubt you deliver me to Caerlaverock for the promised bounty."

He shrugged. "It would not be unwelcome, to be sure, but I never rely upon any windfall until it is in my hand."

Of course, he did not. He did not dream or hope. He would rely only upon what he held in his hands. He was more rock than man and a thousand years would not weaken his convictions. Elizabeth could have admired that, if he had not been so set upon delivering her to Caerlaverock.

They sat in silence, only the crackle of the fire between them. Elizabeth would have his tale, no matter how hard she had to battle for it. "It cannot be whim that brought you to these shores."

"'Twas not."

There was a puzzle here and one he would not solve for her. He appreciated logic and good sense, so Elizabeth would endeavor to reason the truth. "You are the son of a mercenary, got upon your mother when she was unwilling. It must be your maternal uncle who trained you for your spurs." She was rewarded with a minute nod. "But why? Your tale is incomprehensible, sir." She sat back. "It might even be said to be improbable, like a bard's tale."

Amaury did not smile. "To be sure, I have thought as much myself."

Elizabeth tried his trick and remained silent as he stared into the fire. The ploy did not succeed. The fire crackled, the dogs snored, and Amaury might have forgotten her presence completely.

Elizabeth doubted that could be the case. He was standing guard over her, whether it seemed like it or not.

"Will you tell me your tale?" she asked finally and he looked up. His expression was surprisingly bleak and she had the ridiculous notion that she should console him. She smiled and he blinked. "'Twould keep me from fleeing, for a while at least."

He snorted and granted her a grim glance. Then he frowned and shook his head, staring into the fire again. "What matter if I do?" he murmured with a rare trace of impatience.

Elizabeth was intrigued beyond all. She leaned closer, determined not to miss a word of what had to be a rare confession.

WHAT MATTER if he confided in the lady? In truth, the weight of his tale grew within Amaury and he knew he had to shed its burden. His sense of injustice might turn his purpose to vengeance, which was no good end. Why not entertain the lady with his tale of woe? She spoke aright that it would ensure she did not flee. He did not truly believe she cared

—she simply sought a diversion. Dawn was mere hours away, and after they reached Caerlaverock, they two would never see each other again.

The prospect saddened him, as he knew it should not.

Impatient with his thoughts, Amaury began. "I was unaware of my parentage for all of my life, until several months ago. I grew up with every privilege, and then it was all taken away." He made a sweeping gesture with one hand.

The memory still burned.

Elizabeth's eyes were bright with curiosity. "What happened?" When Amaury did not speak, she moved closer, against every expectation. He did not move when she sat down beside him, then Grise moved to lean against her other side. The lady seemed to be unaware of their proximity.

Amaury could not ignore it.

"Please tell me," she urged and he glanced down at her, his heart leaping to find her gaze fixed upon him. She looked soft in the firelight, but also strong.

Alluring, but not his to touch.

Amaury turned to the fire again with a frown. "I was betrayed and as a result, I made a choice in anger."

"How were you betrayed?"

"Not three months ago, I was the oldest son of Gaston de Vries, a knight and a champion at the jousts, a man assured of the bounty of his future. Then Gaston insisted that I accompany him to the funeral of Jean le Beau, the mercenary who had years before seized the de Vries holding to make it his own. He secured this claim by forcibly wedding Gaston's sister and my aunt."

"When was this atrocity committed?"

"Before I was born. The *Loup Argent* is the result of their union."

"Another arranged match?" the lady asked with an arch of her brow.

"A forced one, for her own father protested it and died for his objections."

Elizabeth paled.

"'Tis not the same as your situation," Amaury told her and she nodded once in reluctant agreement, then swallowed. "There cannot be two men alive as vicious and violent as Jean le Beau."

"One can hope," she said softly.

Amaury continued. "When Jean le Beau died, I saw no reason to attend this funeral, but Gaston was adamant. I accompanied him in poor temper, to be sure. I had intended to ride to Paris, to visit friends. We planned to ride to hunt in a merry party and I was to assess a stallion, perhaps court a lady's affections while there. A funeral did not compare to such pleasures, let alone a funeral for a villain who would not be laid to rest in sacred ground."

"You knew Jean le Beau?"

"Only slightly and I did not like him."

"But you went to the funeral."

"I was not in a position to refuse a command from Gaston de Vries," Amaury said. "And so it was that I learned I was not, in fact, Gaston's son. The man I had called father all of my life shared no blood with me."

"You learned Jean le Beau was your father at his funeral?" She was incredulous.

Amaury nodded, humiliated even at the recollection. "Gaston stripped my legacy from me before the company. Evidently, he and my mother had been betrothed when Jean le Beau forced his affections upon her. Gaston wed my mother as previously arranged, knowing that she carried another man's bastard, in order to claim her dowry." He shook his head. "I had absolutely no notion of this truth before that day."

Elizabeth was visibly surprised. "Did your mother not tell you?"

"She died in the delivery of me. My father—" he corrected himself with impatience "—*Gaston* wed twice more. I have two younger brothers, half-brothers, in truth. I also learned that day that the *Loup Argent*, Maximilian de Vries, who I believed to be my cousin is, in fact, also my half-brother." He sighed. "It was a humbling afternoon, to be sure." They sat in silence for some moments.

"I am sorry for your misfortune."

"It is kind of you to say as much, but sympathy was not the point of my tale." Amaury shook a finger at her. "My point is that I had no notion that anything could go awry. Nothing had in my life to that day —and then all did."

The lady blinked. "We have that in common," she said, to his surprise. "I did not believe anything could go awry when I fled Beaupoint and learned differently. We share the experience of unexpected disappointment."

Their gazes locked with a potency that stirred Amaury deeply. He knew better than to wish that circumstances might be different between them, but when the lady shivered, Amaury lifted the side of his cloak, inviting her to take shelter against his side.

She did not move.

"You have my knife," he reminded her.

"You have shown yourself adept at divesting me of weapons."

"You had best be warm for your lesson. Cold fingers are clumsy."

She shook her head and remained where she was, drawing Grise a little closer.

Amaury was encouraged that she had at least considered the possibility of moving closer. It would be a victory to earn this lady's trust.

"Then what?" she asked.

"Gaston told me that I could keep my horse and my hounds and the garb upon my back, but no more than that. I was no longer welcome in his hall."

"Fiend," she said with heat, shocking Amaury that she took his side at all. "But it could have been worse."

"Could it? He could not take Zephyr, for the stallion was a gift from my uncle, along with my spurs and my sword. He could never take these dogs from me, for they are loyal to no other. But he ensured I had no means to ensure their welfare and that, I confess, dismayed me."

She tipped her head back to study him. Her eyes sparkled, which surprised him as much as her teasing tone. "Surely you of all men did not make an emotional choice." She feigned shock and if the topic had not been so serious, he might have smiled.

"Surely I did. I had no notion what to do that day and so I accepted Maximilian's offer to accompany him to Scotland. Anger led me false. I erred, and I would repair my mistake."

"By returning to your uncle's abode?"

"Where I should have gone first. He has always been my ally, but in that moment, in the face of uncertainty, I forgot."

Her gaze clung to his. "I sense a moral."

She was right in that. "In fleeing your home, you neglected your duty and broke your uncle's pledge. That is no small deed. It is your obligation to set matters to rights. Duty and honor demand no less."

Her lips thinned before she looked back at the fire. "And you will see it done, whether I am willing or nay."

Amaury pressed his argument. "To decide against a man with a glance makes no sense. You are not witless. You reason well."

"I thank you for that."

"You must recognize the folly of your choice."

The lady, however, sighed and remained silent.

Amaury wanted to convince her. "How did your own parents make their match?"

He earned another hot glance for that. "They met at the altar on the day of their nuptials."

"An arranged marriage between strangers." Amaury sensed victory. "And how did their match fare?"

She sighed, her eyes flashing with annoyance. "They came to love each other deeply."

"You see? All will come aright. Your husband will treat you with honor. Your uncle's plan will be proved aright. In no time at all, you will be happy in your match, your affections secured."

"And if they are not?"

"It is right and good for a widow to make her own choice."

She laughed under her breath. "My father used to say as much. I must believe, though, sir, that hoping for my husband's demise might diminish the chances of our having a happy match."

Amaury had no argument for that. He looked back at the fire with an effort.

"If I fled, could you not let me go?" she asked finally, but there was no heat in her question. She sounded resigned to her fate.

Amaury shook his head, resolute. "Where would you go? How would your safety be assured? I could not allow you to be endangered again."

To his relief, she did not ask why. "What would you do?"

He met her gaze again, letting her see that his conviction was unshakable. "I would do whatever was necessary to deliver you to your betrothed. I would deliver you bound hand and foot if necessary."

She caught her breath, but Amaury was not done.

"But consider this, my lady. You are reluctant to wed this man. You have fled from him once and that is no balm to a man's pride. If you are delivered to him unwillingly, he may spurn you and the match."

She smiled with delight. "I cannot dislike that prospect."

"Or he may ensure that you pay in private for the assault upon his pride."

Elizabeth's gaze flew to his "What do you suggest?"

"That you go to him willingly, even with enthusiasm." He cleared his throat. "In your place, I might concoct a tale to show myself in better light."

Her eyes sparkled in a most beguiling way. "A tale? Do you mean a falsehood?"

"Not precisely. What if you did not flee your home to avoid the match?"

"But I did."

"What if you were *taken*? What if your absence was through no fault of your own? Any blow to your betrothed's pride would not be your fault and he could not blame you for it. Who knows the truth other than you? No one will be able to challenge you."

"The reivers who seized me know where I was taken."

"But they cannot know why you were there. You might have fled another captor first. And how likely is your betrothed to discuss you with reivers and outlaws?"

Elizabeth smile dawned and Amaury could not look away. "You prompt me to question my assumptions, sir. Is it fitting for a knight to tell a falsehood?"

"If it means a lady's welfare is assured, I believe an exception can be made."

"As you did once before," she whispered.

Their gazes locked and held for a potent moment, one that made Amaury taut. He yearned for what he could not take and he dared not indulge himself. He looked back at the fire. "Of course, you are not a knight, so you have no such constraint."

"But you would have to support my tale at Caerlaverock. They would believe you, if not me."

"I would do so."

"You would?"

"I would." Amaury spoke with conviction.

"You would lie again to ensure my welfare." This notion clearly pleased her.

"Without question."

Her smile was radiant. "And that is like a bard's tale, even though we both know that life does not resemble such entertainments."

Amaury could only smile back at her. He liked how she became unafraid to challenge him. He liked her quick wits and her sparkling eyes. Again, the heat rose between them as they stared at each other. A new light dawned in the lady's eyes, one that affected Amaury most strongly. His heart skipped and his gaze fell to her ripe lips. A desire filled him to show her that men need not be feared. He wanted to give her more than a dagger—he wanted to prepare her for her future, but that was far beyond the bounds of propriety. Nay, he wanted to introduce her to the pleasure that could be shared between man and woman.

The temptation was so potent that he knew he could not deliver her to Caerlaverock soon enough.

Indeed, he already suspected it would tear the heart from his chest to leave her there and ride away.

ELIZABETH WAS warm to her toes, filled with the confidence that she had lost since Beaupoint. Amaury's expression had softened slightly and his pledge that he would support a lie for her welfare, filled her with a glorious sense of satisfaction.

She could have stretched forward, just an increment, and given him the boon he had suggested just hours before. She could have kissed him, but recalled herself in time.

Surely it was his intention to dismiss her fear of him?

Surely he should not have succeeded so readily?

But Elizabeth could not deny his allure, or her own newfound trust.

She looked away, her heart skipping, lest he guess his effect upon her. She could not help but consider his words. What if Amaury was right and she did come to love Calum, as her mother had come to love her father? Alys and Maximilian loved each other, despite their match beginning in adversity. Perhaps love did conquer all, as the troubadours insisted. She was tempted to take Amaury's suggestion and follow his advice, but one detail could not be denied.

"If I shirk his embrace or flinch from his touch, will that not reveal my fears?"

"It might. A maiden can be shy on her nuptial night, though."

Elizabeth remained silent. She was no longer a maiden and she feared the import of that. Her silence probably told Amaury that truth or at least suggested it—if he had not guessed already.

But what could she do? Her choices were few and her heart filled with despair. Amaury would not take her to Kilderrick and she doubted she would reach there safely alone. Neither would he avert his gaze or fail to be vigilant this night.

By this time on the morrow, she would likely be wed to Calum.

By this time on the morrow, Calum might have taken a vengeance upon her. Or they might be happy in their nuptials and commencing upon a future together. Elizabeth wished she did not have to wait a day to know the outcome.

"If I do this, what assurance have I of happiness?" she asked, not truly expecting a reply.

"What assurance of happiness do you have otherwise?" Amaury asked, as maddeningly calm as she might have anticipated.

She looked up at him. "Do you tell the truth about your cousin?"

He touched his heart, solemn. "As I live and breathe."

"Give me your vow," she insisted.

"You have my word of honor, my lady. My cousin is happy beyond compare in her match."

Elizabeth frowned.

"You have need of a plan, my lady," Amaury suggested quietly.

"Why? I have no choices."

"There always are choices." Bête collapsed beside Amaury and put his chin on the knight's thigh, and Amaury rubbed the dog's ear. "There was a time, not so long ago, when I always expected matters to proceed according to plan."

"Perhaps not since Gaston's revelation?"

"And in that I have, to my embarrassment, learned something from the *Loup Argent*."

Elizabeth looked up.

"I was unprepared for bad tidings and chose badly as a result. Emotion ruled my decision, as it should not have done."

"You have made this point…"

"But I would make another. Maximilian was also to be disappointed at the funeral of Jean le Beau. He had long believed, for he had been told as much, that Château de Vries would fall to him upon Jean le Beau's demise. He arrived, expecting the seal to be placed in his hand. Gaston, however, after denouncing me, declared that he would claim Château de Vries himself, passing Château Pouissance to my younger brother." Amaury's eyes were a vehement blue. Elizabeth realized he was not so impassive as she had believed, but that she had to look more closely for hints of his reactions. "But the *Loup Argent* was not caught unawares," he continued. "Maximilian was prepared for disappointment, even though he arrived in hope of triumph. He had a plan, in case matters went awry."

"What was his plan?"

"He calmly asked for the seal of Kilderrick, claiming he would take that holding as his legacy. Gaston was more than glad to be rid of the burden of a distant and ruined holding. They went together to the treasury, purportedly for the seal but truly so that the master of the *Loup Argent*'s arsenal should know the treasury's location."

Elizabeth's thoughts flew as she reviewed the *Loup Argent*'s company. "Rafael?"

Amaury nodded. "Aye, truth be told another half-brother and son of Jean le Beau."

She inhaled sharply at this detail, but she did not doubt Amaury's word. How many bastards had that mercenary bred? She was not certain she wished to know.

"Then Maximilian left Gaston to his prize. He did not truly leave, though. He invited a small company from the household to flee with him and awaited them in the forest, for Maximilian protects those loyal to him." Elizabeth nodded, seeing that the brothers had that trait in common. "When they had arrived and darkness had fallen, when the window of the treasury lit with Gaston's arrival to count his prize, Rafael cast Greek fire at that tower, setting its interior aflame."

"The *Loup Argent* had his vengeance." He destroyed what had been taken from him rather than let another possess it. To Elizabeth's thinking, that was the choice of a mercenary. She did not like that Amaury obviously respected this.

But she was wrong about the reason for his admiration.

"More importantly, he had his plan. He knew what he would do if he was denied, and he made preparations for that possibility," Amaury said. "In contrast, I had made neither plans nor preparations. I accepted Maximilian's offer, even though I should never have joined his company. If I had paused to think, I would have recognized that my uncle would have a place for me in his household. If I had considered duty and honor, instead of choosing in anger and disappointment, I would have made a wiser decision. Better yet, I might have planned for the eventuality of Gaston denying me a legacy. I could have wed an heiress years ago." He met Elizabeth's gaze as she wondered whether he had a specific lady in his thoughts. "And what of you, my lady? What plan have you, if your betrothed does not wed you gladly?"

Belatedly, Elizabeth saw his point and admired it. "Why would he not?"

"Is he a man of generosity and kindness? Is he austere? Does he delight in the pleasures offered by life? Or is he prudent and careful beyond all?"

"I do not know."

"Does he care overmuch for the opinions of others?"

"I cannot say. I will guess that he intends to keep the goodwill of his laird and patron, Robert de Maxwell. He is sworn to that man's service."

Amaury nodded and when he spoke, his words were thoughtful. "Let no one know of the dagger, at least until you are assured of your spouse's good will."

Elizabeth was startled by his warning. "What do you think will happen when I wed him?"

Amaury shrugged. "I think he will wed you and I hope you will be happy as his spouse." He raised his gaze to hers. "But it is possible that he will not like that you fled the nuptials originally or that he may take a reckoning from you for the delay. He may wait to do as much in privacy, perhaps in the nuptial chamber, rather than let others witness his dismay."

Elizabeth swallowed. "It is better to be prepared," she said quietly.

"Before the sun rises, I will give you some guidance in the use of the weapon."

"I thank you," she whispered, glad of her unexpected ally. "And we are agreed upon the tale?"

"So far as I know, you were taken from your home against your will and would have come sooner to your betrothed had it been safe for you to do so."

Elizabeth nodded.

"The match must have been for some advantage and the agreement made after much deliberation," Amaury said, chiding her slightly. "I fear you have convinced yourself that the situation is more dire than it is."

"Like your cousin, Felicia."

"I would wish you all her happiness."

Elizabeth accepted what she had to do. She would wed Calum and hope for the best.

But still there was one detail that stood in the path of that joyous resolution—the possibility that she would flinch from his touch.

"I would ask a favor of you, sir," she said on impulse. She felt her face heat as she sought the words. She was keenly aware that Amaury was watching her intently. "I would know what it is to welcome a man's kiss," she managed to confess. "I have learned only to fight or run, even to faint, but your counsel is wise. I must welcome Calum to allay any doubts he may have, and I do not know how to do as much."

In truth, that was not the only reason she wished to have Amaury kiss her, but Elizabeth would not admit that, even to herself.

He blinked as if astounded. "You would grant me a kiss?"

"I would ask that you grant me one." Her cheeks were burning with the audacity of her request, but Amaury stood up and turned toward her. He was serious but his gaze heated in a way that warmed her to her toes. Elizabeth caught her breath and put her hand in the breadth of his, her heart thundering as she let him raise her to her feet. His eyes fairly glowed with admiration as his other hand rose to her face. His fingertips grazed her cheek, as if he thought her too fragile to touch, and the slide of their warmth into her hair almost made Elizabeth dizzy. She could not look away from the glow in his eyes.

She felt beautiful. Cherished. It was a thrilling combination and had to account for the fire in her veins.

"You grow bold, my lady," Amaury murmured, his low voice making her quiver with yearning. "I cannot imagine that your spouse will be displeased to have such a bride." His fingers eased into her hair, his hand cupping her nape as he lifted her to her toes. His caress was heavenly, both gentle and filled with power. Elizabeth found her lips parting in anticipation.

And that was before Amaury claimed her lips in a persuasive and satisfying kiss.

CHAPTER 5

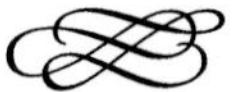

To have Elizabeth request a kiss was sufficient to shatter Amaury's resolve. He wanted her to know that there could be sweetness between a man and a woman, as well as mutual pleasure, but it was delicious torment to have her soft lips against his own.

He had to remember that she was not his to claim.

It was a lesson, no more than that, a request from a lady he was compelled to fulfill.

All the same, he felt his grip tighten upon her waist, his fingers spreading as he pulled her closer instinctively. She felt good against him, slender but sweetly curved, her breasts against his chest. He knew his eyes closed as he slid his free hand into the silk of her hair. He had never known the like of her and knew no other would ever compare. He lifted his head, breaking their embrace, even as he raged for more.

Calum, he reminded himself savagely, would not be able to keep from cherishing her.

He deliberately put distance between them, hoping that she did not notice his agitation.

He was aware that Elizabeth's hand rose to the lips he had just sampled—but not thoroughly enough—and she smiled.

"Oh," she said, then smiled more broadly at him.

Temptation rose hot. Amaury turned his back upon the lady, striding to the other side of the fire and ignoring her as best he could.

Elizabeth did not seem to be troubled by his rudeness.

"Is it always thus?" she asked quietly and once more, Amaury was fool enough to look at her. She held his cloak wrapped around herself, that expression of wonder still upon her face. She seemed radiant to him, alight with the pleasure of their kiss, and that only twisted the knife, for Amaury knew he could never touch her again.

He should not have touched her this once.

He should not have let her touch him.

But this lady had the ability to make him forget duty and responsibility. Her power was perilous.

"It can be," he managed to say finally. His tone was gruff but she did not seem to mind. "When lovers meet, I wager it is."

"And that is the sum of it. Well." She took a deep breath and donned his cloak.

"That is the start of it," he felt compelled to note.

Her eyes widened. "It improves?"

"It quite reliably does."

"Oh." She caught her breath and looked over their camp. "In marriage as well as in love?"

"It can be so, I am given to understand."

"Then why would anyone leave their bedchamber?"

Amaury snorted with laughter, surprised into it.

He fell silent when Elizabeth closed the distance between them and touched a fingertip to his mouth. Even that sent a surge of heat through him. "I like your smile," she whispered and desire raged through him unchecked.

She was irresistible. He could not deny himself one last taste but he did not trust himself to kiss her lips again. Amaury held her gaze as he turned his head the slightest increment. Pleasure flooded through him as he kissed the softness of her palm. Something flared in her eyes, a flush stained her cheeks and it took all within him to step away.

This was too much temptation. Amaury knew when he reached his limit. He retreated and bowed to her, formal again as his desire burned. "I shall endeavor to follow your counsel, my lady."

"Am I your lady?"

She was thinking of tales, no doubt, in which a knight serves the whim of a married lady, but that was no game for Amaury. "For this night alone, I wager. Your husband will not welcome my service, to be sure."

She sobered then. "No, I suspect he will not." She bowed her head as she settled before the fire again and he felt a cur for having disappointed her in any way.

Her resolve was impressive—indeed, it was far more fascinating than he would have expected—but Amaury knew what had to be done. He had promised her a lesson with the knife, and perhaps this was the moment. She looked to be in no mood to fight but Amaury could change that.

He would provoke her, with the advice he had been given but had never found compelling himself. "A lady," he said firmly. "Should be demure."

Elizabeth flicked a lethal glance his way. "Demure?"

Amaury nodded, thinking of Sylvia and the burden of her companionship. She had been demure, to be sure. "Also biddable and amenable to her husband's will."

"Biddable," Elizabeth repeated with undisguised annoyance. "Like a dog."

Amaury nodded again. "Beautiful and a pleasure to the eye."

"Like a tapestry," she said, her tone sour.

"Those are the traits of an admirable lady. Undoubtedly you were taught the same and should you embrace these notions, your marriage will fare well." He nodded, as if pleased with his own conclusion.

Then he deliberately averted his gaze, granting her an opportunity.

Of course, she took it.

Amaury had expected no less.

~

How wondrous a single kiss could be!

Elizabeth had no notion of the pleasure that could be conjured with such a caress shared willingly—until Amaury had shown her. She felt warm to her toes and yet shivery. She both savored the sensation and was hungry for more. Much more. The fact that she had requested the embrace and partaken of it by choice had changed all.

'Twas inappropriate that she should share more than a single kiss with this man who defended her, but Elizabeth could not keep herself from wishing to feel his caress again.

If nothing else, Amaury's kiss gave her hope. It prompted her to recall that her parents had found happiness in their arranged marriage, and that they had certainly enjoyed pleasure abed together. She had been told often that she had been conceived in love and merriment. How had she forgotten that detail? The memory, the kiss and even Amaury's argument reassured her that she might indeed find contentment in her match with Calum.

Indeed, the kiss—and the choice of whether to even welcome it—reawakened Elizabeth's confidence. She could choose. She could decide her own fate. She could welcome the future with Calum or turn it aside. She felt bold, as she had that long-ago night when she had fled Beaupoint, confident that she could determine her own fate.

And that fed her resolve to follow her uncle's bidding, to wed Calum, and to know comfort and security again. He would not find her a meek bride, content to do as he dictated. Perhaps Calum would not desire a wife with fire in her eyes.

Elizabeth would not be otherwise, though she would do her duty.

How curious that the kiss which had set her very soul afire seemed to have turned Amaury to stone once more. She felt as if she had awakened from a long sleep, but he was even more grim than ever.

She wanted to provoke his response again, which meant she had to surprise him. She wanted to see his eyes flash, to see him smile—even to prompt his laughter. 'Twas only fair that she nudge him to wakefulness again as he had awakened her. They both had decisions to make and futures to discover, and she wanted him to have his own dreams fulfilled. That would never happen when he was grim, if not bitter.

But then, Amaury erred.

He gave her advice that she could never accept.

Elizabeth was prepared to grant this assured knight a surprise, if not two.

~

AMAURY DID NOT HAVE to wait long.

Elizabeth lunged toward him, unfastening the clasp of his cloak so that it fell to the ground behind her as she sprang. His own dagger flashed but he spun and snatched for the weapon. He missed, and Amaury knew that the sight of her in his chemise, her curves silhouetted by the fire, was a surprise and a distraction. She also switched the knife to the other hand and drove it against his other side, moving with impressive speed. It nicked his chemise and pricked his side before he seized it from her. When he would have grabbed her, she kicked him hard and retreated, eyes blazing as she put the fire between them.

"Biddable," she echoed, her opinion of that most clear.

Amaury struggled against his urge to laugh. "Predictable," he countered and her eyes blazed.

What a beauty. The firelight favored her, gilding her skin, caressing her face, putting glints of red and gold in her hair. She might have been made of flame herself, as filled with fire as a phoenix in a tale. How would she greet him abed? When she was not fearful, Amaury could only imagine that she would be a wondrous lover, welcoming and seductive. He would not resent Calum's good fortune. He would not regret his own lack. He glanced down, knowing that temptation would not serve either of them well, and put the dagger in his belt.

"Is that how you grant a gift?" she demanded, indicating the blade.

"You will have it back soon enough," he said and her lips tightened in disbelief. She folded her arms across her chest and watched him warily as he walked to the end of the shelter. Had she known the alluring sight she made, she would have seized the cloak again. It took some effort for Amaury to feign disinterest and turn away.

Her gaze fairly bored a hole in his back. He could not truly be surprised that this lady's fire stirred him beyond every expectation.

"When?" she demanded.

"Once our lesson is completed." He chose a stick from the old roof and broke it in half, taking his heavier knife to whittle the shape.

"What are you doing?"

"We will use sticks," he explained.

"Sticks?" She drew closer to him, frowning at the shape he carved of the first stick. It was close to that of a dagger, but with a blunted point.

"Weapons of peace," he said with a nod. "That way, neither of us will be injured inadvertently."

"It seems less than ideal."

He cast her a glance. "Because you cannot cut out my heart with a stick?"

She laughed, surprised by his charge, but did not deny it. Indeed, she blushed in a most enticing way.

What a glorious creature she was.

Amaury frowned and looked back at his task. "My uncle found it suitable. I trained for two years with sticks before I felt the weight of a sword in my hand."

"He taught you well, then?"

"'Twas his responsibility."

"Duty again," she muttered. "But not all men would have welcomed such a task, or performed it well."

Amaury nodded, then considered the end of the stick before whittling it a bit more. "Raymond is an honorable man, who fulfills his obligations with joy."

"You miss him."

"And why not?" Amaury did not wait for a reply, but stood and offered her one of the sticks.

"You miss France," she suggested quietly instead of taking it.

He was shocked that she had discerned anything of his thoughts and feelings.

"It would be irrational not to miss the life I knew there," he said tightly.

"Do you miss anything or anyone else?" Her curiosity was beguiling, but Amaury would not be tempted to confide in her. They had only this night together and she already knew too much of him. If he shared more, she might guess the truth in his heart—she might not do her duty to Calum and it would be his fault. Amaury could not abide even the suggestion that he might provoke her to abandon her responsibility.

He handed her one of the sticks instead.

He strode into the motte so there was space, then held up his own, inviting her to fight. When she muttered something unflattering beneath her breath then came after him with purpose, he knew that she would certainly try to do him injury, even with a stick.

Indeed, he welcomed the challenge.

~

Elizabeth should have known better than to expect another confession or explanation. Perhaps she had been saved by a sphinx. Amaury certainly shared that creature's affection for riddles and enigmas.

He was due for a surprise.

Elizabeth gripped the stick as she concocted a plan.

Amaury had stepped into the motte, away from the fire and the shelter, and even without his hauberk, he was no vulnerable opponent. They circled each other. He watched her, waiting and wary, leaving her to make the first move. He was poised to spring, his every muscle taut, and Elizabeth doubted she could defeat him.

Was it possible to surprise a hunter of such experience?

She could only try.

Oliver was sound asleep from the sound and the horses dozed. The rain had stopped and the clouds had cleared. There were stars overhead but no wind. The air was cool and the ground of the motte was rapidly drying. As they circled each other, Amaury's features moved from being lit by the fire into full shadow over and over.

That was the key. Facing the fire, Elizabeth knew she would be fully revealed. When Amaury faced the fire, she would be in silhouette and her actions just as clear to discern. She would strike when she was half in shadow, when it was harder for him to discern what she did with the obscured hand.

She had to admire his patience. He did not taunt. He did not try to provoke her. He simply moved in silence, his gaze locked upon her. Patience was his great gift and she did not doubt it had been learned.

He might be infuriating but he was also intriguing. How she wished she might spend more than one night in his company.

The greater concern was to defeat him.

When her hand was shadowed, Elizabeth suddenly lunged toward

Amaury. She lifted the stick at the last moment, guessing he would deflect the blow. He did, their sticks cracking against each other, then spun to seize her wrist. But Elizabeth passed the stick to her other hand and struck at him from behind, aiming a blow at his blind side. The stick brushed across his tabard on the back of his shoulder, and she saw his eyes light with surprise. He released her wrist, casting her away from him and retreated.

"Well done," he said, but his tone did not hold the warmth she had hoped to hear. They circled each other again, but Elizabeth's heart was beating more quickly. "Can you use your left hand as well as your right?"

"Better," she admitted. "My inclination is to use my left. I had to be taught to favor my right."

"That is a gift."

"I did not think it at the time."

He made a sound that was neither a snort nor a breath of laughter, but his eyes shone more brightly. "But it gives you the chance of surprising an opponent as you just did. That is an asset, indeed."

Elizabeth could not ignore the rush of pride prompted by his words.

"Aim always for points of vulnerability," Amaury continued, his words low and steady as they circled each other anew. "The face. The eyes. The groin. Keep surprise on your side. Step inside a blow and strike quickly. Use any advantage you can find. Subterfuge and surprise."

"And if I have no knife?"

"Your fingernails can be weapons. A knuckle in the eye will cause pain. An elbow or a knee can distract an opponent, as can a heel brought down hard on a toe. You have struck me with the top of your head. That is good. Cast sand in the face of your assailant. Use any means you can contrive. And run. Run whenever you can. You are agile and quick. Know your strengths."

"Surely that is cheating."

"Surely there are no rules when a lady is assaulted."

This time, she feinted with her left hand and switched to her right. As she expected, Amaury anticipated her, but when he caught one wrist and then the other, she had planned for that. She dropped the stick, then bent and drove her head against him. Her onslaught sent him staggering backward, but when he might have seized her, she lifted her head abruptly. She caught him under the chin with the back of her head. He grunted as he released her, then retreated.

This time, his gaze simmered as he lifted one hand to his mouth and studied her. "I bit my tongue." He stared at her, surprised that she had achieved even this small victory, and Elizabeth smiled in triumph.

"But you relinquished your grip," she said with satisfaction, bending to retrieve her stick. A second too late, she knew she had erred.

In a flash, Amaury was upon her. He kicked the stick away just before her fingers closed over it and caught her around the waist. He scooped her up and flung her over his shoulder, but Elizabeth kicked and struggled. While he battled to retain a grip upon her, she flung herself from side to side. He wrestled to hold her fast and she spied his bare forearm.

She bit him, recalling the way Alys had bitten Maximilian, and he swore with unexpected heat as he struggled to move her and keep his balance. Elizabeth kicked the back of his legs and he fell, cradling her against his chest so that he took the brunt of the impact. He landed hard upon his back and froze as if winded. Elizabeth seized the opportunity to grab the dagger from his belt and twisted around to touch its blade to his neck.

Amaury blinked but did not move. Elizabeth was atop him, almost seated upon his chest, a bit winded herself and warm. His arms were locked around her and he was so very close. She could feel the breath he took and could not look away from the vivid blue of his eyes.

"Well done," he murmured. "Three times in a row."

"Perhaps I learn to be unpredictable."

"Perhaps you do."

And then he smiled.

God in Heaven, what a sight. The smile curved Amaury's lips slowly, so slowly that Elizabeth was reminded of the sun cresting the horizon each morning. His features softened and his eyes lit, making him more handsome than ever. 'Twas as if she watched him thaw and when that dimple finally made its appearance, her heart clenched tightly at the sight.

He raised one hand, keeping his other arm locked around her waist, and lifted the dagger from her hand. His hand was warm, his touch gentle but firm. His gaze never swerved from hers and the heat in his eyes was undiminished. "You are a marvel," he said, the words low as if he had not meant to utter them, and Elizabeth was enchanted.

She leaned closer, unable to resist temptation, and touched her fingertip to his mouth. "You should smile more often," she said. "It makes you look so much less fearsome."

"I cannot believe that to be a good thing," he murmured, sobering anew, and would have moved her aside.

Elizabeth bent on impulse to touch her lips to his again.

She felt Amaury's shock but he neither pushed her aside nor surrendered to the embrace. He did not seize or claim her, but let her do what she would with him. She felt possessed of a power she had not realized she held.

A kiss, willingly given, could be a greater weapon than a blade. Elizabeth was astounded by that, and by the heat that suffused her body as her lips rested upon his. This man seemed determined to challenge her every expectation and this one she would abandon readily. She had never felt pleasure with a man, not until this night, and one taste had only made her hungry for more.

She wanted more.

Her braid fell heavily to one side and her breath caught, but Amaury let her kiss him. He was hers to command and that was a sensation she would not readily surrender. All the same, it seemed to be a less than satisfactory embrace. She did not know how to touch a man. She did not know how to improve upon her beginning.

Embarrassed, she lifted her head and knew she flushed crimson. "I am sorry."

"Do not apologize for such a gift," Amaury said, his voice husky. "You offer a boon and most unexpectedly." He was deadly serious now, his gaze dark. His hand trailed down her cheek and she felt both the warmth of his touch and his tenderness. That he should temper his strength for her was potent indeed.

"I do not know how..." she whispered.

"You began well," Amaury murmured. She watched him swallow. "If you wished to try again, I would not protest." That teasing glint was in his eyes again, the one that made her feel daring and bold.

Elizabeth smiled at him, reminding herself that she had nothing to fear from this man. "Truly?"

Amaury smiled outright. "Truly, my lady. I am your captive at this moment."

Elizabeth laughed, her heart fluttering, then touched her lips to his again.

~

A MAN SHOULD USE caution when making a wish.

Amaury had not truly expected Elizabeth to kiss him again, but she challenged his expectations again. This time, she angled her mouth over his, demanding as she had not been before. He felt her lips part. He tasted her breath, and Amaury feared she might kill him with a caress. He heard himself moan softly, then he could resist no longer. He rolled Elizabeth to her back, bracing himself over her, and let his passion flood their kiss. Too late, he feared he might frighten her, but yet again, she defied expectation. Elizabeth gasped but did not pull away.

To his delight and surprise, she locked her fingers in his hair, drawing him closer, demanding yet more. She fairly blossomed beneath him, welcoming him, mimicking his moves so that his blood turned to fire. A flick of his tongue prompted an echo from hers; the graze of his teeth made her nip at him. She was intoxicating, so ardent and willing that Amaury forgot all he knew to be true. There was only Elizabeth, only her sweet desire, only the ardor awakened from first glimpse but fed to an inferno on this one night.

Amaury deepened their kiss, savoring her, but when she arched her back and let her leg twine around his, he knew it went too far.

He had to halt while he could.

He would not become like his blood father.

He was not like Jean le Beau.

Amaury broke the kiss and rose abruptly to his feet. He marched toward the fire as he put distance between himself and temptation.

Who would have expected a kiss to shake him as vehemently as this one had? To be sure, it had been a kiss of short duration, but its power was staggering—and more than enough to make him forget his principles.

Duty and honor, he reminded himself sternly, even as desire burned hot. His very blood was on fire, his heart raced, his body was taut with need. He clenched his fists, battling for control, then belatedly recalled his manners.

He pivoted and returned to Elizabeth, formally offering his hand to her.

She regarded him as if mystified by him then smiled, the sight melting his resolve. Amaury swallowed and looked toward the gate. The lady slid her hand into his, the very motion a caress, her hand a delicate weight within his, then let him lift her to her feet. She did not move away and he could feel her studying him. Amaury risked a downward glance and wished he had not, for she was flushed and her eyes were sparkling. On the other hand, he could not regret the beguiling sight of her pleasure.

He spied his cloak, abandoned for their 'lesson', and seized it, carrying it back to her. "You will be cold," he said gruffly, nearly casting the garment at her. "It will not be long until the dawn. I suggest you sleep." He did not wait for her reply before pivoting to leave her side again.

He stood on the cliff overlooking the river, letting the cold air diminish his desire as the lady settled to sleep. He thought she would not flee, but he would be certain. He waited and he watched. The skies lightened in the east and a mist rose from the river.

Two kisses and he was shaken to his marrow.

Elizabeth made Amaury sharply aware of all he had lost. He knew he had possessed every advantage and had not appreciated his good fortune until it was gone, but now he saw more. Sharing even part of his tale with her had made the truth clear.

He was Amaury de Vries no longer.

He was not Gaston's son, which meant he was not of the lineage of de Vries. The insignia of the griffin rampant, associated with that family, was no longer his to bear. He had no right to wear his surcoat, emblazoned with that insignia, or to put the caparisons similarly embellished upon Zephyr. He should pack them up and deliver them to his younger brother, Philip.

Who was he?

Denied by Gaston, Amaury could not be denied by his mother and her kin. That blood bond was beyond dispute. Elizabeth had guessed aright that he admired his uncle. He would call himself Amaury d'Evroi, after the holding of his uncle, his mother's family—and his destination. At Evroi, he would create a new future for himself.

He spared a glance toward the lady beneath his protection. After he took her to her betrothed at Caerlaverock, he would never see her again. Elizabeth would wed Calum. She would see the merit of duty. She might be with child by the spring. Amaury had given her his best dagger and she had given him a kiss that had shaken his world. They had exchanged all that could be shared honorably and Amaury could not—or would not—admit to wishing for more.

He began to pack the caparisons away.

He was a knight to his marrow, even if he was no longer Amaury de Vries.

ELIZABETH AWAKENED, halfway thinking she was home in her own bed again. She was enveloped in fur, warm beneath a wool cloak, one dog curled against her belly and another behind her knees. She felt the sunlight on her face and opened her eyes to a sky of glorious blue.

She had slept late. The sun was high and the day was already pleasantly warm. The fire had died down to ash and the caparisons that had hung from the rafters had vanished. There was also no sign of Amaury and Elizabeth feared for a moment that he had abandoned her.

How curious that she feared that first, rather than seeing an opportunity to flee.

Elizabeth sat up hastily and saw immediately that she was not alone. Oliver was polishing the destrier's hooves on the far side of the shelter and the palfreys were all tethered there as well. If Amaury had left, he had done so on foot.

No doubt the boy watched her in the knight's absence.

And where would Amaury have gone? He would not abandon all his possessions without good cause. Why would he take the caparisons but not the destrier? Elizabeth doubted he would hunt again this morn since he intended for them to ride to Caerlaverock. Perhaps he assessed the road they must take.

She would not think about parting ways with the man who had challenged her notions so effectively. She could not bear the notion that she might never see him again. She admired him and trusted him, because of his principles, and she could have become accustomed to seeking the subtle hints of the passion he strove to hide.

What would he be like when he lost his heart?

Elizabeth would never know.

She roused the dogs so she could get to her feet. Oliver was working diligently, as if he might not complete his tasks in time. Zephyr's dark mane had been braided and bound with blue ribbons. The great beast's neck was arched and his nostrils flared as he was tended, evidence that he was just as vain as every other warhorse Elizabeth had ever known. Oliver bowed to her and continued to brush the destrier to a gloss, his hands fairly flying over the creature's sides.

"You are diligent," she said to him after they had greeted each other.

Oliver shook his head. "He says we must be splendid this day, so that you arrive to your nuptials like a queen."

"Splendid?" Elizabeth echoed, curious at the choice.

"He said much about pageantry and appearances influencing results. I could not heed it all, not with so much to do." The boy frowned. "His plate armor has not been polished in a month and there are four horses to tend." He flicked a look at her. "He said we would ride out as soon as you awakened."

"May I help?"

"Of course not, my lady." Oliver smiled and inclined his head. "I apologize for my poor temper."

"The horses look beautiful."

He paused to survey them. "I thought they all should have their manes braided, not just this proud beast." Zephyr twisted around to nip at the boy's hair, and Oliver laughed as he brushed the stallion's head aside.

Splendid. What a notion. Elizabeth herself had no chance of being so splendid on this day. She could only regret the kirtles she had left behind at Beaupoint, the slippers and cloaks, the belts and veils and circlets. She understood Amaury's meaning as Oliver insisted he did not. Appearances did influence the welcome one gave and received. She did not want to appear at Caerlaverock as a ragged waif. It would not have been all bad to be arrayed in finery for her nuptials, but on this day, she would settle on being clean.

Grise followed her as she walked to the old latrine, the dog taking her own relief in the short growth near the edge of the cliff. A moment later, Grise peered over the lip and barked, tail wagging like a banner. It was a joyous bark, which was answered by a man's response.

Amaury.

Warmth flooded through Elizabeth at just the confirmation that he was near. Though she had not been able to look upon him when he had washed the night before, their kisses had fed her curiosity and her boldness—and at this distance, he might not notice her perusal. She eased to the edge of the cliff when she was done and caught the scruff of the dog's neck, as if to ensure that Grise did not slip, and then she looked.

Oh.

Amaury bathed in the river below. Of course, he was nude. The water rose only to the midst of his thighs, which left plenty of tanned skin exposed to her view. Once Elizabeth looked, she could not do otherwise, though she felt the heat of her blush all the way to her toes.

Amaury was magnificent, wrought as perfectly as a man could be. The drop was not so great that she could not discern details, and she found herself studying him avidly. He turned away from her, bending to immerse himself in the water and Elizabeth could only admire the taut curve of his buttocks and the power of his thighs. His shoulders were broad, his back muscled and tanned, and he moved with grace. She knew his body was hard for she had felt as much during their fight, but she greatly liked the sight of it.

He straightened and flung back his head, the droplets of water catching the morning sunlight. When he pivoted, she could see the tangle of dark blond hair upon his chest, the way it grew in a vee that pointed downward. It was only natural to follow the line and her eyes widened at the sight before she blushed. Still she did not avert her gaze. He speared his fingers through his hair, pushing it back from his face in a tangle, and she stared.

Then his expression lit with surprise.

Elizabeth retreated quickly, certain he had spotted her. Amaury moved with purpose toward the bank and she halfway thought he might climb it to confront her. Instead, he crouched down in the shallows, then bent over something she could not see. She leaned forward but he was out of her view. What was he doing?

"Ha!" he muttered with satisfaction. When he became visible to her again, something glinted in his hand. He washed it in the river water, then strode to the bank a little downstream. Elizabeth watched as he dried himself, then donned his chemise, chausses and boots. The cloth clung to his skin, revealing his body still. He marched toward the entrance to the motte, tossing that item in one hand and catching it.

She returned to the fire, holding her hands to its warmth as if she had not been watching him. The dogs ran to meet him at the gate, barking with delight.

"Good morning to you," she said when he bowed to her from the other side of the fire.

He held up the item he had retrieved. "It is already a day of good fortune."

"How so?"

"The corpse had not washed away in the night. I was able to retrieve my bolt, after all."

That was what he had taken from the fallen man the night before. "And you did not flee." His satisfaction was clear.

"I scarce had the chance."

He granted her a very blue look. "If a way could have been found, you would have discovered it, my lady." He said this as if it was neither praiseworthy nor a fault.

"Because I am not biddable?" she asked and he almost smiled.

"There is that."

"I understand we are to be splendid this day."

His eyes glinted. "We shall do what we can. We leave shortly," he added, as if to urge her to hasten, and Elizabeth took the hint.

Amaury beckoned to Oliver, who immediately brought a dagger and a mirror of polished silver. The boy held the mirror while Amaury checked the sharpness of the blade, then carefully shaved his whiskers.

Elizabeth's chemise was stiff after drying in the night air, but it was her own and the cloth would soften in the wearing. Once she would have been troubled by her lack of maid or attendant, but she had learned to lace the sides of her own kirtle and braid her own hair well enough. By the time she tied the lace at the end of her braid, Amaury was dressing with Oliver's assistance and she openly watched.

On this day, he evidently had chosen to wear his full armor, not just the mail hauberk, thus Oliver's earlier complaint. The knight's hair was drying in the sun, looking more blond than it had earlier, the waves gilded by the light. He donned a red padded aketon over his chemise. It was laced down the back and tightly fitted, making her keenly aware of the lean power of his body. His hauberk went over his head and was laced in the back, as well. It fell to his knees, shining like silver after Oliver's efforts, and Amaury's boots were polished to a gleam. Oliver darted around Amaury, fastening buckles and tightening straps on the plate armor as the knight directed him in a rumbling undertone.

Over the mail, Amaury donned arm defenses that were tied at the elbow. He wore steel cuisses over his thighs and greaves over his calves, and sabatons of shining silver over his boots. She was surprised that he wore his dark tabard over the armor, for it seemed plain in contrast. She recalled knights wearing a shorter and more fitted surcoat, emblazoned with their insignia, but not Amaury. It seemed to her that his surcoat should have matched the caparisons that had vanished. They were not on the destrier, but she had not imagined them.

White with a blue griffin rampant.

If they were to be splendid, why had that raiment vanished?

Amaury buckled on his sword, this scabbard studded with gems that caught the sunlight. He hung a different dagger from his belt on the other side. A mail aventail hung to his shoulders. Oliver crouched to buckle on his spurs as Amaury donned his gauntlets, made of leather with lattens around the wrist and more steel gleaming on the fingers.

The sunlight reflected off the polished armor, making him look as bright as the sun.

His cloak was deep indigo lined with white fur flecked with black, cut full and long, clipped over his shoulders. That lining could only be ermine and Elizabeth noticed that he hesitated a moment before casting it over his shoulders.

But she wore the plainer one and the wind was too chill to be without a cloak in this season.

Oliver led Zephyr from the shelter and the destrier tossed his head and stamped his feet, clearly proud of his appearance. The two of them armored the horse with a chain mail trapper that had to be heavy. It fell to the steed's knees and covered him from chin to rump in shining rings of steel. There was armor for his head and a padded saddle with stirrups hanging from its sides. With his mane braided and tail tied, Zephyr was as elegant as his master.

Amaury circled the horse, bending to buff one hoof, straightening a ribbon in his tail, adjusting a stirrup. It had been a long time since Elizabeth had seen the like of either of them. Oliver handed Amaury his bassinet and the pair of them turned to her, the knight's expression as impassive as it had been the night before.

How she yearned to see his smile one last time!

CHAPTER 6

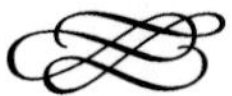

"You both are splendid indeed," Elizabeth said, moving closer to admire the horse. She did not say that she felt quite plain in comparison.

"You shall not appear as a woman come to beg for mercy, but as a lady come to grace her betrothed with her hand. It would be neither fitting nor strategic to appear otherwise."

Amaury spoke formally, as if they were strangers.

"The finery is yours," she had to note.

"And I am pledged to your service." Amaury continued when she did not reply. "The splendor of a servant reflects upon the one he serves."

Again, he was thinking of Calum's reaction and she appreciated his impulse.

He gestured to Oliver, who combed his own hair hastily and strove to neaten his appearance.

"What happened to the caparisons?" she asked.

Amaury's gaze flicked, a subtle hint that she had found a matter of import. "They are embroidered with an insignia that is not mine to wear." He spoke stiffly but with resolve.

Ah. "And who would know?"

His sidelong glance was hot. Elizabeth felt a surge of satisfaction that she had provoked a response from him. "*I* would know," Amaury said. "It would be wrong to wear them or my surcoat."

Duty and honor again.

Elizabeth wondered whether she could provoke his smile again before they reached Caerlaverock.

"Surely the cloak is in the house colors," she said lightly.

His lips tightened. "But it bears no insignia."

Elizabeth lifted the plain cloak from her shoulders. "Would you prefer that I returned this one?"

He surveyed her. "You will be cold."

"We could trade."

His eyes glittered and she thought he would not respond, then he swept the finer cloak from his shoulders and offered it to her. Truly, both were far beyond the richness of any cloak she had ever owned, even at Beaupoint, but the blue and white one was majestic. Elizabeth felt like a queen when it was upon her shoulders and she knew she stood taller.

Amaury was watching her and the intensity of his scrutiny made her heart flutter again. "My apologies, my lady, I should have offered it sooner. The hue suits you well."

God in heaven, she wanted another kiss from this man before their paths parted forever, but he was so grim that she feared he would decline if she asked.

'Twas then she noticed that there was a ribbon tied on the scabbard for Amaury's sword, at the top where it hung from his belt. The ribbon was as red as blood, a narrow, curled frippery that had no place in a knight's finery.

It was a lady's trophy. She had heard of ladies granting such favors to the knights they admired. The lady would tie her ribbon to the knight's lance before he jousted, taking it from her hair or her girdle, a public sign of her interest.

Or affection.

Elizabeth's heart sank like a stone, for a riddle had just been solved. That was the reason Amaury turned aside from her and their kiss. His heart was claimed, undoubtedly by a lady far to their south. *She* was the reason he would return to France. She was the one who prompted his smile and thawed his demeanor. Undoubtedly, she was both biddable and beautiful.

That lady and Amaury's commitment to her was the reason he had turned to stone again. He would believe that any attention to any other woman was a sign of infidelity.

Even though Elizabeth rode to wed Calum, she was disappointed. She could only hope that her betrothed stirred her as readily as this man did.

Her throat tightened but she would not be fearful.

"May I carry Persephone?" she asked, as if the bird had drawn her attention.

"Of course." He offered his hand to her. "Shall we ride? You should be with your betrothed by midday."

She took his hand, ignoring the little stab of disappointment that had no place in her wedded-life-to-be. "I thank you, sir," she whispered, her gaze clinging to his. "For all you have given to me."

"I am honored to have been of service," he said with another of the little bows that made her want to draw his own blade against him.

One palfrey had a saddle upon her back, a much simpler one than Amaury's, and he adjusted the stirrups, glancing between her and the straps to gauge the height. It was the palfrey with the white star on her brow, a pretty mare.

"This is Esther, is it not?" she asked Oliver, who nodded agreement.

Amaury lifted Elizabeth to the saddle, releasing her quickly, and she hooked one knee around the front of the saddle, locking her other foot into the stirrup. He checked the length again, ensuring that her seat was secure. She kept her gaze fixed upon the leather gauntlet Amaury bound to her arm, then sat straighter as he put the bird on her fist. Persephone's weight was welcome and the jesses felt good in her grip.

Amaury walked around the horse, adjusting Elizabeth's cloak so that it spilled evenly on all sides.

"You will arrive in splendor, my lady," he told her with an intent look that made her mouth go dry.

"Borrowed splendor."

"But magnificent all the same." He whistled and the dogs gathered around the destrier as he swung into the saddle.

Their little party rode out of the motte, Elizabeth on Amaury's left and Oliver behind with the other palfreys, then left the old bailey behind. By the time they crossed the river Annan, the mist was rising and the dogs were running ahead. Soon their ways would part forevermore, but Elizabeth could not think of one word to say.

She simply held her chin high and hoped for the best.

~

ELIZABETH LOOKED GLORIOUS.

There was a new confidence about the lady this morning, and that gave her a radiance that Amaury found most attractive. She sat tall in the saddle, her chin high, and he thought her majestic, despite her worn garb. She rode with grace, her long auburn hair loose and shining in the sunlight, brushed to a gloss. She was not a maiden come to beg forgiveness of her spouse, but one who rode to him in triumph. Amaury could scarcely bear to look upon her—nor could he stand to look away.

He was glad she had offered to carry the hawk, for he wanted his hands free. They might be assaulted on their way, or they might not be welcomed with joy at Caerlaverock. It was good for Oliver to be similarly unencumbered.

He wondered whether the lady had guessed as much. She was not a fool, to be sure.

He was absurdly proud of her for having chosen to fulfill her duty. 'Twas not his concern, but he could only feel his influence had been good in this case.

That gave him a rare sense of accomplishment.

"You are pleased with yourself this day," she said, her tone wry. "Is it because you wear your armor?"

"Why would that be of import?"

"You do not need me to tell you again that you look most attractive."

It did not trouble Amaury to hear the words again, all the same. "I am content that you do your duty and keep your uncle's pledge. There might have been a purpose in my coming to this land, after all."

"I am glad to have provided a justification," she said and they rode in silence for some moments.

Amaury understood that she still had concerns about the match with Calum, but there was little more he could do about that. Time—and the man himself—would undoubtedly improve her view of the match.

"Tell me of Caerlaverock," he invited.

"The keep has a distinctive shape," Elizabeth said, her tone was as formal as his had been this morning. He told himself to be glad that their thoughts were as one, but he missed her passion. "For it was built in the shape of a triangle. There are four towers, two forming a gatehouse and the other two more distant. It has stood almost a hundred years, stronghold of the Maxwell family, but was seized and destroyed in recent years. It was restored to Robert de Maxwell who has rebuilt and fortified it again this past decade. I am not certain whether the repairs are completed. The drawbridge is between those two close-set towers."

She spoke crisply, as one certain of her facts, and Amaury wondered whether her father had ensured that she had a particularly good education. One heard of sole daughters being so taught. Either way, what she told them now was most useful.

"A great moat surrounds all, so my father said."

"You have not visited it?"

She shook her head. "But he came after Robert de Maxwell reclaimed the seal, and admired it greatly. There is an abandoned keep to the south, not far from the new one. It is closer to the firth: the old keep had a harbor as well as a moat. We will ride past the ruins, no doubt."

"It is now abandoned?"

She nodded back toward the place where they had spent the night. "Much like that one, and for much the same reason. Flood waters were high repeatedly for some years. When the keeps flooded, the lairds moved their abodes to higher ground. At Caerlaverock, old and new are close together, while at Annan they are miles apart."

"Annan?" Amaury repeated.

"We took shelter in the old motte-and-bailey of Annan, built by the de Brus family. They now abide at Lochmaben."

"What of your family home?"

"Beaupoint?"

Amaury nodded. "Is it near the waters of the firth?"

"It overlooks the firth."

"Was it moved to another site as well?"

Elizabeth shook her head. "It was always built upon a headland. The high waters still did not come near it." She pointed into the bright light over the firth. Amaury could only see the faint outline of the opposite shore. "Beaupoint is there."

So near and yet so far. Amaury did not doubt that she could pinpoint the precise location of her home, but one would have to ride all the way back to the eastern edge of the firth, doubtless south to Carlisle, then along the opposite shore to Beaupoint. It had to be ten times the distance that a crow could fly between the two.

She was betrothed to a man in the service of a laird, and Calum was not a laird in his own right, which only meant Amaury was right: Beaupoint could not be a very rich holding. The property had passed to her uncle on her father's demise, for he had been her guardian: perhaps there were male cousins who would inherit after his demise. Elizabeth was not an heiress, let alone a rich one. All the same, Amaury could see the strategic importance of an alliance on both sides of the firth. There had to be trade sailing to Carlisle. Perhaps there were tolls to be earned, or at least, control to be asserted. Robert de Maxwell undoubtedly liked the notion of one of his men having a link to Beaupoint.

"The bounty will be a welcome gain to you, no doubt," Elizabeth said finally, and her tone was slightly tart. "It will surely fund your return to France."

"If it is paid."

She cast him an assessing glance. "Should I be insulted on behalf of my betrothed that you doubt his pledge?"

"I mean no insult, I simply endeavor to learn from the *Loup Argent*."

"No expectations," she said with a nod.

"Or plans for every eventuality."

She cast him a pert glance. "Then what are your plans?"

"If the bounty is paid, I shall seek passage on a ship to France. Where would be the best place for that?"

"Carlisle," Elizabeth said without hesitation, pointing back. "You could reach it in less than a day's ride, though I have no notion how many ships there are at this time of year."

"I suspect Oliver will return to Kilderrick," Amaury said and the boy nodded the affirmative. "Which means the palfreys belonging to the Loup Argent will have to accompany him—unless the bounty is paid and I can purchase two of them."

"I will not sell them at a bargain," Oliver warned.

"I would be surprised if you did." Amaury was aware that Elizabeth watched him. "If the bounty is not paid, I will ride south alone, with Zephyr and Persephone, and seek another quest along the way. I would still hope to reach France by the spring."

"The better to find your heiress." There was a yearning in Elizabeth's voice and Amaury knew he had to ensure she had no whimsical notions about him.

"If Fortune smiles upon me, I might already know her," he said with confidence.

"Indeed? Is she biddable and beautiful both?"

He allowed himself to smile, as if in reminiscence, then touched the token upon his scabbard that he had neglected to remove. "Fair Sylvia," he said with a sigh. "I can only hope she has not wed in my absence and still holds me in esteem."

Elizabeth's lips tightened and she looked ahead of them, touching her heel to the palfrey's side. "It cannot be far now," she said. "Soon our ways will part forever." And her tone hinted that moment could not come soon enough.

WRETCHED MAN.

How could he kiss her thus and hold another woman in esteem? Elizabeth only hoped Amaury had not been thinking of Sylvia during their embrace. She was more vexed with him than she should have been, and his inscrutability did not improve her mood.

They rode in silence until a structure appeared on the rise ahead of them, its distinctive shape clear from her father's description. A pair of pennants snapped against the blue sky, one flying from each of the gatehouse towers. She recognized the black saltire of the de Maxwells on its white field.

That was when she realized the import of his packing the caparisons away. "If the de Vries insignia is no longer yours to bear, what is your name?"

"Amaury d'Evroi," he replied. "I choose my uncle's holding as my name."

"What is it like?"

Again, he smiled slightly at mention of France and she understood that he would never have remained in England. "Magnificent. It is some distance south of Paris and the château dates from the twelfth century." He did not continue but seemed to be lost in recollection.

"Amaury d'Evroi," Elizabeth echoed. "I think it suits you well." She swallowed, thinking of that token on his scabbard. "I shall expect to hear tales of your exploits sung by the bards, sir, and to hear the tidings of your marriage to the beautiful Sylvia."

"I thank you."

"And I thank you for your assistance."

His gaze flicked to hers. "I hope your gratitude will increase in time." And he urged Zephyr to greater speed, riding ahead of her.

Aye, he would put this duty behind himself, claim the bounty and return to France—and Sylvia—with all haste. Elizabeth frowned and rode onward, resigned to her duty.

But Amaury would lie for her. It was a small concession, but it was more than she would have expected from a man of such principle.

His choice pleased her mightily for all of that.

CAERLAVEROCK WAS as magnificent as Elizabeth's father had said. The keep rose from the ground to an imposing height, that pair of towers flanking the gate in an impressive show of strength. The keep was indeed triangular, surrounded by high curtain walls and a moat of considerable breadth. They had to ride around it, for the gates faced the north, giving ample opportunity to admire the structure. Amaury did not disguise his approval as they entered the small village clustered outside the gates.

In but a decade, much progress had been made in restoring the fortress: the towers of the gatehouse were built high and the curtain wall enclosed the bailey completely, even if the walls were not as tall in some places as others. The sound of hammering and the cloud of dust revealed that the masons were busily at their labor. She might have been returned to Kilderrick for all the activity.

There was wealth here aplenty, which meant the Moffatts had allied themselves well.

Elizabeth felt that all turned to watch her ride through the village and she kept her chin high. Would Calum greet her warmly? Would he be a good spouse? Doubts assaulted her and she almost turned the palfrey to ride away.

But Amaury was as steady as a rock. He rode on, not changing his speed as they rode toward the gates. Elizabeth heard the whispers spread through those gathered behind them, the awe at Amaury's appearance, the curiosity about Oliver and the baggage on the palfreys.

"This is a fine fortification," Amaury said as they drew near the gates. "That old tale must be true."

"What tale is that?"

"The Roll of Caerlaverock," he said with satisfaction. "I heard the poem sung once though I do not recall the words. It included a fine listing of all the attending knights and their colors, as well as a bit of their natures."

"Truly? I do not know it."

"The tale itself is fairly short. The English king attacked this keep with over eighty knights but was held at bay for days. When finally they took the keep, they discovered that a mere dozen men had held it against them. That was in the summer of 1300. It looks as if the fortifications have been damaged since then." He tipped back his head to survey the towers. "But I can see how it was done." He flicked a glance her way, his eyes that fearsome blue. "Even a warrior in service to this holding will be a man of some affluence."

Elizabeth knew he meant to reassure her and she nodded, her mouth dry. The portcullis was open and a sentry revealed himself, stepping into the middle of the path that ran beneath it and calling a challenge.

He spoke in Gaelic but Amaury did not reply. Belatedly, she recalled that he was as her servant.

"I am Elizabeth d'Acron," she replied, speaking with an authority she did not quite feel. "I am the betrothed of Calum Moffatt and this knight, Amaury d'Evroi, escorts me to my nuptials, having saved me from ruffians and reivers."

"Welcome, my lady," the sentry said, after a moment of delay that indicated his surprise. "Your betrothed will be glad to welcome you." He bowed, then stood out of the path, inviting them onward with a gesture.

The passageway between the towers was narrow and dark, compelling them to ride in single file. It also was long, having several chambers on each side. Amaury went first, and Elizabeth knew his hand was on the hilt of his sword. She followed and Oliver came last with the palfreys. It was cold beneath the shadow of the towers and she shivered a little, as much from that as a portent of doom.

Deep shadows on either side of the passage disguised the chambers in the two towers flanking the gate. She spotted a glimmer of metal and realized the chain from the drawbridge extended down into the back chamber on the right. Beyond the passageway was the courtyard, filled with morning light and still spotted with puddles from the rain the day before. Elizabeth was surprised by the generous proportions of the contained space.

On the right of the courtyard rose a stone structure, two floors in height, built against the curtain wall. Only the second floor had small square windows. The stairs were wooden and located between the building and the gate tower. Smoke rose from a squat building beyond this larger one and the smell of bread made Elizabeth conclude it was the kitchen. On the opposite side of the courtyard was a low wooden structure, evidently the stable.

Three boys came from the stables, accompanied by a burly man who could only be the ostler. The courtyard filled with speculative whispers, but Elizabeth ignored them.

Amaury dismounted, then took the reins of her palfrey. He had removed his bassinet and tucked it beneath his arm, his armor distinctive in this company clad in boiled leather jerkins and chain mail. He looked wealthy and foreign, as well as imposing and handsome, and he captured every gaze—as well as Elizabeth's own.

Oliver accompanied the ostler and the horses toward the stable, leading Zephyr himself under Amaury's watchful eye. Elizabeth was so busy studying Amaury that she did not realize their host had appeared until Amaury bowed. The couple who stepped out of the fortress into the bailey were more finely dressed than the others and that, as well as the deference of the company, clearly revealed their identities.

The man was older, with streaks of silver in his dark hair and beard, and a stranger to Elizabeth. He wore chausses and boots and a tabard of deep green that fell almost to his knees. He wore no hauberk or other armor, clearly believing himself safe within these walls. Behind him was a woman close to his age, her hair bound back beneath a veil and circlet, her kirtle dyed blue with woad. She wore a girdle of gold with keys hanging from it and Elizabeth knew she was the lady of the keep. She had a kindly face. Another woman in fine garb, also older than Elizabeth but younger than the lady of the keep, stood behind them. Elizabeth guessed she was an unwed daughter.

Her gaze was locked upon Amaury and her expression left no mystery as to her impression of him.

Her parents exchanged a glance that annoyed Elizabeth.

"Welcome," the man said, inclining his head to Elizabeth. He turned then to Amaury and continued in Norman French. "I am Robert de Maxwell, Second Lord Maxwell and Laird of Caerlaverock. Name yourself and your errand here, sir."

"I escort this lady to her betrothed, one Calum Moffatt, that her nuptials might be celebrated."

The laird turned a stern look upon Elizabeth and her heart quailed. "You are late by the better part of a year, my lady."

"I was seized by reivers near my father's home," Elizabeth said, holding the older man's gaze. "I escaped them with the aid of Alys

Armstrong at Kilderrick but feared to journey here alone. When this knight arrived at Kilderrick, he offered his assistance in ensuring my safe conduct here that I might fulfil my uncle's pledge."

There was a moment of silence while the laird considered this confession and Elizabeth could not decide whether he believed her fully or not. She parted her lips to add to the explanation then recalled her father's counsel that a liar always seeks to embellish the tale and closed her mouth. The laird lifted a hand and his lady glanced across the bailey with a smile. A man descended a ladder from the ramparts then strode toward them, his steps decisive. His gaze locked upon Elizabeth and her heart fluttered in trepidation and recognition.

She forced a smile, glad that she had Amaury's dagger in her garter.

"Calum!" the lady said. "There are merry tidings this day. Your betrothed, Elizabeth d'Acron, has arrived to take your hand. We shall have a wedding to celebrate."

But when her betrothed bowed before her and took her hand in his, Elizabeth felt far from celebratory. She had arrived to keep her uncle's pledge, but her dread of Calum was tenfold what it had been a year before.

Surely she was mistaken.

Surely Amaury's prediction was right.

Elizabeth could only hope.

AMAURY HAD ERRED.

He could scarce believe it himself, but the truth was inescapable. With a single glance, he disliked Calum Moffatt, and this despite his conviction that it was illogical for Elizabeth to declare the same response. He had been certain that her opinion was a manifestation of being denied her own choice, but now he wondered.

He had never disliked anyone at a glance before. But no matter how closely Amaury scrutinized the man, how carefully he listened to Calum, how much he wished to dismiss his immediate distrust, he could not deny his dislike.

Worse, there was no discernible cause for his conclusion. Calum was handsome and neatly attired; he spoke politely and greeted Elizabeth with courtesy. While his garb was not as rich as Amaury's, it was of good quality and well-tended. Calum was tall and broad, of an age with Amaury, dressed in a mail hauberk, boots and a plain tabard. His head was bare and he did not wear a mail coif around his neck. He had dark hair that hung to his shoulders in waves and moved with the economical power of a warrior.

Perhaps it was his eyes that unsettled Amaury, for they were silver-grey and so cool that he was reminded of a wolf. But a man could not be blamed for the hue of his eyes. And the color of his eyes could not determine his nature. The very notion was foolish.

All the same, Amaury could not deny his distrust.

The other man's manners were gracious and his smile, when he spoke with Elizabeth, was warm. He treated her with honor, as a lady should be treated, escorting her to the hall and murmuring pleasantries into her ear, no doubt telling her of the members of the household as he made introductions.

He prompted her laughter.

Was Amaury jealous? Did he dislike Calum because that man had a glorious bride, the one that Amaury himself would have been honored to make his own? If so, he was unkind as well as unfair, and selfish as well.

He was greeted with enthusiasm by the laird, who insisted upon describing the new fortifications of the keep. Oliver had disappeared with Zephyr and the palfreys, overseeing their placement in the stables, then returned to take Persephone from Elizabeth. Amaury could only contrive to be a good guest. Elizabeth had vanished into the hall in the company of the ladies. 'Twas Calum who returned his cloak, that man's gaze steady as Amaury put it over his arm. They bowed to each other, formally polite, and Calum thanked him for his service to the lady.

There was no mention of the bounty and Amaury thought it rude to ask.

The nuptials were to be held three days hence, for Calum's relations would be summoned to partake of the celebration. Amaury offered to hunt for the kitchens, for he did not know how he would occupy himself otherwise and he would not leave without being certain of

Elizabeth's security. His suggestion was accepted with gusto by the laird. Calum's assessing gaze meant that Amaury would ride out early and with only Oliver. He knew full well how readily accidents occurred.

He made an excuse to leave the men, then sought out Oliver in the stables.

He discovered that the ostler was so impressed with Zephyr that he had granted the destrier a stall of his own. The three palfreys were tethered in the next larger part of the stables, alongside other horses. A quick glance revealed that none of the horses were as fine as even Maximilian's palfreys and Zephyr had no competition. Most, indeed, were shaggy ponies, indistinguishable from the pair that had become part of Amaury's entourage.

Oliver had placed Amaury's baggage in the stall with the destrier. Persephone was tethered on a makeshift perch and Amaury stroked her chest, murmuring reassurance. She had need of a flight, but would have one the next day. The dogs were already dozing in the straw.

"And so the lady will wed," Oliver said, and something in his tone hinted that he shared Amaury's lack of enthusiasm for that. "When do we leave?"

"We will stay for the nuptials three days hence," Amaury said, not truly wishing to ride away from her at all. Oliver nodded, and bent to help him remove his armor. The pair conferred quietly in Norman French and though Amaury expected few could understand their words, they both kept their voices low. "I would sleep a while this afternoon."

"Have you a chamber?"

"Here will suit well enough," Amaury said, not wanting to leave his possessions. "On the morrow, we will ride early to hunt."

"Have they paid the reward?"

Amaury knew he should be accustomed to the boy's blunt questions by now. Truth be told, he did not find Oliver's curiosity as unseemly as once he had. He shook his head. "You could accompany me south," he said then. "I would be glad of your assistance."

Oliver smiled, not ceasing his labor. "I would return to the *Loup Argent*."

"You are loyal to him."

"Aye." Oliver nodded once. "He is no angel, but he never claimed to be one. He has been good to me, and that suffices."

"Will you tell me of it?" Amaury asked and the boy was visibly startled. "I would not delve into your secrets, but I wonder how you came to ride with him."

Oliver averted his gaze, frowning as he laid Amaury's greaves aside. "I joined the Compagnie Rouge, but not by my own choice."

"How then?"

"Jean le Beau came to our village. I was born in Ghent. There was a dispute between two lords over the toll on a road and the taxes on cloth. It was woven in one town and dyed in the other, so both felt entitled to all the coin, instead of each taking their portion. Jean le Beau was hired by the other lord to besiege our town and subdue it." The boy swallowed. "My mother was beautiful."

Amaury winced, then shrugged out of his hauberk. "I fear I can guess this part of the tale." He rolled his shoulders, then stored his armor away as if he were the squire. He had best become accustomed to doing his own labor.

Oliver glanced at him, then picked up a brush. "Aye, I suspect you do," he said in measured tones as he began to brush down Zephyr. He worked for a while, lost in memory as Amaury brushed the palfreys. "Our door was kicked in when we barred it against the intruders. My father was cut down when he would have defended my mother and I." He shook his head and Amaury knew the memory had to be troubling.

"You were young?" he asked when the boy fell silent. He took off Esther's saddle. At Oliver's glance, he shrugged. "Two will finish the labor in half the time."

Oliver nodded. "I had seen seven summers. I tried in my turn to defend my mother, though I only echoed my father. I did not understand the mercenary's intention, not until I was vanquished and cast out the door. His men guarded the portal while she screamed and I thought I could not endure anything worse." He visibly gritted his teeth and his voice dropped low. "I felt such futility."

"Aye," Amaury said, and reached to touch the boy's shoulder. "I can well imagine."

"But the worst part was when she fell silent." Oliver held Amaury's gaze. "There was not a sound when Jean le Beau left our home. He laughed at me, like it was all a jest, and then he walked away. I attacked him from behind, furious but too weak to win. I was struck down, beaten by him and his comrades, and left for dead in the dust, my mouth full of blood."

It had been a fierce lesson, to be sure. Amaury said nothing, simply worked and waited.

"When I awakened, it was dark and the town was burning. My home was yet intact, but I could not leave. Instead, I went to look. The interior was in ruins, everything broken and scattered, my parents' bodies on the floor. And the blood." Oliver's throat worked. "I was not prepared for the blood, the smell of it and the sight of it, not then." He eyed Amaury again. "I do not know how long I stood there, but *Loup Argent* found me. He flung open the door—I learned later that he was ensuring none of his men were left behind—and I was terrified of him. He took one look, then spoke to me. I was so shocked and shaken, but I was impressed by him, not only that he addressed me but that he changed languages until I responded to his words."

Amaury nodded, well aware that he did not share Maximilian's alacrity with language. Oliver shared that trait and Amaury admired it greatly.

"I did not reply but must have made some indication that I understood, for then he continued in that tongue. He was a fearsome sight, a warrior in black silhouetted by the flames, his features so handsome that I thought a demon spoke to me. He asked if it was my home, if these were my family, if there were others missing. He asked if I had witnessed their demises. I admitted to only seeing my father fall. He asked why I had returned, but I had no other place to go. And then he nodded and surveyed the detritus of our home, his decision made. I dreaded his words for I knew he had decided my future, but he bade me choose one item. A token, he said. A memory. I immediately went to the corner where my mother hid her treasures. They were few, but they were hers and they were untouched. I took a strand of beads, one that my father had given her when they were courting and which she wore when she was happy. Their value is small, but great to me."

Oliver tugged at the neck of his chemise and Amaury saw the beads in question around his neck. "The *Loup Argent* examined them and I thought he would claim them himself. He said they were rough garnets and gave them back to me. He asked if I could ride, evidently skeptical but it was my task to tend the mules. He then said there was always room in his company for a boy willing to learn. And so I came to ride with the Compagnie Rouge, as the *Loup Argent*'s squire. He took me from that town, taught me to be a squire, defended me and saw me fed. He taught me to speak the tongues of many and even to read. I know the tending of armor and how to ensure that we are not cheated. I have seen much of the world riding in his company, and I will never willingly leave his service."

"Your loyalty is complete."

"It was earned, sir."

"Aye, I see that. I do not recall seeing your mother's gems before."

Oliver's smile was quick. "The *Loup Argent* keeps them in trust for me. He gave them back to me when he commanded that I ride with you, in case I did not return."

Amaury nodded. The Maximilian he had come to know these past months did more than defend those who followed him: he ensured they had their due.

"If I am paid the bounty, I will buy two palfreys from Maximilian as pledged and surrender the coin to you. Be sure to negotiate a fair price with me, or he will be displeased."

The boy's smile flashed.

"And you may take the one of your choice and ride back to Kilderrick."

"Ghita, sir," he said without delay, indicating the dapple. "I have long ridden her."

"And if I am not paid the bounty, you will take them all back to Kilderrick. I will continue south with Zephyr and the dogs."

The boy surveyed him for a long moment. "You will not be able to manage your armor, sir." He seemed to find this concerning.

Amaury shrugged as if it was of no import. "I will wear only my hauberk until I find assistance."

Oliver flicked a glance over his shoulder then lowered his voice yet more. "I do not see joy in him at her arrival," he said quietly, his gaze fierce.

"Nor do I," Amaury admitted. "I compelled her to come here and if I was wrong, I will not abandon her."

"Nor I, sir."

"Then let us learn what we can until the nuptials are celebrated." Amaury met the boy's gaze. "The truth will become clear that night."

"And you may be paid the bounty after their vows are exchanged."

They two exchanged a glance and a nod of agreement, their path clear.

CHAPTER 7

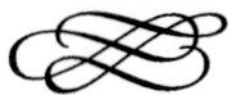

Amaury rode out on three successive mornings as the sky was barely tinged with pink. In a way, he enjoyed leaving the confines of the keep and escaping the watchful gazes of the company. Oliver accompanied him, riding Ghita, the dogs ran with him and Persephone excelled in adding to the toll. They spoke openly when they were far from the keep. He felled a deer each day, earning the gratitude of the cook.

Who was not, it had to be said, so talented with a sauce as Denis, the cook at Kilderrick. How curious to feel any longing for that place, but Amaury knew it was more a case of not feeling at ease at Caerlaverock. His motives were suspected and he knew it—indeed, he would have been surprised if it had been otherwise. He was unknown and foreign, neither of which counted in his favor. He knew he was watched and his actions reported to the laird. He wished he did not have to rely upon Oliver to understand what was said in that heathen tongue of theirs.

Robert de Maxwell was a gracious host, though, and one inclined to be more fulsome about his keep than Amaury might have thought wise. The laird showed Amaury the prisons beneath the towers, walked the ramparts with his guest, and enthused about the defenses being rebuilt.

He also complained politely about the *Loup Argent* hiring so many of the best masons of late. He tried to discover *Loup Argent's* construction plans for Kilderrick, but Amaury did not have to deceive his host. He did not know how large a fortress Maximilian planned.

"Oh, to have a mercenary's treasury," Robert de Maxwell said with a laugh, as if he made a jest, but Amaury heard little humor in the comment.

At least his host was not so trusting as to reveal the location of his own treasury. Amaury would have guessed it to be somewhere in the gatehouse compound.

Of Elizabeth, Amaury saw little, though he fretted for her.

In the meantime, he learned much of the keep. The great hall was on the second floor behind the gatehouse towers and filled the width of the space. It had a high carved ceiling and a fireplace at either end, as well as two windows overlooking the courtyard. The chain for the drawbridge was visible against one wall, where it passed through the floor to the room behind the gatehouse.

The ground floor of that stone structure inside the courtyard was used for storage, and there was no doubt that the laird was prepared for a siege. Amaury only had a glimpse inside the shadowed space but it was stacked so high with provisions that there was scarcely a footpath from end to end. Exterior stairs granted access to three chambers on the second floor of that building along the inside of the western wall, linked by a narrow corridor running between them and the curtain wall.

There were arrow slits between the stones in strategic locations, and machicolations at the summit of the rebuilt towers to allow for dropping missiles on attackers. The drawbridge was a marvel, both stout and long, and the moats were impressively deep.

Amaury found much to admire, to his host's obvious pleasure. They walked the high walls and talked of politics in France, of favored tactics at the hunt. There were tales told at the board each night, but often in Gaelic. Oliver learned little of import and Elizabeth might as well have been at the king's court in Sterling for all Amaury saw of her. At least Oliver would have some tidings to take back to Maximilian.

Amaury continued to hope for one clear sign that Elizabeth was content. Of course, he still hoped for the bounty to be paid but as each day passed, his expectation of that diminished.

That did little to improve his opinion of Calum Moffatt, to be sure.

~

THREE DAYS at Caerlaverock and Elizabeth felt her frustration rising like soup coming to a boil. How would she survive in this place? She was surrounded by strangers and watched all the time. She could not even use the latrine without someone lingering nearby.

What did they expect her to do?

Why did they care?

So many maids had tended her in the bath that first day that there had been no opportunity to hide Amaury's knife: there had been silence when it was spotted, a collective inhalation when she insisted it was hers, and then it had vanished forever in the grasp of Lady de Maxwell. Elizabeth doubted she would see it again, and she felt that she had betrayed Amaury's trust in losing it so readily.

Lady de Maxwell was kind enough, but it was clear that Calum was merely a warrior sworn to her husband's service. Her daughter, Meriot, was also kind, but obviously believed herself too far above Elizabeth even to befriend her. She understood that she would have no special rank in the household. She was not even certain whether Calum had a chamber of his own, or where they might sleep. On their nuptial night, they were to be loaned a chamber with a great bed, the one used by the laird's son and heir when he visited, and the discussion made it clear that Elizabeth should not expect such luxury in future.

Why had her uncle betrothed her to this man? Why had Calum even desired her as his bride? There was some detail she did not know, some tale that would ensure all made sense. Perhaps the challenge of solving a riddle would give satisfaction.

Worse yet, she had to appear to be joyous about the union, as if she were willing—even delighted—to place her hand in Calum's. Amaury's final warning circled in her thoughts and Elizabeth dared not give Calum any hint that her doubts were undiminished. She could not read her betrothed's thoughts or even be sure of them, for his gaze was always cool no matter how warmly he spoke. He gave her shivers, just as he had that first time, but Elizabeth pretended otherwise. She was as good as his possession and no one in this hall would aid her if all went awry.

She had to keep it from going awry, even if she had never been a skillful liar. Evidently, she would be compelled to learn and she had best do it quickly. The sole detail about her situation in favor of that was that no one sought her opinion on any detail: they simply decided for her, as if she was too witless to have a thought of her own.

Against every expectation, Elizabeth found she preferred to be told she was wrong, and to argue the matter with a certain stubborn and confident knight. She reviewed their conversations of that single night a thousand times, savoring every confession, remembering every small hint of his thoughts. How fortunate the distant Sylvia was to hold his admiration.

She ignored Amaury utterly at the evening meal each night, taking the excuse of following his own advice. She knew her days would be bleak when he left and there was no longer a chance of even catching a glimpse of him—or a word of admiration for him in the lady's chambers. Meriot was quite taken with him and chattered endlessly of his deeds each day, and Elizabeth found herself listening hungrily to the details.

Those three days both took an eternity to pass and were over all too soon. It was the last day of November, a grey and rainy day, that Elizabeth found herself surrounded by women again, being dressed for the wedding vows she did not wish to exchange.

And once again, she had no choice.

If the lady had given any sign of discontentment, Amaury would have intervened. But Elizabeth was radiant at her nuptials. Garbed in a russet kirtle with gold embroidery on the hem and cuffs, with a golden girdle around her waist and her hair arranged in a corona of braids, she was as gloriously beautiful as only a happy bride can be. Amaury watched as the pair exchanged their vows, as Calum kissed Elizabeth's cheek, as she shyly dropped her gaze and flushed with pleasure at her husband's touch.

Amaury's gut writhed. Never had he been so dismayed to find himself correct. Elizabeth followed the path of his cousin Felicia but with greater speed—in mere days, she had come to adore the man chosen for her.

He would have left immediately after the service if the hour had not become so late, regardless of the discourtesy. He had wanted to see Elizabeth married, but now darkness was falling. It would be folly to ride out at night, though he was impatient to be gone. The sight of her happiness should have given him joy or at least satisfaction.

Instead, it was torment.

He paused for a moment in the bailey, not minding the rain, instead of following the rest of the company to the great hall.

"And she is wed," Oliver said in Norman French, appearing suddenly beside him.

"Aye. Our task is complete."

"You need not sound so sour about success."

Amaury looked quickly at the boy only to discover that his eyes twinkled. What was this? Truly, he seldom knew what to expect from this squire.

Oliver inclined his head. "May I speak outright?"

"You have never refrained from doing so in the past."

The boy grinned. "It is most clear that you admire the lady…"

"I never gave a hint of that."

"And were so fastidious in ensuring that she had no notion of your feelings that she might have concluded you despised her."

"'Twould be safer thus," Amaury said stiffly.

"But I was not fooled, sir."

"You did not tell her as much."

Oliver chuckled. "That kiss removed her doubts, I am certain."

Amaury felt the back of his neck heat that the boy had witnessed it. "It was a mistake."

"But not an embrace you regret, I am sure." At Amaury's quick sidelong glance, Oliver continued. "The heart of the matter is this, sir: if you desire the lady, you must act."

"She is wed, as arranged."

"But is she happy?"

Amaury turned to the squire. "What do you suggest?" He dropped his voice low. "I will not follow the lead of the *Loup Argent* and simply seize the woman of my choice. I will not compel any lady to welcome or accept me, for *I do not claim what is not mine to possess*." He held Oliver's gaze until the boy looked away.

"If you do not choose, others will choose for you," Oliver murmured. "This is what I learned in the Compagnie Rouge."

"I have chosen and so has she."

"Then there is no reason for foul temper."

"Nay, there is not." Amaury spoke sharply and immediately regretted it. He frowned and softened his tone. "I am vexed. I am disappointed. My lack of resource chafes at me, but I have no choices on this day other than duty, which is fulfilled." He glanced toward the hall and the sound of merriment. "If the lady were discontent with her situation, though, I *would* choose." And he met the squire's gaze steadily.

Oliver smiled approval. "I am glad to hear of it, sir. In such circumstance, I would be honored to offer my assistance."

"But she is content." Amaury was compelled to acknowledge the truth. "And we will ride out at dawn." He would have to sort his belongings before he slept if the bounty was not paid. He would have preferred to take all that was graced with the insignia of de Vries and deliver it to Philip himself, but without more horses, he would be compelled to leave it behind. He would take his armor and be glad of it.

"Very good, sir."

"Let us sit together at the board this night," Amaury suggested.

Oliver was visibly surprised. "I thought you would insist upon rank being maintained."

"We are comrades on a quest," Amaury said. "Perhaps I have learned something from Maximilian, after all." He smiled at the boy. "I have grown fond of you and will miss you after the morrow."

Oliver smiled. "I feel the same, sir."

They entered the hall and found two places together. Amaury could not bear to glance toward Elizabeth at the high table. He dropped his voice to a whisper. "And if you see any hint that she only feigns satisfaction, then I will choose."

Oliver's smile was bright. "As is only fitting, sir." He cleared his throat slightly. "Perhaps you should check before we ride out."

Perhaps Amaury should.

~

IT WAS NOT the wedding that had once filled Elizabeth's maidenly dreams. In those visions, she put her hand in that of a gallant knight—a handsome man of honor, a man, it must be noted, much like Amaury d'Evroi—and her heart was filled with joy. Her father was there and she was wed in the chapel at Beaupoint. Her kirtle had been made for the occasion, lavishly embroidered by herself and her ladies in preparation for the anticipated day. Her veil was cloth-of-gold, she wore her mother's circlet and carried a rose from Beaupoint's garden. The chapel was gloriously decorated with flowers, the day was sunny and clear, and familiar villagers lined her route to the chapel, wishing her well as she approached the knight awaiting her at the doors. Her heart thundered when their gazes met and his smile warmed her to her toes, and she knew with complete conviction that they would be happy forevermore.

Instead, she was at Caerlaverock, an unfamiliar keep, and surrounded by strangers, being wed to a man she still distrusted. Her kirtle was hastily made of borrowed cloth, although kindly offered, she had neither veil nor circlet, much less a rose from Beaupoint's gardens. Her father was dead. Beaupoint was distant.

The steady rain suited her mood perfectly.

Elizabeth did not know how she survived the exchange of their vows. She had the definite sense that a trap closed around her. She had been right to run from this match. She should have fled again. But Amaury would have hunted her and brought her to Calum, regardless of how far she fled and how often. He had vowed as much and she believed him.

He could have taken her back to Kilderrick. He could have let her flee. But nay, he meddled in what was not his concern, insisting that he had to see to her security, and compelled her to come to Caerlaverock.

Duty and honor.

The provenance of men. Why was it impossible for them to let a woman make her own choices? Why did they all assume that she was no more than a pawn, with no desires of her own to be fulfilled?

She could not ignore the fact that Calum spoke to all around them and not to her, nor that he kept a firm grasp upon her hand. When congratulations were offered to them after the service, he accepted them, clearly expecting Elizabeth to remain silent. Amaury was not alone in his admiration of biddable brides, to be sure.

She seethed inwardly that this would be her life henceforth and missed her father heartily. How her parents had disputed every matter! How her father had invited her mother's opinion and Elizabeth's too! Evidently what she had thought was common was rare—and she had not appreciated it sufficiently at the time.

The company returned to the hall and the high table, but Elizabeth did not look for Amaury. He could not ride away soon enough, for the damage was done.

As the venison was served, Elizabeth wondered why Calum himself had not sought her out over the past year. It seemed his desire for her did not burn so brightly as to cause his own inconvenience. Coin, though, he would spend coin. Was it his own? How did he come to have so much coin as a warrior pledged to serve the de Maxwells?

"My lady." Calum indicated the trencher they were to share, inviting her to take a piece of meat. Elizabeth was grateful that he did not see fit to feed her from his own hand, like a pet dog.

She missed Grise and even Bête.

God in Heaven, she missed Amaury, her conviction that he would defend her and his solemn manner. He listened to her and aided her, as irksome as his manner could be.

It was only reasonable that she was haunted by his kisses.

She chose a small piece, thanked Calum for his courtesy, then dared to ask a question. "Is it true that there was a bounty to be paid for my delivery here?"

Calum smiled at her. "Do you not think it would be worth any price to me to see my betrothed at my side?"

"I am honored that you would make such an offer, no less that you had such concern for me."

"A generous offer, too," Robert de Maxwell interjected. "Calum is not one to let an investment be lost so readily as that."

"An investment?" Elizabeth echoed, pretending to be more witless than she was.

The laird's smile broadened. "You cannot imagine that your uncle simply chose your intended," he chided. "Calum made a persuasive argument for his own selection."

"You two and your schemes," Lady de Maxwell said, her manner tolerant.

"You will be glad enough of the gain once it begins to flow into our coffers," her husband said mildly, earning his wife's smile.

Elizabeth was confused. What scheme did they have?

She was keenly aware of Amaury, sitting in the company, the gleam of his mail a glint of silver in her peripheral vision. She stole only the barest glance in his direction, for Calum watched her intently and his grip upon her hand was firm. To her surprise, Oliver sat beside the knight and they seemed to be conversing amiably. It appeared that they were comrades, which she would never have anticipated.

"When will you ride out?" Lady de Maxwell asked Calum and Elizabeth glanced up.

"Your bride is surprised by the hint of departure," the laird said jovially. "Have you not told her the good tidings? I should think she would be gladdened by them."

"What tidings?" Elizabeth asked.

"We ride to Beaupoint," Calum said smoothly. "The rest of my men should arrive in several days. I sent word to them once you arrived, but some were far afield."

"Beaupoint? But why?"

Her husband smiled but it was not a merry expression. Indeed, he looked ruthless for a moment, then his expression changed. Had she imagined the change? Elizabeth shivered, reminded of the hungry wolves that had invaded the camp at Kilderrick. "To claim the prize, of course." He leaned closer. "Surely you would be glad to live at Beaupoint again?"

"Of course. I have missed it dearly," Elizabeth said, her thoughts spinning. "Has my uncle fallen ill?" The demise of that man was the sole justification she could imagine. In James' absence, her husband might try to claim the holding himself.

"Not yet," Calum said smoothly, laughing with the laird at some private jest.

Elizabeth did not understand but she feared their implication.

"And what of your guardian?" Calum asked her, serious once again. He nodded toward Amaury and Elizabeth took the chance to fill her gaze with the sight of him. Amaury did not look up, though she thought he stiffened slightly—as if aware of the weight of her glance.

"What of him?"

"He arrived at Kilderrick in the company of the *Loup Argent*?" the laird asked.

"He did."

"Why?" Calum asked. "He does not look like a mercenary."

"Far from it," the laird added and again they chuckled together.

"I think he is glorious," Lady de Maxwell said. "It is too long since you have taken me to watch the knights joust, my love." Her daughter nodded with enthusiasm, sighing as she openly studied Amaury.

The laird shook his head indulgently, but Calum was still waiting for Elizabeth's reply.

"I do not know why he joined that company," Elizabeth lied. "Perhaps he sought adventure, but it matters little now."

"How so?" Calum asked.

"He means to return to France. He escorted me here because he left Kilderrick himself. He said it was his knightly duty to defend a lady."

"Such a man," Meriot said with approval.

"When does he sail?" Calum asked, his impatience to see Amaury gone more than clear.

"I do not know." Elizabeth cleared her throat, seeing how she might show her gratitude to Amaury. "I believe he has little coin and passage for that destrier will be expensive." She opened her eyes wide and looked at Calum, a little disconcerted to find him watching her closely. "If there is a bounty, its payment could ensure his quick departure from these shores."

Her new husband smiled. "I shall ensure that it does," he vowed, then beckoned to the steward to give instructions. Elizabeth dared to look back at Amaury and her heart skipped to find him watching her, as inscrutable as ever. His gaze followed the steward and she felt bereft when he looked away.

But then, she would never have the chance to speak to him again. She had best reconcile herself to that.

"How is the meat?" Calum whispered beside her, a reminder that he remained attentive.

"Delicious," Elizabeth said, granting him a smile. "You should have this piece, sir, for it looks to be most tender."

"Feed it to me, my lady," he commanded, his voice silky, and Elizabeth knew she could do naught else.

AMAURY HAD ANTICIPATED an interrogation since their arrival at Caerlaverock, but it was not until the wedding feast was finished that it came. An older man, the steward of the keep, was summoned by Calum and given instructions at the end of the meal. He nodded and bowed, then made his way to Amaury, clearly on a mission.

"May I?" he asked, indicating the place on the bench opposite Amaury. Amaury nodded agreement, even as the others at their table moved away.

How interesting that the steward was feared.

He looked pointedly at Oliver, who did not move. Indeed, the boy smiled at him with utter confidence, then continued to clean his trencher.

The man inhaled sharply. "I would speak to you alone, Amaury d'Evroi."

"My squire and I have no secrets," Amaury said easily. "The boy has not eaten well of late and I would not dismiss him from the feast."

The other man's lips thinned. "What ails him?"

"My lack of coin, no more and no less."

The older man's gaze turned shrewd. "I might be of assistance with that," he said, placing a sack upon the board. Its contents jingled and there had to be a goodly number of coins within it.

The bounty.

Which was not yet in Amaury's hand.

He did not reach for it, wondering what this man desired of him.

"How so?" he asked mildly and sipped at his ale. Something was afoot in this hall and he disliked that Elizabeth would be left in the midst of it. He would have liked to have known what scheme was contrived, though truly it was not his concern.

The other man was perhaps double Amaury's age with lines of experience upon his brow. His features were weathered and his gaze was shrewd. He wore a boiled leather jerkin that only emphasized the breadth of his chest. His hands were worn and tanned, the hands of a man unafraid to labor, and he had a number of small scars. There were two on his right cheek, more marks on the backs of his hands and Amaury did not doubt that the man's garments hid more souvenirs of war. He would be no small opponent, to be sure.

"I am Murdoch Douglas, steward of Caerlaverock." He did not offer his hand, merely his steady stare.

In Amaury's experience, a steward did not tend to be a warrior but a man with skill at organizing the household. He was accustomed to stewards like Yves, now at Kilderrick, a paternal and particular man with a strong sense of how domestic matters should best be accomplished and little knowledge of warfare—though much skill with chess. Yves had been the son of a steward and raised to take his post. In this wild land, it seemed that all men were warriors, and as they aged, they were pressed into service in other roles.

"I have not seen your like at Caerlaverock since the king's last visit," Murdoch continued, speaking Norman French as fluidly as Amaury. He beckoned for a cup of ale and surveyed Amaury as it was poured, a critical gleam in his eyes. Amaury expected such a man to be blunt and he was not disappointed. "How did you come to be in Scotland at all? Your kind are usually at the king's court in London or Smithfields, if on this isle at all."

"I joined the company of the *Loup Argent* when he rode to Kilderrick," Amaury said, leaving a number of details unsaid.

The other man's brows rose. "I have heard of his assault upon that keep. A ruin and a cursed spot. No one would care if it was not such a fearsome mercenary intending to claim it as his own."

"He has claimed it, and Alys Armstrong as his bride."

"Why?"

"He would make his home there."

Murdoch turned his crockery cup in the wet mark it had left on the board. "And join with the reivers to raid the borders, I assume." The older man's gaze was downcast, his thoughts hidden.

"Nay, that is not my understanding," Amaury said, earning a sharp glance. "He conferred with the king when last I saw him, about defending the borders against their attacks." He could not mistake this man's interest in that detail.

"Which king? Scottish or English?"

"Robert II of Scotland."

The other man's lips tightened and he looked across the hall. "If you speak aright, there will be a missive arriving for my laird." His tone made Amaury bristle.

"Do you challenge my word, sir?"

Murdoch almost smiled. "Not yet." He sipped his ale. "You cannot blame any man for having doubts of tidings that are unexpected."

Amaury did not reply to that, but finished his ale. He might have risen and excused himself, but the other man spoke again before he could.

"When do you return to the *Loup Argent*?"

"Never. Kilderrick does not suit me."

"Why did you leave now?"

"To save the lady, of course."

"Why?"

Amaury bristled and knew his reaction was noted. "She was abducted from Kilderrick when the *Loup Argent* rode to the king. I pursued her captors to ensure her welfare."

"Why?" The man was relentless, and Amaury felt that he was being interrogated, a most unsuitable situation for a guest.

He glared at Murdoch and spoke crisply. "Because she was under the protection of the *Loup Argent*, a companion of his lady wife, and her welfare was therefore my responsibility along with the defense of the keep."

Those brows rose again. "He left you in command."

"He did."

"Yet you abandoned your command for the lady." It was clear this man thought the choice had been a bad one.

"I ceded the command to another, for I believed myself to be the best candidate to find her."

"Why?"

"I hunt," Amaury said, biting off the words. "While once I hunted for pleasure and sport, since arriving at Kilderrick, I have hunted daily to see the company fed. I track, I pursue, and I locate my prey. I was therefore best qualified to find the lady with speed."

Murdoch nodded. "What happened to her captors?"

"Their corpses are in the river near the old keep of Annan. They assaulted her. I could not honorably stand by and watch."

"Their names?"

Amaury shrugged, not troubling to hide his indifference.

The other man nodded, sipped and nodded again, his gaze fixed upon the floor. He looked up so abruptly that Amaury might once have been startled. No more. He had become accustomed to adversity in Maximilian's camp and stared steadily back at Murdoch. "Did you then partake of her charms when the competition was dismissed?"

"Nay!" Amaury rose to his feet, outraged that such a suggestion should be made. "I would never despoil a lady."

"You rode in the company of a known mercenary."

"And I am not of his ilk."

The older man nodded, appeased. "Sit down, sir. I would learn more of whatever tidings you bring."

"I did not come to Caerlaverock to bring tidings."

"But you left the *Loup Argent*'s company, despite the fact that he had once entrusted you with the command of his keep. Some would think that a good indication of future responsibility and reward. Unless he has changed his opinion of you?" The older man surveyed him. "Or did you choose to seek better opportunity?"

"I do not owe you any explanation."

"Nay, you do not." Murdoch's smile was chilly. "And I do not have to permit you to ride out, whenever you would choose to depart."

"You would not halt me." Amaury guessed this to be true, for no one wanted an armed knight within their walls whose allegiance was uncertain.

"But I might feel compelled to keep a toll from guest with a reluctant tongue. That is a fine stallion you ride. I have been seeking one of his ilk for years." Again, that shrewd gaze met Amaury's steadily.

And now he was threatened, while a guest at the board.

Barbarians. They were all barbarians.

"I intend to return to France with all haste," Amaury confessed.

"The hardship was not worth the adventure?"

"The rewards are markedly less than anticipated."

The older man chuckled. "Where in France?"

He had no lack of questions, to be sure, but Amaury would not sacrifice Zephyr.

Nor would he confess more than was necessary to this man.

"Wherever I can find a tournament. I will joust again." He did not reveal his doubts about that strategy, or his hopes that his uncle would have gainful employment for him instead. What mattered was departing this place freely.

Murdoch shook his head, appearing to be amused. "Aye, the truth of battle is never as glorious as the mockery of it." He wagged his finger at Amaury. "And there are far fewer wealthy noblewomen present to admire a man's armor in a true battle." This time, his survey was derisive, but Amaury did not care.

"I leave at dawn, if not before, with my destrier."

"Aye, that would be a wise choice. If you ride east to Carlisle, you might yet find passage on a ship." The steward drained his cup, having made his dismissal more than clear. "Godspeed to you, Amaury d'Evroi." He pushed the sack of coin across the board. "Do not forget your reward."

"I will not." Amaury understood that he had been dismissed and he was glad of it. He stood, tucking the coin into his purse and refusing to glance toward Elizabeth. He would count it later, but the purse had a heft to it. Gold or silver, it should be enough to ensure his passage to France, along with Zephyr and at least one palfrey.

He bowed to the high table, but did not approach to speak to any of them. He would not feed any rumor that there was more between himself and the lady than was the case. He then headed for the stables, Oliver fast behind him.

"Cur," the boy muttered when they reached the bailey.

"They have a strange notion of hospitality in this land, to be sure," Amaury said. There was no one in their vicinity, for most remained in the hall to celebrate. He spied two sentries on the walls and did not doubt there were more. The silhouette of the gatekeeper was clear, as was the portcullis barring the way. His dogs came running and he bent to greet them as if naught was amiss.

He could not leave this keep soon enough.

Oliver's suggestion was a good one, though. He had to speak to Elizabeth and verify that she was content. How would he manage that? He spared an upward glance to the chambers on the second floor of that structure to the west. She would be there, doubtless, and though the distance was short, she might as well have been in Paris. The laird's chamber would be there, as well, and undoubtedly the daughter's.

"You lied," Oliver declared with a smile. "I have eaten well enough of late."

"I wanted your impression of him and what he said."

The boy sobered. "He wants rid of you."

"Which makes no sense. I am one man within an armed garrison and pose little threat." Amaury shook his head as he strolled onward. He nodded to the ostler who sat in the shadows by the door to the stables, and kept his voice low. "Something is afoot in this place, something they do not wish us to witness. Either they want us gone with haste, or we will not leave this place alive."

Oliver nodded agreement. "They paid the bounty."

"They may plan to steal it back."

Determination lit the boy's eyes. "Only one of us should sleep this night."

Amaury nodded. "And we shall plan for all the possibilities, including the lady having need of our aid again. I must verify that she is content before we leave."

"What will you do?"

Amaury considered that. "I may indulge too much this night or at least appear to have done so." Their gazes met and Oliver's smile turned mischievous.

Then the dogs came to them and Oliver halted at the stall, scanning the space with suspicion. Amaury halted beside him, also sensing that something was amiss. Persephone was asleep on her makeshift perch and the horses dozed. There were bones in the straw, evidence that the dogs had been distracted. His gaze fell upon his luggage and he approached it slowly. Oliver was beside him, his manner just as intent. The boy inhaled deeply, then looked around with narrowed eyes. Aye, Amaury smelled the intruder as well.

Someone had been in the stall in their absence.

Their gazes met and they nodded as one.

Amaury opened one bag and raised his brows at the disheveled surcoat hastily pushed in the top. He exchanged a glance with Oliver, knowing all had been carefully arranged.

Someone had searched his belongings and looked at his surcoat.

Someone had sought his insignia. But why?

He nodded at Oliver then raised his voice, feigning anger. "What do you mean, there is no wine?" he roared. "You know I need my wine before bed! Cursed boy! And my surcoat is not folded with the precision I demand." He strode across the stall. "Look at this mail! It needs to be polished. And this blade has not been sharpened in a week. Will you never learn your responsibilities? Now I must fetch the wine myself while you complete your duties."

"I will go, my lord," Oliver said in deference.

"How can I rely upon you? Even the simplest task is performed badly. I should have left you behind in France." Amaury paused halfway across the stables and shouted back at Oliver. "The sooner we regain those shores and I can replace you, the better!"

"I am sorry, my lord," Oliver said, his manner so contrite that no one who knew the boy would have believed his performance. "I shall do better, my lord."

"Not while I draw breath, I am certain," Amaury snarled then marched toward the ostler. "Who has wine in this abode?" He held up one of his newly gained coins. "I will pay."

CHAPTER 8

Elizabeth's heart was racing when she was left alone in the bedchamber with her new husband. The sound of the merry-makers faded as the new couple eyed each other across the room. How she wished she could read Calum's thoughts! He smiled slightly, strolling around the chamber, examining trinkets, as if he had never been in the room before.

In truth, there was little in the chamber. The bed occupied most of the space, its wooden posts stretching to the carved ceiling. It was hung with heavy curtains, which were open to reveal the marriage bed. The floor was devoid of so much as a strewing herb. There was a table beside the door, with a small window above it, and a brazier stood near the bed on its tripod, radiating some heat. The rain pattered incessantly on the roof and a cool breeze came through the shutters.

There were three chambers in the space above the great hall and this was the furthest from the stairs, at the end of a short corridor. The largest one was first and the haven of the laird and lady. Elizabeth had been granted her bath there, and it was a sumptuous chamber. The daughter of the house and the maids slept on pallets in the middle chamber while most of the household slept in the great hall, in the kitchens or in the stables.

Elizabeth had been undressed by the women and left only with the chemise granted to her. The garment of fine linen fell to her ankles and she wished she still had Amaury's dagger—as well as her confidence. Her breath came quickly and she could not keep her hands still. She pleated the linen between her fingertips, watchful and wary of her new spouse.

Was he displeased? Was he filled with anticipation? Would their mating be merry? Elizabeth could not tell and that troubled her deeply. She hoped for a kiss like the one Amaury had given her, but she feared that was optimistic. She waited, wishing Calum would simply say what he would and take his due.

He abruptly pivoted to face her, his gaze so cold that she jumped.

His smile was no better.

That he conjured Amaury's dagger was not reassuring. Elizabeth should have guessed that it would be surrendered to him.

"A trinket of yours?" he asked, his voice low and dangerous.

Elizabeth flushed. "Aye. It is mine." She reached out her hand. "I thank you for its return."

He did not surrender it. "It cannot be yours with this insignia upon the hilt. This is not the mark of Beaupoint."

"It was a gift to me."

"From whom?"

Elizabeth faltered. "A comrade," she managed and Calum's smile broadened.

"Is that what you call him?" he mused. He walked closer to her, his expression unfathomable. He held out the dagger before himself, not giving it to her, and she wondered whether he would use it against her.

Elizabeth retreated a cautious step.

"Why does your *comrade* not wear his insignia? Did he hide it so that this blade could not be identified as his own?"

"Nay!"

"Did you mean to deceive me?"

"Nay. Of course not."

"Then tell me the name of the comrade who gave this to you."

Elizabeth squared her shoulders. "Amaury d'Evroi."

"Why did he give it to you?"

"So that I could ensure my own protection."

Calum scoffed. "Such a fine blade as this? A gift of such value might indicate a much stronger relationship than you imply."

Elizabeth swallowed. "He is a knight. He thought it a fitting gift."

"And you accepted it, which means you thought it fitting as well."

"It was not like that. His was an act of kindness."

"When did he give it to you?" Calum asked, interrupting her.

"After he saved me from the ruffians."

"Perhaps after some other event," her husband suggested, his voice soft with accusation. He moved suddenly, seizing Elizabeth's chemise and drawing her to her toes. Now there was fury in his eyes and the sight terrified her. "Do you truly think you can bring your lover before me and I will be fooled?" he demanded in a hoarse whisper.

"He is not my lover!"

Calum released the chemise and shoved her hard, so hard that she fell to the floor. The blow stung as did her landing and she knew she would be bruised. She eased away from her husband, hoping she had the chance to bruise.

"I know you are not a maiden," he said, his tone mild again.

"Because of the reivers," Elizabeth said. "I was seized by reivers outside Beaupoint and taken captive. That was why I did not wed you as planned. And to my shame, they had their due of me. There was nothing I could do, sir. I was but one against many."

"You were not seized from Beaupoint," Calum corrected. "You were seized by reivers *after* you fled Beaupoint,"

"I did not flee Beaupoint," Elizabeth insisted, but she saw in his eyes that he knew otherwise.

How could he be so certain of that?

There was solely one way, but Elizabeth could not believe it.

He crouched down before her, turning the knife as he spoke. "You were a maiden the first time I had you," he said calmly and her eyes widened. He had led the reiver's party! He had been the one to abuse her.

He had been brutal and rough, which was no good indication for her future. Elizabeth eased backward a little.

"I cannot expect you to be one this time, as well, but I do not expect you to have shared your favors with other men since that night."

"You!" Elizabeth whispered in horror. "It was you."

"Reiving is my trade, you must know that. My brothers have claimed all the holdings granted to our family." Calum's eyes glittered. "When I saw that you were not enamored of our match, I came to Beaupoint to take what was mine. We intended to breach the walls but to my surprise, I found you far beyond the village." He leaned closer. "You fled."

Elizabeth swallowed.

He clicked his tongue reprovingly. "You should have known you could not run from me." His eyes flashed and he drew back his arm, brandishing the dagger. He moved and she saw the blade flash close to her face as he buried its point in the wooden wall. She looked between it and her calm spouse. "Who would have guessed that you survived all this time at Kilderrick?"

"You never sought me," Elizabeth said. "You knew I had been freed there. Yours must have been the party that was waylaid."

"By witches." He grimaced. "My men would not return to Kilderrick, even if I had suspected that you remained there." He shook his head as he surveyed her. "Nay, I believed that either you would die in the forest or a treasure-seeker would find you. The bounty saved me many miles and much searching." He straightened then and crossed the chamber, leaving her upon the floor. She watched as he unfastened his belt and laid it aside, then tugged off his boots.

The moment she dreaded was nigh upon her. Elizabeth sat up, then stood up. She heard Amaury's counsel again: *If you fight someone larger and stronger and intend to win, you must use your wits.*

What could she do?

"Where will we go?" she asked, wanting to keep him talking. She might yet find a way to evade him. She might convince him to be kinder than he had been that first time.

"I told you. We ride for Beaupoint."

"But I still do not understand. My uncle resides there as its lord."

"Not for much longer. I paid dearly to gain your hand, wife of mine, but truly I paid for Beaupoint."

Why was everything about Beaupoint?

"But I am not its heiress."

"Yet." Calum paced the room, apparently content to explain to her. Elizabeth would take every moment to conspire against him—and learn his plan for her uncle. "Robert de Maxwell proposed an alliance, that I should claim a base on the other side of the firth that might control its traffic. Why should we not command both sides of the western march?"

"My father was the English Warden of the Western March."

Calum smiled. "I know. He has need of a successor."

"But my uncle…"

"He will have no chance against my company of men." Calum scoffed. "While I am certain that his ledgers are in order, I know his walls will not be well defended. Sadly, he cannot be allowed to survive. Does he have sons? I cannot find out for certain."

"He is a cleric," Elizabeth said tartly.

"Which does not preclude the existence of sons."

She shook her head. "There are none."

"I hope not. I have waited long enough for my due, and such complications would be unwelcome."

"But you cannot gain a holding by such treachery!" Elizabeth had to protest. Surely the king would uphold justice?

"Who will oppose me?" Calum demanded calmly. "Baron de Clyfford has said openly that he is desirous of a warrior for the post your father held." He referred to the Lord Warden of the Marches, a man whose holding was south of Carlisle.

"He has a son," Elizabeth said.

Calum laughed. "Who you refused, and your father indulged you." He shook his head. "I have learned much of your willfulness, wife of mine. Recognize that such defiance will not be tolerated here." He removed his tabard and set it aside. "Your uncle will die. We will claim Beaupoint. After some negotiation, the baron will surrender the post to me, especially since I am wed to the daughter of the house. Be gladdened, my lady, that you are of use to me for the moment. After I hold Beaupoint, you may not find that you remain so."

Elizabeth swallowed. "But you will need a son," she said, striving to keep her tone light.

She won a near-lethal glance for that. "A son," he echoed, his tone scathing. "Do not imagine that you will present me with a blond and blue-eyed brat inside the year and I will be fooled."

"I would not," Elizabeth said as he cast his chemise aside. "I did not!"

Calum stalked toward her in his chausses, his intent more than clear. "Good. You should learn how to please me. That will be your sole chance of salvation."

Elizabeth doubted that she would feel pleasure in whatever he desired of her.

She backed up and found only the bed behind herself.

He seized her hair and drew her forcibly closer. "Kiss me," he growled. "Sweetly."

Elizabeth swallowed. His grip in her hair was painfully tight but she touched her lips fleetingly to his.

"That is not a kiss," he charged. His eyes glinted. "One might think you unwilling, my lady."

Elizabeth took a breath. She leaned closer and pressed her mouth against his. She thought of Amaury's kiss, how he had cajoled her to join him in the pursuit of pleasure, and she tried to echo his movements. She tried to entice her husband and make him forget his anger.

And she failed.

She thought Amaury had been wrought of stone, but Calum was even less responsive. She surrendered and eased away from him, only to find his gaze burning into hers.

"Harlot," he muttered. "Someone has taught you to kiss and it was not me." Before she could argue, he raised his hand to strike her again.

Elizabeth scrambled onto the bed to avoid the blow, but lost her footing when the mattress sank low. Calum chuckled. She tried to crawl across its width but he seized her ankle in a relentless grip. He smiled as he pulled her steadily closer, as she struggled and the chemise rode up her thighs. She kicked and thrashed but he grabbed her other ankle and spread her legs wide, his eyes gleaming as he looked upon her.

Subterfuge and surprise are your allies.

Elizabeth heard Amaury's advice as if he whispered in her ear. She saw that Calum was intent upon the prize he would claim, that he would force her as he had once before, that he did not care if she was injured.

She had to trick him.

She had to surprise him.

There was only one way.

Elizabeth shuddered as if in surrender. She let her body become limp and Calum drew her closer, chuckling at his triumph.

"Aye, that is the way, wife of mine. Obedience will suffice." He bent and grazed the inside of her thigh with his teeth, then nipped at her as if he was a wolf in truth. He laughed at the dismay she could not disguise, then reached for her waist to draw her against him.

When he surveyed her with satisfaction, Elizabeth kicked him, hard, in the groin. He staggered backward with a cry and she dove across the bed for the dagger embedded in the wall. Before she could reach it, Calum's arm locked around her waist and he hauled her close again. She was on her knees, unable to evade him.

"I do not mind this way, either," he said and Elizabeth tried to kick him again. She missed and he struck at her legs, gripping her shoulder with one hand and her hair with the other as he forcibly held her down.

Elizabeth twisted suddenly and bit his hand. When the weight of his grip loosened and he swore, she twisted and drove her knee into his belly. He ducked the blow and rolled across the mattress himself, tumbling from the edge and landing on his feet.

He beckoned to her, eyes glinting. "The lady likes a fight," he mused. "I enjoy one myself."

Elizabeth began to move toward him, but then lunged over the bed and grabbed the knife instead. She dove at him then, brandishing the blade. In the last moment, he stepped aside but she had passed the knife to the other hand and jabbed upward with it. He swore when she nicked the back of his thigh, then seized her wrist. His grip was tight, so tight that she was compelled to drop the dagger, and she gasped when it fell to the ground. He kicked it aside and released her so abruptly that she stumbled.

Elizabeth retreated, wishing she could retrieve the knife. How else could she surprise him? Calum pursued her with measured steps and she continued to retreat—until the wall was behind her and she had nowhere to run.

"Whore and harlot," he muttered through his teeth, his eyes glittering in triumph. "Now you will have your just reward."

He raised his hand and Elizabeth closed her eyes, knowing that he would beat her blue. No one in this hall would defend her against him.

Nay, she would not let him do this without a fight. When he was but a step away, Elizabeth straightened and charged him. Her head collided with his chest and he staggered backward. He swore. Then he caught her shoulder and spun her around, slapping her so hard across the face that Elizabeth saw stars.

She fell to the floor, dizzy, her hair spilling loose, her chemise bunched around her thighs. She spotted the dagger, too far away to be retrieved, but she would not despair.

'Twas her last chance.

Elizabeth glanced up at Calum as he unfastened his chausses, then when they were around his knees, she moved like lightning. She dove at his knees, flinging her full weight against him and he toppled backward. There was a loud crack as he struck his head on the corner of the table, then he collapsed upon the floor.

Elizabeth knew she would pay for her defiance. She struggled to her feet, trying to put distance between them, expecting to feel the weight of his hands at any moment.

But he did not touch her.

She struggled to catch her breath as she looked back upon him, sprawled on the floor. His chausses were around his knees and one hand outstretched, but he did not move.

All she could hear was her own terrified breathing. Slowly, her heart returned to its normal pace. Still Calum did not move.

Elizabeth straightened slowly, warily, her gaze locked upon him. She feared a trick or another blow, but still, he did not stir.

Was he breathing?

She dared to creep closer to him. His eyes were open and he stared at the far corner of the room, as if he spied a horrifying specter there. The chamber was empty, though, save they two. The hair pricked on the back of Elizabeth's neck and she stifled an urge to shiver.

He was dead.

This was her chance.

Elizabeth retrieved Amaury's dagger and gripped it in shaking fingers, unable to look away from Calum's corpse. Her cheek still stung from his blow and her heart raced with fear. She donned her kirtle again and shoved the dagger into her garter, trying to calm herself. She could not leave the keep during the night and she did not wish to be discovered in this chamber with Calum's corpse.

What should she do?

If ever there had been a time for clear thinking—a moment when a plan would be wise—this had to be it. Elizabeth was well aware of the silence of the keep, and knew that all had retired to slumber by this hour. It was dark beyond the window and the adjacent chambers were quiet. She could hear more than one man snoring, but not at close proximity.

Were they *all* asleep?

She dared not assume so. Even if she were so fortunate, she would not be able to get through the gates alone. Elizabeth sat on the bed and the ropes holding the mattress creaked. She bounced there, trying to mimic the rhythm of intimacy, as her thoughts churned. She moaned and grunted at intervals, hoping to make the ruse plausible as she contrived a plan.

If she appealed to the laird, she did not doubt she would be promptly wed to another man loyal to his hand. Robert de Maxwell would seal her fate before her uncle even learned of her situation, given the plan to claim Beaupoint. She had to assume the scheme would continue without Calum. Would the reiving party still attack Beaupoint? When?

She had to warn her uncle.

Somehow.

She could not think of slipping out of the keep, so she considered the first challenge before her. She had to leave this chamber. She opened the door and the narrow corridor beyond was filled with shadows. She pulled Amaury's dagger and took a hasty step into the darkness, closing the door behind herself.

No sooner had the latch dropped than she was seized from behind.

A man locked his arms around her, his palm closed over her mouth, and her fear was reborn with new vigor. Elizabeth made to drive the blade behind herself, twisting against his strength, then felt his breath against her ear.

"'Tis only me," he murmured.

Amaury!

The very man responsible for her wretched situation! Elizabeth spun in his embrace with relief and fury.

AMAURY HAD REMAINED in the great hall until all the others had retired. He had consumed a quantity of terrible wine, pouring more of it into the rushes, and feigned sleep at the board. When all the others slept or had retired elsewhere, he crept up the stairs from the great hall. The hall and courtyard had fallen into darkness. The stone walls shone dark and wet from the rain. The wooden stairs were slippery.

He eased past the laird's chamber on silent feet. The laird snored loudly as did his lady, leaving no doubt that they were asleep. The sound of gentle snoring carried also from the second chamber. There was only one other chamber.

Was Elizabeth in the second or the third with Calum? Amaury did not know. He stood in the shadows, uncertain, until he heard a repetitive sound coming from the third chamber. The rhythm was unmistakable, the creaking of the bed ropes leaving little to be doubted of the occupants' current activity.

Elizabeth had to be there.

The sound, at least, disguised his approach. Amaury eased closer to the door and bent to peek through the lock. He could not see anything in the darkness beyond.

The creaking continued with regularity and he found himself marveling at Calum's endurance. It went on and on, a relentless rhythm that indicated extraordinary fortitude. There was a moan and then a gasp from the chamber, and Amaury stood in the shadows, uncertain he should be listening at all.

If they two met abed with such enthusiasm, perhaps Elizabeth was well pleased.

Perhaps she was exhausted.

Truly, the man had an unholy endurance.

Amaury looked at the ceiling. He counted to a hundred and still the sound continued, with unswerving regularity. He began to feel a measure of compassion for Elizabeth, for she would not be able to sit at the board on the morrow at this rate, then there was a little cry of pleasure.

Hers. The very sound made his own blood quicken and his fist clench.

It was followed by a muffled grunt, less readily identified as being that of Calum—but who else could it be?

The lady laughed a little and made some playful comment. Though the sound of her delight stabbed at Amaury's heart, it could not be denied that he had the answer he sought.

She was content.

He and Oliver would leave without her.

He had scarce taken a step than he heard the latch on the door. He backed into the shadows of the darkest corner, hoping he would be hidden from whoever left the chamber, but not having time to do anything else.

The door swung open and a lady stepped into the hall, a lady in a russet kirtle. A dagger shone in her hand and Amaury knew it was his own.

Elizabeth!

She might scream and no good would come of his discovery here. She took one step into the corridor then Amaury seized her from behind, closing one hand over her mouth and lifting her to her toes. He saw her grip the dagger and knew she would fight him, but touched his lips to her ear.

"'Tis only me," he murmured and she exhaled, collapsing against him in relief.

To Amaury's surprise, she spun and jabbed a fingertip into his chest. "You!"

she whispered with heat and he saw her eyes flash. "'Tis all your fault. I am wed to that villain and now he lies dead and I will be forced to wed another cur by dawn." She poked him again in frustration. "You and your cursed *duty*. If I had returned to Kilderrick, this could never have occurred."

She did not step entirely out of Amaury's embrace and he was nigh overwhelmed to find his arms full of the lady's soft heat. She was close, too close for him to think of any detail other than that kiss they had shared. It took him a long moment to comprehend her words and her anger.

Calum was dead?

Amaury struggled to make sense of what the lady told him, no easy task when he was so beguiled by her. "But you gave every indication that you were pleased to wed Calum."

Her eyes flashed dangerously. "I was advised to disguise my true feelings. You might recall that counsel."

He had suggested as much himself. But she had been uncommonly persuasive. Amaury had thought her reconciled to her duty. "You convinced me," he said and she jabbed at him again.

"You would be readily convinced that duty was satisfactory. Fool!"

Her frustration was more than clear, but Amaury had to know all. "You say Calum is dead?" In a way, he was not surprised. That man's amorous feat might have cost him dearly.

"You may look upon him yourself, if you do not believe me." Her tone was hostile and Amaury tried to calm her.

"I believe you, my lady."

"He was displeased that I had your dagger. They took it from me in the bath the first day. We argued." She took a quick breath and her voice trembled when she continued. "He fell and did not rise again."

She was troubled, it was clear, and Amaury could not blame her for that. She might never have seen a man die before, and he wished she had not witnessed this death.

"I knew he was not to be trusted," she said with heat. "He was the reiver who seized me a year ago." She grimaced. "He was *proud* of his deed. He said he knew I would flee and that he intended to teach me a lesson. Blackguard!"

Again, Amaury was astonished. Calum had been the one to assault her outside Beaupoint? He could scarce believe a man would treat his intended so cruelly. He was horrified at the other man's deeds, but more appalled by his own part in the lady's misfortune.

He had compelled her to come to Caerlaverock, believing that fulfilling her duty was most important of all.

He had put the lady he honored in peril.

Amaury was shaken by the magnitude of his own error—and the price she might have paid.

"He did not care if I died," she said, perhaps taking his silence for doubt, and Amaury heard tears in her voice. He wished he could see her more clearly.

"My lady, I owe you a thousand apologies. I compelled you to come to this place, against your own will and instincts, and I can never repay my debt to you." He continued when she did not reply, his voice hoarse. "I, too, had my doubts of his nature and at a glance. I should have trusted your reaction. I erred and mightily."

She stared at him. "You admit that you were wrong?" She sounded surprised.

"I was utterly mistaken," he admitted and bowed his head. "I sought to protect you but instead put you in danger." His voice broke. "That my insistence upon duty could have cost you all is a debt I will never repay. No deed of mine can ever compensate, my lady."

Elizabeth was evidently astonished to silence but she recovered. "I never thought to hear you admit you had erred."

"I will do so again, if you desire."

"I wish I could see your eyes."

"Then let us leave this place. I will escort you wherever you desire and with all haste." He took her elbow, but she did not turn. She looked up at him though he could not discern her expression.

"Suddenly you heed me," she said. "That is a sweet change."

"I erred. Command of me what you will and I will strive to make amends."

Elizabeth looked over her shoulder at the empty corridor, then moved closer to him instead of leading him to the stairs. "I would like another kiss," she whispered. "Here in the darkness."

"That is scarcely sufficient reparation."

"True, but in this moment, I would like to be consoled." There was a quiver in her voice, one that made him fear to learn whatever had occurred before Calum's death.

Amaury could not refuse such a simple request, never mind one that allied so well with his own desires. He framed her face in his hands, and cursed himself when he felt her tremble at his touch. He thought of that rhythmic creak and could not imagine how sore she might be as a result.

"How did you endure such a long ride?" he asked softly.

"I did not," she said, which made no sense. "I needed time to think when he died," she confessed. "I bounced on the bed alone."

Amaury bent closer. "My lady, you fooled me truly. That is twice in rapid succession, for I believed you happy in your match."

"And you trusted that I was content, even though you also disliked him." She shook her head, chiding him. "There are moments when you can be a fool, sir."

Aye, he was a fool for this woman and that, Amaury guessed, would never change.

He could say no more for she eased even closer, her gaze wide as her lips parted. Amaury could not resist her silent appeal. He slid one hand into the silk of her hair and surrendered to temptation, bending to capture her lips beneath his own. Elizabeth rose to her toes, welcoming him, inviting him onward, one hand on his shoulder and the other trapped between them with his dagger. Her kiss was a heady pleasure, one that he knew he should not savor overmuch. He slanted his mouth over hers, hungry for more than this mere taste, and let her taste his satisfaction that she was safe.

He would do any deed for her.

He would take her to Kilderrick.

He might linger in Scotland, even in service to Maximilian, to see her defended.

Even lost in the splendor of her kiss, Amaury was vaguely aware that the air stirred beside them—as if the door to the chamber opened again. No sooner did he have the thought then he heard the other man's triumphant whisper.

"I knew it," Calum said.

Amaury broke the kiss and spun, pushing Elizabeth behind him. Calum stood in the doorway, far from dead, dressed in only his chausses. The light from the chamber spilled around him, making his anger clear. There was a bruise rising on his temple and fury in his eyes. "You contrived this, the two of you. Do not imagine that I will stand aside while you savor my bride."

Amaury drew his second dagger from his belt, thrusting the lady toward the stairs. "Run!" he bade her, glad that she obeyed without hesitation or argument. He heard her footsteps as she raced down to the bailey, then he dove toward Calum. He had only his small knife but he would do what damage he could, while he could.

"Stop her!" Calum shouted, brandishing his own blade. "Awake, all! *Awake!* Do not let her escape!"

The household began to stir at the hue and cry, and Amaury knew there was no chance of a covert escape. They were well and truly outnumbered and only speed could aid them.

Or deception.

Yet again, he realized he had no plan and that the lack might cost him dearly.

"O-li-ver!" Amaury bellowed, hoping the boy guessed his intent, then jabbed at his opponent's chest. His desire to take a price from Calum's hide for so abusing Elizabeth would give him the strength of ten men.

Though Amaury doubted even that would be enough.

Elizabeth ran.

Amaury roared for his squire behind her and she heard blades clash. She dared not look back.

She made the base of the stairs before anyone tried to stop her, then easily evaded the grasp of the sleepy cousin who grabbed at her in the bailey. She was terrified yet pleased beyond all.

Amaury had apologized.

And he had admitted that he had erred. Elizabeth had never expected to see or hear such words from him, and that he pledged himself to her service, that he vowed to make amends, made her heart soar with joy.

And his kiss. His kiss melted her reservations and heated her blood. It had been both gentle and powerful, even more potent than the last. What a vexing, challenging, honorable and glorious man.

Elizabeth knew then with utter conviction what service she desired of him.

She hoped she could summon the audacity to ask.

In the meantime, they had to escape Caerlaverock.

Where were the horses in the stable? How could she reach them without being caught. She whistled on impulse, mimicking the way Amaury called his dogs, and Grise trotted out of the stables, ears up. She barked in recognition of Elizabeth, her tail wagging as Oliver appeared behind her. He had all of the horses saddled and loaded, as well as Persephone on his fist, and his relief at the sight of her was clear.

"What is the plan?" Elizabeth asked in a whisper and the boy's surprise was clear.

"There is no plan, my lady."

"How can this be?" Elizabeth was incredulous. After all his talk of the merit of plans, Amaury had no strategy?

"Who could have anticipated that you would wish to leave with haste?" Oliver asked, his tone so reasonable and measured that he might have been the knight himself. "You appeared to be content."

"You might recall that I had advice to give a willing appearance," she replied and the boy blinked, then grinned.

"And you were most persuasive," he said. "I salute you, my lady." He bowed.

"Oliver!" that knight bellowed again and they both looked up in alarm. There was a crash, then the two men tumbled down the wooden stairs to the bailey, grappling for supremacy the entire way. Calum wore only his chausses and Amaury, Elizabeth was alarmed to see, was not wearing his hauberk.

"Where is his hauberk?" she asked and Oliver nodded toward the baggage. "But he might be injured!"

"He does not sleep in it," the boy said, his manner impatient. "How could he anticipate this fight?"

For a man who heralded the merit of planning, Amaury needed to include more possibilities in his schemes, to Elizabeth's thinking.

Calum landed atop Amaury in the bailey and jabbed for his throat. Amaury rolled, landing his knee in Calum's groin, who then managed to flick the dagger from Amaury's grasp. They both turned to watch as the blade danced across the ground, then lunged after it as one.

Oliver looked at the dagger in Elizabeth's hand, then paled. "He has only the small blade?" he asked, but it was not truly a question.

Elizabeth nodded and he shoved Persephone toward her. She had barely taken the falcon before Oliver burrowed in the luggage, seizing the scabbard of Amaury's sword. He pulled the blade free as he hastened toward the battling men. The dogs circled around Elizabeth, growling as they watched Calum and Amaury battle.

"Sir?" Oliver said, bowing as he presented the weapon.

Amaury glanced up and his eyes lit. He drove his elbow into Calum's face, then bounded to his feet. He seized the sword and spun around, swinging it hard at Calum. Calum had just risen to his feet, and he took a step back but not quickly enough. The tip of the blade sliced a thin line across his chest, and a red line appeared from shoulder to shoulder. Calum stared down at it in shock for a moment.

Then he spat an insult, jabbing at Amaury with his dagger. When the knight stepped back, Calum darted for the ladder to the ramparts. A sentry granted him a sword when he reached the summit, and Calum seized it, spinning to confront Amaury as that knight reached the top of the ladder. He slashed at Amaury's hands but the knight bowed his head and lunged upward with a bellow.

Amaury slashed at Calum's knees with his own sword and Elizabeth feared he would lose his grip and fall. The rain pattered down steadily and she feared Amaury might slip. Calum darted backward, inadvertently granting Amaury the opportunity to bound to the top of the ladder. Once on the top of the ramparts, Amaury swung first at the sentry who made a snatch for Calum's abandoned dagger. He fairly lost a hand for that, and staggered backward to escape Amaury's blow. Amaury thrust at Calum, then pivoted and kicked the sentry in the chest. That man fell into the bailey, landing hard on the timber roof of the stables. He rolled to one side, dazed but alive.

Calum and Amaury faced each other on the summit of the wall, swords at the ready.

Yet Elizabeth, Oliver and the horses were trapped inside the bailey. What could she do? The portcullis was down and the drawbridge was up. The gatekeeper stood in that narrow passageway between the gatehouses, silhouetted against the opening and looking like a formidable barrier. He was watching Calum and Amaury fight and paying little attention to her. All around them, sleeping men stirred to wakefulness. There were masons and servants, Calum's relations and warriors aplenty. In moments, any opportunity to flee would be lost, for their little party would be vastly outnumbered.

Elizabeth guessed that little good would come of their capture, which appeared to be inevitable. She had no doubt Calum would take a reckoning from her and she feared she might not survive it.

Calum and Amaury's blades clashed with force, then to her horror, the pair disappeared from view. She heard a splash as they fell into the moat and saw her chance.

"My husband!" she cried, racing toward the gatekeeper. "He cannot swim. We must save him!"

And the gatekeeper, visibly appalled at the prospect of Calum's death, opened the portcullis.

Half the puzzle was solved!

CHAPTER 9

The two men's blades clashed, the force of Calum's blow making Amaury stagger. 'Twas clear the other man intended to win at any price. Amaury was well aware that those warriors who defended the keep were mustering and the opportunity for escape—such as it was—was dwindling quickly.

But this man had despoiled Elizabeth. He had captured her and injured her, and Amaury could not let that pass unchallenged.

"So, you do desire my wife," Calum said as he swung at Amaury. Amaury took a step back, then glanced down to check his distance to the lip of the wall. It was but a handspan away. Far, far below, the dark water of the moat glinted. The rain fell steadily upon them, the land around the keep wreathed in mist and shadows. "I wager you sampled her."

"I know you did," Amaury retorted and struck hard. "Almost a year ago, *before* you were wed."

Calum grunted but parried the blow. They moved down the wall, weapons raised, each eying the other. "She was mine to take."

"Not before your nuptials. You dishonored her."

Calum laughed. "But not you? Delivering her to another man for the coin is noble?" He spat and their blades clashed again.

"I erred on the side of honor. Clearly, that was a miscalculation with regards to you."

Calum swung again and Amaury parried, but he pretended to falter. Calum stepped closer to strike the final blow, his eyes alight with triumph, but Amaury moved suddenly to slice at Calum's legs. The other man danced backward in his surprise and Amaury moved closer —only to have Calum use a similar feint. His eyes glinted, the sole warning Amaury had, and he lunged directly at Amaury.

The blade sliced the outside of Amaury's thigh and he stumbled, more because it was expected than due to a great injury. Calum laughed and kicked Amaury in the chest so that he fell backward toward the edge of the wall. Amaury pretended to lose his balance but seized Calum's ankle and hauled him closer with a hard tug. The other man fell toward Amaury, his expression astonished, and Amaury did lose his balance in truth.

They went over the curtain wall together, swords flying out of their grasps, and landed in the midst of the moat with a splash. The moat was deep enough that Amaury could not feel the bottom and the water was so dirty that when he ducked beneath the surface, he could see nothing at all. His sword was upon the bank, but he could not see where Calum's had fallen. That man obviously thought it was in the water, for he was feeling beneath the surface with desperation, even as he struggled to remain afloat. There was shouting and the noise of activity within the walls but Amaury had this dispute to finish first.

He dove at Calum, drawing him forcibly under the water. The man flailed and kicked, struggling until he broke the surface again.

"I cannot swim!" he roared.

"How sad," Amaury said, not believing the tale. He dragged Calum down again, holding his breath. Calum kicked and freed himself, seizing upon a rock in the curtain wall to hold himself up. 'Twas clear that he found a footing there and Amaury reasoned that there was a narrow lip of earth against the foundation of the wall.

"You..." Calum began, but Amaury decked him before he could say more.

Calum fell backward and Amaury seized him, casting him toward the middle of the moat. The other man sank beneath the surface, disappearing from view.

All was still.

The water did not move. Amaury moved his arms, remaining afloat, and turned slowly in place, suspicious. He could not have conquered Calum yet. He knew it instinctively.

Victory had been too easy.

In but a moment, he was proven right.

Suddenly Amaury was seized by the knees and pulled under the surface. He had time to take a breath, then wrestled with Calum under water. The other man was as slippery as an eel and much stronger. Only the water kept either of them from landing a fierce blow.

Amaury reasoned that Calum must have need of a breath, for he had been beneath the surface for a while. Amaury had taken a deep breath and could wait. They battled against each other furiously, Amaury ensuring that neither of them made it to the surface.

Just when Amaury felt his need to take a breath grow, Calum twisted and jabbed his elbow into Amaury's throat with savage force. Amaury choked and took a mouthful of foul water. Calum wriggled free, surging for the surface. Amaury swam after him and caught him around the waist just as he took a great gulping breath, flinging him against the curtain wall hard.

Calum exhaled and swore, then sank bonelessly beneath the surface, but Amaury would not be fooled again. He found his footing on that slippery ledge, gripping the stone of the wall with one hand. When Calum drifted near him, apparently unconscious, Amaury seized him.

He pulled the other man from the water and waited until his eyes opened warily. Amaury decked him and heard the other man's nose crack. He pummeled him against the wall, landing two hard punches in the gut. Calum groaned and reached for Amaury's eyes, but he rammed his opponent hard against the stone. There was a loud crack and Calum went limp.

Amaury let Calum sink but held fast to him, alert for any movement. There was none. Blood rose to the surface in a stream of crimson. He hauled his opponent to the bank, casting the other man to dry ground. Still, Calum did not move.

Amaury checked and discovered that the other man's pulse was gone. That could not be a feint.

It was done.

And now, the lady had to be rescued. Amaury picked up his sword and turned to survey the high walls of Caerlaverock, only to discover that the lady had saved herself.

~

THE GATEKEEPER HAULED on the rope for the portcullis, pulling it hand over hand. Though he worked with speed, Elizabeth could only wish he would move even more quickly. The rope groaned as the portcullis was steadily raised. She could hear splashing but had no notion of how Amaury fared.

She could not bear it if he died in defense of her.

Another man emerged from the other gatehouse and clearly did not approve of what he saw. He looked to have been awakened by their discussion and was rubbing his eyes, even as he scowled at the first guard. "What is this?" he demanded gruffly. "'Tis too early to open the gates. The sun has not yet broken free of the horizon."

"We must save Calum Moffatt from drowning," the first man explained, securing the rope for the portcullis. It was open, though the drawbridge was yet raised against the curtain wall. It was a formidable wooden bridge, as wide as a man was tall and several times higher. Elizabeth recalled the chain in the one chamber that secured it. "He battles against that foreign knight and they have fallen in the moat."

"Nay!" The second considered Elizabeth with suspicion. "Has the laird given the command to open the gates?"

The first man hesitated instead of replying.

"Must the laird give the command to save a man's life?" Elizabeth demanded. "You will linger and my husband will die! Will the laird not be displeased that you did not act to save a warrior sworn to his service? Calum cannot swim!" She did not know this for certain, but they had to be urged onward.

The pair exchanged a glance. The second made to return to the bailey, perhaps to seek the laird's counsel. The first folded his arms across his chest and waited.

Men! It seemed the only one who listened to Elizabeth was Amaury.

Oliver had urged the palfreys into the narrow passage and the space was crowded with circling dogs and impatient horses. The second man made slow progress down the length of the space and clearly was displeased about it.

He was not so discontent as the destrier, however. She heard Zephyr snort and stamp with impatience, no doubt because he was last instead of first. She could see the dark silhouette of the destrier's head as he fought the bit, and she wondered that Oliver had not settled the steed. They had sufficient challenge without an outraged destrier.

"Step aside, step aside," the second guard said. People were visible in the bailey behind the warhorse, whispering and pointing. Elizabeth's heart skipped that their small party was trapped in this narrow space. It could not end here.

She turned on the first man, intent upon gaining her way. "Why this delay?"

"He speaks right, my lady. We must await the laird's command to open the gates."

"What nonsense! A man will die because of your reluctance to use good sense."

The guard looked to be troubled by this.

"Surely you can begin," she suggested. "Surely it is no quick task to lower a drawbridge of such size. Why, it must be the length of three men!"

"Five," that man corrected solemnly. "And the chain three times that."

"Truly?" she said with awe. "I have never heard of such a marvel."

"Aye." He nodded proudly and pointed upward, warming to his explanation. "It runs through the wall of the great hall itself, then down to this chamber where the chain is coiled and secured." He seemed intent upon explaining it to her, and Elizabeth chose to encourage that.

"How is it secured?" she asked.

He stepped through the doorway to the chamber with the coiled chain and gestured. "There is a wheel that it is wound upon, and this pin to secure it, and..."

She looked around the chamber, noting that the guards had clearly taken their leisure in this space the night before. There were four empty crockery cups and a large pitcher that had evidently been filled with ale at some point.

She could hear the second guard complaining in the passageway and apparently Oliver had ensured he had not progressed far. "Make way," the guard commanded with impatience. "Make way!" Zephyr continued to stomp and snort in outrage, then whinnied with fury.

"I am sorry, sir," Oliver said, sounding so contrite that Elizabeth knew he was responsible for the destrier's agitation. "I do apologize, sir. He can be most difficult, sir."

Then she heard a bellow of indignation from the stallion. She and the guard stepped out of the chamber in time to see Zephyr throw his head back. The horse tossed his head, his nostrils flaring, baring his teeth. Elizabeth thought he might rear. The second guard shouted, trying to get out of the way of the destrier's hooves. The dogs barked and circled beneath the horse's legs, adding to the confusion. The palfreys nickered and stamped, jostling each other and trying to flee.

Zephyr did rear, his massive hooves pawing the air. He landed so hard that the ground shook and the palfreys crowded toward the closed drawbridge. Bête growled, Esther shied and Grise barked.

Zephyr then lifted his tail like a majestic plume and defecated.

Elizabeth blinked in surprise. Oliver had a wicked grin, which meant he had planned the feat.

The second sentry swore as the scent of dung filled the narrow passageway. The volume was impressive and a considerable obstruction, deposited as it was in the middle of the narrow passage. The smell was sufficient to bring tears to Elizabeth's eyes. Those in the bailey began to laugh, then laughed harder when the sentry slipped and fell in his haste to reach the laird. He swore, slipped again and then fell silent as the destrier stamped and fumed.

"Bert?" the first sentry called. "Are you hale?"

Elizabeth gave him a hard shove, but her effort to trip him failed. He was too large for her to push off balance and he only stumbled against the wall of the passageway. She needed another weapon and the cry of the bird on her fist gave her an idea.

The guard spun back to her, his expression hostile. "What is this?" he demanded but Elizabeth had removed Persephone's hood with a quick gesture.

She flung the bird toward his face, releasing the jesses. The peregrine raised her claws and screamed as she took flight.

The sentry stumbled back into the chamber where the chain for the drawbridge was secured, his hands over his face. He fell against the great coil of chain and Elizabeth gave him another shove. When he fell to the floor, she seized the locking pin. The chain began to unfurl with remarkable speed and considerable noise.

"Nay! Not so fast!" he cried and grabbed for the chain with his gloved hands. It rolled through his grip even as he struggled to stop it.

As soon as he turned his back upon her, Elizabeth seized that crockery pitcher and broke it over his head. The guard fell to the floor, the chain rattling as the drawbridge was unsecured.

Persephone screamed, a triumphant cry that meant she flew high overhead and was free of Caerlaverock.

The drawbridge hit the opposite shore of the moat so hard that Elizabeth feared it might shatter, but she did not delay. At her whistle and gesture, Bête and Noisette ran across the drawbridge. The palfreys took one look at the light of the clearing beyond and cantered toward it, without being so guided. Elizabeth urged them all ahead of her, Oliver waved her onward, then she made to follow the horses.

A man suddenly lunged out of the gatehouse on the other side and snatched at her. He moved so quickly that she had no chance to evade him, but Grise jumped for him, snarling. "Cursed beast!" The man stabbed his blade at the dog, but Elizabeth had time to draw Amaury's knife.

She stabbed it at the man's face, horrified when the blade sliced open his cheek. He gave a cry and staggered backward, another sentry appearing then in the passageway.

"Run, my lady," Oliver cried and Elizabeth did not delay. She was across the bridge, Amaury's dagger in her hand and Grise by her side. The horses were ahead of her, men were slipping in the dung behind her as they tried to follow from the bailey. Oliver thrust and parried on the narrow drawbridge with the sentry who had given chase. They were evenly matched, though Elizabeth hoped Oliver would win.

Persephone swooped out of the sky toward the battling pair, screaming as she dove, talons extended. When the sentry looked up at the bird in horror, Oliver kicked his feet out from under him. The man fell into the moat with a splash. When he broke the surface, he shouted and shook his fist, but they were all across the bridge. A command was roared from inside the walls and the portcullis dropped as the drawbridge began to rise again.

Oliver laughed as he swung onto Ghita's back and Elizabeth was already in the saddle on Esther's back. She wrapped Amaury's cloak over her arm and raised her fist, whistling for the peregrine. The sun had just crested the horizon and the light was silvery in the light rain.

Persephone called and turned, a majestic shadow against the pearly sky. The peregrine then dove for Elizabeth's fist, landing with such vigor that Elizabeth's arm dropped past her knees. She hooded the bird and murmured to her, then looked for Amaury.

He stood on the bank, dripping wet, beside a fallen man who could only be Calum. There was blood on his chausses and he was filthy, but he was alive. And as relief flooded through her, he looked up at her and shook his head.

Elizabeth's heart stopped then skipped, for yet again, she could not guess his thoughts. He was inscrutable again, eyes narrowed as he surveyed her, then she watched his lips curve into a reluctant smile.

"Well played, my lady," he said, his low voice and his praise making her heart sing. "Well played." He dropped to one knee and bowed his head to her. "I apologize for compelling you to come to this place, my lady. I erred sorely."

Elizabeth's heart melted and she almost slipped from the saddle to lift him to his feet, but the first arrow buried itself in the ground beside him, quivering as he glanced at it.

Amaury rose to his feet with haste and ran for Zephyr.

~

THE LADY WAS A VISION. Elizabeth was as beautiful as Amaury recalled, but there was a new resolve about her. He had seen her raise her fist, imperiously summoning the peregrine, and call with every confidence of being heeded. She was meek no longer and he savored the change. Once he had admired her for her beauty alone, but now his admiration deepened into far more, a change that was only possible because she gained confidence and poise. It might even have been due to her fearlessness in telling him when he was wrong. His heart soared when she turned to face him in triumph, the bird on her fist, more glorious than any lady he had ever seen.

When her gaze collided with his, his heart stopped and his chest tightened. He forgot the ache in his thigh and the dull pain in his jaw, and no longer wondered if he had lost a tooth to Calum's punch. He was unaware of how cold and wet he was, unaware of activity in the keep, or even the unholy stink of moat water upon him.

There was only Elizabeth.

In that moment, Amaury knew with utter conviction that no other lady would ever challenge her custody of his heart. The maiden who had captured his heart with a glimpse had been only a pale shadow of the lady she became. He wished he could see the woman she would ultimately become.

He had time to salute her and apologize again before the first arrow struck. No doubt, it would be followed by another.

He limped toward Zephyr, cursing the pain in his thigh.

"You are injured," she said with concern, circling the palfrey around him.

All Amaury wanted was to see her away from these walls.

"It is naught," he said grimly, hoping he could swing into the saddle. "Ride on."

"You are bleeding!" she added crossly. "You are injured in truth."

"We have not the luxury of time, my lady," Amaury said, gaining the saddle with an effort. He closed his eyes, wincing at the pain, and hoped she did not notice. Oliver brought him the scabbard for his sword and he sheathed the weapon, even as he gave the destrier his heels.

Of course, Elizabeth did notice.

"You cannot simply ride on," she chided, matching her palfrey's pace to that of the destrier. They cantered beside each other, leaving the keep behind but not quickly enough for Amaury's taste. The lady, though, was determined to chastise him. It was impossible to believe that he had once thought her meek. "You are wet..."

"And we are besieged," Amaury said, interrupting her. He pointed to the summit of the walls and the archers that had become visible in silhouette.

"God in Heaven," she whispered as a score of arrows were loosed in their direction.

"Release the hawk and ride," he instructed. "She will follow."

Elizabeth did as bidden—not questioning him, for once. He would not have been the man he was to fail to find satisfaction in that. Persephone soared high, crying as she did. Still she looked back at Calum's corpse, her uncertainty clear.

"Is he dead in truth this time?" the lady asked.

"He will dishonor you no more," Amaury said and looked at her fully for the first time. The sun was cresting the horizon and in the light, he saw the mark upon her cheek. It was already turning color and swelling. "He struck you," he whispered in dismay.

"Twice," she said and dropped her gaze.

Amaury almost turned back to cut out the villain's heart, but Elizabeth shook her head.

"I am hale," she said.

"You are not hale," he corrected her. "You are injured and were nearly abused and it is my fault for bringing you to this cursed spot..."

"And it is your fault that I left that chamber alive," she said, interrupting him.

Amaury looked at her, not understanding.

She smiled a little. "You taught me that I should fight back. I would never have dared before I met you." Her eyes shone. "So, I was imperiled by doing my duty, but saved by your instruction. You cannot take the blame without the credit, sir."

Amaury did not know what to say to that. In truth, the warmth of Elizabeth's gaze and the splendor of her smile provoked such a vehement response in him that he could not think coherently.

"I am glad," he managed finally, speaking even more gruffly than was his inclination. He bowed his head to her. "And I thank you for seeing all through the gates."

She nodded once. "I believe we are in each other's debt, sir." She gave him another smile, one that made his heart thunder.

There was a roar from the keep behind them. This was their opportunity to ride fast and hard.

Amaury glanced back, then slapped Esther's rump. "Now ride!" The mare took off at a frantic gallop and Amaury gave Zephyr his heels. Oliver raced behind them upon Ghita, holding the reins of Flora. The horses' hooves pounded against the ground.

As Caerlaverock erupted in fury and the sun rose pink in the east, Amaury's entire company galloped eastward. He knew he was not the sole one glad to leave that fortress behind.

THE RIVER ANNAN was ahead of them before Amaury allowed the horses to slow to a walk. Elizabeth noted that the tide was out and the wet flats extended far into the estuary.

Amaury looked back over his shoulder with concern, disinterested in the tides.

Elizabeth expected that would shortly change.

Even though they halted, he moved quickly, instructing her to remain in the saddle.

"I do not think we have been pursued yet," he said. "The situation will not last."

He jumped down from the destrier's saddle and she winced as she watched him limp toward Flora and the baggage she carried. Oliver was already unpacking items.

"A clean chemise and chausses, sir," he said. "And your hauberk, of course."

Amaury stepped behind the palfrey, out of Elizabeth's view. She knew he stripped down because she saw garments hit the ground. He sneezed mightily and she bit her tongue rather than chide him again for being reckless with his own welfare.

"Have you a cloth?" he asked Oliver. "I would wipe some of this filth from my hide."

Oliver ran to the river and filled a pail, then returned to scrub the knight down with haste. "We ride to Kilderrick," Amaury said. "And with all haste, as the lady originally requested."

"Kilderrick?" she echoed.

Amaury cast her a glance over the palfrey's back. "Aye."

"Nay," she argued. "We must ride to Beaupoint."

His expression became stern again. "Why?"

"I did not tell you all that Calum said. They mean to storm Beaupoint and take it as a haven. His family are reivers and they wish to have a refuge within England. They mean to seize Beaupoint for that purpose."

"Then they would be able to raid further south," Amaury guessed.

Elizabeth nodded. "He paid a great deal of coin to win my uncle's agreement that he might wed me."

"Coin from reiving?"

"I wonder if Robert de Maxwell contributed. My uncle will not survive the attack, by the plan, and Calum intended to claim Beaupoint himself."

Amaury nodded. "For his marriage to the lady carrying the blood of the holding would buttress his argument. Would the king grant it to him?"

Elizabeth shrugged. "The baron who is the king's justiciar might do as much." She bit her lip. "But the Moffatts are Scottish and known to be reivers. Thomas de Montgomerie, Baron of Clyfford, is known to be most fair."

"You know him?"

"He was my father's overlord, a man I have known all my life."

"Perhaps there would be coin to encourage his decision," Amaury said.

Elizabeth frowned and did not protest. She could not imagine that the baron could be so cajoled, but Calum and his kin must have had a plan. Perhaps the baron was ill. His oldest son, Gavin, might well accept a bribe if it was a rich one.

"But Calum is dead," Oliver contributed.

"I do not believe they will abandon the scheme so readily," Elizabeth said.

"It would be a considerable advantage to have a sanctuary, especially as Maximilian joins the effort to stop the reivers," Amaury said.

"Aye. They could simply remain in England and amass their wealth there," Oliver acknowledged. The three nodded in appreciation of the scheme.

Amaury donned his hauberk and turned to look across the firth. Elizabeth watched him trace a path along the north shore to the shrouded end of the estuary then west again. "'Twill take days to ride to Beaupoint," he said softly, then frowned. "Nay, we must take these tidings to Maximilian." He nodded at Oliver. "We can reach Kilderrick by dusk, if we ride hard."

"Aye, sir. We can turn north here and cut a shorter path."

"Aye." Amaury put his hand on the destrier's saddle but Elizabeth cleared her throat.

"I do not ride to Kilderrick," she said.

Amaury cast her an impatient glance. "We have just decided..."

"You have decided and you have erred before, sir," she said and his eyes narrowed. "I must ride to Beaupoint, alone if necessary, and warn my uncle of his peril."

"My lady," Amaury began to protest. He held her gaze, as likely to cede to her will as a mountain.

Elizabeth did not surrender. She leaned forward and argued her side. "My uncle is a cleric, inexperienced in matters of war. Another man might be prepared for assault, but I wager he will not be." She raised her brows. "No doubt his ledgers are in perfect order but that will scarce defend the walls."

Oliver's smile flashed, but he flicked a glance at Amaury and sobered with an effort.

"Beaupoint is not my concern," Amaury began.

"But it is mine. My uncle is my sole surviving kin," Elizabeth replied. "I will warn him, whether you accompany me or not."

And leaving the knight with one hand raised to dispute the matter with her, she turned Esther and rode into the firth. She took a deep breath of the familiar scent of the flats and noticed the mist that had gathered over the water ahead. The far shore could not be seen, but she knew the distance well. The rain fell lightly, much diminished from the night before. It would halt by noon, she wagered. She spoke to the palfrey, who was unfamiliar with the flats, but Esther gained confidence with each step as the water grew no deeper.

Beaupoint was but hours away.

Elizabeth did not glance back, though she wondered what Amaury would do.

DENIED HER WAY, the lady would willingly end her life.

Amaury stared after her, astounded that she would be so foolish.

"What madness is this?" he called after her, but she neither halted nor looked back. The palfrey walked steadily into the water. Amaury swore beneath his breath and pursued her on foot. His boots were already wet.

"Have you lost your wits, my lady? Why would you see to your own destruction over a difference of view?" To his surprise, the wet sand beneath his feet was firm and the water did not grow much deeper, even as he left Oliver and the other horses behind. It was scarcely to his ankles when he managed to seize Esther's reins, but the shore was so distant that the squire could not have heard them.

Elizabeth looked down at him and he caught his breath at the sight of her. He would promise her anything to keep her safe, and could not bear the possibility of a world without her in it. Her lips set with resolve. "I told you: I ride for Beaupoint."

"You ride into the sea," Amaury corrected.

She shook her head, eyes shining with a conviction he could not explain. "I use the weth to cross the firth. It is quicker."

Weth. He had never heard the word before. What was a weth?

"Save for the fact that you will drown," Amaury countered.

She shook her head again and he had the sense she laughed at him. "The water is shallow when the tide is out. It is still flowing outward, so there is time to make the southern shore." She raised her brows. "Unless, of course, you would stand here half the day and dispute what I know to be true." There was a challenge in her dark eyes.

Ride across the firth? Amaury was skeptical. He turned and looked, though, and wondered whether she spoke the truth. The flats shimmered in every direction, silvery-grey with water, but it seemed the water above the sand was not deep. There was a fog ahead and he guessed the water was deeper there, in the middle of the firth.

He was reminded of Mont St. Michel on the north coast of France, which was only accessible at low tide. The road was beneath the sea otherwise and the mount became an island twice a day. "How deep does it get?" he asked and was rewarded with her smile.

"You listen to me!" she said with satisfaction and Amaury felt his neck heat.

"This is most wondrous. I had not anticipated it."

Her smile grew brighter then she turned to gesture. "At the deepest point, it will crest Zephyr's knees, but that will not be for long."

"You have ridden this route before?"

"Not this one. There are many weths, at least four that have been well known for eons. I have watched from Beaupoint as this one was used, but have only ridden on the shortest one to the east." She smiled, but the expression was tinged with sadness. "My father forbade me to use the longer ones. Timing is of greater import with them."

"But there is time on this day?" This was not an error Amaury wished to make.

She pointed downward. "Watch the water. It still ebbs away to the sea."

Amaury looked and saw that it was true.

"There is time," she insisted and he believed her.

He could escort her to Beaupoint, sending Oliver to Maximilian to share what they had learned. He could then ride to Carlisle, losing little if any time at all before finding passage to France. There was coin in his purse for the passage. This was an unexpected advantage, and one he would never have known about if not for Elizabeth.

That alone meant he should escort her. "Then we shall do it," he said, watching her smile light her features. "Come back to the shore while I send Oliver on his way. I vow to be quick."

Shock replaced her pleasure. "You dismiss Oliver?"

"He was loaned to me only by the *Loup Argent*." He spared her a glance. "Like you, he is fond of his own choice, and his is Kilderrick."

"But he cannot ride there alone."

"He has ridden alone in worse places, I imagine. He will be fine."

"But how can you manage without a squire?"

"I will find one, and until then, I will survive." Elizabeth did not comment upon that, and it sounded like folly even to Amaury. It seemed that with every passing week, more advantage slipped from his grasp. Soon he would have nothing left at all. The dogs barked and ran toward him from the shore as he led Esther back to Oliver.

"You call it a weth," he said aware that Elizabeth rode in silence.

"It is an old word, for the paths have been known for centuries. My father said that was why the Romans continued Hadrian's Wall along the south coast of the firth, for they knew the weths created a point of weakness on the border."

Amaury nodded. He had been right. She knew so much of this land and its history, that her father had ensured her education.

And because of that, they would evade whoever followed them from Caerlaverock. Truly, he was fortunate to have this lady as his companion.

To Elizabeth's relief, Amaury was quick in dismissing Oliver. It seemed the arrangement had already been made and the knight had given the boy a payment for Esther and Flora. Amaury's baggage had been packed accordingly and she appreciated anew that Oliver was efficient. The pair exchanged a few words, Amaury thanked Oliver and shook his hand, a choice that visibly startled—and pleased—the squire. Then they wished each other Godspeed and parted ways.

It was not long before Elizabeth and Amaury were on the flats again, far from the shore. He had whistled for Persephone and Elizabeth had the bird on her fist. She held the jesses tightly. Amaury led Flora by the reins, scanning the water as if he expected it to suddenly become much deeper. The dogs stayed close, their ears folded back. To her relief, he was limping less and there did not seem to be fresh blood on his chausses.

"We make slow process," Elizabeth said.

"Aye, but I do not know the depth of the water. I have been soaked once this day and would avoid a second time. Although the firth is cleaner." He spared her a warm glance. "Tell me how you managed to escape the keep."

Elizabeth told him the tale, which prompted his chuckle and his admiration. Zephyr's contribution made him laugh aloud, a wondrous sound.

"How did Oliver encourage that?" she asked.

Amaury patted the horse's neck. "It is something he does when vexed. Always has."

"But how could Oliver have known?"

Amaury considered this. "He is clever, that boy, and observant of detail. Oliver must have noticed that I provoked him before we boarded the ship from France." He slanted a glance at her. "It is preferable to leave such a burden behind."

"I can well believe that."

"Zephyr will never soil his stall either and he has not ridden out since yesterday morn."

"Oliver would know both those details."

"And he used that information to good effect." Amaury nodded. "He has learned much from Maximilian, to be sure."

"Do you think he will become a knight?"

Amaury shook his head. "It is tradition to dispatch a boy at eight summers of age to his maternal uncle to be trained for at least seven or eight years. Oliver is much older than that, probably fifteen summers. He has no living kin. I do not believe he was nobly born. And even Maximilian, if he chose to sponsor the boy, has no maternal uncle who would indulge his request."

"You could train him."

The notion clearly surprised Amaury. "I could teach him the skills, but I have no fortune or holding, no ability to grant him the gifts of knighthood. His destrier. His armor. His sword and his spurs."

"Would you have done it if you had not been disavowed?"

He considered the question, which she had not been confident he would do. "Six months ago, no, I would have done no favor for Maximilian. I disliked and distrusted him and would have rejected any suggestion that a boy without noble blood was worthy of earning his spurs."

"And now?"

He met her gaze steadily. "And now I wonder how many opportunities I lost because of my convictions. Oliver would make a fine knight. I see his merit as I never would have before."

"Just as you see that of the *Loup Argent*."

He nodded, his gaze seeking hers. "Among others. My convictions suffer deeply in this land."

What other convictions of his had been compromised? Elizabeth wondered.

There was something about the stillness and the broad surface of the shallow water that made it seem as if they were alone in all the world. She felt as if she could tell him anything at all, and ask for his confessions as well. The quiet made her bold.

Even so, she refused to look at the token bound to his scabbard. "But you must still believe that a woman should be silent and do as she is bidden." She heard the challenge in her own tone but he did not take umbrage.

Amaury slanted a glance her way, but that elusive smile was tugging at the corner of his mouth. "Though you would dispute this notion."

"How can I not? We find a way to reach Beaupoint sooner because I shared my knowledge with you."

Amaury glanced down at the water, which rose to Zephyr's knees. "We are not there yet," he murmured.

"Do you doubt my word?"

"I would be certain of the accuracy of your information before offering congratulations."

Perhaps his expectation of women had not changed, after all. Why was it that Elizabeth could not leave the matter be?

CHAPTER 10

Demure and biddable," Elizabeth said when they had forded the deepest part of the firth and she saw the tension ease from Amaury's shoulders. He checked the course of the water again, and she knew he also saw that the tide was turning. He eyed the shore and began to move more quickly. "Indeed, sir, you would confuse a lady with an ornament, or a tapestry skillfully wrought."

"Not so much that."

"Then what *do* you expect of a woman? What do you expect of a wife?"

He shrugged but his eyes were vividly blue. "That the union would result in children."

"Not sons?"

"I would hope for more than one. Sons and daughters." He nodded. "And that my lady's presence would fill my heart with joy."

Elizabeth could not hide her surprise. "You, of all men, would argue the merit of love?"

Amaury spoke with familiar resolve. "I would argue the merit of respect and kindness in a match, of mutual consideration, of honor and —" he shook a heavy finger at her "—even though you might argue its value, of duty."

"Then you would not expect either husband or wife to take a lover for passion's sake? It is oft thus in the troubadour's tales."

"I would never condone or tolerate that," he said with heat.

Elizabeth was intrigued that they shared this expectation. "But the match itself would be made dispassionately, rooted in alliance and advantage."

"You need not scorn what has worked well for many."

"You need not dismiss the notion of love being a good foundation in itself."

"But is it? Love leads the heart astray. Love makes one forget obligation and duty. Love compels one to think only of one's own desire, and tempts one to forget all else one knows to be true." Amaury nodded, so persuaded of his own thinking that Elizabeth could only listen. "Love persuades a man to put his own needs aside that he might serve the lady who holds his heart captive, no matter what misfortune results. Results are often ill-fated as a result."

Elizabeth heard the echo of truth in Amaury's words, and noticed that he was uncharacteristically fulsome. He had surrendered his heart, perhaps to the lady who had given him the token, perhaps to the much-admired Sylvia, and it had changed all for him.

"I do not have to wed for love," Elizabeth ceded. "But I would hope to find love in marriage, and I cannot believe that it will grow when I am desired only for whatever advantage I can bring to the match."

"How so?"

"If a man wishes to satisfy himself with me abed, but does not care for my pleasure, then I cannot hope even for courtesy, let alone love. I have learned that. If a man yearns for some other asset that might be gained by wedding me, I similarly cannot hope that he will suddenly have a care for my concerns, especially when they differ from his own."

Amaury frowned. "Then what would you wish from a suitor?"

"That he desired me for myself alone," Elizabeth said with conviction. "That I was the prize he sought, my company and no more." She smiled. "I would be courted for myself."

"For that situation, you believe, will lead to the love you seek."

"You scorn my words again."

"I do not. I think you forget a detail."

"How so?"

His eyes glinted as he teased her. "You also wish to be heeded."

Elizabeth could not hold back her smile. "Indeed. Is that so wrong?"

He stared at her for a moment then frowned and bent to scoop up Noisette. "I think of practicalities, having been so recently reminded of the merit of comfort and affluence." He was so calm that Elizabeth wished again to provoke him. When he argued with her with fire in his tone, when his eyes flashed, then Amaury was irresistible.

When he kissed her, she would happily surrender her all to him.

Was she a fool? Or did he hide his feelings overly well? How she wished she knew.

Amaury continued. "The man who has the right to wed you for yourself alone must be as wealthy as a king, for then marriage could bring him no asset that he did not already possess."

"That would mean he was aged. I have no desire for an elderly spouse."

Amaury shook his head. "Then he must have naught but himself to offer."

"That might suffice."

"You know better," he chided with impatience. "In that case, you would have no abode, no income, no gems and clothes, no servants or horses, perhaps even no food. I suspect that love would not survive long in such circumstance."

"Why not?"

"It is an emotion of luxury, not one fed by hardship."

"You are certain of this."

Again, she earned a very blue glance. "You are not so impractical as to believe otherwise, my lady."

Elizabeth stopped her palfrey and fog swirled around them. She felt audacious but she knew what she desired. "*You* have only yourself to offer, sir."

Amaury halted. He granted her a piercing look, his disapproval clear. "Do not suggest such folly, my lady," he said gruffly. "It would bring us both to misery."

"Misery?" Elizabeth echoed, her temper rising. "Then those kisses we shared were less potent for you than for me. I would give much for another such caress."

"Would you give all?"

"Aye!"

He shook his head slowly. "It is a kiss. The flesh responds to sensation. Do not make more of such incidents than they deserve."

Elizabeth exhaled. She knew he had thawed for those kisses. She knew her touch had an effect upon him. Undoubtedly, he thought to protect her still.

"I do not jest," she replied, endeavoring to echo his restraint. She had to make a logical appeal to convince him, it was clear. "When we reach Beaupoint, my uncle will see me wed to another suitor with all haste. I am only useful to him."

"How can you be certain?" Amaury's eyes glittered.

"Calum paid richly for the right to take my hand. The coin was what guaranteed my uncle's support." Elizabeth was resolute. "Coin is no reason to make a match."

"It should not be the sole reason, to be sure."

"It is only logical that he will repeat his choice and simply wed me to another."

"You were the one who insisted upon going to Beaupoint."

"You!" she said beneath her breath, unable to hide all of her annoyance. "Always, you would credit duty and good sense, instead of instinct and passion."

Amaury remained impassive. "'Twas impulse that led me to this land, if you recall."

"And so you argue that emotion leads one awry. I would insist instead that it is duty that guides one false."

He was evidently surprised. "Duty?"

"Aye, *duty*," Elizabeth said. "'Tis duty that compels me to ride to Beaupoint to warn my uncle of the plans of those across the firth. But my loyalty will be rewarded only by another match being made for me without my consent." She was bitter and could not hide it. She gave him a scathing look, knowing her own eyes simmered. "You offered me a boon, sir. You offered to serve me and make amends for compelling me to ride to Caerlaverock. You invited me to demand what I would of you."

"Aye," he agreed warily.

"Then wed me, before my uncle can commit me to another."

Amaury stared at her, his reaction hidden as she might have predicted.

Elizabeth continued with heat. "As vexing as you can be, I admire that you adhere to your principles. I trust you as I have never trusted a man since my father." She felt her cheeks heat as he held her gaze, his own intense. "I liked your caress enough to desire more, and that is unusual, too. No matter how much you insist that flesh responds to sensation, I believe our kisses were mutually satisfying beyond most." She raised a hand before he could protest. "Though I will allow that might be whimsy." She bit off the word, noting how he averted his gaze. Did he fight a smile? She could not say.

Elizabeth took a breath and continued. "I believe you would treat your lady wife with honor and respect, and though I doubt your heart would ever be at risk, I believe we would find satisfaction with each other."

His gaze flicked to hers and then away, a reminder of the cursed Sylvia and her boundless charms.

She raised her chin when he did not reply and added to her argument. "You have some coin. I could journey to France with you, once my uncle knows of his peril and our marriage. You may be sure that I will endeavor to bring *joy* to you with my presence, sir."

Amaury began to walk again, his attention fixed upon the water. Elizabeth's heart fluttered at her own audacity, and she consoled herself that he had not immediately refused. The shore drew near and the horses moved more quickly of their own inclination, clearly glad to climb to dry land again.

Elizabeth waited as long as she could endure but still Amaury did not speak.

"Have you lost your tongue?" she demanded finally. "Has my sensible argument so astonished you that you cannot reply?"

He put down Noisette, who shook herself, then turned to face Elizabeth. His manner was intent, so intent that her heart nigh stopped.

"Know this, my lady," he growled. "You are the most remarkable woman I have ever encountered."

"Is that not a good trait?" she asked, hoping for some encouragement.

A smile curved his lips for a moment. It faded all too quickly but his avidity did not.

"You challenge expectation," he continued. "Indeed, you *defy* expectation. There are men who would find such a tendency alluring."

Elizabeth guessed immediately that he did not count himself in their number and her heart sank like a stone.

"You seem to believe you can say anything to me without repercussion," he continued.

"Because I trust you."

"Because you believe that any challenge will be ignored. You believe that no man will heed you, whatever you say, and that I am in that company as well."

"And if I do?"

"I should teach you a lesson, my lady."

With another man, Elizabeth might have dreaded the import of his words. With Amaury, she was filled with anticipation. "How?"

"I should wed you. I should accept your offer and see you proven wrong." Amaury shook his head with resolve. "But I will not do you such disservice. I will not watch you learn that my forecast is correct." His lips set and he urged the horses onward. "But I will not," he concluded with force.

Wretched man! Elizabeth urged Esther after him with annoyance.

AND NOW SHE WAS FURIOUS.

Amaury did not dare to look at Elizabeth. He could feel her vexation with him like a red tide at his back, and he knew that if he so much as glanced her way, if he glimpsed her eyes alight with determination, he would lose his own resolve to do what was right.

He would not watch disappointment consume her and know himself to be responsible.

He could not endure it.

He could not be the one responsible for seeing the fire fade in her eyes, or the one who ensured that she learned the harsh truth of the world. He would not be the one to tell her there was no coin, no food, no shelter.

He would not watch her realize that love was insufficient.

How curious that this woman beguiled him all the more thoroughly with every increment that her confidence grew. She would never be biddable or demure and Amaury was glad of it. She could not know how tempted he was by her proposal, or impressed by her argument.

He knew the bitterness of losing all resource and he would not inflict that upon her.

She could wed better.

"You!" she fumed behind him. "Even an argument of good sense will not sway you from your chosen path."

"You desire an argument of good sense?" Amaury retorted, hearing his own frustration in his tone. "Your uncle is a cleric by your own admission."

"He is."

He spun to confront her. "And so he will know, better even than most men, that a marriage that has not been consummated can be annulled. How far is it to Beaupoint?"

"But a few hours ride."

"If we are to find a chapel this very moment and pledge each to the other, how should this match be consummated before we arrive at Beaupoint?" He watched her lips set. "What is to halt your uncle from annulling the match immediately? He does, after all, wish to see you wed for his own advantage, and there is none to be had with me as a suitor."

"I would not say as much."

"But I will, and so will he."

She heaved a sigh. "And so you would surrender me to my uncle's will, and I should be sold into marriage again at his dictate, and all that transpired in this past year might not have happened. Truly, you cannot expect me to be content with this solution."

"I do not," Amaury said mildly.

"And you do not care if I am discontent?"

"I have another suggestion."

"You will sell me to another suitor yourself," she guessed, her tone bitter.

"If I knew of one in these parts, I most surely would make the introduction." Amaury earned a hostile look for that, one that might have flayed a man alive. "But I do not."

"How unfortunate."

"And so only a deception can be proposed."

She drew her palfrey alongside his as if she wanted to see his face more clearly. "You, of all men, propose a deception? Again?"

"It will not be of long duration, and it will serve the greater good."

"I am astonished," she said softly, but Amaury ignored her wry tone.

"We will tell your uncle that we are wed, but we will not be wed."

"A lie?" she asked with raised brows.

"A timely falsehood. We will tell him we have been wed a month, since immediately after that day you aided Persephone."

"Where were we wed?"

"We pledged to each other in the forest of Kilderrick. Marriage is the sole sacrament that does not require a witness beyond God himself. As a result, our match has been consummated many times over, and so it cannot be annulled." He glanced at her, triumphant with his tale.

"For a man so concerned with honesty, you are adept with a falsehood."

Amaury fought his smile.

"But why would it be for short duration?"

"Because either Calum's kin will pursue us and they will seek a reckoning, or they will endeavor to claim Beaupoint as originally planned. It will not take them long. I will linger to defend you and your uncle from that assault." He doubted he would survive that challenge, for many reasons, but saw no reason to distress her with that truth—if indeed, she would be distressed. "I will abandon you afterward, and you will be able to wed to advantage."

"And you will return to France to enter the lists in the spring," she said with some hostility. "Never to be seen in these parts again."

"You will be a widow once over and abandoned by a scoundrel."

"You are no scoundrel..."

"Your uncle will be indebted to you for warning him of a potential attack. You will be able to choose, perhaps a man with nothing to his name."

"I think it a sensible plan," Amaury said.

"I think it, like most plans wrought by men, ignores my desire in the end."

"You will not be despoiled," Amaury retorted and she must have heard the sharpness of his tone, for she met his gaze with new wariness. "You will not be disappointed by another match." He leaned closer, unable to bite his tongue. "And I will not have to watch you learn to despise me."

She was startled by his words, he saw it well. Her lips parted and she studied him, shaking her head slightly. "I never would..." she whispered.

"I will *not* risk it." He looked away from the appeal in her eyes, told himself he made the right choice, and wished he had not confessed so much. He scanned the road before them, ignoring Elizabeth. "Which way Beaupoint?" he demanded, hearing the impatience in his own tone.

He meant to defend her. Elizabeth should have guessed as much. Even as she longed to shake Amaury, she wondered whether his plan might have results that surprised him.

"We shall have to behave as man and wife," she said lightly after she had indicated the direction to Beaupoint.

He nodded once. "Of course."

"We shall have to be affectionate before others," she continued.

"Not all couples are so."

"But they know me well at Beaupoint. All know that if my heart was lost, I would be unable to hide that truth. I would be most fulsome with my affections."

Amaury glanced toward her.

Elizabeth smiled, sensing his discomfiture. Aye, he thought he might lose his admirable restraint. He should have guessed that she intended to undermine it. "We shall have to share a chamber and a bed," she continued. "Lest my uncle or the servants conclude that our match is not a merry one."

He swallowed and she saw his fingers tighten on the reins. "It would only be good sense," he said tightly, never glancing toward her.

"And since you have no squire, I should have to help you disrobe. And it would only be a courtesy to the servants that we should share a bath." She furrowed her brow as if she did not notice his quick sidelong glance. "I wonder whether there is yet a maid at Beaupoint, or whether you will have to help me with my laces?"

"You dressed yourself well enough these past days."

"But I shall have finer kirtles to wear and all must be right if we are to appear as a happy union." She smiled at him. "But then, even though flesh responds to sensation, it would not be good sense to indulge any urges."

"It would not," he agreed with such heat that she wondered who he endeavored to convince. Then he stopped and frowned. "You have need of a ring." He retrieved a small gold ring from his purse, one too small for even his smallest finger, and reached out to offer it to her between his finger and thumb.

"It was my mother's," he confided quietly and pleasure suffused Elizabeth at the sentimentality of the token. "It is the sole item I have of hers."

"I think that is not true," she said, and his expression became puzzled. She pushed her finger through the band of gold so that it was on her finger and admired the look of it there. Then she looked up to find him watching her. "Your father and your step-father were both cruel and selfish, but you, sir, are a knight of honor. That must be your mother's legacy to you."

Amaury stared at her, apparently astonished, and she watched his throat work. He was utterly at a loss for words and his gaze clung to hers, until he abruptly looked away. He nodded at Beaupoint's tower, rising to an imposing height on the cliff ahead. "This then, is the abode of your overlord, the baron?" His voice was hoarse but Elizabeth knew she had glimpsed the heart he tried to hide.

"No," she said mildly.

"Then Beaupoint lies yet further?"

Elizabeth shook her head. "That is Beaupoint." She watched closely for a response but barely discerned one. Amaury's brows rose, as if he had believed her home to be a modest holding, then he was so impassive that once again he could have been wrought of stone.

She would have wagered her all that he had not known the truth of Beaupoint.

They passed through the village and she was aware of how keenly Amaury looked about himself. No sentry stepped forward to challenge them, either in the village or on the path to the keep. Children and chickens emerged from houses to look upon them and it seemed to Elizabeth that there were fewer villagers than she recalled.

And fewer men, to be sure.

"You did not tell me you were an heiress," Amaury said finally.

"I am not," Elizabeth admitted, though she wished otherwise in this moment. "My uncle holds Beaupoint."

"Not for long, I fear," he said grimly.

"What do you mean?"

"There is nary a sentry or a guard to be seen." He spoke with restraint but she heard his outrage. "Who defends these walls? Who protects this village? What travesty is this?"

"No doubt, my uncle thinks the holding sufficiently safe in daylight."

Amaury pivoted to confront her. "Were you not seized between the village and the tower gate?"

She had to nod agreement. "It was in the evening."

"Day or night is of no concern." He swept out a hand. "The entire village should be walled. It would take at least a dozen men to see such a vast territory well defended, though I should wish for twice that." He nodded at her. "Your uncle is a fool. If the Moffatts come for Beaupoint, they will take it readily."

"I thought you were uncertain they would follow."

"I was, until I saw the prize. Where will we find your uncle? We will not have much time."

~

No gatekeeper barred their path and no ostler strode from the stables to greet them. Elizabeth was shocked at the change in her home, which appeared to be deserted. Finally, Hamish, the cook, came to greet them, his surprise clear. He was a rotund man who had once been inclined to laughter. Now he looked drawn, thinner and much older than she recalled. He welcomed Elizabeth, then admitted that Edmond, the seneschal, had been dismissed and that Simon, the ostler, had left the village in search of another post. Her uncle, it seemed, had divested Beaupoint of many of the trappings of wealth and comfort over the past year.

Amaury asked about the gatekeeper, the sentries and the knights in service to the hall.

"My husband, Hamish. Amaury d'Evroi."

Hamish bowed then answered Elizabeth. "There is only myself, my lady, my wife Nelwyna and Harriet, a maid from the village. His lordship would be rid of her, but Nelwyna insists the girl is needed. They argue about the wage regularly."

Elizabeth knew the girl had been paid a pittance and her lips tightened at James' frugality.

"A tower four stories in height with three in its employ," Amaury muttered. "It cannot be so."

"Many have left the village, my lady." Hamish smiled apologetically. "Matters are not as they were."

"So, I see, Hamish. I thank you for these tidings. Is my uncle in the hall?"

Hamish nodded and retreated to the kitchens.

Amaury tethered the horses in the bailey, then followed Elizabeth into the hall. On the ground floor of the tower, there were storerooms and she could not help but note how empty they were. The great hall was on the second floor. There were no strewing herbs on the floor and the hearth was cold. Only one candle burned, in a small chamber in one corner. Her father had kept his ledgers there but now it fairly overflowed with scrolls and other volumes.

Uncle James was alone in that small chamber, consumed, as ever, with his books. He looked no different than Elizabeth recalled. He was tall, like her father had been, but a lean man instead of a broad one. His face was lined and his gaze was dark, but inclined to seem fixed upon some distant point. He was often distracted, in her experience, and she wondered if he would even recall who she was.

He wore, as ever, simple dark garments that were worn on the elbows and knees, along with boots that had done their service in full. His hair fell to his shoulders in silvery waves and his brows were bushy, just as silver. He bent lower over a page as she studied him from the portal, then tapped his lip as he considered what he had just read.

"Uncle James," Elizabeth said softly and he jumped, visibly startled despite the low timbre of her voice. "I have returned."

He spun to survey her, a glint that might have been assessing lighting his eyes when he looked beyond her to Amaury. His smile was thin. "Elizabeth. Welcome, my dear. And who is this? I am not so aged that I cannot see it is not Calum Moffatt."

"This is Amaury d'Evroi, Uncle." Elizabeth straightened. "My husband."

James' brows rose. "Indeed? What of Calum?"

"He is dead."

Her uncle gave a sigh of relief. "Then he will not expect the return of his coin. Good. Good. It is well spent and that would have been inconvenient." He would have turned back to his reading, but Amaury stepped past Elizabeth.

"Sir." He spoke so sternly that James jumped again and turned to look at him. "May I enquire, sir, as to the defenses of this tower?"

"Whatever do you mean?"

"How many knights serve you, sir?"

James smiled. "None. I am rid of them all." He shook his head. "Knights and their horses and their squires. They are expensive all of them. Such appetites!"

"None, sir?" Amaury's shock was more than evident. "Then you have other warriors who serve you?"

James tore his gaze from his parchment, his expression mild. He shook his head. "There are only four of us within these walls and even that is two too many. I suppose I cannot expect Hamish to evict his wife, but that girl! There is no cause for me to pay that girl, no matter what Nelwyna says."

Amaury looked about himself, surveying the great hall behind them and glancing toward the upper floors. "Four," he echoed and James smiled.

"I should like a clerk, to be sure, but I have yet to find one young enough to accept the wage I would pay. For the moment, I manage on my own." He returned to his book. "Welcome home, Elizabeth." He began to read again.

Elizabeth did not dare to look at Amaury. She could feel his outrage.

"Sir," he said again, this time more forcefully. "You said Calum's coin was spent."

"Indeed."

"Upon what?"

"Well, I managed to obtain this marvelous manuscript of Bede…"

"Sir! This keep is of strategic import and considerable value. It is your responsibility as lord to see it defended, as well as all those within its walls and its village. It is your duty to the king."

"God will defend us," James said with a dismissive wave. He was searching for the prized volume.

"He may be otherwise occupied in your moment of need."

"Then whatsoever results, sir, will be His will." James gave Amaury a hard look. Elizabeth saw that her uncle earned a more resolute look for that.

"What of Laurent?" Elizabeth asked, endeavoring to make peace as the pair glared at each other. "My father's captain-at-arms. He was yet here when I departed."

"And he is gone now," James said with satisfaction. "Such demands for coin! I could bear it no longer. He wanted more knights and another wall, one that surrounded the village. Always he spoke of the reivers and the threat they offered, and his warnings became more dire after you departed, my dear. I am glad you did not have to endure them."

"He sounds a man of good sense," Amaury said. "Where is he now?"

"I have no notion. He is gone, oh, a week. Perhaps two." The older man's voice rose querulously. "Will you leave me, please? I must finish this passage today."

Elizabeth did not know what to expect. She felt Amaury simmering with indignation, and feared he might challenge her uncle anew. Instead, he pivoted crisply and marched through the hall. She heard him say something to someone, but could not discern his words. By the time she had bidden her uncle good-day, closed the door and followed, Amaury was striding toward the village with resolve.

Harriet stood in the bailey, holding the reins of the horses, her expression bewildered. Elizabeth remembered the young girl who had worked in the kitchens for several years. She had to be fifteen or sixteen summers of age and was slender, with a mop of curly red hair and freckles across her fair skin. Elizabeth did not have to ask Amaury's destination, for the younger girl spoke immediately.

"A whore, my lady," she said with surprise. "What need has your husband of a whore? Hamish said you were wed."

In the doorway to the kitchen, Nelwyna covered her smile with her hand. She turned and disappeared into the kitchens at Elizabeth's quelling glance but Elizabeth felt her color rise.

A whore? And within moments of his arrival?

How could Amaury so embarrass her?

She squared her shoulders and summoned a smile. "Will you help me take the horses to the stable?" she asked Harriet sweetly. "I understand Simon is gone."

"Aye, my lady. He departed with Laurent and all the other men." The girl sighed. "It is so quiet, my lady. It does not seem right for the hall to be so empty."

No, it did not.

And yet Amaury had sudden need of a whore.

Wretched man.

Elizabeth led the horses to the stable, her very blood simmering. The dogs cavorted around her, apparently unaware that she was irked —again—with their master.

But Elizabeth's heart rose at a familiar nicker as soon as she stepped into the shadows of the stables. A silvery shape moved in the darkness and there was another nicker, a more joyous one.

"Blanchefleur!" she cried, and flung herself into the mare's stall with joy. She could not fail to note that her mare was the only horse left in what had once been a crowded stable. The horse seemed as delighted as

Elizabeth, for she nibbled Elizabeth's hair and nudged her, stamping her feet and swishing her tail.

"He could not sell her, my lady," Harriet confessed. She tethered the two palfreys then tried to claim the reins of Zephyr. The destrier, a glint in his eyes, was more interested in Blanchefleur. He arched his neck and snorted, undoubtedly trying to impress her with his majestic appearance. Blanchefleur flicked her tail and ignored him so studiously that Elizabeth knew her indifference was feigned.

She was glad to hear that her uncle had some sentimental notions. "Because she was my beloved steed, and daughter of my father's favored destrier?" she asked.

"No, my lady. Because she is of a kind with a knight's steed, but is a mare. No knight desires a mare, and no farmer desires one born of a destrier. She is too proud to draw a plough and she eats a great quantity. He did not sell her, but not for lack of trying." The girl dropped her gaze. "He has talked of her becoming a stew, my lady, for there has been little meat, but Hamish will not hear of it."

"I should hope not!" Elizabeth said with indignation. How dare her uncle even consider such a choice? She leaned her head against the mare for a moment, glad that she had returned home despite the challenges, then Zephyr's impatient stamp recalled her to her tasks. "They must all be brushed down," she said to Harriet. "And the luggage taken into the hall."

"Will you and your husband use the solar, my lady?"

"Does my uncle not sleep there?"

"He prefers his small chamber and sleeps on a pallet there," the maid confessed. "Truth be told, he burns a candle most of the night, reading. The rest of the hall is empty save for the wind." She heaved a sigh. "It could be haunted, my lady, with the joy of former times."

Elizabeth refused to weep over what was gone. Instead, she turned and looked toward the village. If Amaury had need of a whore, he could have made his request in her very presence. There was only one whore at Beaupoint, or at least that had been the case a year before.

"Does Heloise still reside in the village?" she asked Harriet.

The younger woman nodded. "Aye, my lady, though not so affluent as once she was, what with all the men-at-arms not receiving their wages." She blushed a little and averted her gaze. "I told your husband how to find her cottage."

Elizabeth gave the maid instructions about the baggage, then set to tending the horses herself. The task had to be done and there was no one else to do it.

She refused to be disappointed in Amaury's choice.

Perhaps all men were vermin in truth.

CHAPTER 11

One thing Amaury had learned in Maximilian's company of mercenaries was where to seek fighting men when they were in or near a town. The village whore would know Laurent and perhaps where that man had gone, and Amaury did not care what price he had to pay to learn the truth.

He could only hope the warriors were not long departed, for Beaupoint had need of them for its defense and soon.

He found his destination readily, thanks to the girl's directions. Heloise's hut was neither the largest nor the smallest in the village, and it was neatly kept. There were several chickens in the yard and a boy, perhaps a few years younger than Oliver, was repairing the thatch on the roof. He looked up at Amaury's approach and halted his labor, curiosity bright in his eyes. His hair was dark and as unkempt as his garments but his gaze was bright with intelligence.

"Is this the abode of Heloise?" Amaury asked in Norman French.

"Who asks?" he said, replying in kind.

"Amaury d'Evroi, husband of Elizabeth d'Acron." Uttering the lie gave Amaury a ridiculous measure of pleasure.

The boy nodded and would have jumped from the roof, but the door was flung open. A woman of some forty summers, curvaceous but not plump, pretty but not beautiful, stood there. Her gaze was assessing and her expression skeptical. That as much as anything revealed her trade. "If Lady Elizabeth is your wife, you cannot be seeking me," she said in challenge.

Tidings traveled as quickly in this village as any other Amaury knew. He became aware that several women had followed him and stood in a cluster, whispering to each other as they watched.

"I seek the former captain-of-arms, one Laurent..." Amaury let his voice trail away, inviting her to add details.

"Laurent de Rousson," she provided. "A fine man of fifty summers, captain-of-arms at Beaupoint these twenty years. The old lord trusted him with all of value in his possession, but the new one—" she sniffed with indignation "—he cares only for his prayers."

"I understand Laurent has left?"

"He stayed as long as he could," Heloise said with heat. "But a man must be paid his wages. It could no longer be endured. The lord has coin, but he spends it on *old manuscripts*!" She flung out a hand in disgust. "Of what merit is a library if the keep is besieged?"

"Indeed," Amaury said and she was evidently surprised by his ready agreement. "Where did Laurent go?"

She folded her arms across her chest. "Why should I tell you? You, a wealthy knight, might simply compel him to return, citing his duty to the late lord. A man must eat!"

"Indeed, he must. How much was Laurent owed?"

She named a sum which was not unreasonable, but her manner remained hostile. "That was for this past year. And the others who rode out with him, they, too, were unpaid."

"How much?" Amaury asked again.

The sum she named was nigh the remainder of the bounty paid to Amaury. He suspected he would have little need of it, unless he left Beaupoint this very day and abandoned Elizabeth. The Moffatts would come for Beaupoint and with its current defenses, the slaughter would be fearsome. He took the coin out of his purse, noting how avidly both boy and woman eyed the small bag. "And you," he said to the boy. "Do you know where Laurent and his company are destined?"

The boy nodded.

"When did they leave?"

"Three days past, sir, for they lingered in the hope that the lord would recall his senses. I wager they rode slowly, too, thinking they might be called back."

But they had not been. Amaury knew without asking. "Can you ride?" he asked and the boy nodded. "What is your name?"

"Alfred, sir."

"He is a good boy, my lad," Heloise said with heat.

So, this was her son. He might even be Laurent's son.

Amaury offered the boy a silver coin. "This is for you, if you will ride in pursuit of Laurent and his party and invite their return."

"And why should they come?" Heloise demanded.

Amaury lifted the bag of coin. "Because I pay their wages and request that they return. Beaupoint and its lady have need of their service. Perhaps they might return in honor of the late lord's memory."

Mother and son exchanged a glance filled with surprise. The villagers behind Amaury whispered.

"I have no horse, sir."

"Then come to the hall and I will lend you a palfrey. Take care to return her in good health, for my lady is fond of her." At his mother's nod, the boy jumped from the roof and followed Amaury. "He will have need of a meal or two to take with him, and a warm cloak," he called back to Heloise, who disappeared into their hut.

Those villagers made no effort to disguise their curiosity.

"The mare's name is Flora," he told Alfred as they entered Beaupoint's stable.

Zephyr took one glance at him and neighed mightily, a sign that something or someone had caught his interest. The red-haired maid was brushing Esther while the other horses nosed in their feed. There was one horse in the stable that had not arrived with Amaury, a large dapple mare who was a proud beauty. She stamped and snorted, too, her attention fixed upon Elizabeth but Amaury did not doubt that she was as aware of Zephyr as he was of her.

"Which palfrey is Flora?" Alfred asked with excitement.

Elizabeth was clearly seething, and Amaury could guess why.

"You are returned quickly," she said. "Was the price too high?"

Alfred blinked and looked between the two of them.

"My lady," Amaury chided, well aware that both boy and maid looked between them. "Fighting men seek predictable pleasures. I sought only tidings." Recalling her warning about showing affection, he leaned closer and stroked her cheek.

"You smell foul, sir," she snapped.

Amaury smiled, untroubled by her manner. "Laurent is only a few days away," Amaury saw her eyes widen. "Alfred will ride after him, in the hope that he and his company can be convinced to return."

Elizabeth looked back toward the village then at him again, her fury visibly fading. "I thought..."

Amaury made a dismissive noise and touched his lips to her temple. "What need would I have of such indulgences with a wife as glorious as mine?" he murmured.

She retreated hastily, flushing crimson. Harriet sighed with satisfaction. Elizabeth did not say more, but Amaury knew that situation would not last.

He saddled the palfrey and was glad to see how Alfred leapt into the saddle with agility. The boy handled the reins with reassuring familiarity as Amaury adjusted the stirrups, proof that he did know how to ride. Flora shook her head, more than ready to run, as Alfred tucked the sack of coin into his chemise.

"Fear not, my lady," the boy said to Elizabeth. "I will take care of her." He inclined his head to Amaury, then urged the mare out of the stables. "Farewell, sir! I shall make such haste as I can." Bête followed them into the bailey and barked as if to wish them well.

"Godspeed to you, Alfred," Amaury said and lifted a hand to wave. The movement prompted a waft of foul air from his clothing and he grimaced at the truth in Elizabeth's earlier claim. He would not persuade anyone of anything when he smelled like Caerlaverock's moat —not even, apparently, Elizabeth. "I have sore need of a bath, my lady. Is there a tub here in the stables?"

Elizabeth pointed to it. "But there is neither ostler nor stableboy to assist you. You have no squire, sir." Her tone implied that she would not aid him, but he had not expected as much.

Ignoring her concerns, Amaury set to rolling the wooden tub to the middle of the floor. It was large but well-constructed and in good condition. "You forget that my uncle trained me for my spurs. I am not afraid to work, my lady."

"I will ask Hamish to heat water for you, sir," the maid offered.

"I thank you, Harriet. Summon me when it is hot and I will carry it. The task will be too much for you."

Harriet smiled. "Thank you, sir."

"And the lady will bathe in the comfort of the keep, no doubt, after our journey."

"In the solar," Elizabeth said. "We are to occupy it as my uncle does not."

Amaury nodded, hiding his surprise. "Is it at the summit of the tower?"

"Aye, sir."

"There must be many stairs to that chamber."

"Eighty-seven, sir."

"Then I will carry that water, as well, if you make all else ready for her."

"Thank you, sir!" Harriet's pleasure was more than clear. She darted out of the stables.

He felt Elizabeth watching him as he began to brush Zephyr. The dogs, reassured by this routine, found places to sleep in the straw. "What of Persephone?" he asked.

Elizabeth pointed to the end of the stables, where he could see a beam of light. "There is a small falconry there, though the birds I remember are gone."

"Their scent will reassure her all the same." He set to work with gusto. First Zephyr had to be tended, then the mare's stall had to be cleaned for he could smell that it had not been swept out in days. Likely Laurent and his men had been the last to clean the stables. He had to find food for the dogs and for Persephone, then his own bath was a necessity...

Elizabeth cleared her throat and Amaury glanced up to see that her eyes were dark. "Why did Laurent leave?" she asked in an undertone, glancing toward the kitchens. "He was captain-at-arms for twenty years or more. My father trusted him utterly."

"But your uncle did not pay his wages."

"Nay!"

"Aye."

She frowned. "Then why would Laurent return, even if Alfred asks him?"

"Alfred takes the coin for those wages, the better to persuade Laurent and his fellows to come back to Beaupoint."

"How? When did my uncle give you the coin for it?"

Amaury scoffed. "Why would he pay the debt now when he refused to pay it previously? Nay, he would surrender no coin for this."

"Then?"

"I used my own, of course," he said gruffly, avoiding her gaze. She would guess the import of that in a heartbeat, he was certain.

"I thought you had no coin," she said finally. "I thought that was why you left France."

Did she think he had deceived her? Amaury turned and met her gaze. "It was, but I earned some, if you recall, as reward for a certain lady's arrival at Caerlaverock. I have it no longer."

He watched Elizabeth's cheeks pale. "All of it?"

"All of it." He turned back to the horse. "It is well spent, my lady. Do not make much of little."

"All of it," she echoed, coming to his side. "Why would you do this deed?"

"Why would I not?" He straightened, knowing he could not deceive her. "They will come," he said, meeting her gaze steadily and watching her swallow. "If the keep is as undefended as it is on this day, the consequences will be dire."

Elizabeth paled and looked away. "I thank you," she whispered. "Again, for seeing to my defense."

"It is not done yet, my lady," he said with false cheer.

Again, he felt her watching him. "I apologize for thinking the worst when you sought Heloise."

Amaury nodded. "I should have anticipated as much and explained."

"I would wager you have a plan for every eventuality."

"I strive to do as much, to be sure. If only I had some clean garments, I might seek the aid of the villagers."

"To do what?"

Amaury frowned. "We will need every blade if the Moffatts attack."

"But they are villagers. It is their duty to work the land. It is the obligation of knights and warriors to fight."

Amaury raised his hands, inviting her survey. "And you see before you the sole warrior within any distance of Beaupoint. I think it would be wise to find assistance as I will surely be outnumbered."

She frowned, thinking. "Perhaps you should speak to Father Owen. All rely heavily upon his counsel."

"An excellent notion. Thank you." Amaury moved around the other side of Zephyr, still brushing.

Elizabeth lingered when he thought she would leave and Amaury turned to see that the dapple mare was pestering her with enthusiasm. Elizabeth brushed away the horse's nose with tolerance but the mare persisted, her affection unmistakable. She bit Elizabeth's braid playfully, her tail swishing.

At least someone at Beaupoint was glad of the lady's return.

"She is your mare," he guessed and Elizabeth nodded, unable to disguise her pleasure.

"Blanchefleur is only here because my uncle could not sell her, I understand." She stroked the horse's nose while the mare nuzzled her shoulder. "And I am glad of it."

"As am I," Amaury said softly, hoping she would smile.

She did, if tentatively, but still it lit her eyes. "Will all be well?" she asked in a small voice.

"I will do whatever I can to ensure as much," Amaury vowed.

Then her smile widened and he could only stare in awe at her beauty. "I know," she said with conviction. "I know that." She heaved a sigh. "I only hope it will be enough."

"As do I," Amaury replied, though his doubts were growing. He frowned and returned to his work with vigor.

Then, against every expectation, Elizabeth came to his side. She put her hand on his shoulder, despite the smell of him, and leaned closer. Amaury froze. Her gaze flicked to his and her smile turned playful, then she brushed her lips across his. Her lips were soft, her caress tentative, but that it was voluntarily granted was a heady pleasure. Heat surged through Amaury, a desire so potent that he had to close his eyes and look away.

"The water heats, sir," Harriet said from the portal and Amaury wondered whether Elizabeth had contrived the show of affection for the maid.

"I will find you some clothing," Elizabeth said, stepping away from him. She lifted a hand to her nose. "Perhaps you might wash my husband's garb for him, Harriet."

"Of course, my lady."

Elizabeth left the stables, her step light, but Amaury could not keep himself from watching her go. She was glad to be home, he knew it well, though he feared she would not be able to enjoy Beaupoint long. He wished heartily that he could do more. He was well aware that the maid studied him, but it could not hurt their tale if Harriet realized his affection for Elizabeth.

He could not even think about spending each night alone with Elizabeth in the solar.

If she resolved to tempt him, she might very well succeed.

ELIZABETH STOOD on the threshold of Beaupoint's solar and surveyed the familiar room, her heart aching. The chamber that occupied the top floor of the tower was filled with memories for her, of her mother at her embroidery, of her father recounting tales as they sat together in the evening, of laughter and of love. She had played on the floor here as a child, matched wits with her father at chess there as a maiden. She had learned to sew at her mother's side here, and stood on a stool at the window that overlooked the firth, following her father's finger as he taught her the landmarks of their abode. She had slept in the great bed as a child, nestled between them on cold nights. She remembered it in light and darkness, cold and warmth.

She walked around the bed now, running her fingers over the carved posts that rose to the ceiling, feeling the weight of the heavy curtains that could enclose the bed in warmth and darkness. It was still piled with pelts of wolves.

On this day, the floor was cold, for the brazier was unlit. The hearth in the great hall two floors below was cold, too, and the very walls emanated a chill. There was dust on the shutters and Elizabeth wiped it away. She looked over the firth, the tide now rolling in. She remembered the rumble of her father's voice in her ear and could almost see his heavy finger as he taught her the landmarks.

It would break his heart to see what Beaupoint, his family pride and joy, had become.

She blinked away her tears and turned to the two great trunks. They were a pair, the mirror of each other, and had been wedding gifts from her grandparents to her parents. One stood on each side of the bed and she opened her father's trunk first. His garb and his armor had been cleaned and placed there after his death. Elizabeth had washed and mended the clothing, and her father's squire had polished his armor to a shine. There were those who said he should have been buried in it, but her father had been too practical for such whimsy. He had dictated that it should be saved and used by another man for his own protection.

Elizabeth shared that practicality and she admired that Amaury showed similar good sense. His hauberk and armor were as finely crafted as her father's and she could imagine her father and Amaury's uncle agreeing that good armor is purchased only once. She knew that her father would have approved of lending the garments to another knight. Amaury looked to be of a size with her father, and she knew he would want to be both clean and well-attired when he came to the board for their evening meal.

She had been a fool to imagine for a moment that the man she had come to respect would abandon her immediately upon reaching Beaupoint, to seek the services of a whore. Of all men, she should know to trust Amaury.

The contents of the chest still had a faint scent of her father and Elizabeth inhaled it, remembering. On top, there was a tabard with her father's insignia, embroidered by her mother, a fine garment but one she knew Amaury would not wear. He did not wear his own surcoat with the insignia that was no longer his to bear—this would be no different. Beneath that tabard and the armor was another simpler tabard, wrought of heavy dark wool and devoid of any ornamentation. She shook it out, recalling that it had been her father's choice for most days. There were dark chausses, too, and fine boots of black leather. She chose two chemises of snowy white linen and a simple broad belt, gathered them up and descended to the stables again. When she had her own bath, she would check the garments she had left behind and open her mother's trunk, too.

She reached the great hall and was startled when someone spoke.

"Foolish girl," James chided softly and Elizabeth spun to find him watching her. Her uncle wagged a finger at her. "You always had a love for tales, but your father would have told you life is no tale."

Elizabeth could not help but recall that Amaury had said the same.

"You look at him with your heart in your eyes. It is all well and good for a woman to love her husband, but do not imagine that your affection is returned."

"I do not, Uncle," Elizabeth said mildly.

"Mark my words, he wed you for Beaupoint and no other reason. It is just as your father anticipated it would be. I can only hope this one proves himself worthy of your esteem."

"He did not wed me for Beaupoint," she insisted. "He knew nothing of it."

James scoffed. "All warriors know of Beaupoint."

"But he is from France."

"Someone would have told him, likely after seeing you in his company." James raised his voice, pretending to speak as a man in a tavern might. "Ah, you have captured the heiress of Beaupoint, fortunate man. Her holding is a worthy one, indeed. You will abide in splendor, my friend!" He laughed, shook his head. "Aye, his scheme is readily discerned. Do not be deceived, my niece."

"But I am not an heiress," Elizabeth noted. "I told him so."

Her uncle harrumphed. "And what of young Gavin de Montgomerie? Time was the Baron's oldest son could not wait to claim your hand. Why would you wed this stranger, as if Gavin never breathed?"

Elizabeth straightened. "I have not seen Gavin in years."

"The baron's own son. One cannot find fault with that match."

"Father did. He forbade it."

Her uncle fixed her with a look. "Yet you did not flee from his edict."

Elizabeth saw no reason to lie. "I had no desire to wed Gavin, in truth."

"Whyever not? He is suitable. If he had offered a sack of coin as great as Calum did, you might be round with his child by now."

"Then I am glad he did not," Elizabeth said. The truth was, she feared, that she knew Gavin too well. They were of an age and their families had mingled since she was a child. He might have been a brother for all her interest in him, though it was fair to note that she had suspected that Gavin felt otherwise. Had the proposed match been his father's notion or Gavin's own? She had never wondered before, but now she did.

Her uncle waved her away, disinterested in whatever she might say. "Every woman wants a babe in her belly," he said, his tone dismissive. "It is the sole achievement that makes them content."

His opinion delivered, he then bent over his parchment again, squinting at the text in the dim light. Elizabeth knew she had been forgotten already. She might have thanked him for keeping Blanchefleur but she knew he had not done as much on purpose.

Still, James' words took root in her doubts as she descended the last flight of stairs. Had Amaury defended her with the hope of claiming Beaupoint? She could not credit the notion. She was not an heiress, but Calum had thought to force the matter upon her uncle's demise, with her as his wife. Amaury might have been inspired by Calum's plan himself.

Someone had to be Lord de Beaupoint.

Or did Sylvia and her inheritance provide a stronger allure?

Their feigned match was a puzzle to her. While it ensured that her uncle did not pledge her to another, she could not discern Amaury's motive in suggesting it. She supposed Sylvia was the reason it could not be a genuine match, that and his plan to return to France by the spring.

Why had he not simply ridden on immediately? What concern to him whether she was forced to wed another, today or in a year?

Elizabeth found herself unable to forget Amaury's words that first day. She could see him yet, his expression skeptical and his tone dismissive.

Surely you have learned that most of us do not reside in tales. If we did, you would have found a champion in the woods and lost your heart to him at a glance, and I would have found an heiress who was immediately enthralled with me. Whimsy, all of it.

But she had found a champion, and they feigned a match. Was it madness to hope that Amaury might stay, or that her uncle might be convinced to cede Beaupoint to him?

Elizabeth could not deny that she found the prospect most attractive.

Water splashed as she stepped into the stables and she halted on the threshold to stare. No matter how often she saw this man at his bath, Elizabeth could not tear her gaze away from him. The tub was deep enough that the water within it could rise to his knees. He was crouched down, scrubbing his hair when she arrived, but then he stood up and Elizabeth stopped cold. She swallowed, eying the muscled breadth of his back, his tight buttocks and powerful thighs. He shook his head and water flew in all directions, then he laughed when Bête barked at him playfully.

She must have made some slight sound because Amaury glanced over his shoulder. His gaze warmed and he smiled, the change in his expression making her heart leap.

"Sir!" Harriet said behind her with a giggle and Elizabeth felt herself blush crimson. The girl rushed past her, surveyed Amaury with open appreciation, then placed a new bucket of hot water beside him. "For your pleasure, sir," she said, then retreated, her eyes filled with merriment as she passed Elizabeth. "I will not return soon, my lady," she whispered, her tone conspiratorial.

Elizabeth thought she might die of embarrassment.

But they pretended to be wed.

And she had told him that they must feign affection for each other. By their own tale, they had been married a month and already intimate many times.

Amaury bent to add the new bucket of water to the contents of the tub. "If you leave the garments, I will come to you shortly," he said.

Elizabeth took a deep breath. "But someone must tie your hauberk, dear husband," she said, speaking loudly so her words would carry to the maid's ears, if the girl was listening. "I could not ask Harriet to do as much." She forced a light laugh, though her chest was tight. "It is not as if I had not done as much a hundred times already."

AMAURY HAD EXPECTED Elizabeth to flee at the sight of him in the bath. He was not surprised by the maid's audacity—though she was young, her manner made him doubt that she was innocent. Elizabeth was another matter, though. Her flush of awareness made her look even more alluring than usual and he ensured that he kept his back turned to her, hoping she left the stables swiftly.

He should have predicted that she would not.

He continued to wash, well aware that she simply stood near the portal and watched him.

"You were injured," she said finally, her voice breathless.

"Not so much as that."

"You were limping," she said, chastising him, and he heard her approaching footsteps.

"And the wound has closed cleanly already. It is of no concern."

At her words, he glanced up to find her closing upon him with purpose, garments clutched against her chest and a pair of fine boots in her hand. "Shall I wash your back?" she asked sweetly, reaching into the tub for the cloth.

She would tease him.

She would provoke him and his restraint would break. Just the sight of her fired his blood and Amaury knew he drew close to his limit.

He *wanted*.

And she was not his to take. If he claimed her, he would do as every other man had done in her experience. Such a deed would undermine all the confidence she had regained—and it would show him to be no better a man than Calum Moffatt.

He seized her hand and let his gaze bore into hers, willing her to understand. "You do not have to do this," he whispered.

"Of course, I do. You have no squire."

She did not understand the tempest she conjured. She did not realize the import of her actions. Amaury surrendered the cloth and turned his back to her, crouching down so that the water rose around his hips. She wrung out the cloth and rubbed across his back, then up his neck, pushing it into his hair. Amaury closed his eyes against the heady pleasure of her touch. He could smell her skin and burned with a desire that could never be satisfied. He gritted his teeth as she rubbed more forcefully.

"The muck is everywhere," she said beneath her breath, chastising him as if he had chosen to leap into the moat.

"I cleaned my hair."

"Not well enough." She set to scrubbing him as if he were a filthy floor. Amaury leaned forward, bracing his hands on the tub, telling himself that his response was not shared. She saw him as a mess to be cleaned, not a man to be touched or seduced.

He would endure this and she would leave him, none the wiser.

She paused to rinse the cloth, then ran a fingertip along the scar on his shoulder. His eyes flew open as her light touch sent shivers over his flesh. "You were injured here." Amaury blinked and gripped the tub, a jolt of need searing through him to his toes.

"A long time ago," he ceded tightly. "My first day of training with sharpened blades, in fact."

She did not speak for some moments. "Are you angry with me?"

"Of course not, my lady."

"You sound angry."

"I sound...aroused." He glanced over his shoulder at her, meeting her gaze and no longer hiding his thoughts. Her eyes widened, evidence that the simmering heat she had awakened was revealed in his eyes, and she swallowed, which made her look both fragile and vulnerable.

He fully expected her to recoil or retreat.

To flee, perhaps to bolt the door of the solar against him.

But Elizabeth leaned forward and looked down his chest. Amaury had no time to sink lower into the water to hide his erection from view. Elizabeth caught her breath, then her gaze flew to his again.

Now she would flee.

To Amaury's surprise, she smiled.

"You like this," she murmured. Her fingertip did not lift from his skin.

"I told you, flesh responds to sensation."

"Like this?" She let her fingertip slide to his spine, then traced a feather-light line down the middle of his back. Amaury inhaled sharply. Elizabeth watched him closely, her smile broadening at even this proof of the power of her touch.

"Your eyes are very blue," she whispered.

"You do not know what you do," he growled.

"Oh, but I do," she whispered, touching her lips to his shoulder so gently that everything within him tightened with vigor. "And you like it."

Amaury looked away from her, striving for control. Elizabeth was bent upon tormenting him, it was clear. She flattened her hand to slide it across his shoulders. Her fingertips fluttered down his arms, finding every tiny nick and scar as they went. Amaury closed his eyes, savoring the gentle sweep of her hands upon him, feeling his body respond in a most predictable way. It would take him all the night to satisfy them both, if not an entire year of nights abed. He wanted to feel her wrapped around him. He wanted to hear her gasp with pleasure, he wanted to make her shudder and shake, he wanted to make her shout, and feel her velvet heat locked around him. He wanted to sleep with her in his arms, to awaken to find her soft against his side, to stir her to wakefulness with a caress...and with every notion, his desire grew more insistent and his grip upon the tub tightened.

But she did not halt her exploration.

"You play with fire, my lady," he felt compelled to warn her.

"I warned you that we should have to show affection for each other." She touched her lips to his shoulder in another light kiss and Amaury could not keep from looking at her. Her eyes sparkled, her trust of him complete. "I am glad you are clean, sir," she whispered, her eyes sparkling.

"I should pull you into this tub," he threatened, watching her smile broaden. "I should show you the response you provoke."

She laughed at him, tapping his shoulder with her fingertip. "But you would not."

It was a dare he could not resist.

Amaury moved like lightning, lunging to his feet and seizing her in his arms. Elizabeth squealed when he swung her into his arms, but her cry was one of delight, not terror. He caught her beneath her knees and held her captive against his chest, liking the press of her curves against him. She smiled up at him, untroubled by her situation.

"Or perhaps, you would," she said, then laughed again.

"You have need of a bath as well, I believe," he said, crouching to lower himself into the water again.

That roused her. "Not in my kirtle!"

"Then take it off."

"Amaury!" Elizabeth gasped and he loved the sound of his name on her lips. She struggled against him, laughing as she tried to wriggle free. Amaury pretended to drop her then caught her again before she touched the water and she laughed, clutching his shoulders. "You would not."

"I am tempted."

She tapped his chin with a confident fingertip. "But you sir, never succumb to temptation."

"Are you sure?"

"I am convinced of it." Her fingertip rose to his mouth and she watched it as she traced the outline of his mouth. "When first we met, I thought you were wrought of stone and a man without a heart," she mused.

"You sound as if you have changed your view."

"Not entirely." Her eyes danced as she met his gaze anew. She was playful and bold, and utterly alluring. "I like to touch you," she confessed softly, so softly that he barely heard her words. Her cheeks burned crimson at her own audacity and her throat worked again. "I like that you let me."

"I told you to demand what you would of me," he murmured.

"There is one favor I would ask," she whispered. Her gaze became searching as her smile faded, then she stretched to touch her lips to his. Amaury felt the familiar tide of heat that was launched by this woman's caress and strove to let her explore him as she would. Her fingers slid across his shoulders and her eyes closed. She angled her head to deepen their kiss, locking her fingers in the hair at his nape, and Amaury could resist her no longer.

He caught her close, tightening his grip upon her, then slanted his mouth over hers to claim her with a demanding kiss. She made a little gasp and he was certain she would demand release.

He should have known better with this lady, who grew more bold by the hour. Elizabeth whispered his name, her voice taut with need, then plunged her fingers into his hair. She sighed and softened, opening her mouth to him as she gripped his hair tightly, demanding more.

Amaury no longer had it within him to deny either of them a searing and highly satisfactory kiss.

Surely Amaury's kiss would set Elizabeth's blood afire. She surrendered to him, welcoming his hunger and secure in the knowledge that he would never hurt her. His kiss was a hundred times more potent than their earlier ones, a kiss intended to awaken every fiber of her being and set it aflame.

And it did. She burned for satisfaction as she never had before. She tingled to her toes, her very blood running hot with need. His kiss was hot and demanding, no longer a gentle tribute but a summons to join him on a descent into pleasure. Elizabeth wanted to be naked, to press her bare skin against his, to meld their bodies together in the pursuit of mutual satisfaction. She knew Amaury could guide her well along that path and she wanted desperately to know all that could be shared between man and woman.

She wanted to discover it with Amaury.

Elizabeth could not have broken their embrace to save her life. She pressed herself against Amaury, wanting more, then someone gave a little shriek of surprise.

Curse Harriet!

Amaury broke their kiss, spinning to put Elizabeth on her feet beside the tub. He seized a cloth and wound it around his hips, then pivoted to confront the maid. She was standing in the portal with a bucket of steaming water, her expression one of delighted astonishment.

Elizabeth wondered whether the girl brought Amaury hot water with such regularity simply so she could look upon him again.

She also wondered whether her own heart would ever return to its usual pace.

"Thank you, Harriet," Amaury said, as calm and composed as ever. Elizabeth glanced at him, shocked that he was unaffected by their embrace. She saw then the tension in his jaw and the way he strove to catch his breath. The signs were there, now that she knew to look, and they gave her great satisfaction. "I will dress and take that water to the solar for the lady. I expect she will have need of several more."

Harriet bowed and left with obvious reluctance, leaving the bucket as instructed.

"Go," Amaury instructed Elizabeth with quiet heat. "I will follow when I am dressed."

Elizabeth took a breath then dared to make an invitation. "My parents often retired to their chamber in the afternoon. Perhaps you should not dress completely." She felt like a wanton in making the suggestion aloud.

Amaury shook his head with purpose even as he dried himself. "You forget that I must talk to Father Owen." Again, he spoke with complete composure, as if they had not shared a shattering kiss, as if her heart was not hammering, as if she had not suggested they meet abed and now.

"Duty calls?" Elizabeth asked tartly and Amaury nodded.

"Aye, my lady, it does."

She spun and left the stables, marching toward the solar, striving to echo the cursed man's composure herself. Elizabeth knew full well that she failed.

An afternoon abed with Elizabeth.

What a beguiling and seductive suggestion. Amaury could have accepted with pleasure, especially after that kiss. Her confidence grew by leaps and bounds, and he wanted to reap the bounty of that change. He knew he should not touch her, he knew he would leave her behind at Beaupoint, but when she kissed him as if she could not be satisfied with a mere caress, when she invited him to her bed, Amaury could not resist.

Elizabeth spoke aright about duty, though. He had little time to muster the resources of this holding to see it defended, but he would do his best.

Perhaps, though, on this night in the solar, when they were alone, she might invite him again.

Invigorated by that prospect, Amaury shaved and dressed with haste. He liked the clothing she had brought him, for it was simple and sturdy, of good quality and well-made. He then carried the hot water to the solar for her, ensuring that he did not look upon her lest he be tempted. He was impressed again by the majesty of her family home, but did not linger in the solar.

The hour grew late and he would speak to the priest.

Her uncle was in his chamber near the great hall, but did not stir or speak. Amaury strode to the village, aware that the same women watched and whispered. Bête and Noisette accompanied him, Noisette racing ahead and looking back as was her wont, Bête keeping pace beside him. He found the priest readily in the cottage beside the chapel.

Father Owen was stout and somber, as well as frequently skeptical, in his manner. Amaury discerned that the villagers did not like James' management of the holding. Matters had changed and they preferred how it had been. The priest expressed hope that all would change with Lady Elizabeth's return and Amaury sensed that the villagers' loyalty had to be buttressed again.

He found himself offering a feast for all in the great hall, to celebrate his nuptials with the lady, and was relieved that the suggestion was well-received. Indeed, the plump priest smiled and was amenable to sending three boys to the keep at first light to aid in the hunt.

Amaury had only to convince James to comply.

CHAPTER 12

Beaupoint was so finely wrought, that Amaury could not help but be saddened by its neglected state. It must have been majestic, and not so long ago as that. He took note of the details as he returned from the priest's abode, considering what he could change quickly. He had no doubts the Moffatts would not readily surrender a claim to this prize.

At least the doors to the lower floor, with the stables and storage rooms, were sturdy and could be readily barricaded. There were few villagers, which was not ideal in terms of willing hands at the defense, but they would all fit easily in the stables and storerooms of the tower.

The great hall was chilly that night, for the fire set upon the great hearth was so small as to burn fitfully and there was a wind from the west. Three places were set on a trestle table close to it, though the chamber could easily have held sixty people. Perhaps more. Amaury was glad that the entire village could be easily accommodated and, in a way, the fact that James had been tight-fisted meant the villagers would be more impressed with less.

Such a hall. Crowded with villages and warriors, perhaps with musicians, the tables loaded with food and the fire blazing, it would be as splendid as any hall he had ever seen. The ceiling was high and wrought of wood, carved and painted most elaborately. The floor was solid, cut of broad beams, and the stone hearth was a part of the very wall. Above it was carved the insignia of Beaupoint, three falcons in a line. The stone had been painted so the birds were black upon a field of gold.

Elizabeth's uncle sat in the place closest to the fire, bent over a piece of vellum. There was a single candle lit on the board and the smell of beeswax filled the hall. There was already a loaf of bread upon the table, one that looked to have been made of dark flour. It was less than fresh.

Elizabeth stood by her uncle, concern upon her brow. She wore a kirtle of deepest green velvet, thick with golden embroidery upon the hems and cuffs. The bruise upon her cheek from Calum's blow was dark but not as large as he had feared it might become. She looked like the noblewoman she was and Amaury could have simply stood and gazed upon her. There was a golden girdle around her waist, but no keys hung from it.

They were on the board near her uncle's fist.

Her auburn hair was braided and coiled into a coronet topped with a veil and circlet, as Amaury had never seen it arranged before. He realized that she garbed herself as a married woman, no longer as a maiden, and he nodded to her, glad she had the wits to realize the change was necessary for their ruse. He would never have thought of it.

Bête and Noisette had followed him and now sat by the hearth, ever watchful. Grise, perhaps predictably, remained beside Elizabeth.

Amaury bowed to Elizabeth and kissed her hand, then greeted her uncle, receiving only a grunt in reply. He and Elizabeth took their places as Nelwyna appeared with a great bowl with steaming contents. Harriet followed with three bowls.

The cook's wife was a buxom woman with dark hair and lips that were pinched tightly shut. Her dark gaze flicked to James several times, her dislike of him more than evident, but she did not speak. Only when she put the bowl down on the board noisily did James look up.

It was a thin soup with a few vegetables from the winter garden, cooked so thoroughly that they could scarcely be identified. The bread was hard and stale, and there was only a bit of smoked eel in addition to the soup. Amaury was amazed to realize that they had eaten better that night in the ruins at Annan.

It seemed an eternity had passed since that night.

James had put his reading aside with regret and ate quickly, making no attempt at conversation. It was one of the most dismal meals Amaury had ever shared.

When they were done and the uncle reached for his document again, Amaury cleared his throat.

The older man ignored him.

Amaury spoke all the same. "I wonder, sir, when you last entertained the villagers."

James looked up with surprise. "Why should I do as much?"

"Because it is your obligation, as Lord de Beaupoint, to host them regularly for meals such as they cannot contrive themselves. It is their reward for their loyalty and part of the exchange between lord and tenant."

James made a dismissive gesture. "They fare well enough on their own."

Amaury kept his tone temperate. "But you have an obligation, sir, and now that your niece is wed, you owe the villagers a celebration."

The older man fixed Amaury with a glare. "I suppose you think it would be fitting for me to expend coin upon them."

"I suppose that their loyalty might be worn thin, given the lack of such generosity from their overlord, and the oversight of your obligation to them." Amaury watched James inhale sharply but continued. "And if Beaupoint is attacked, we shall have need of every knife, indeed of every hand, to see it defended."

"You concern yourself overmuch with matters of war."

"I concern myself greatly with seeing my wife's family holding defended. If you might recall, sir, the lady herself was captured by reivers, just beyond the village."

James glanced up, surprised, and eyed Elizabeth. "Is that so?"

"It is why I disappeared, sir," she said with patience.

"Well, that is audacity indeed." James frowned. "But there is no reason for them to return. Beaupoint's treasury is bare." He chuckled as if pleased with that state, which made no sense at all.

"Beaupoint is a prize in itself," Amaury insisted. "It is a splendid keep and yet in good repair. I would imagine that many might desire it."

"Would you?" asked the uncle slyly.

"Any man would, but I recognize it is not mine to claim," Amaury replied. "There were those at Caerlaverock who believed the lady should have wedded one of Calum's kin. They might arrive to argue the merit of their view."

James regarded him shrewdly. "You never explained to me how my niece ended up as your wife."

"She and I met at Kilderrick where she had found sanctuary after being abducted by reivers, and we wed."

"But you were betrothed to Calum," James said to Elizabeth. "I took his bride price."

"I thought never to see him again," Elizabeth said. "I thought never to return to Beaupoint again."

The uncle's eyes narrowed.

"But the lady was later seized, for Calum had offered a bounty for her delivery. I followed to defend my lady wife. Calum insisted he had the prior claim and we fought." Amaury shrugged. "He lost."

James studied him, considering this tale, and Amaury thought he might not accept it. "Then why would his family believe she should wed one of them, if she is wed to you?"

"They chose not to believe that we were wed."

"Perhaps because a price had been paid by Calum for my hand," Elizabeth added. "They believe I have been bought."

James sighed. "I suppose you have a scheme to address this and it will cost me coin."

"I have invited Father Owen to bring the villagers to feast at the hall, in celebration of the lady's nuptials," Amaury said.

"My hall! You have an audacity," the older man complained.

"We have need of their aid since you have dismissed all of the men-at-arms. I issued the invitation as if it came from you."

James shook his head. "It is not their place to fight."

"They will defend their homes, if suitably encouraged. And there is no one else to defend Beaupoint, thanks to your choices."

James shook his head. "You are a man of war, so you think of war.

Beaupoint has not been attacked in the last year and it will not be so now."

"I believe otherwise, sir."

"What will this cost me?" James demanded querulously.

"It may save your life, sir," Amaury said. "But I will hunt on the morrow that there is abundant meat."

"There is nothing amiss with soup," James complained but a gleam lit his eyes at the prospect of a more substantial meal.

"Then we will have a soup, as well," Amaury said smoothly. "Perhaps my lady might plan the meal. Are there eggs to be had? Wine? Ale?"

"You will see me impoverished!"

"I would not see your manuscripts damaged, sir."

"Witless soul. Reivers do not steal manuscripts!"

"Nay, sir. They *burn* them."

James caught his breath and considered Amaury with horror. "A feast then," he said tightly. "Be certain to tell Hamish so that he can complain of having too little assistance."

Amaury rose to his feet and bowed. "I thank you, sir. I think your choice most wise."

"Aye, because I ceded to you," the older man said testily. He looked to Elizabeth. "Perhaps you should invite Gavin de Montgomerie," he said and she spun to face him.

Elizabeth stared at her uncle, her shock unmistakable. She had paled and Amaury saw that her hands had clenched. "Gavin?" she said, her voice unsteady.

"Aye, Gavin, the baron's oldest son," he said with impatience. "You remember him well. We spoke of him earlier this very day." James bent over his document. "He was always most interested in the match you might make, as I recall. Indeed, your husband might be interested to know that Gavin offered for you himself."

"Father declined his suit," Elizabeth said stiffly.

"Because he said you were both too young. That was five years ago, so the same argument could not be made now." James looked up. "He has come often to ask after you in your absence."

"He has?" The lady's surprise was evident, as was her pleasure.

"Indeed. In fact, he had intended to match the bride price offered by

Calum. He insisted upon it, but you vanished before he returned with the coin."

"You never told me of this," Elizabeth said.

"I was not certain he would keep his word. I meant it to be a surprise for you, but by the time he had the coin, you were gone." James shrugged. "'Twould seem only courteous to invite him to share your good tidings."

And there it was: the practical choice of suitor. Son of a local baron, a man well known to the family, a marriage that would bring an alliance between two houses, a match that would ensure Elizabeth's safety and security.

No wonder Amaury despised this Gavin, without the need to know more of him.

He watched as Elizabeth considered her uncle's revelation. She could not hide her dismay and disappointment, which meant Gavin was not the only one whose affections were involved. "There is no messenger who might invite him," she said finally, then spun to march toward the stairs.

James waved with impatience when Amaury remained. "Go now. Leave me to read and savor this costly fire we have set this night." He looked after Elizabeth then back to Amaury. "Go, do what wedded couples do and leave me in peace."

That was the last thing Amaury would do this night.

"I would ask for another candle, to light the way," he said as Elizabeth's steps slowed on the stairs. "And some wood for the brazier that the lady's comfort might be assured."

James glared at him. "You begin to vex me, young man."

"I know we share a concern with Lady Elizabeth's comfort and safety."

James fairly growled. "Ask Nelwyna for what you desire, and mind it is not too much!"

At least, victory over the feast had been won more readily than Amaury might have expected. At worst, he knew a truth he could not forget.

Grise raced after Elizabeth and he went to the kitchens, the other dogs following him. He saw the amazement in Nelwyna's expression when she granted him a lit candle, and she said she would send Harriet to light the brazier. He knew Elizabeth had bitten her tongue in the hall, but still he was surprised when they reached the solar and she spun to confront him.

"A feast?" she demanded.

"Gavin de Montgomerie?" he asked, his tone cold, and she flushed scarlet.

"I have known him all of my life."

"Aye, I assumed as much. And he has asked for your hand before."

"My father said we were too young." She flushed again and dropped her gaze, even as Harriet's footfall sounded on the stairs. "It was the sole time we ever argued."

Amaury did not need to know more.

He had glimpsed the solar and the view earlier but at night with the shutters open, he saw what a vantage point it was. The skies were clear now and the moon was in its first quarter, shining silver light over the countryside. He put down the candle on a chest and strode to the window overlooking the firth, then gazed in wonder as Harriet entered the chamber.

"Admirable," he murmured beneath his breath. "Truly a marvel."

Of course, men aspired to claim Beaupoint. It was a gem beyond most. Amaury's chest tightened. And the lady was a prize beyond all.

He would leave as soon as the Moffatts were repelled. He would vanish in the night, leaving no word, and Elizabeth, abandoned, would be free to wed this Gavin.

He would not consider the wasteland of his future with no chance of seeing her again. What was of import was her happiness and security.

Gavin, the practical choice, would see all aright.

THERE WAS no mistaking Amaury's favorable impression of Beaupoint. Indeed, he was so impressed with the holding that he seemed to have forgotten her. His eyes were gleaming as he surveyed the solar, then his face lit further when he viewed the firth. He braced his hands upon his hips and simply looked, his pose so much like that of her father's familiar one that tears pricked Elizabeth's eyes.

But her father had invited her to look with him. Amaury seemed unaware of her presence, which rankled.

It was more than her pride that suffered—it was her expectations. She had hoped to welcome him abed this night, but as with all men, his attention was claimed by Beaupoint.

She heard Harriet's step upon the stair and went to his side, as if theirs truly was a happy union. He moved so that she could look out the window as well, but Elizabeth was keenly aware of the distance he left between them.

"Where is Annan?" he asked as Harriet bustled at her tasks, no doubt listening avidly.

Elizabeth pointed. "In the sunlight, you can see where the river joins the firth."

"I think I glimpse it."

"And Caerlaverock is there, to the west." She pointed and spoke, recalling her father's words as Harriet set a fire in the brazier behind them. "And Carlisle is there, where the water disappears to the east. It is a little south and impossible to discern from this window."

"And beyond?"

"Galloway to the north and west, the islands. Kilderrick is over there but far from view."

"What a vantage point," he said with satisfaction. "Is there a place for a sentry to share this view?"

"Down there." Elizabeth pointed. "To the east and another to the west."

"Unmanned now, I wager," Amaury murmured and she nodded. There was no one to fill that post.

Harriet left the chamber, closing her door behind herself.

Amaury frowned and Elizabeth thought he might utter a word against her uncle, but his words surprised her. "My uncle Raymond possessed a most artful device, a reading stone that allowed one to see better at a distance. I believe it came from Byzantium." He shook his head. "That would be a most useful tool in this eyrie."

Elizabeth could not help but smile. She went to her father's trunk, opened it and reached down to the bottom. She found the cool quartz stone by touch and presented it to Amaury. "Like this, perhaps?"

It was half of an orb of rock crystal, polished on all surfaces, the smooth bottom almost the size of her palm. She had been fascinated by it as a child, for when one looked through it, items at a distance appeared to be larger and closer. She supposed it could be used to read, but her father had used it here.

She was glad that her uncle had not claimed it.

Amaury clearly recognized the instrument, for his eyes lit. He accepted it from her, then lifted it to look. "Admirable," he said again. He continued to speak softly, so softly that she had to stand close to him. "I would confer with you so that no other can hear us," he murmured. He was scanning the darkened firth again and anyone who saw them at the window might not guess they conferred. "What did Calum tell you of his plans?"

"That they would attack."

"But when?"

"You truly seek my counsel."

"I have learned to rely upon it," he said to her pleasure. "When?"

"He said it would take two or three more days for his kin to gather."

"And we have spent one of them," Amaury mused. "Would he know of the weths?"

"I cannot say. Robert de Maxwell would know of them, for certain."

Amaury nodded. "But another day. And if they ride around the firth?"

"It would take a company two days at least, less if they did not halt at night."

"And is there a time that one would not use the weths?"

"At high tide, or if there is a storm. Some will not cross it in rain or fog, for fear of losing their way." She considered the possibilities. "Those first two men did not want to cross the Annan in the dark. Calum's kin are from further north, for the Moffatts live west of Kilderrick and a bit to the north. They might not trust the water."

"Three days then at worst," Amaury concluded. "And perhaps four or five, more likely. Depending upon the weather." He put down the glass and shook his head, his dissatisfaction sobering. "We will plan the feast for the night after tomorrow and hope the attack does not come that night, when all are sated and sleepy."

"Such a meal cannot be arranged sooner."

"Yet it must be done as soon as possible, to fortify the loyalty of the villagers." He frowned and rubbed his brow. "They are all we have to defend the keep, unless Alfred finds Laurent in time."

"Surely he will."

"If you are inclined to pray, my lady, you might make an appeal."

He did not say more but Elizabeth could guess his thoughts. He feared 'twas not enough and dread rose within her. Before she could ask, he turned away.

"I must ride to hunt on the morrow. I will be gone when you awaken."

"I would accompany you and contribute my share."

"You must be here and watch in my absence."

"Surely they cannot arrive so soon."

"Surely we do not know." Amaury shook his head crisply and turned back to the window.

Elizabeth felt dismissed.

"On this night, I will take the watch." He spoke without emotion at all. "If you would unlace my hauberk again, my lady, I would be most grateful."

Elizabeth did not know whether to feel relief or dismay that he had no amorous expectations of her. Once again, he was impassive and inscrutable, but this time, she sorely resented the change.

ELIZABETH HESITATED to comply with his request and Amaury knew she watched him, trying to discern his thoughts. He would not be so weak as to tell her of his despair. Her home would be lost within days and he doubted he could repair the matter. No matter how he worked, they would be outnumbered. Most everyone within Beaupoint would die, including himself. And Elizabeth, Elizabeth would be seized and claimed again, if she was not killed.

It was enough to break his heart.

He bowed his head, hating that he had so few options, and waited.

He would teach her better to defend herself. Just as that short lesson with the knife had allowed her to escape Calum's attack, more instruction might save her life.

It was not enough, but it was all Amaury could do.

Finally, he could feel Elizabeth's presence close behind him. She freed the lace and he heard her take a breath. She would speak. She would invite his confidence. She might even appeal to him.

And Amaury would be lost. He could not afford to be tempted, not now.

Amaury stepped away from her, bending to let his hauberk fall over his head to the floor. Then he crouched to examine it, apparently engrossed in assessing its state though he knew precisely what had to be done. He could feel her gaze upon him as surely as a touch, but he ignored it, fetching a cloth and a steel then settling on the floor to begin the cleaning of his armor.

He had spent many days at such tasks while training for his spurs and he gave it his full attention this night.

Save for his awareness that the lady exhaled in frustration.

Save for his interest in the sound of her laces being pulled free.

Save for his intense desire to turn or even glance over his shoulder to watch Elizabeth disrobe.

He would not dishonor her now, not when he had so little time left.

AMAURY DID NOT SLEEP that night. Nor did he look upon Elizabeth as she slept, Grise on the bed beside her. The other dogs laid on the pallet he had brought to the solar and snored with contentment as was their habit. He kept watch all night, and in the first light of the dawn, he noticed the stones to the west of Beaupoint's tower.

They were cut square and set in the ground, like the foundation for a building. But what construction would there be at Beaupoint? They had to be two hundred paces from the west wall. Was it an abandoned site? Amaury was curious.

James was awake, his candle burning in his small chamber. Amaury asked for a few silver pennies for the boys who would help him at the hunt, and though the older man was disgruntled, he consented.

Amaury had a glimpse inside the locked trunk that was his treasury and was shocked to see how barren it was. What had James done with Calum's coin? Had he spent it all on manuscripts? He certainly had a considerable collection.

Amaury found three grubby boys awaiting him in the bailey, all of them lanky and unkempt. The one who proved to be a girl on closer inspection was the sole one who admitted to being able to ride. He asked one of the boys to lace his hauberk, then saddled Esther for the girl. The boys would run and beat the scrub for him. He hesitated for a moment, then saddled Blanchefleur instead of Zephyr, guessing that the mare had not been out of the stables since Laurent and Simon's departure. She stamped in her enthusiasm, arching her neck and clearly ready to run, while Zephyr nickered in protest.

The children gave him advice about the location of deer and other game, the girl pointing to the forest to the south and west of the keep. Amaury slung his crossbow over his shoulder and rode out, the dogs racing ahead and the boys struggling to keep up.

It was a fine day to hunt.

When Elizabeth awakened, Amaury was gone. She dressed with Harriet's assistance, then kept vigil at the windows for him. There was not a flicker of movement to the north and the sunshine allowed for long views, even without the glass. She heard his company's return, close to noon, and turned to look to the west.

She was distracted by the stones set on the ground, as if they were laid for a foundation. They had not been there before, and they were not accidental. They had been chiseled and placed with deliberation, the work of a mason. She could not explain it.

The sound of the horses grew louder and she looked to the south. Evidently, Amaury had learned that the game was abundant in the forest that was part of the holding. He rode Blanchefleur, who cantered with a satisfaction that could not be disguised. A girl rode Esther, and

Elizabeth used the reading glass to verify that it was Twyla, the smith's daughter. She was the best rider of the village children and Elizabeth liked that Amaury had not given her a lesser task because of her gender.

Of course, that would not have been practical.

The boys were Tyson and Roydon, the brewster's twins, younger than Twyla but often competitive with her. Someone had lashed together an arrangement of branches—she could guess that Amaury had done as much—and the boys hauled two deer back to the hall upon it. There were hares hung from Amaury's saddle and grouse aplenty from Esther's. Persephone was on Amaury's fist and his crossbow hung from his saddle. Amaury's deep voice carried to her ears as he encouraged the children and she could see their proud smiles.

Elizabeth reached the bailey in time to see him surrender a silver penny to each of them as he thanked them. Hamish and Nelwyna were fussing over the game, and Amaury turned away, only to have Twyla clear her throat.

"I could help, sir," she said and he glanced back at her. "I know of horses, sir, for my father is the smith. I could brush them down and such, sir."

"There is a smith in the village?"

She colored. "There was, sir. He has gone to Carlisle in search of a post, sir, leaving us here until he is certain of one."

"I see," Amaury said. "I would be glad of your assistance, Twyla, but let me speak to his lordship about a wage."

Her face lit with joy. "Thank you, sir. It need not be much, sir. We wish only for some bread, sir."

Amaury nodded once, inscrutable again. Elizabeth could fairly feel his disapproval though. "I would ensure that you can be paid before you begin," he said to Twyla.

"I will brush down the horses, sir," the girl said with a quick bow. "The task must be done and I do not mind."

"The midday meal is laid," Elizabeth said to Amaury as he strode toward her, his features set.

"Good, for I have matters to discuss with your uncle." He spoke grimly, then paused beside her. "What are the foundation stones to the west of the tower?"

"I do not know," she confessed. "They were not there when I left a year ago."

Amaury nodded once then continued to the great hall. She followed behind him and sat at the board, embarrassed that there was only another thin soup.

She was not surprised by her uncle's vehement protest in response to Amaury's query.

"Coin! You warriors are all the same. Coin, coin, coin. And for what? The tending of horses we do not even require. It does not grow upon trees, sir. I have precious little to spare."

"The girl works hard and must be compensated."

"The horses should not even be here."

"Is it true that the smith has left the village?" Elizabeth asked.

"I do not know," her uncle said. "Why should he stay if his trade is the tending of horses?" He leaned toward Amaury. "I suppose you will have him back next, and insist that I pay him."

"Nay, I will not."

The pair glared at each other, then ate in silence.

"What are the stones to the west of the tower, sir."

James smiled, his expression triumphant. "It is Elizabeth's bride price."

Amaury's confusion was clear. "You would build another structure, not a hundred steps to the west of Beaupoint's tower? Why, when you do not tend to this structure?"

"It will be the chapel of St. Joseph, the heart of a monastery I have endowed here at Beaupoint. The documents are all in the treasury of the keep."

Elizabeth caught her breath. Beaupoint would become a religious house?

James drew on the table with a fingertip, his enthusiasm clear. "There will be a cloister, with healing plants, and a chapter house beyond for the brethren to live. But the detail of import is the church, for it is here that people will come to worship."

"There is a chapel in Beaupoint village where people worship," Elizabeth reminded him.

"But it is too small," James insisted. "I have a prize for this chapel, a treasure that will bring pilgrims to pray here."

"A treasure?" Amaury echoed.

"A holy relic, and one of great significance. There is a family in the east of Scotland, far beyond Edinburgh, a family that hails from the east. Lammergeier is their name, Avery Lammergeier is the one I knew years ago. Officially, he traded in cloth, silks and samites, and some dyes, his expertise being in all the fibers woven in the east. On occasion, though, he acquired relics and sold them here or in France, tokens of the saints to bring miracles to the faithful. Some twenty years ago, he showed me one such." James raised his brows. "A cup."

"A cup," Elizabeth repeated.

God in Heaven, he had spent the legacy of Beaupoint on an old cup.

And Calum's coin on masons, while Beaupoint itself was virtually abandoned.

Her father must be stirring in his grave in outrage.

"A cup said to have been the one used by Joseph of Arimathea to catch the blood of Christ as he died, a cup long associated with Tintagel, a cup that had found its way—who knows how—into Avery's hands. Of course, he wished to sell it. He was a man less interested in items than the price they could fetch."

"How could you be certain of its provenance?" Elizabeth demanded.

Amaury simply listened, his silence evidence that he was as astonished as she.

"I could not." James lifted a finger. "Until I held it in my own hands. I knew immediately that it was genuine. I could feel its power and it shook me mightily. I knew that such a prize should be defended and also shared, that its power should be offered to those in need. I asked Avery to keep it for me. Avery, being Avery, demanded regular payments to continue to do so. It cost me nigh everything and Percival gave me the last payment."

"Percival?"

"My brother. Elizabeth's father."

"Surely your prize is not here?" Amaury protested.

James laughed gleefully. "Fear not. It is safe."

Amaury exhaled and pushed away from the board.

"A thief might overlook it, even in a treasury, for it is a simple cup of plain design. It does not reveal itself with a mere glance."

"You would build a monastery and create a church for pilgrims, that they might come to see this cup," Amaury concluded.

James nodded. "'Twill be magnificent and a fitting legacy to my brother." His satisfaction was undisguised.

Elizabeth could not share his view. She was glad she did not have to remain to see it. It would be easier, given these tidings, to ride to France with Amaury and never see Beaupoint again.

She saw the knight shake his head as if in disbelief.

They finished the meal in silence, James stealing glances at his current choice of reading material, then Amaury rose.

"Your lessons must continue, my lady," he said. "Join me in the bailey, at your convenience, if you please. I hope there might be a quintain there."

Beaupoint turned to a monastery. Amaury had never heard a notion that was such a travesty. This keep was a marvel and it would be left to crumble to ruin, while a monastery was built alongside it.

For the love of God, he had never heard such folly.

Actually, he supposed James' plan was for the love of God.

He should leave. He should ride out of these gates this very day, head to Carlisle and find passage to France. He should forget about Elizabeth and Beaupoint and any misguided notion of responsibility for her welfare.

But Amaury could not do it. He could not abandon her, not until he was certain of the motives of the Moffatts.

Nay, not until Laurent returned.

If Laurent returned.

Amaury grimaced as he entered the bailey. He looked down the road, knowing it was too soon to hope for aid but unable to help himself. When the captain-of-arms was back at Beaupoint, his duty would be done. He would depart without delay and ride south to secure his future.

He would.

Twyla came out of the stables, flushed from her exertions. The horses had been tended admirably and he complimented her on her efforts. He could not fail to note her pleasure when he granted her another coin.

"I will come each day, sir."

"I cannot say when there will be more coin," he felt compelled to tell her.

"But I have two silver pennies, sir!" she said with delight. "I will work until the Yule for this sum."

"It is not sufficient."

She straightened. "When there is none, sir, a small sum becomes sufficient."

Aye, there was that.

"Is there a quintain in the stables?" he asked. "My lady must practice her skill with a knife."

"Can she throw a knife, sir?"

"I learn, Twyla," Elizabeth said from behind Amaury. "At my husband's insistence."

"My father taught me," the girl confessed. "He said it is often of greater import for a woman to be armed than a man."

"I should like to meet such a wise man," Amaury said and Twyla beamed.

"I shall send him to you when he returns, sir." She smiled. "He will want to see your destrier, to be sure."

The quintain was found and propped up in the bailey. 'Twas clear it had not been used of late, but Amaury was glad to find it at all. It was a pole with a wooden shield mounted upon it, at the height of a shield carried by a man on horseback, used in training with arms. Amaury drew two lines on the shield with a piece of coal, dividing it into quadrants.

He returned to Elizabeth's side, drawing his plain knife. Twyla hunkered down to watch. "Name your target," he said to Elizabeth.

"You cannot aim so precisely." He granted her a look and she sighed. "I will not be able to do as much."

"Not unless you believe it possible," he said.

"Top right," she said, folding her arms across her chest.

Amaury fixed his gaze upon that quadrant, raised the knife and flicked it hard. The blade sank into the wood in that section and Twyla cheered. He retrieved the knife and handed it to Elizabeth, hilt first. "Now, you."

She took an unsteady breath, gripping the knife as he had instructed her, then flinging it. The blade buried itself in the wall of the stables behind the quintain.

"A noble effort, my lady," Twyla called as she raced to collect the blade.

"You must step into it," Amaury said. "Consider your entire body to be a projectile, pointed at your target." He demonstrated again as she watched.

She frowned when Twyla went to retrieve the blade.

"Never in anger," Amaury advised softly.

"Passion will lead me astray?" she asked and he nodded.

"Indeed. Do not think about it overmuch. Let your thoughts be serene. Be confident of your success."

When Twyla came back with the blade again, she smiled at Elizabeth. "Like this, my lady," she said, then made a perfect throw.

This time, Amaury was the one to applaud.

He saw Elizabeth's lips set as she lifted the knife and eyed the target. She took a breath and he watched the tension ease from her shoulders as she calmed herself. When she lifted her hand, he knew that she would conquer this challenge soon.

CHAPTER 13

It was late when Elizabeth finally climbed the stairs to the solar and the keep was quiet. Grise was by her side and she stroked the dog's back on the stairs. She was a bit sore after her training with Amaury this day, for she had used muscles she had forgotten she had. But she had made progress and was hopeful of some encouragement from him.

It had been impossible not to notice how often he had looked toward the road, obviously in hope of Laurent's return. Thus far, there was no sign of the warriors who had left Beaupoint.

There had been much to resolve in the kitchens this night. Not only had Amaury brought a great deal of meat for the feast, but there were villagers aplenty gathering in the kitchens, as well. It had been chaotic when Elizabeth arrived to confer with Hamish. She learned that the fields had been left fallow the past year, which explained the lack of bread. As vexing as that might be, it also meant that many in the village had not done their days of service owed to the lord. She had found them in the kitchens, intent upon giving their assistance now. That was welcome, for Hamish had need of all the helping hands he could get.

They also brought eggs and chickens. Miriam had begun to make ale when Elizabeth and Amaury had returned, and she offered it for the feast though it would be still thin. Others brought vegetables from their gardens, cabbage and turnips, much of which was mounded upon the tables in the kitchens. Still more loaned knives and pots, and the noise of all their chatter was nigh overwhelming.

Hamish and Elizabeth decided upon the dishes to be served, and Nelwyna began to assign tasks. The activity had settled into a rhythm, still filling the chamber with chatter, but also with purpose. More than one villager congratulated Elizabeth on her match, more than one woman rolled her eyes and smiled at the mention of Amaury, and even Father Owen made an appearance to ensure all was well.

It took hours to set all to rights, but Elizabeth enjoyed it, and the memory of former times. She sent the enthusiastic Twyla home to her mother, thanking the girl again for aiding her with learning to throw a knife. In truth, Elizabeth had never seen so many merry smiles in her father's hall.

It was good to be home.

Her uncle was murmuring to himself in his small chamber, bent over some manuscript or other, his features illuminated by the single candle that burned there. Elizabeth bade him a good night but he did not reply.

The solar was quiet when she reached it and she assumed that Amaury watched at the window. Instead, she found that he dozed upon the straw pallet the dogs had used the night before, still in his hauberk and boots.

But when had he last slept? Before they left Caerlaverock.

Elizabeth shook her head and lifted the reading glass from his limp hand, knowing what he would ask as soon as he awakened. The tide was in, the moon shone over land and water, and nothing moved to the north that she could discern. There was no activity on the road to Carlisle either, which was less good, but she doubted Laurent would ride at night. Grise nosed Amaury's hand and he jumped to wakefulness, looking around himself with alarm.

"The glass," he said, surely thinking he had dropped or lost it.

"I have it," Elizabeth replied. "And I looked but no one approaches." She bent and tugged off his boots. "You must sleep, sir."

"I must keep the watch," he protested.

"I will keep the watch," she insisted. "Lean forward that I might reach that cursed lace."

To her surprise, he did as bidden, barely stifling a mighty yawn. "I should…"

"Sleep," she said, pushing the hauberk over his head. He rolled his shoulders as she had seen him do a dozen times once relieved of its weight. In truth, it was heavy, so heavy that she wondered how he bore it all day. "And now to bed, sir."

He opened his mouth to protest, but Elizabeth waved him to silence. "You will not be able to defend Beaupoint if you are tired beyond all."

It had to be a sign of his exhaustion that he followed her bidding, though still he looked one last time to the east and the north. He would have slept on the pallet, but she pointed him toward the bed sternly.

He disrobed and nearly collapsed into the bed, closing his eyes in rapture, and then he fell soundly asleep.

This dutiful, responsible, honorable man.

Elizabeth watched him as she undressed and he did not even roll to one side. She pointed and Grise jumped onto the bed beside him, yawning noisily before she dropped her head and closed her eyes. Bête and Noisette again shared the pallet and Elizabeth wrapped herself in Amaury's cloak before lifting the glass and looking across the firth.

The tide was rolling in, the rhythm of the water most soothing to watch. No one could use the weth for some hours now. She moved to the east-facing window to watch the road instead.

She listened to Amaury's steady breathing, watched the tide and hoped Laurent arrived soon.

SUNDAY, the day of the feast dawned clear and sunny.

Still there was no one on the road to Carlisle.

Amaury bathed and shaved in the stables, dressing in his own clothing which had been cleaned. He wore his simple dark garb and brushed his own boots to a gleam. No sooner was he prepared than Elizabeth appeared, dressed in yet another kirtle he had never seen before. This one was a deep sapphire blue that favored her coloring admirably. James came into the bailey behind her, looking up at the sky, then led the way to the chapel in the village without a word. Amaury commanded the dogs to remain in the stables, then offered his arm to Elizabeth.

On a morning like this, he could hope for the best.

In Beaupoint's chapel, he could see why Elizabeth so loved her home. Villagers came forward with smiles to greet her and welcome her back. He felt that they walked to the chapel on a tide of goodwill. Elizabeth introduced him to so many people, and he admired that she knew all their names, even remembering their children and livestock. There was Miriam, the brewster, plump and smiling, grateful for what her sons, Tyson and Roydon, had earned the day before. Twyla's mother, Anna, greeted him with pleasure and Twyla pushed her younger brothers Thomas and Robert forward. Even Heloise inclined her head to him, before an older man fell to his knee before Elizabeth.

"My lady," he said with a wheeze. "I took Magdalena and Maeve into my care in your absence. I hope you do not mind."

"This is Frederick," Elizabeth said to Amaury. "He was my father's falconer."

Amaury knew then who Magdalena and Maeve had to be. He reached to help the older man rise to his feet again.

"I could not leave the peregrines there alone, my lady. They need to hunt..."

"Of course, they do," Amaury said kindly. "Will you bring them back to the keep? My own falcon, Persephone, would benefit from the company of her own kind."

The man's eyes lit. "Another peregrine?"

"A fine one," Elizabeth said. "Perhaps you might assist in tending the three of them. No one can contest your knowledge, Frederick."

"It would be a pleasure, my lady!"

"More expense," James grumbled but Amaury and Elizabeth ignored him.

Amaury met the healer and midwife, Erwina, and her daughter, Audry, who was a bonesetter. There was a miller, Clive, who looked less affluent than most millers of Amaury's experience, and his thin wife, Merry, who did not look merry at all. There were many others but Amaury lost track of their names. His overwhelming impression was that there were too many women.

He looked again down the road to Carlisle as they approached the chapel, but it remained empty.

Father Owen greeted them at the door, welcoming the entire village into the chapel for the mass. It was not an ornate building, but there was much to admire in its simplicity, and Amaury guessed that it was old. The floor was of stone, many of the chiseled stones marked with crosses, and he guessed that Elizabeth's family were buried in the crypt. Certainly, she bowed her head and was silent, likely in recollection. There were greens on the altar and beeswax candles burning, and Father Owen had a booming voice that made much of the service.

Amaury felt a sense of history and community, one that reminded him greatly of his uncle's holding. While Evroi was much richer, there had been a similar bond between its residents.

When the service was done, he and Elizabeth followed James out of the chapel. The mood turned jubilant as the villagers headed for the keep.

Children ran ahead of them, older villagers following with their spoons and napkins. More than one carried a musical instrument of some kind and it felt festive. There was an excited chatter as they reached the hall and found their places, and the smell from the kitchens was most enticing.

There was a roar of approval when Hamish appeared with the roast venison and cups of ale were raised in salute.

"All hail the lady Elizabeth and her new husband," cried Miriam the brewster.

"All hail!" echoed the company and drained their cups. There was a smattering of applause, then the dishes were carried from the kitchens and passed to fulsome approval. Amaury felt he was the sole one in the company who did not share in the celebratory mood. Indeed, fear rose cold within him.

It was the third day since they had left Caerlaverock. The assault would come soon, but Beaupoint was virtually undefended. The village would be set alight. The walls would be stormed. There were so many women and children, and the men were mostly elderly.

They would all die.

He should have ridden to Kilderrick and asked Maximilian's advice.

Murdoch Douglas had spoken aright—Amaury knew little of real war. He knew of jousting and combat on the field *à plaisance*. The assault upon Beaupoint would not be for pleasure and the residents were woefully unprepared. He had hoped for a few more men in their numbers, or a few more women who, like Twyla, had learned to fight. They were villagers, though, content and merry, undoubtedly adept with the tilling of fields and the plucking of chickens.

They would not be so for much longer.

He was looking down at the table, sickened by their prospects, when Elizabeth reached over to kiss his cheek. "You should smile, sir, lest they conclude you regret your choice of bride," she whispered.

There was much Amaury regretted, but not the defense of this lady. He took her hand in his, holding her gaze, and kissed her palm slowly. She flushed and smiled, then he bent down to kiss her fully, much to the satisfaction of all.

She would pay the highest price of all and he knew it well.

Amaury could only hope that Laurent made haste.

Amaury was uncommonly quiet during the feast. He rose several times, leaving the table, and Elizabeth knew he checked the road to Carlisle. Finally, fearing that others might think him rude, she sent Twyla to the solar with her bowl of stew to watch in his stead.

Still he was restless and discontent. His smile never reached his eyes. They retreated to the solar amidst many merry wishes, sent Twyla to meet her mother in the bailey, and he became even more grim.

Harriet came with hot water, flushed with delight after the feast. She chattered as she filled a bowl for Elizabeth and helped with her laces, the girl's words seeming loud in the solar. Amaury was oblivious. His brow was furrowed as he moved from the north window to the east one, watching, always watching.

Elizabeth tried to wait for him to speak. She dismissed Harriet then shed her kirtle, expecting at least a glance of curiosity. There was none. She removed her chemise and stood nude in the chilly solar as she washed. He did not appear to notice. Finally, she dried herself and donned a clean chemise, then extinguished one candle.

Still, he did not move.

She braided her hair and tied it, then fixed him with a look.

"You are grim," she said finally.

He shrugged, acknowledging her words but not replying to them.

He moved to the north window yet again. "The tide flows out," he said.

Elizabeth moved to his side and looked out over the water. "It will take hours before anyone can use the weths," she said, intending to reassure him.

She earned a hot glance for that. "And you think I will sleep during that interval?"

"Why not?"

He frowned and shook his head, raising the glass to his eye. The silence descended again. "I will sleep when I am dead."

"Nonsense. You should come to bed."

Amaury shook his head, resolute.

"You are irked," she said, when his next bout of silence had stretched too long to be endured.

He flicked a glance her way, one so intent that she nearly retreated a step. "Aye," he said and she heard now the fury in his tone.

"What have I done?"

"You?" His surprise could not be mistaken. "You have done nothing at all. The errors, and there are many of them, are entirely mine. Worse, they cannot be repaired, not now." He shook his head. "It has all gone awry and the sole mercy is that I will not have to reflect upon my failure for long."

What was this? The feast had gone well, to her thinking, better than she had expected.

"I cannot imagine what you mean," Elizabeth said. "The villagers are content, as you desired them to be. Your plan worked most well in regaining their loyalty. I had not expected them to participate with such enthusiasm after this past year."

Again, she was treated to a glare one that silenced her.

"It is three days since we left Caerlaverock. The attack we anticipate may come at any moment."

"But we knew that."

Amaury exhaled. "These villagers, whatever their enthusiasm, cannot face them with success. They are women and children."

"That does not mean they are defenseless."

"It nigh does," he said. "I had hoped for a few more men, some doughty farmers, or vigorous young women. They are older and complacent, or merely children."

"But..."

"They will *die*, my lady. The only mercy is that it will be quick." She was startled by his vehemence. "It will only take a dozen men to seize the keep, if that, and they will succeed within moments." He bit off the last few words precisely and Elizabeth chilled.

"They might not attack."

"And surrender the prize of Beaupoint willingly. Nay. They will come." He turned to face her, his eyes snapping. "I will die in your defense, my lady," he said with conviction. "I will protect you to the very end, but the end will come. We will be out-numbered and we will lose. Your uncle will surely die. Most of the villagers will die, unless they have the wits to flee. I will die and you will be claimed again, quite possibly in this very chamber." Elizabeth felt her eyes widen. "Beaupoint will be seized, according to the original plan, and you will either be forcibly wedded to one of them to secure their claim or you will also die."

Elizabeth caught her breath. "You do not gild the tale, sir."

"It is all my error!" he roared. "I killed Calum Moffatt. I sent Oliver back to Kilderrick with no suggestion that we might need Maximilian's aid. I brought you to Beaupoint instead of riding to Kilderrick, where Maximilian's aid could have been won. They will follow us here, bent on vengeance, and we will be defeated." He paced to the eastern window, his every muscle taut with anger. "Never could I have imagined that my failure would be so very complete."

The air sizzled between them, Amaury's agitation filling the chamber like a tangible force. But Elizabeth knew he was vexed with himself, that he set his expectations high, and she was far from disappointed with his efforts.

"I should never have thought to say as much," she said lightly. "But you, sir, talk overmuch."

He fairly snarled at her, then fixed his attention upon the road to Carlisle. "You should sleep," he said tightly. "I am fit company for no one this night."

Elizabeth disagreed. She knew he could only be so angry because he was roused, because he cared, and his sense of responsibility only made her admire him all the more.

"I do not regret a moment in your company, sir, or a single choice we have made," Elizabeth dared to say.

"It has been a lie, and perhaps that is why it has gone so badly wrong."

"You encouraged me to defend myself instead of meekly accepting whatever was granted to me." He granted her a skeptical glance. "You ensured that I left Calum's bedchamber alive with that gift," she reminded him. "And you freed me from a most unhappy match." She watched his lips set and moved closer. "But most importantly of all, you brought me home to Beaupoint, as I requested."

Amaury looked up when her voice caught.

"If I am to die soon, it will be here at Beaupoint, which gives me great consolation. I am here, with my forebears, with their ghosts and their legacy, and there is no place in all of Christendom I would rather be. I always hoped that my demise, when it came, would be here. I thank you for that."

"It should not come so soon as this," he said gruffly.

"My uncle would say it was God's will."

"You will forgive me for saying that your uncle is a fool."

Elizabeth smiled. "I will. My father often said the same thing of his brother."

Amaury did not reply.

"Tell me of your uncle."

"Why?"

"Because you admire him so. I would know more of him."

Amaury exhaled. "He is a man of honor who tends his responsibilities."

Of course. "But would he blame you on this night as you blame yourself?"

Amaury stared across the room, then shook his head. "He could always find merit or some detail to praise, even in the darkest situation. That was what made him a good teacher."

"I can imagine as much."

"He oft said that a man should live each day so that he would have no regrets, if he were not to see the morning's light. He never retired without making amends or making an apology. He never left any deed to be done the following day. He balanced his accounts, so to speak, each and every day. I always admired that."

"If you were to die this night, would you have regrets?"

"Scores of them," Amaury said with heat.

"I would have only one," Elizabeth said and he glanced toward her warily. She smiled. "I have never known the pleasure that can be shared between man and wife."

Amaury shook his head and took a step back.

"I would have my boon of you, Amaury d'Evroi," she said firmly. "And I would have it this night, while still we have the chance."

"You have had your boon. We feign a match."

"The falsehood does not satisfy," she said, reaching to run a fingertip down his arm.

He looked down at her hand but did not move.

Nor did he look away.

"You do not know what you ask," he said gruffly.

"No, I do not." She flattened her hand, caressing his shoulder. "That is why I ask you to show me." He stared down at her, eyes simmering. Elizabeth reached up and wound her arms around his neck. Amaury became completely still, a man of stone once again, but Elizabeth saw the fire in his gaze. She smiled, then once again touched her lips to his.

For a moment, he did not respond. She feared he would turn her aside, that he would decline to indulge her. Then she felt him shudder and knew his resistance crumbled. He caught her around the waist, lifting her against his strength, and angled his mouth over hers, deepening his kiss as if he could do nothing else.

It was wondrous. Tender and exhilarating, so ardent that she could only close her eyes and enjoy. Each time, he embraced her, the pleasure was more than the time before—each time she grew more bold beneath his caress. She slid her fingers into his hair, drawing him closer, wanting all he had to give.

When Amaury finally lifted his head, there was an awe in his expression that made Elizabeth feel invincible. "It is your last chance to step away," he said in a husky rumble. "I will not be able to turn aside if you kiss me again with such ardor."

Elizabeth was delighted. "Then I do have power in this exchange?"

"You have all the power in this exchange." He swallowed and caught his breath, his throat working. "And if you wish to halt, tell me as much, and I will endeavor to serve your will."

She knew he would do it. She knew he would conquer his own passion for her own sake, for she had seen him struggle for restraint. As a result, she trusted him completely. "I would have you proceed, sir, if you please."

To her delight, Amaury's lips curved into a smile. "I do please," he murmured with heat. He turned his head then, his gaze still locked with hers, and pressed a hot kiss to her palm. It was a gesture that thrilled her each and every time. "For I can only surrender to my lady's command."

Elizabeth had a moment to smile with delight, then Amaury swept her from her feet, capturing her lips in a triumphant kiss as he carried her to the bed.

This would be the night she learned all.

Amaury could not resist Elizabeth or her request. If this was to be his last night alive, he would ensure it was one to remember. If it was to be her sole opportunity to enjoy the pleasure a couple could make abed, he wanted her to experience all of it.

And her enthusiasm could not be denied. She was glorious, not just a beauty but clever and the more bold she became, the more he admired her. She had unbound her hair and it fell gleaming to her hips, the light from the candles snared in its glossy waves. He could never decide the hue of it, for it seemed brown sometimes, and reddish in others. On this night, the candlelight gave it glints of gold. And the softness of it! It felt like silk, but the tresses curled around his fingers as if they would ensnare him forever.

Her eyes were wide this night, and seemed darker than he knew them to be. They were fathomless pools, filled with secrets, thickly lashed. She studied him, then glanced downward, suddenly shy, when he untied the lace of her chemise. She did not move away, though and the flush in her cheeks revealed her interest. She bit the fullness of her bottom lip, tempting him to taste her again, and he savored how readily she responded, meeting him halfway and sharing in the kiss. She participated, as she had not the first time, and he welcomed the change.

He swept the chemise from one shoulder, baring her skin to view, then cupped her breast in his hand. Her eyes widened, but she smiled, then she gasped as he slid his thumb across the nipple. The nipple tightened beneath his hand and he watched her lips part in wonder. He brushed his mouth across hers, then bent and took that nipple gently between his lips. Elizabeth's fingers locked in his hair as he teased the nipple to a point, grazing it with his teeth, flicking his tongue against it, and sucking it gently. Her skin flushed and she moved her hips with agitation, all signs that he made progress in ensuring her arousal.

He swept the chemise from her other shoulder, letting it pool around her waist, and Elizabeth shook her wrists free with an impatience that was most satisfying. Her eyes were sparkling with anticipation now, with no indication of fear. Amaury smiled at her and bent again to his delightful task. The other nipple was given similar attention and responded with just as much enthusiasm. He could smell the sweetness of her skin and the heat of her arousal, and loved the sweet weight of her against him. He teased the first nipple with his finger and thumb, his other hand lost in her hair. Her incoherent moan gave him a satisfaction of savage power.

"You wear too much garb," she protested breathlessly, after he had kissed her lips again. Amaury stepped away from the bed and their gazes locked once more with the potency he came to expect. There was nothing in all the world save this lady, but Amaury refused to wish for more than could be. Not on this night.

He shed his tabard, glad he had not worn his hauberk this day. He watched for her reaction as he shed his own chemise, and when he cast it aside, she surveyed him openly. He removed his boots but not his chausses, for he needed a reminder of his resolve to stop once she had been pleased.

She was not his wife in truth and he would not dishonor her now, not when the end was so near. He would ensure her pleasure only.

Her welcoming smile meant that he returned quickly to the bed. He took her in his arms again and they shared a kiss, longer and more hungry than those that had come before. When Amaury lifted his head, his heart was racing. Elizabeth flushed, then reached to touch him. Amaury closed his eyes at the wave of pleasure he felt at the weight of her exploring fingertips, and let her touch him as she would. His choice seemed to embolden her, for she placed her hands flat against him. She ran her hands across his shoulders and his chest, moving with greater surety in every passing moment. She pushed her fingers through the tangle of hair on his chest and even gave it a little tug, then pinched his nipple as her eyes sparkled. It responded to her caress and she hesitated only a moment before closing her mouth over it and mimicking what he had done.

Amaury closed his eyes and caught his breath, his hand rising to tangle in her hair again. He caught her nape in his hand and lifted her face so he could kiss her again. He wanted to feast upon her, to take her to the summit of pleasure, to ensure that she learned to welcome this deed with anticipation. She rolled to her back, fairly pulling him atop her, but Amaury remained by her side. He slid his hand down the length of her, then eased his fingers into the slick heat at the top of her thighs. She jumped a little when he touched the spot that would give her pleasure, then gasped into his kiss when he caressed her there. She was wet and hot and sweet, her body revealing her pleasure and lack of fear.

On impulse, Amaury moved lower, pushing aside her chemise and closing his mouth over her. She stiffened for a moment, then he moved his tongue against her, and she fell back upon the bed with a moan of pleasure. He teased and caressed her, driving her to the height of distraction, then slowing his touch again. He used his fingers and his mouth, waiting until she was flushed and aroused. Her pulse was quick and her skin was flushed, and he moved against her decisively, casting her into an abyss of delight.

She cried out and shook from head to toe, then trembled in the aftermath of her release. "Amaury," she whispered in awe and he could not help but smile at her delight.

With regret, he turned away from the sight of temptation and pushed a hand through his hair. He was raging with need, but it would not be right to satisfy himself here on this night. He washed, taking his time at the task to compose himself. He kept his back turned to Elizabeth but was aware of the weight of her gaze. The keep was silent and chill, the view out the windows all darkness when he checked. There was not even a moon this night.

It was when he reached for his discarded chemise that he felt her hand land upon his shoulder. He had not even heard her rise from the bed but did not dare to turn and look at her. If there was an invitation in her eyes, he would be unable to resist. Even her fleeting touch sent fire through him.

"Amaury," she murmured again and he closed his eyes at the alluring sound of his name upon her lips. He felt her arm slide around his waist from behind and her bare breasts press against his back. Her nipples were taut, her skin soft, her hands bold in their exploration. One swept downward, following the line of hair to his navel, but faltered there. He knew he should move away, maybe even leave the solar this night, but her caress was the most seductive sensation he had ever experienced.

Her breath was on his skin, then she touched her lips to the back of his shoulder. Amaury gritted his teeth, unable to bear it yet unwilling to ask her to stop.

"Impossible man," she whispered, laughter in her voice. "I entreat you to finish what you have begun." Elizabeth spread her fingers wide, fanning them across his skin, and Amaury's eyes flew open as her hands slid downward. Her hands eased beneath his chausses, her fingers exploring and Amaury was lost.

He spun and caught her in his arms, claiming her lips in a triumphant kiss, and carried her to the bed again.

He would face the repercussions on the morrow, but on this night, he would do as she asked.

ELIZABETH KNEW her words changed all. It was thrilling to know that she had dissolved Amaury's reservations with her touch and her words, that she held such power over this warrior.

They tumbled to the bed together and his hands roved over her, caressing her with surety. His kiss was so fierce and hungry that she wondered how she could even have thought him dispassionate. She pushed down his chausses and he kicked them off with impatience. She stole a glance at him and her chest tightened, but she knew he would not injure her.

As if he had noted her trepidation, Amaury gathered her into his arms again. He held her captive against his chest, feasting upon her mouth, his fingers moving between her thighs once more. His sure touch could not be denied and she felt her heart race as she shivered in need. Already she learned what she needed from him, what release he could grant to her. She opened her legs to him and Amaury inhaled sharply then moved between her thighs. As ever, he braced his weight atop her. He cupped her shoulders in his hands, his gaze more intent than ever she had seen it as he eased inside her.

Elizabeth could not look away from him. He moved ever deeper inside her, powerful yet moving in steady increments, his entire body tense. She felt the shiver beneath his flesh and admired his control, then gasped aloud when he was fully buried within her. She gripped his shoulders and pulled him closer, demanding his kiss, and he buried his face in her shoulder.

"My lady," he whispered hoarsely. "You do not know the spell you cast."

Elizabeth smiled and pushed her fingers through his hair, liking the feel of him, the sense that they shared this act together. She ran her hands over his shoulders and down his back. "There must be more," she whispered and he lifted his head, granting her a smile that heated her to her toes. His eyes were glittering and he considered her as if she was a marvel.

A man of stone. How could she have ever imagined as much?

He lowered his head and kissed her as if he could not do otherwise, and Elizabeth felt the heat rise within her again. And then, he began to move inside her. As pleasurable as it was, she caught her breath in recollection of another night.

Amaury caught her around the waist and rolled immediately to his back, so that she sat astride him. Elizabeth knew her astonishment showed, but he fitted his hands around her waist. He lifted her up and down. "I am in your thrall," he said, letting his hands fall to her thighs once he had shown her. "Take of me what you will."

He was serious in this. Elizabeth moved tentatively, watching how Amaury caught his breath and his eyes darkened. He did not seize her, though, and he did not drive himself into her in pursuit of his own satisfaction.

He waited.

This glorious maddening honorable man.

"Do you like this?" she whispered, fearful that his pleasure had been compromised.

Amaury's slow smile left no doubt of his reply. "What do you think?" he murmured and Elizabeth laughed aloud. His manner gave her the confidence to explore. She moved atop him, she changed the speed of her movement, she rolled her hips and it seemed that all she did only heightened his response. She walked her hands down his chest and caressed his nipples again, kissing his smile and feeling his hands tangle in her hair.

"Seductress," he whispered, eyes glowing.

Elizabeth laughed for she had never considered herself to be such. "Perhaps I shall not release you from this spell," she teased.

"Perhaps I will not struggle overmuch."

She braced her hands upon his shoulders and moved rhythmically again, watching him as the heat rose once again between them. She saw his jaw tense and felt his hands lock around her waist, urging her with greater and greater speed. Elizabeth followed his suggestion, keeping that pace as her own blood nigh boiled, then Amaury moved one hand between her thighs.

He touched her with surety, caressing the spot he had so pleasurably tormented before, and Elizabeth felt again that she was cast into the stars. She cried out with the power of her release, then Amaury rolled her abruptly to her back. He drove deep inside her one last time, then roared with his own satisfaction. He collapsed atop her, breathing heavily, then touched his lips to her shoulder.

"Enchantress," he whispered and Elizabeth gathered him close. Her heart slowed its pace and she felt both languid and warm, content to doze with Amaury in her arms and she in his.

It was idyllic. Wondrous. A feat that fairly demanded repetition.

Elizabeth fell asleep smiling, more than content.

AMAURY COULD SCARCE BELIEVE IT. He had added to his errors, yet he could not regret his choices in the least. Love did lead a man astray, to be sure. He lay in the great bed, Elizabeth curled against his side, her hair cast over his chest and her breath upon his skin. Never had he known such satisfaction. He wound a lock of her hair around his finger, amazed by her passion and beauty. Never had he anticipated that they might touch like this.

He wanted more, far more, a lifetime by her side and yet more than that.

And yet he would not have it.

Impatient with his own folly, Amaury rose from the bed. He washed less quietly than he should have done and realized as much too late.

"What is amiss?" Elizabeth asked, her voice sleepy. "Why did you leave?" There was a warmth in her tone, one born of pleasure, one that invited him to return and make her cry out again.

"I take the watch," he said, keeping his tone curt.

She laughed a little, probably not realizing how sultry she sounded. "Have you not earned a reprieve?"

He glanced at her, braced on her elbows, breasts bare, hair spilling over the linens. And that smile. Never had he seen a woman more alluring and Amaury was struck to silence by the sight of her. The magnitude of his error might have overwhelmed him, and how far love had led him astray, but he was horrified yet more that he could not summon a whisper of regret. If she entreated him again, he would succumb again.

Elizabeth sat up and wrapped her arms around her knees, her smile fading. "You are silent, sir. Do you mean to remind me that flesh responds to sensation?"

Amaury turned away from temptation. "Can you have any doubt?" His words were hoarse, his resolve in ruins.

"There was more to our mating than that."

He shrugged, feeling a cur. It was the moment to make a sweet confession, but he could compound all his errors but uttering three words, resonant with truth.

He would not do it.

He felt the change in her mood as surely as the sudden crackle of a flame. He heard her rise from the bed, and knew she moved with impatience. He was not surprised when she halted beside him, when he smelled the sweet musk of her skin, when he glimpsed the glorious spill of her hair. "I suppose you were thinking of Sylvia and not me," she said, her words tight with anger.

She offered him the perfect excuse.

Still he could not look at her while he encouraged her error. "Sylvia," he breathed, then shook his head. He reminded himself that his choice was for the greater good, but he felt cursedly cruel.

"Demure, biddable and beautiful," Elizabeth said. "A paragon among women."

Amaury nodded once.

He thought for a moment that she might strike him.

He was quite certain that he deserved no less.

But Elizabeth pivoted and marched back to the bed, threw herself into it and pulled the linens over her head. Her back was turned to him and she ignored him, save for one last muttered comment.

"Wretch!"

Amaury knew he deserved far more. A part of him wanted badly to console her, to apologize, to make matters right between them, but he had erred in loving her this night and he would not compound the mistake.

He did not sleep.

She did not sleep.

Her breathing did not slow and the air in the solar fairly crackled with tension. Grise jumped onto the bed with Elizabeth and settled with a satisfied grunt. If Elizabeth wept, he would not be able to stay away. Instead, she seethed with vigor.

Amaury paced the chamber. He refused to think about what could not be. He would not be the one to disappoint her. He opened the shutters and looked out, seeing the land cloaked in darkness. The moon was behind a cloud, the shadows were deep.

And that was why the line of lights moving across the firth could not be missed.

The reckoning had come, and it was too soon, by any accounting.

"Awaken, my lady," he said softly, knowing she would hear him. "They come."

"Nay!" Elizabeth was beside him in a heartbeat and looked across the firth. He watched her eyes widen in fear, then her lips set with resolve.

How could he do anything other than love her completely?

"Make haste," Amaury advised, seizing his own clothes. "Secure yourself here with your uncle. I must alert the villagers."

CHAPTER 14

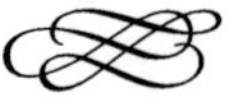

It was madness.

They could not win, but Amaury was unable to surrender.

He left the dogs in the solar with Elizabeth and raced down the stairs. James was yet reading in his chamber and he urged that man to the solar.

"I cannot leave my manuscripts," that man protested, rising to his feet.

"Three," Amaury decreed. "Choose three and secure the door of the solar behind you."

"Three? How can I choose only three?"

Amaury strode into the chamber, seized the one James had been reading and two others, then pushed him toward the stairs, shoving the manuscripts into his arms. "Three. Now make haste."

"But..."

Amaury bent down and stared into the man's eyes. "They come for you," he whispered, then touched the signet ring on James' finger. "And this. Do not make it a simple conquest."

James' alarm was clear and he stumbled toward the stairs.

Amaury watched that he began to climb, then hastened down to the ground floor. He roused the three in the kitchens and dispatched

Harriet to the village. He retreated to the stables, and had donned his hauberk by the time the first villagers arrived. They came with scythes and shovels, with knives and pots, their faces pale with fear. They also followed his instructions. When they were counted, he secured the portal, insisting that they remain within.

"I hear the ponies!" whispered one and a frisson of fear passed through the company.

"They will kill whoever obstructs them," Amaury told them. "They come for the lord, the seal and Beaupoint. They will take the lady to secure their claim. You can let them pass to save your own lives."

"Nay," Miriam said, stepping forward and brandishing a rough knife. "We stand with Lady Elizabeth."

"In memory of Lord Percival," said Hamish, waving a fearsome blade from the kitchens. The villagers cheered.

Frederick loosed the jesses of the falcons at Amaury's instruction and removed their hoods, letting them fly free. The horses were untethered and Amaury stroked Zephyr's neck, perhaps for the last time. Father Owen led a rousing chorus of prayer as Amaury seized his sword and bolted back up the stairs.

He raced back to the solar, as the hoofbeats of the arriving force grew louder. Twyla was fast behind him with her dagger drawn and he could not keep the girl from the battle. They were almost at the summit of the stairs when Elizabeth screamed a warning. Amaury barged through the door, only to find a hook over the base of the window on the eastern side. He pointed back and Twyla slammed the door, securing it with the beam across the back.

A man's gloved hand appeared at the window and Elizabeth stabbed at it with her dagger. The man swore and lost his grip but not for long. His hand reappeared and Twyla darted to Elizabeth's side, the pair of them driving blades into the man's hand.

Amaury loaded his crossbow and when the hand vanished, he stepped between the women and loosed the bolt at the face of the man just two arm's lengths below the window. He gasped, choked and fell heavily toward the earth. He clearly dislodged other climbers as he fell since there were shouts and curses from below. He seized his knife and endeavored to cut the rope, but it was thick and doughty.

"Fiends," Elizabeth said and Amaury followed her glance to see that the village had been set alight. Bright flames licked against the darkness and the smell of smoke rolled toward the windows.

There were shouts in the hall and the sound of weapons clashing.

It all happened too quickly.

A hand appeared at the west window, where another hook had landed. Twyla sliced at those fingers but the man grabbed her with his other hand, holding fast. Elizabeth slashed at his wrist furiously as Amaury shot another man who appeared at the east window.

It would all be over too soon.

James looked between the two windows and the door, clutching the few manuscripts he had brought with him.

"Divine intervention would not be unwelcome on this night," Amaury said and the older man fell upon his knees to pray.

There was a shriek from below and the sound of footsteps on the stairs. Amaury loaded another bolt and loosed it straight down from the east window, hoping it would injure more than one man climbing the rope. He went to the west window and did the same, then heard footfalls on the roof.

"God in Heaven," Elizabeth whispered, looking up. "They are like rats."

"A plague of vermin," Amaury agreed. He listened to the creak of the wooden roof, then climbed upon one of the trunks, jabbing suddenly upward with his sword so the blade slid between the planks. A man cried out, then screamed as he fell.

"Well done, sir," Twyla said, then the ramming began at the door.

Amaury continued to stab at the men on the roof, though it was harder to discern their positions with the noise. Elizabeth slashed at the hands and faces of those who appeared at the east window while Twlya did the same at the west. James frantic prayer filled the air, along with the smoke from the village.

Then the bar securing the door cracked loudly and the door slammed back against the wall, hitting so hard that the wall trembled.

Three warriors stood in the portal, each carrying a sword and a dagger, each wearing full armor. The one at the front was older, his expression so grim that Amaury knew he would not be readily turned aside.

They had lost. Amaury's heart sank to his toes, then he feared he would have to watch Elizabeth being despoiled.

"Laurent!" the lady exclaimed with delight.

The grey-haired warrior nodded to her gruffly and almost bowed. Then he marched into the chamber with the other two fast behind him. They seized one metal hook, hauling it forcibly into the solar, then flung it out the window. There was a resounding crash as the reivers were flung to the ground. They did the same with the other hook, then Laurent paused to shake Amaury's hand.

"Well met, sir," he said with satisfaction. "It is good to return to Beaupoint."

THE TIDE of the battle changed in their favor with Laurent's arrival. Elizabeth did not know how many of her father's men had returned with the older man, but clearly they were of sufficient number to make a difference. She heard the clash of steel on steel from the bailey and the cheers of the villagers as the reivers were defeated.

The two warriors who had arrived with Laurent were Oscar and Bertram, valiant men who Elizabeth had known for at least ten years. Oscar was tall and fair, missing several fingers and most of his hair, and inclined to monosyllabic replies. Bertram was short and dark, a nimble man with flashing eyes, a scar on his cheek, and a fulsome manner with women. They often fought back to back, a partnership that appeared unlikely but which had always worked well. Once the ropes were cut and the attackers were trapped on the roof, they made a sport of jabbing at them with their swords, taking inspiration from Amaury but enjoying it far more. Indeed, they made a contest of who injured more reivers.

Laurent pointed out the window as the attackers began to flee. Several raced toward the firth, but the tide had changed and was now rolling in.

"They will not make it across," Elizabeth said. "The firth is too wide here."

Laurent nodded. "The ponies will manage to swim to shore. The men, perhaps not." He shrugged, indifferent to their fate.

A smaller company of attackers, presumably those with their wits about them, rode to the east. Amaury had loaded his crossbow and picked them off with his usual impressive aim. "They ride too fast," he muttered when Elizabeth reached his side. "Soon they will be too far away."

'Twas clear he wished to fell them all. Elizabeth opened his purse and handed him another bolt to assist him.

"How many are left?" he asked without glancing her way.

Elizabeth counted the bolts in the purse. "Six."

He grimaced. "Then we must make them count." Amaury loosed four more bolts in rapid succession, each one striking a reiver in the back of the neck or between the shoulders. They fell from their ponies and did not move again.

The two remaining men gave their heels to their steeds, their figures silhouetted in the road.

"Which do you think is Murdoch Douglas?" Amaury asked.

Elizabeth seized the reading glass and looked. "The one on the right is more his size."

"I think the same," Amaury replied and loosed the bolt.

Elizabeth was startled when the man on the left fell heavily to the ground. His pony raced away at a gallop. The man on the right looked back in alarm, and she could see his features through the glass. "We were right!" she said with satisfaction, surprised when Amaury lowered his crossbow. He tossed the last bolt into the air and caught it again, watching the steward flee.

"I thought you would strike him down," Elizabeth said.

"It is too far," he said, with a shake of his head, then gave her a sidelong glance. She was surprised to see a twinkle in his eyes. "Someone must take the tidings back to Robert de Maxwell. I thought he would be the most credible."

Elizabeth smiled her agreement, her heart so full that she could not summon a word of thanks for him. Amaury rested his hand on her shoulder for the barest moment, as if he understood, then turned to Laurent. The two men shook hands, Amaury thanking the former captain-at-arms for returning with such haste. James watched from the corner he had chosen, clutching his manuscripts, his features drawn. Oscar and Bertram were introduced to Amaury, all of them shaking hands, and Amaury acknowledged Twyla's contribution. The girl flushed with pride at his praise.

"We must see to that fire," Laurent said, leading Oscar and Bertram from the solar with purpose. None of them acknowledged James, which did not surprise Elizabeth. When Amaury made to follow them, her uncle cleared his throat and Amaury paused.

"You were right," the older man said with annoyance. "You were right and I was wrong. I owe you an apology, sir."

"You owe more than that," Elizabeth said to the surprise of both of them. "Amaury paid their outstanding wages with his own coin so that they would return."

James grimaced. "I will repay you, then."

"If you expect them to remain, you must add to that," Amaury added.

James visibly struggled with this, then sighed and nodded. "I will pay for them to remain through Epiphany, then we can review this matter."

A little more than a month. Elizabeth watched Amaury, wondering whether he would think it sufficient.

He nodded once. "It is a start."

"How long will you stay?" James demanded when Amaury turned to the portal again. Elizabeth watched Amaury stop and bow his head for a moment. "You came to warn me, so Elizabeth insisted. I have been warned and defended. Will you remain?"

"I have no place here," Amaury said and Elizabeth knew then that he had planned to leave soon. With or without her?

"Stay through Epiphany," James said, his grumpy tone making the invitation sound less gracious. "Someone must ensure that these men do their tasks and I have no understanding of it. I would have value for the coin!" When Amaury hesitated, James continued. "I will repay you then and only then."

Amaury sighed. "There is much to be done this day. We shall talk of this later."

He left, Twyla hastening behind him, then James muttered something and followed. Elizabeth found herself alone in the solar, with Amaury's purse clutched in her hand and tremendous uncertainty in her heart.

He would not leave Beaupoint without her, would he?

But it had been his plan to vanish and leave her to wed another once the safety of Beaupoint was assured.

She had no doubt that Amaury would ensure that all the injured attackers were dead, that the fire in the village was extinguished, and that he would retrieve his bolts. In the meantime, she would see that any injuries among the villagers were tended and the hall was once again set to rights. They would each fulfill their duties, as if they were lord and lady of the keep, but they were not and never would be.

Beaupoint, a religious foundation. She could not even think of it.

'Twas when she would have put Amaury's purse aside that she felt there was something else within it. She was startled to see that he had kept her red silk purse, the one that she had once cut to make a hood for Persephone. It seemed a thousand years ago that she had found the peregrine with her jesses snared on a branch, an eon since that day she had first glimpsed Amaury. How her heart had leapt then, as if recognizing that their futures might be entwined. How much he had taught her in less than a week; how much he had helped her to heal from the scars of the past.

And this man, who insisted he had no regard for emotion, had kept a token from that day.

She straightened, her heart warmed by the discovery, hoping it meant he would not abandon her now that his perceived duty was done.

Then she recalled the tribute from Sylvia bound to his scabbard and doubted his regard for her anew. He defended and protected her, to be certain, but Elizabeth doubted that would be sufficient to change his chosen course.

This man had a will of iron and convictions set in stone, and affection would never influence either.

'Twas in that moment Elizabeth realized she had lost her heart to Amaury.

~

AMAURY WORKED the rest of the night alongside Laurent and his companions, dousing the fire and gathering the dead. In addition to the former captain-of-arms, four warriors had returned to Beaupoint. Oscar and Bertram had been the two to follow Laurent to the solar, while Ealhard and Hugh had fought in the bailey and hall, defending the villagers. They were all gruff men and effective warriors, not dissimilar to those who followed Maximilian.

The ostler, Simon, had also returned with them. He was a merry fellow of about Amaury's age, and one who moved with brisk efficiency. Four boys accompanied the party, though Amaury did not hear their names, and Alfred, too, was in the company. Amaury praised the boy for his efforts and could see that he was pleased.

By the time the hall was in order, the horses had been brushed and fed, and the stables swept. Frederick was fussing over the peregrines, once again hooded and tethered to their perches, and Amaury could fairly hear James grumbling about the expense.

For his part, Amaury had never been so glad to see such a company of warriors in his life.

It proved that only one hut in the village had been burned to the ground and it had been an unoccupied one on the perimeter. The fire had leapt from roof to roof and many of the huts needed to be thatched anew. By the time, Amaury had seen the last of the dead gathered at the chapel, Father Owen was already organizing the repair of the roofs. Boys were gathering thatch and women bound it into clusters, more boys climbing the roofs to make the repairs. Heloise ordered them about with authority, and there was much merry whistling as they worked.

Amaury sent Laurent and his men to the kitchens to eat when the worst of the work was done, for they had ridden through the night to reach Beaupoint. Fortunately, there was stew and soup left from the feast, as well as some of the thin ale. The hall sounded right to him then, filled with warriors taking their ease, laughing and jesting with each other, recounting tales of the night before. The stables were no longer lonely and empty, and the boys bustled at their tasks.

Yet this place would become a religious house. It was beyond belief.

Amaury refused to consider James' request, not when there was so much to be done, but it grew in his thoughts as tasks were completed. His inclination was to leave with the dawn, for his duty was done. The hall had been defended and would be so through Epiphany. He did not think the reivers would return soon if ever, and there was the ideal match for Elizabeth in this Gavin de Montgomerie.

He should ride to Carlisle, despite his unwelcome desire to linger. Amaury could only take that as a reminder of love leading a man astray.

This time, he would choose for practicality and good sense.

IT WAS LATE in the afternoon when a party appeared on the road that ran from the village to Carlisle. It was a small company, on horseback, led by a man whose armor flashed in the sunlight. His destrier was a fine beast, a dapple with a dark mane, much like Elizabeth's mare. Amaury straightened and shaded his hand to look. The knight's insignia was of deepest green, graced with a white hart, but he did not recognize it.

Another knight rode slightly behind him, one who appeared to be younger, then two squires followed. They were all splendidly attired.

"Sir Gavin de Montgomerie," Simon muttered beneath his breath as if that were not a good thing.

Amaury's heart sank.

Elizabeth's ideal suitor had arrived.

It was time for him to leave.

Simon took his silence for a lack of information. "His father's holding is south of Carlisle, sir. He offered once for the lady's hand, but her father declined."

"I was told as much." Amaury watched Laurent step forward to greet the arrival. It was clear they knew each other, for their voices were hearty and this Gavin laughed merrily.

"His younger brother, Nigel, rides with him," Simon said, more approval in his tone. "He is a fine man, the echo of his father even now."

Once again, Amaury knew a profound dislike of a stranger, without hearing a word from that man's lips. Truly, Elizabeth's whimsy tainted his own choices. Impatient with his thoughts, he strode forward to greet the guest.

Gavin de Montgomerie was perhaps a decade younger than Amaury, proud and handsome, a man with chestnut hair and bright green eyes. He had the assurance of a man raised in wealth, a confidence Amaury had once shared. To his eyes now, it made the other man appear young. Gavin's smile was ready and his laughter quick, but Amaury's initial dislike only grew stronger when they spoke.

There was something in the other man's manner that seemed assessing. Though he possessed a certain charm, which he was unafraid to use, it seemed to be only a patina. He never halted in his survey of Beaupoint and Amaury could fairly taste the other knight's lust for this holding.

Elizabeth's father had declined his suit because he thought them too young. That could no longer be a concern.

He recalled Elizabeth's confession that she had argued with her father over the matter and guessed that her choice had been made years before. So be it.

"I bid you welcome to Beaupoint," Amaury said.

"Laurent, you did not tell us that there was another warrior in Beaupoint's service," Gavin said with a smile that did not light his eyes. He surveyed Amaury, and Amaury did not fail to note that the other man failed to introduce himself, and did not offer his hand.

"First warrior, to be sure, sir," Laurent replied. "For Lady Elizabeth is wed to him."

Gavin's brows rose. "Wed? Why did we not hear of these joyous nuptials?"

"The lady and I met at Kilderrick," Amaury said smoothly. "And pledged to each other there."

"I thought she was to wed Calum Moffatt."

"The lady had other notions." Amaury offered his hand. "I am Amaury d'Evroi."

"Gavin de Montgomerie, of course," the other knight said, spurning Amaury's hand. He touched his heels to his steed. "I must confer with the lady and ensure her welfare. How terrifying it must have been for her to endure this assault." His tone almost implied the attack was Amaury's fault. "Elizabeth!" he called, as if to ensure that all knew he was sufficiently familiar with the lady to address her with such familiarity. His squires followed behind them, each of the three boys splendidly attired.

Elizabeth stepped out of the keep and Amaury heard her voice raised in greeting. The new arrival dismounted and bent low over her hand, the sight of them together making it clear to Amaury that they were well acquainted—and that the other man's arrival was welcome. Elizabeth laughed at some comment he made, her manner almost flirtatious.

Laurent cleared his throat. "I was at Clyfford Manor when Alfred found me, sir," he said gruffly. "I rode there in search of a post, for it is the finest holding close to Beaupoint and the baron is known to be fair. I had no notion Sir Gavin would follow us."

"But he did not follow in sufficient time to come to the lady's defense," Amaury felt compelled to note.

"Aye, though his steed is finer than mine," Laurent said, shaking his head. "But then, a gentleman could not be expected to ride so hard as we did. He would have taken his comfort at night at an inn."

"Of course," Amaury agreed smoothly, knowing that he would not have halted for any reason if he had believed Elizabeth to be in peril.

"I apologize, sir, that my departure caused him to arrive so suddenly as your guest."

"The lady is pleased so all is well," Amaury said. "What can you tell me of him and Clyfford Manor? Forgive me, for I am not of these lands and do not know the reputation of men and houses."

Laurent nodded. "Sir Gavin's father, Thomas de Montgomerie is the Baron of Clyfford, and also Lord Warden of the March."

"I do not know this term."

"It is he who appoints the three lords who serve the king as guardians of the border." Amaury must have looked blank, for the older man continued. "There should be three, sir, on each side of the border, appointed to keep the peace. On the Scottish side, the Warden of the Western March is Sir Archibald Douglas, and indeed, he fills the other posts as well. On the English side, the Warden of the Eastern March is Lord Henry Percy, first Earl of Northumberland and he defends the Middle March, as well. The wardship of the western march has been unassigned since the demise of Lord Percival de Beaupoint."

Amaury turned to the other warrior in surprise. "Lady Elizabeth's father was the Warden of the Western March?"

Laurent nodded again. "Aye, sir. And reivers did not have such success in his time, to be sure."

And so Beaupoint had greater value even than the keep itself, or the charms of the former lord's daughter. The man who claimed it might also be awarded a post of both esteem and responsibility—if it did not become a monastery.

No wonder the lady's hand was so keenly pursued.

Elizabeth had told him that Beaupoint was always at root and he could see why.

"But it has been several years since his death," Amaury said. "Why has the post not been reassigned?"

Laurent smiled. "Who can say? Perhaps there are not seen to be any suitable contenders."

James came out of the keep then to greet Gavin and both warriors watched him. Neither commented, but Amaury watched Gavin and Elizabeth laugh together, utterly at ease with each other. Even James greeted the younger man heartily and Amaury felt his mood turn foul.

"We must move the rest of the fallen to the chapel before we halt," he informed Laurent and turned back to the labor that had to be done.

Their guest could wait for his attention.

Amaury did not doubt that Gavin would be content to speak with Elizabeth in his own absence.

TRUST GAVIN TO arrive at a most inconvenient time.

Elizabeth wanted to speak with Amaury but duty consistently intervened. She had only just restored the solar to rights and ensured that all was organized in the hall. She had greeted Laurent and his men when they came to dine and ensured that they felt their efforts were appreciated. And now, in the moment she was free to pursue Amaury, Gavin arrived.

What a gift he had for being irksome.

He was as handsome and gracious as ever, confessing a concern for her welfare, even troubling to charm her uncle. Elizabeth felt obliged to welcome him to Beaupoint and even to speak with him. Amaury himself would insist it was her duty.

But would Amaury remain until Epiphany? She had a sense that the promise of his coin being repaid to him had not been compelling. No doubt he was intent upon riding to France and Sylvia without delay.

She had to speak to him and soon.

But Amaury did not come to the hall. Elizabeth should not have expected otherwise. He would see every task completed first. There were injured villagers to be tended and corpses to be gathered for blessing and burial. She had noticed that he ensured that he spoke to those who had fought for Beaupoint, encouraging them and their efforts, invariably leaving each with a more satisfied expression than before.

There were four of them, Gavin and his younger brother, Nigel, as well as a pair of squires. Nigel, it was clear, had earned his spurs since last she had seen him. Elizabeth congratulated him, always having liked the younger son of the baron. He was quiet but his manners were courtly, and he had always been in awe of his more flamboyant brother.

Upon their entry to the hall, her uncle retreated to his little chamber, so she alone was left to entertain the new arrivals.

Elizabeth had the curious sense of having been abandoned.

"Well, Beaupoint is not what it was," Gavin said, surveying the hall with dissatisfaction. "Truly, my lady, you might as well live in the village for all the comfort of your hall."

"You will recall, sir, that the keep was besieged just hours ago."

"But still." Gavin kicked at the rushes on the floor, many of them stained with blood. "One must see the servants well trained."

"There is only Harriet at this moment and she does her best."

Gavin sighed.

"Perhaps you should return to Clyfford," Elizabeth suggested. "Where there are more comforts to be savored."

Gavin granted her a brilliant smile. "Ah, but there is no lady so admirable in that hall."

How strange that once his praise had made her heart flutter and now it left her cold.

"I rather like your mother," she said quietly and Nigel smiled at her.

"You understand my import better than that, Elizabeth." Gavin fixed her with a look of admiration, then took the best seat at the board. He cast an imperious glance at the dwindling fire on the hearth and one of his squires hastened to kindle a brighter blaze. The other ran for wood. "Tell us of Calum Moffatt. Were you not wed to him?"

"I was but briefly. He died."

Gavin's eyes brightened. "And you are returned to Beaupoint, a widow?"

Nigel cleared his throat. "Laurent said…" he began but Gavin waved him to silence.

"Always let a lady recount her own tale, Nigel," he chided. "It is discourteous to do otherwise."

Elizabeth wondered what she had ever found attractive about this man. They had known each other since childhood, of course, but it seemed a year away had lifted the scales from her eyes. Gavin was always gracious, but now she sensed an anger in him, as if he believed himself to be owed a due. Had he always been thus? Had he changed or had she not discerned his truth? Her distrust of him was undeniable.

Still, he was a guest.

"I returned to Beaupoint, wed to the knight Amaury d'Evroi," she corrected, amused that she sounded so demure.

"But why?" Gavin asked, leaning closer. "Elizabeth! Who has ever heard of him? Who arranged this match? What do you know of his family and his connections? It is a most unacceptable arrangement. I must speak to your uncle about this matter."

"*I* chose," Elizabeth said as Harriet brought a pitcher of ale into the hall. The girl halted at her lady's tone and looked between lady and knight.

"*You* chose?" Gavin laughed. "Truly, Elizabeth, you have learned the most absurd notions. It must have been at Kilderrick. One hears much of the witch and virago Alys Armstrong. No doubt you were in her debt and fell under her influence. We shall see such foolery rapidly dismissed."

Elizabeth nodded to Harriet, who poured ale for the knights, then vanished into the kitchens again. She sat down stiffly at the board, having declined a cup herself, and wished Amaury would arrive. "A widow has the right to choose for herself. So my father always insisted."

"And yet, Beaupoint was assaulted. Was this the result of your nuptials? Is your new husband so despised that battle follows him?" He shook a finger at her. "You have a responsibility to those in this keep, Elizabeth."

"I do not, not any longer. Beaupoint is my uncle's holding."

"But not for long, surely. He will die, and without a son. The holding will come to your lord husband's hand, as sure as the sun rises in the east each morning. You must dissolve this match and contrive a better one, Elizabeth. Your uncle grows no younger. Make haste in this matter." He sipped his ale, obviously confident as to who the better choice might be.

Elizabeth stood up. "You speak out of turn, Gavin."

He shook his head and spoke as if contrite. "After all these years, I thought there could be frank speech between us, Elizabeth. I am solely concerned with your welfare."

He was solely concerned with Beaupoint and she knew it well.

"That is kind of you," she said with a tight smile. "But I am convinced that I will be very fond of France."

He blinked. "France?"

"My uncle intends to turn Beaupoint to a monastery, as is his right as lord." Elizabeth spoke with a confidence she did not feel, and savored Gavin's dismay. "My husband and I will leave for France after the Yule, where he will enter the lists again. He was a great champion at the joust."

Gavin watched her as he sipped and she could sense his thoughts racing. Then he shook his head again and smiled, as if she were a fool. "You cannot truly believe that to be his plan? Elizabeth, you have become credulous."

"Why should I not believe him?"

"Because it is clear that he desires Beaupoint! Look at how he administers the holding as if it were in his own hands already."

"Amaury does what needs to be done. He is a man greatly concerned with responsibility and duty."

Gavin smiled sadly, as if she were witless.

Amaury strode into the hall then, followed by Alfred and the three dogs. Elizabeth heard his low murmur as he gave the boy instruction, then he came to the board and Alfred went to the kitchens.

"My lady." He bowed to her, his manner so formal that she could not guess his thoughts. Again. "Father Owen asks you to attend the funeral mass this afternoon for those who fell in defense of Beaupoint. There will be another for the fallen reivers. Father Owen prefers to keep the services separate and I agree with him. I hope that is suitable to you as well."

"Of course."

He glanced toward her uncle's favored chamber. "I must speak to your uncle. I am certain he would also attend."

"Of course." She gestured. "You have met Gavin de Montgomerie and his brother, Nigel?"

"One but not both," Amaury said, offering his hand to Nigel. He barely glanced toward Gavin. "I trust that you have both had a warm welcome."

"Very warm," Gavin said, and Elizabeth had the sense he meant to sow doubt in her husband's thoughts. "Elizabeth and I are old friends, of course. We fairly grew up together! Of course, I have a great interest in her choice of spouse."

"Indeed, she has done me the honor of putting her hand in mine."

"And that you travel to France for the lists."

Amaury nodded, clearly wondering at Gavin's queries. "The season will begin after Easter, as always." He bowed. "If you will excuse me, my lady. I will tell your uncle of Father Owen's arrangements, then wash before coming to the board."

Elizabeth nodded and watched Amaury go to James' chamber. They exchanged a few words then Amaury departed, Bête and Noisette trotting behind him. Gavin sipped his ale, watching Amaury go, and grimacing when Grise came to sit beside Elizabeth.

"I cannot abide dogs in the hall," he said. "They are so dirty, their fur filled with vermin."

"I like dogs," Elizabeth said. "And Amaury's dogs are most clean." Grise placed herself between Elizabeth and Gavin, fixing her gaze upon him like a silent accusation. Elizabeth patted the dog, feeling as if she had an ally in her husband's absence.

"When did you wed him, Elizabeth?" Gavin asked softly. "Is it so long ago that the match cannot be dissolved?"

"It was a month ago," Elizabeth lied and held Gavin's gaze in challenge.

His brows rose and he coughed delicately. "Yet I heard you wed Calum only a few days ago."

"He claimed he had a prior right…"

"Do you not see, Elizabeth? If you wed this knight first, then you were not a widow and the choice was not yours to make." Gavin dropped his voice to a confidential tone when Elizabeth could not think of a reply with sufficient speed. "I think, Elizabeth, that you are as ill at ease with an untruth as ever you were. I think that you are not wed to this man at all and that somehow, something has put you in his power."

Elizabeth cursed her own weakness, for she flushed crimson.

"I will not stand by and let you be abused, Elizabeth. I certainly will not let this fiend take you away to France."

"The choice is not yours!"

"But it must be," he insisted. "Do you not see? You will not survive to see France. He will abuse you and discard you. He might not even be a knight! Why has he even come so far north? You know nothing of him, his family and his reputation."

"I know all of Amaury I need to know," Elizabeth insisted. "He is a knight and a man of honor."

"And one successful in the lists," Gavin mused. "We shall see." He sipped his ale, his manner enigmatic, and she feared what he might do.

CHAPTER 15

Amaury returned to the board to find Elizabeth looking discomfited and Gavin clearly pleased. Their guest made an elaborate show of moving from the best seat, but Amaury did not take it. James scurried into the hall and sat in the lord's place while Amaury seated himself at Elizabeth's side. She flicked a quick glance his way and he knew that she was concerned about some matter.

Their meal was simple but hearty, and welcome after the night's activities. Amaury was breaking his fast at midday and was glad of the stew. Gavin chatted to James about the plans for the monastery during the meal and evidently the older man felt interrogated, for he was quick to excuse himself and retreat to his chamber again.

"Liar," Gavin said beneath his breath when James was gone.

Amaury glanced up in surprise, seeing that the knight's younger brother was also startled by the word. "I beg your pardon?"

"You are not wed to the lady," Gavin said.

"I have told you that we are wedded," Elizabeth said.

Amaury took Elizabeth's hand. Her fingers were cold. "My ring is upon her finger."

"And who witnessed this joyous union?"

"Marriage is the sole sacrament that requires no witness other than God."

"When were you wed?"

"A month ago, or so." Amaury smiled at Elizabeth. "When first we met at Kilderrick, we knew our hearts were as one."

"And what of Calum Moffatt?"

"He thought to disregard our match, and also assaulted the lady. We battled and I won."

"I think you lie. I know you lie. If you are wed to the lady, which I heartily doubt, you had no right to take her hand in yours." Gavin stood and cast down his gloves on the board. "I challenge your honor, sir."

"There is no need."

"There is every need," Gavin insisted, his eyes bright. "A lady I admire has been compelled to support your falsehood and I will defend her honor."

"But..." Elizabeth began to protest.

"You will not take her from this keep without a fight," Gavin said.

Amaury watched him. "You might take care whose word you dispute," he said, giving the other man a chance to recall his words.

"Because you have been a champion at the joust?" Gavin scoffed. "I doubt that tale, as well." He leaned on the table. "I think you have charmed Elizabeth for some dark purpose of your own. I would defend her honor. If you are such a champion, it should not trouble you to meet me on the field." He sneered this last and Amaury struggled to keep from responding in anger.

"The prospect does not trouble me," Amaury said finally. "But I think it unnecessary."

"I challenge you, whoever you are and whatever you call yourself," the other man said boldly. "In the name of Elizabeth d'Acron and for the memory of Percival d'Acron."

Elizabeth caught her breath. "No," she said, but Gavin raised a hand.

"No one will truly be injured, my lady," that man said, his eyes glinting in a way that told Amaury his intention was otherwise. "A duel of honor is like a jest, an entertainment, as your *husband* could tell you. If he has been such a champion, he should find it amusing to display his prowess."

"Save that I see no reason to do so," Amaury said.

The other knight reached into his purse and dropped a sack on the board. It jingled, fat with coin. Amaury realized he had prepared for this moment, that he had come to Beaupoint specifically to provoke a fight.

He had found one.

"*There* is a reason," Gavin said with challenge. "It seems that those residing at Beaupoint could use a measure of coin."

"Name your terms," Amaury replied and Elizabeth touched his arm. He closed his hand over hers, not averting his gaze from Gavin's.

"If you defeat me, the coin is yours." The other man opened the sack and let the coin spill on the board. It was a considerable sum.

"And if you defeat me?"

"You will leave the lady and Beaupoint without delay."

The terms should not have troubled Amaury, for he had every intention of leaving, but Gavin's words irked him so that he had to ensure his response did not show.

"Weapons of war or of peace?" he demanded.

"War, of course," Gavin said. "Only those in training fight with weapons of peace."

"*À plaisance* or *à outrance*?"

Gavin smiled. "*À plaisance*, of course. We are not barbarians."

Amaury wondered. Still, the other man was a knight. He was rich and local. Amaury did not doubt that Gavin meant to injure him, regardless of the rules, and would simply pay a fine for so doing.

And then he would wed Elizabeth once Amaury was gone.

It might be an ideal solution for the lady, but the truth was that Gavin's attitude annoyed Amaury. As much as he strove to remain impassive, he wanted to thrash this man before witnesses.

"We have an agreement," he said and thrust his hand at the other man. "We will meet Saturday next, here, in the space between the village and keep. Three bouts, whoever wins two will be triumphant, and you will chose the first weapon."

Elizabeth gasped outrage, but Gavin's eyes lit. "I will see you then, sir," he said heartily, and they shook upon it.

If each grasped the other's hand a little more firmly than was necessary, only they two knew that truth.

Though Amaury suspected both Elizabeth and Nigel guessed as much.

~

ELIZABETH FUMED for the rest of the day. Whether by accident or design —she could guess—she had no opportunity to speak to Amaury.

Even when he finally came to the solar, the dogs running ahead of him, Alfred and Twyla followed him.

"If you please, sir," Twyla said. "We would invite your decision."

Amaury raised a hand, inviting their question.

"I would ask to be your squire, sir," Twyla said. "But Alfred insists the task would be his."

"I do not have need of two squires," Amaury said.

"But you must have one to aid you at the joust in France," Alfred said. "It is thus in all the tales."

"And I would do it best," Twyla said.

Elizabeth wondered what he would say, but she did not interrupt.

"I think you would make a fine squire, Twyla," Amaury said finally. "You are clever and quick, and you already have skill with a knife." She smiled at this praise. "But that does not change the fact that it would be a most uncommon task for a maiden." He raised a hand when she would have protested. "People would make suggestions and accusations, for a squire must aid his knight at the bath, and I would not have any person in my service shamed for so doing."

Twyla's expression was downcast and Alfred's expectant.

"However," Amaury said and the girl looked up with hope. "My lady has need of a maid and I very much like the notion of her maid possessing your skill with a knife. My lady also has need of someone to continue her lessons in fighting. The other tasks of a maid are similar to those of a squire, tending of garments and so forth, but I think you would be a most excellent candidate for my lady's service." He cast a glance at Elizabeth. "Though the choice is the lady's, of course."

Elizabeth could never have resisted the appeal in Twyla's eyes. "I think it a wondrously good suggestion," she said. "Would you come at first light with hot water, please?"

"Aye, my lady. Of course, my lady. Thank you, sir!"

"And you, Alfred, I will meet you each morning in the stables. I must train this week and you must learn more of armor."

"Aye, sir!"

Amaury pointed to his back. "The lace of the hauberk, Alfred."

The boy unfastened it.

Dismissed, the pair raced down the stairs, laughing in their satisfaction, and Amaury closed the door. He sighed, pushing his fingers through his hair, and Elizabeth knew him to be tired beyond all.

"That was kindly done," she acknowledged as he bent to let his hauberk fall over his head.

"A decision worthy of Solomon himself," he said, rubbing his brow, then fixing her with an intent look. "I hope you did not feel that you had no choice in it."

"I thought it a perfect solution."

He studied her, no doubt seeing that she was vexed with him. He spoke, though, as if she was not. "You should train with weapons half the day and set aside time to wrestle with her here each day as well. The dogs will have to be locked outside, lest Grise take your side." He pulled off his boots and went to the windows, looking in each direction as had become his habit. She knew that he was pondering some matter.

Finally, he spoke and his tone was grim. "If ever you are assaulted, it will not be *à plaisance*, my lady. There will be no rules of fair conduct and you will be fighting for your life. Discuss this with Twyla. Her father and I share similar views, I believe."

His counsel was similar to earlier advice, but more dire. "Do you expect an assault?" she asked.

"I endeavor to prepare for all eventualities. No more than that." Amaury closed the shutters and sank down to the pallet with obvious relief. He closed his eyes and leaned his head back against the wall, even as Bête joined him there. "I shall sleep a week," he murmured, but Elizabeth refused to be swayed.

"You shall not sleep until we speak of this folly," she said and he opened one eye. "Your own uncle advised that no words should be left unsaid when one retired, and I would take his counsel."

"Aye," he murmured. "I thought as much." He closed his eyes again, but beckoned with one hand. "Tell me."

He was so calm, so implacable, that Elizabeth's annoyance soared anew.

"I should kill you myself," she said with heat and his eyes opened again. "I should take your own dagger and drive it into your heart while you sleep, if you insist upon such folly."

"You mean Gavin de Montgomerie."

"Of course, I mean Gavin! How could you agree to such a contest? How could you accept such a ridiculous challenge!"

"He assaults my honor. I cannot let his insult pass unchallenged."

"You might have defended yourself verbally."

Amaury was dismissive of that. "I saw no reason to prolong his visit to Beaupoint. He came in search of a fight. He intended to provoke me, at any price."

"You did not have to grant it to him."

"It was simplest. He is, I think, a man accustomed to claiming what he desires."

Elizabeth suspected the same but would not agree with him yet. "Why did you want to hasten his departure?"

"I did not like him," Amaury said mildly but did not elaborate.

"You do not know him." Elizabeth unfastened her own laces with a vengeance.

"I do not need to."

"I thought you could not find against a man before you knew him" She cast her kirtle toward a trunk. "I thought that was *irrational*."

He almost smiled but he did not so much as glance toward her. "It seems your convictions taint my own, my lady." His tone ensured that she felt no satisfaction in her influence upon him.

Indeed, he sounded as if she had done him an injury.

"I cannot see why you should be insulted by idle words," she continued. "He taunted you, no more and no less."

Amaury's next words were terse. "He said our match was not made. He called me a liar."

"Our match *is* a lie!"

He granted her a glittering look. "Then I should have agreed with him, ceded the point and ridden away this very day? Truly, my lady, we must contrive a signal that you might grant when you wish me to absent myself."

It was rare for his voice to rise, but Elizabeth did not heed it. "Of course, I do not wish you to stand aside, but you need not die for the sake of pride."

"Die for the sake of pride," Amaury echoed, shaking his head. "Your conviction that I will lose is most heartening."

"The divine favors justice in such combat. Our match is a contrivance and you will lose."

Amaury scoffed. "The divine has more important matters to attend. The winner will be the better warrior."

"He is younger."

"And I am more experienced."

"'Twas you who said you grew too old to joust."

"And maybe I have little choice in this matter." His eyes shone with conviction. "No one calls me a liar, my lady, without challenge."

Honor, duty and responsibility. Elizabeth could not overlook that he fought for all these things but not for her. Of course, Gavin had stung Amaury's pride in questioning his honor. "What does *à plaisance* mean?"

"For pleasure, of course."

Elizabeth flushed. "I understand that, but it seems to have a specific meaning in this instance."

Amaury nodded. "The alternative is *à outrance,* which is to the utmost."

"Then you will surrender when you are bested."

He gave her a look. "I will not surrender. I will win."

"I do not wish to be widowed!"

"I doubt you will be for long."

Elizabeth stared at him, aghast. "You also think you will lose," she whispered.

Amaury spoke with a temperance Elizabeth did not share. "I think your former suitor is not a man who concerns himself overmuch with rules or other constraints. I believe his primary interest is in the triumph of his own will, no matter the cost to others."

"You are unkind. You do not know him!"

"I do not want to, truth be told."

"You have found against him on the basis of an impression, no more and no less."

"I am advised that such instinct is a worthy guide."

Elizabeth studied him, knowing there was some suspicion he did not share. She paced the room, then crouched beside him. "Do you think he will cheat?" She could scarcely utter the horrific possibility herself.

Amaury flicked a glance her way and she thought he would not reply, but then he did. "I think you would be advised to watch matters closely, my lady. If he does as I anticipate he will, you may have a claim against him. The king or his sheriff might grant you a reward for your loss and that would grant you more choices than you might have otherwise. If he does not, then no harm is done in your scrutiny." With one last intent look, he stood, stretched as if they discussed nothing of greater import than the weather, and moved to open the shutters to look out the window over the firth again.

Elizabeth surveyed the solar, not even seeing it as she considered his words, and shook her head. "How is it that I should come to be wed to a man so irksome as you?" she asked, not truly expecting a reply.

"Perhaps your next marriage will bring you greater satisfaction." He looked across the firth one last time, then closed the shutters and laid down. He tugged his old cloak over himself and closed his eyes as if weary beyond all. Bête clearly found this satisfactory and Elizabeth watched his hand slide into the dog's dark fur.

"How can you speak so lightly of this?"

"How can I not?" he asked. "I assure you that I will do my best to influence results, but what will be will be. Ask your uncle. He will tell you about God's will."

Elizabeth stared at him but when he did not open his eyes, she shook her head. "I *should* kill you in your sleep," she muttered.

"And your uncle would wed you to Gavin on Saturday for that sack of gold. It would be most expedient."

"Wretch!" she whispered, then flung a slipper at him. Grise sprang after it and brought it back to Elizabeth, her tail wagging.

"I could sleep on my feet this night," he murmured.

"If you leave your wife so irked, you might not awaken in the morning. I would be justified in taking a reckoning from you."

"Rumor will be fed if I sleep in the stables this night."

"I do not understand."

"I would wager that your admirer found himself a spy before he left." Amaury spoke with utter confidence and Elizabeth wondered whether he was right. There had been a time when all servants and villagers were loyal beyond all, but her uncle's frugality had likely changed that.

Noisette curled against Amaury's leg and he stroked each dog.

Elizabeth watched and waited, but he said no more.

She shed her chemise and washed, keenly aware that he did not even contrive to steal a glimpse. She climbed into the bed alone, feeling cold and disappointed. Amaury did not move but she wondered whether he was truly asleep. Grise, with her now customary familiarity, jumped onto the bed and laid down beside her. Elizabeth blew out the flame of the candle, then laid back, wide awake. "I suppose," she said finally. "That Sylvia never disliked a person on sight."

"I never heard her speak against anyone, man or woman," Amaury said. "She was a paragon of grace and elegance."

Elizabeth rolled over so her back was toward him, vexed by his praise. How curious that she should know without doubt that she would despise Lady Sylvia, yet she never had or never would meet that woman herself.

A paragon of grace and elegance—likely with all the opinions of a well-crafted tapestry.

AMAURY ROSE EARLY and left Elizabeth sleeping in the solar. His fate might lie in the hands of the divine, but he would do what he could to influence results. Grise remained with the lady but the other two dogs galloped down the stairs with him. It was barely dawn, but he had a great deal of training to do.

Praise be that Laurent and his fellows had returned. He had need of opponents to hone his skills again.

He passed Twyla on the stairs as she carried a bucket of water to the solar. He smiled at her enthusiasm, and found Alfred awaiting him in the stables with just as much.

How curious that a mere day ago, Amaury had been prepared to die in defense of Elizabeth. Now that he saw what awaited her in his absence, Amaury was determined to survive.

THERE WAS little chance to speak with Amaury that week and Elizabeth wondered whether he contrived as much deliberately. He was always at battle in the bailey, conferring with Laurent about the defense of the keep, listening to the concerns of the villagers. She found him helping with the thatch of the roofs one day, and even in conference with her uncle. He came late to the board and left it early, the surrounding company ensuring that Elizabeth could not have a word with him in private. He bathed in the stables and was often to be found teaching Alfred. He came late to bed, long after she had fallen asleep, and the sole sign of his presence in the morning was a chemise left upon that pallet.

For her own part, Elizabeth taught Twyla her new responsibilities. She ensured that the girl was clean and gave her an old kirtle, even braided her hair though it was short. The expressions of wonder when they first descended to the hall after the change were most gratifying. In the morning, Elizabeth threw knives in the bailey with Twyla and in the afternoon, they wrestled together in the solar while Grise whined outside the door.

She yearned for Amaury and wished beyond all to know his plans. On the night before the duel of honor, she tried to remain awake. Like every other night, though, the strenuous activities of the day ensured that she was asleep when he arrived.

She awakened in the night when Grise moved and found moonlight shining through the shutters on the eastern window. Amaury slept on his pallet, his breathing slow and deep. Elizabeth rose and crept across the room, crouching down before him.

"You avoid me, sir," she accused softly. There was the merest hitch in his breathing but otherwise no indication that he had heard her. Elizabeth chose to believe he was listening. "I think you fear to hear what I intend to tell you," she continued softly. "But I will do it all the same."

There was no acknowledgement of her words and the floor was cold. Elizabeth would say it and be done.

"I fear for you, sir, not because I doubt your skill. I fear for you because I cannot bear the possibility that I might lose you so soon as this." She swallowed, wondering whether she imagined that he seemed taut with attention. "Please triumph on the morrow, even if you must return to Sylvia. I could not bear to know that you were not yet in the world, even if we are parted." She leaned forward on impulse and touched her lips to his cheek. "I love you, Amaury d'Evroi," she whispered. "With all my heart and forevermore."

Her voice broke on those last words but he gave no indication that he heard her. He did not seem to breathe and she watched him sleep for a moment, glad that she had confessed the truth even if only Bête knew it.

She did not see his eyes open when she stood and returned to the bed.

Nor did she see the fierce resolve light within them.

SHE LOVED HIM.

Amaury rose early on the day of the duel of honor, unable to sleep after Elizabeth's unexpected confession. She was sleeping deeply, her braid over her bare shoulder, and he drank in the sight of her. Grise, also on the bed, opened her eyes and wagged. Amaury held a finger to his lips as Bête and Noisette sat down. Their impatience was evident. He dressed quickly in his chausses, chemise and boots. He planned to wash and don his armor in the stables with Alfred's help. His hauberk, sword and dagger were in the solar and he picked them up, then noticed Sylvia's token tied to his scabbard.

Enough.

No one would guess that he had such an abhorrence of deceit to look at his choices since leaving Kilderrick. On this day, he might die in service to this lady and it was time she knew the truth.

There were embers in the brazier and he stirred them to life, coaxing the fire to burn with greater enthusiasm. Elizabeth stirred as he cast the red ribbon into the flames. The smell was acrid and immediate, so strong that he knew it would awaken her.

And she would guess the import of what she found.

His beloved was keen of wit, after all.

Amaury beckoned and left the solar with all three dogs. Should he survive this day, there would be truth between himself and Elizabeth.

Elizabeth awakened when Grise jumped from the bed. As ever, the dog walked across her legs, so there was no missing her departure. Elizabeth grimaced and rubbed her eyes. She had slept badly, both dreading this day and wishing it might be over. She had spent hours regretting her confession and wishing Amaury had heard it, then wondering whether he might have.

There was a foul smell in the solar and she wondered at the cause. As soon as she opened her eyes, she saw the stream of smoke rising from the brazier, where there should be no smoke. She rose from the bed, frowning at the red ribbon coiled on the edge of the brazier. Half of it had already burned to ash and the rest would soon follow.

She knew this token all too well. It was the favor of Lady Sylvia from Amaury's scabbard, a token of that lady's esteem from some long-ago tournament. The sole grace, in Elizabeth's view, was that the lady herself—a paragon of grace as she understood—was also distant.

But Sylvia's token could not be burning by accident. It had been securely tied to Amaury's scabbard, doubtless by the lady's own hands, and had been there for as long as Elizabeth had known him.

Amaury had removed it.

Amaury destroyed it.

Because Amaury *had* heard her.

Of course, he would not make a similar confession, not until this contest was behind him. Impossible man. Elizabeth's heart sang all the same and she was digging in her mother's trunk when Twyla appeared.

"My lady?" the girl asked. "I thought you meant to wear the blue kirtle."

"Nay, Twyla," Elizabeth said, pulling her mother's favored dress out of the trunk and giving it a shake. She smiled, recalling her mother wearing it for the first time, on the day her father had been invested with the seal of Beaupoint by his own father. It was a majestic garment of black silken velvet, thick with gold embroidery in the shape of falcons. Essentially, her mother had worn the insignia of Beaupoint and she had been a glorious sight.

Elizabeth turned to see Twyla staring at the garment in awe.

"Today," Elizabeth informed her. "I arrive in splendor."

AMAURY WAS NOT the only one to stare when Elizabeth appeared, but he guessed his heart soared highest in admiration.

The day was crisp and clear, and there was a thin coat of frost upon the ground. There was no wind and Amaury could not fault the weather. He was standing in the bailey with the other men and the boys, Alfred fussing over his tabard. The boy had polished every item to a gleam and was determined to master all of his responsibilities with haste. His enthusiasm convinced Amaury he had made the right selection of squire.

Gavin had arrived with his younger brother, their horses had been tended, and seats were arranged near the hall. Gavin's armor shone in the sunlight as well, his fitted and short surcoat of green and white similar to the one graced with the insignia of de Vries that Amaury no longer wore. He did not wear a surcoat over his armor on this day. The weapons were laid out for their selection and three of the men-at-arms —Laurent, Bertram and Hugh—would judge. James had taken his seat and Nigel sat near the older man, one space between them. They waited only for Elizabeth and Amaury caught his breath when she stepped into the bailey.

She might have been a visiting queen. She wore a magnificent kirtle Amaury had never seen before. It was black, as deep a hue as the night sky, on one side and gold on the other, divided in half directly down the front. He thought it might have been made of silken velvet given its sheen. On the black side, falcons had been embroidered in gold upon the cloth in groups of threes, then in a line along the hem. The gold side had been hemmed and bordered in the black. It was tightly fitted to her slender figure, a line of golden buttons extending from the square neckline to her hips.

The sleeves were long and fitted, made of the black velvet, with golden buttons from wrist to upper arm. Long tippets hung from the sleeves above the elbow to the ground, made of shimmering gold. That square neckline was bordered in black and she wore a cross of amber stones set in gold that gleamed against the pale skin of her throat. Her gloves were fine golden leather as were her slippers, and her hair had been braided and coiled above her ears. She wore a golden circlet and a gossamer veil of gold that hung down her back. Her cloak was black as well, sweeping the ground and cut full. It was lined in silver fur that had to be from half a dozen wolves.

She swept to the central seat, her chin high and surveyed the gathering. Amaury found himself smiling as he bowed to her, though he could feel Gavin's surprise. She took a seat between Nigel and James, acknowledging each with a nod. She beckoned to Amaury then, a regal gesture he would not refuse, and he dropped to one knee before her.

"You have need of a favor, sir," she said softly, offering a black and gold ribbon. He turned the hilt of his sword toward her and she knotted it there, her gaze fixed upon his with rare intensity. He bowed his head and thanked her, kissing the favor while he held her gaze. Color touched her cheeks and he knew their thoughts were as one, a conviction that only increased his determination to triumph.

Father Owen blessed the contest. The villagers crowded into the bailey to watch. Twyla—a maiden transformed with Elizabeth's guidance—stood behind Elizabeth and James sat at her side. The older man fidgeted, clearly wishing he could be elsewhere. As Lord de Beaupoint, it was his duty to oversee. He raised a hand, indicating to Laurent that they should begin.

Amaury and Gavin strode to the middle of the bailey and shook hands. They both swept off their cloaks, surrendering them to their squires, then bowed to James and Elizabeth. Laurent indicated the weapons with a gesture.

"Swords," Gavin said, making the first choice. He handed his helmet to his squire. "Without helmets."

Amaury nodded and handed his helmet to Alfred, drawing his sword.

The hourglass was inverted and the match began.

Swords.

Without helmets.

'Twas clear the warriors thought this a more impressive choice than Elizabeth did. Both knights' helmets were of the basinet style, which fit like a cap with a chain mail aventail laced to the sides. The aventail covered the neck and top of the shoulders when the helmet was worn: without the helmet, their faces and throats were exposed.

Elizabeth could scarce sit still as Amaury and Gavin began to fight. She had hoped they might circle each other until the sand had mostly run out, but that was not to be. Gavin leapt forward immediately, slashing at Amaury, and his blade rang out as it struck Amaury's breast plate right above the heart. He fought in deadly earnest, but Amaury met him blow for blow.

This was no contest for pleasure alone.

They fought hard, back and forth across the bailey, the vigor of their blows making the crowd gasp. Each knight stumbled more than once. Gavin's blade cut Amaury's cheek when he lunged forward and Amaury retreated, but not quickly enough. Elizabeth gripped her hands together in her lap. Amaury nicked Gavin's chin with the tip of his blade, the ease of his gesture indicating that he could have delivered a more lethal blow if he had chosen to do as much. The warriors nodded approval of this. Their blades clashed again and Elizabeth did not know how she would endure three rounds.

Just before the sand ran out, Gavin lunged at Amaury, driving the point of his sword directly at him. Amaury spun out of the way, seized Gavin's wrist and flung him after his sword. Gavin spun in the last moment and jabbed upward, catching Amaury beneath the chin with the point of his sword and Elizabeth almost rose to her feet in fear.

"Time!" Laurent cried and the men stepped away from each other. Their faces were ruddy from exertion but they both moved with resolve. Neither was ready to cede.

Laurent conferred with Bertram and Hugh, then raised his voice again. "The first bout to Gavin de Montgomerie of Clyfford," he said and there was a bit of applause.

"I thought your father might join us," Elizabeth said to Nigel.

That knight shook his head. "He said the king does not approve of such private contests and that he would not be privy to one. Gavin wished him to adjudicate. In truth, my lady, they argued mightily over this match."

Elizabeth, yet again, was convinced that the baron was a most sensible man.

She took a breath as Laurent lifted a hand, inviting Amaury's choice.

"Crossbows," that man said crisply and Elizabeth exhaled with relief. Their blows would fall upon a target, not each other.

The quintain was brought from the stables and positioned near one wall.

"Shall we say nine shots?" Laurent said, his tone indicating that his was not a query.

Both knights nodded agreement, loading their weapons.

"If the lady will choose," Laurent said, indicating the sixteen sections that now divided the white shield. Elizabeth sent Twyla, who chose the uppermost left section then retreated to safety.

Amaury lifted his crossbow, aimed and his bolt buried itself in the middle of the section.

Gavin missed by a handspan.

Elizabeth sat back with relief, for she knew Amaury would triumph in this bout. She also knew he could not be injured.

Her relief was short-lived, though. Amaury hit all nine of the targets, while Gavin made six. The villagers greeted this result with enthusiasm. The younger knight's annoyance was more than clear, and it showed in his choice of weapons for the final bout.

"Maces," Gavin said, biting off the word. Even Amaury glanced toward him with a measure of surprise. Twyla's fingers dug into Elizabeth's shoulder, for both of them knew that a single blow from such a weapon could maim a man, if not kill him.

À plaisance. Elizabeth wanted to growl. What utter nonsense.

MACES.

If ever there had been a weapon that lacked subtlety of any kind and required no skill to wield, it had to be a mace. Amaury should not have been surprised by Gavin's choice. In this bout, he would be injured for certain unless he could keep his wits about himself. He had a nick on his arm and another on his thigh from Gavin's sword, neither of which were worthy of concern.

But a mace. All one had to do was let the spiked ball fall on a victim and bones would be crushed beneath its weight. Each of the two provided for the bout were the same, graced with a grip the length of two fists, a short run of chain, and then the spiked ball. These were of considerable size, bigger than a man's fist but smaller than a head. Amaury grunted beneath the weight of his weapon when he picked it up.

He could see the glitter of Gavin's eyes as he swung the mace in his place, his posture taunting as he faced Amaury. Laurent called the start and the other man swung hard, obviously intending to strike a lethal blow at the offset. Amaury evaded him and struck back, and they parried back and forth, Gavin aiming for damage and Amaury deflecting his blows. The maces hit the bailey heavily time and again, hard enough to make the ground leap.

The time was half gone when Gavin swung his mace with his full power. On impulse Amaury chose not to move away quickly enough. The spiked ball caught him across the right shoulder, the blow blunted by his armor but still enough to take him to one knee. He heard Gavin's triumphant hiss and chose to trick the blackguard.

He rose slowly to his feet, favoring the shoulder that had taken the blow, as if it was more injured than it was. Predictably, Gavin aimed at the same place, intending to compound the damage. Amaury deflected the second blow, but grunted as if in pain. Gavin moved quickly then, intent upon finishing what he had begun, and not paying sufficient attention to detail. He swung his mace high and struck Amaury on the same shoulder again. Amaury had ducked before the blow but collapsed to the ground as if the mace had taken him down. He rolled before the spiked ball could land upon him and it hit the earth heavily beside him.

The villagers gasped.

Amaury pretended it was a struggle to rise to his feet and let his right arm fall limp.

"Do you cede?" Gavin demanded.

"Of course not," Amaury replied, passing the weapon to his left hand. "One hand is as good as another." Gavin chuckled but Amaury moved quickly, swinging the mace at him and kicking at his feet. 'Twas clear his agility was unexpected, for the spiked ball struck Gavin's chest. His armor was dented and he darted out of range, fairly snarling in his fury.

"A lucky blow," he whispered in anger and Amaury dropped to his knees, as if the blow had nearly finished him. He bowed his head, as if to bolster his resolve.

The sand was running out.

Gavin would err now.

Amaury was still on his knees. Gavin lunged at him, swinging the mace with furious vigor. Someone cried out, but Amaury waited, holding his ground until Gavin was committed to the blow. Then he swung his own mace across the ground, letting the chain catch Gavin around the ankle. The other knight fell with a roar, then struck his head against the ground. His own mace swung into the air over his head and he did not move.

He had to be dazed.

Amaury lunged for the weapon and caught the spiked ball in his gloved hands. It was just a handspan above Gavin's head. The other man's eyes opened and their gazes met. Amaury saw the other knight's expectation that he would let the weight drop.

"Enough," he whispered, then cast the spiked ball aside beside Gavin's head. He saw the other man pale and close his eyes in relief, then noticed Gavin's lip curl as Amaury turned away.

It was a warning he would heed.

"Time!" Laurent called as Amaury walked toward Elizabeth with deliberate steps. He could see that she was ashen and her eyes were darker than he had ever seen them. This battle was not done and he knew it. He took another step then saw alarm light her eyes.

He spun to see that Gavin had risen to his feet, obviously intending to attack. In one smooth move, he punched the other knight in the face, liking the crack of his nose a little too well. Gavin staggered backward as blood erupted from his nose and he looked at Amaury in horror and hatred.

"Time was called," Amaury reminded him tersely, then pivoted to his lady again.

The moment had come for truth.

Elizabeth could scarce take a breath. She had been terrified that Amaury would be injured and now he walked toward her, as calm and confident as ever, while her knees trembled.

He said nothing, but turned to Laurent and extended one gloved hand, palm up.

Laurent hesitated only a moment before surrendering the bag of coin.

Amaury turned then and walked toward Elizabeth. His gaze locked with hers and she knew his decision had been made and he would not be swayed from it.

Whatever it was.

Her heart nearly stopped when he dropped to one knee before her. "My lady Elizabeth," he said, his voice husky and his eyes that vehement blue. Her heart fluttered just as it always had in his presence. "Will you repeat our vows this day, with this company standing witness, that there can never again be a doubt that we are wed?" He swallowed and her heart clenched as his words became husky. "I have only myself to offer you, my lady, but I am yours, heart and soul, forever."

There was no doubting that his words were heartfelt and sincere, not when his gaze clung to hers with such heat.

This man. Elizabeth swallowed and blinked back her tears, wondering how he could have any doubt of her reply.

But then it was Amaury: perhaps he did not.

The company murmured as Elizabeth stood up and offered her hand to him.

"Aye, sir," she said, smiling through her tears. "Aye, sir, I will."

The villagers applauded and cheered. Amaury rose to his feet and took her hand, touching his lips to its back. He turned her hand as he had before, and pressed a hot kiss into her palm, one that made her heart leap.

Elizabeth fairly flung herself at him and his arms closed around her, holding her captive against his chest. His armor was dirty. There was a bruise rising on his cheek and a cut on his lip. She knew he was hurt by the taut line of his jaw, but he stood as sturdy as a rock.

"We could go to the chapel on the morrow," she suggested in a whisper, fearful that he was more injured than she had guessed.

"Now," he insisted, his eyes flashing with vehemence.

"Now," she agreed with a smile. She had time to meet his resolute gaze before he bent and kissed her soundly as if indifferent to whoever might see. His kiss was filled with a passion he could no longer disguise from her and Elizabeth welcomed it with all her heart.

The company hooted, but Elizabeth did not care.

CHAPTER 16

Her second wedding was more consistent with Elizabeth's dreams. On this glorious December day, she put her hand in that of a handsome knight and a man of honor. Her heart was filled with joy. Amaury wed her for herself, not for Beaupoint. He wed her against his own conviction that matches should be practical: he wed her because he loved her.

Elizabeth could find no fault with that.

They walked to exchange their vows in the chapel at Beaupoint, and though her parents would not stand beside her, they had been laid to rest in that very chapel. Elizabeth felt that they witnessed the marriage and knew that her father would have approved of Amaury as a choice.

It was perfect that she had chosen her mother's most glorious gown for this day. The ribbon with Beaupoint's colors was both braided into her hair and bound upon Amaury's sword. The villagers accompanied them to the chapel, wishing her well, their admiration for Amaury already clear. Elizabeth's heart thundered when she glanced up at him on the threshold of the chapel and saw how he smiled at her. The sight warmed her to her toes and made her heart leap with anticipation of their night together.

He pledged himself to her, heart and soul.

She could desire no more than that. Oh, Amaury would protest about coin and shelter, about his future prospects and other such pragmatic concerns, but entering the chapel with him, Elizabeth knew her every desire to be fulfilled.

They were together and that was all that was of import.

Father Owen had hurried ahead and he greeted them at the door to the chapel. Elizabeth halted there beside Amaury. She was aware of her uncle on her other side, of the company gathered to witness their vows, but truly, there was only Amaury, the strength of his hand beneath hers, the heat of him beside her, the low rumble of his voice and the conviction that filled her heart.

She could scarce take a breath when he turned her to face him, then took her hands in the strength of his. He was bruised and battered, but resolute, as confident and certain as ever. His voice was resonant and deep as he made his vows, and she was thrilled to hear him pledge himself to her. No soul could doubt his devotion. He took the ring from her finger, the one that had graced his mother's hand, and held it over each finger—for the Father, for the Son and for the Holy Ghost—before sliding it onto her finger again.

It was impossible to believe that she had ever thought him impassive. Now, she saw the small lift at the corner of his mouth, felt the surety in his grip upon her hands, saw the determination and the love in his eyes.

This man. This glorious, infuriating, handsome and beguiling man. She hoped he would vex her and defend her and enchant her for all her days and nights.

There would never be another for Elizabeth and she knew it well. She did not care if they were destitute. They would have each other and that was more than blessing enough.

She would prove it to him.

Then the priest blessed them and Amaury's eyes shone so brightly that she could not look away. His fingertips rose to her cheek, his touch warm and gentle, then he bent to touch his lips to hers. He still held her other hand captive as his fingers slid to cup her nape and he lifted her to her toes, deepening his kiss. Elizabeth closed her eyes and surrendered, wanting more, yearning for all he had to give. Amaury angled his mouth over hers, his kiss turning hungry, and she placed a hand on his shoulder, drawing him closer, forgetting where they were.

"And that is celebrated sufficiently well for the moment," Uncle James said with impatience.

Amaury lifted his head, his gaze flicking to her uncle, and Elizabeth knew there was a twinkle in his eyes. The priest cleared his throat and invited all into the chapel to celebrate of the mass and Elizabeth felt that she led the company in triumph.

Despite the marvel the day had been, she could not wait for night to fall.

"FROM THE GROUND UP, ALFRED," Amaury said with patience. The boy was crouched behind him in the solar, endeavoring to remove his plate armor. "*Sabaton, greave, poleyn,* then *cuisse.* It is the order of the buckles. You will not manage it another way."

"Aye, sir. Of course, sir." The boy rubbed his brow.

"It is not like you to be uncertain," Amaury said. "What is wrong?"

The boy frowned. "I have not slept, sir. My mother has many guests since Laurent and his men returned, and I must wait until they are gone to go to bed myself." He yawned mightily. "I am sorry, sir."

"You always do your best, Alfred. No man can ask for more."

The boy smiled at that and continued as Amaury wondered what might be done.

He was exhausted himself. He had shed his gloves and unfastened his own sword belt, wincing at the weight of the scabbard. He would be black and blue on the morrow, no doubt.

But he was alive.

And Elizabeth had wed him in truth.

That was a detail to make his heart sing. He had retreated to the solar to wash and dress for the feast and he could not wait to sink into the hot water in the tub.

He was far from alone with Alfred in the solar. The tub that Elizabeth used had been placed in the middle of the chamber and a veritable stream of servants and villagers carried hot water up the stairs from the kitchens to fill it. The dogs darted back and forth and Elizabeth gave directions to no avail.

"It is like a king's court in here," she complained, then cast him a smiling glance. "They *all* wish to speak to you."

She was right. Virtually every person bowed before him and congratulated him on his victory. Most also offered felicitations for the marriage to Amaury and Elizabeth both, and he wondered how many of them had doubted the tale that they were already wed. Each then took his or her vessel back down the stairs and was replaced by another well-wisher. There was a loud ruckus of chatter and laughter from the great hall and he assumed that ale had been poured.

He hoped they had a great quantity of it for he did not intend to leave this chamber soon. The only mercy was that he did not need a bonesetter. Erwina, the healer from the village, had brought herbs and salves, pronouncing that her daughter Audry's skills were not needed. Elizabeth had listened to Erwina's instructions and sent her away.

When the tub was full, Elizabeth was behind Amaury, unlacing his hauberk.

"The water will become cold," she said and he let the hauberk fall over his head. His aketon had to be peeled free of the blood against his skin, which made him catch his breath. Elizabeth gasped.

"It is naught," he said.

She scoffed. "I thought there was to be honesty between us, sir." She ran her fingertips across his shoulder and Amaury guessed that the bruise from the mace was rising. "*À plaisance*," she said beneath her breath with evident disgust. "Only a man could believe that term was fitting."

Then she turned to Alfred. "Take what you can now and return later for the rest."

"But," the boy began to protest.

"I will tend my lord husband," Elizabeth said firmly. "Take the dogs when you go and close the door."

"Aye, my lady," Alfred said, his uncertainty clear.

He left, though, whistling for the dogs, who all descended the stairs noisily.

"He likes routine," Amaury said, rising to his feet and pleased to discover that he was less sore than he had feared.

"Do not tell me that this will become routine," Elizabeth said.

"With the armor. He polishes the pieces in order. He is quite fastidious."

"He will not be polishing much on this night," she said.

"Do you think Heloise would be offended if the boy came to live in the hall? He could help Simon when I had no tasks for him."

"Heloise will accept whatever you decree. Come to your bath, sir."

Amaury waved away her assistance and climbed into the tub himself. "I am not so far into my dotage as to need assistance into a bath." He sank down into the hot water and closed his eyes.

"And I am glad that you may yet have the chance to become elderly." Her vexation made him smile.

He heard her lacings being unfastened, a sound that he had come to find most arousing, and opened his eyes to find that she was shedding that fine kirtle. Her boots and stockings were already cast aside, along with her girdle, and he dared to watch her openly as she shed the fine garment.

She smiled at him. "It was my mother's," she said. "Made for the day my father was granted the signet ring to Beaupoint."

"She wore his colors."

"She did." Elizabeth blushed a little. "I thought it was a day to be splendid."

Amaury chuckled as he leaned back in the hot water. "And so you were. I have never seen the like of you before this day. Do you change for the feast?"

"I thought to scrub your back."

"Did you?" His interest stirred. "I have never understood that nudity was required for that task. I shall have to tell Alfred."

"Was that a jest?"

Amaury only smiled.

Elizabeth lifted the cloth and he opened his eyes to find her enticingly close. "I do not trust that I might remain dry."

"I like a woman with her wits about her."

"You said you liked a woman who was willing," she charged, her eyes shining.

He had said that, though it seemed years had passed since they had made camp at Annan. "On this day, I cannot continue your lessons with a knife," he said.

"On this day, I would have you continue another lesson," Elizabeth said, untying the lace at the neck of her chemise. In the late afternoon light, he could see the shadows of her curves beneath the garment and could imagine the silken softness of her skin. The last light of the sun vied with the light from the candles in the chamber to illuminate her beauty. "I will have this match consummated before you leave this chamber, sir," she said and walked toward him with purpose.

"I believe it to be consummated already."

"It is the order that matters," she chided, her tone scolding but her eyes dancing. "Vows first, then consummation. To invert the sequence means you must begin again."

He leaned back in the tub to watch her. "I apologize. My experience with marriage is limited."

Elizabeth laughed, a most merry and delightful sound. "I do not intend that mine shall become more extensive." She shook a finger at him. "Nor yours, sir."

"You have a moment, my lady, to consider that I still have nothing to my name."

"Then why did you wed me?" She began to wash his back. Amaury leaned forward and closed his eyes in pleasure.

"Because I am not facing such a challenge willingly again."

She bent down, her face close and her eyes gleaming. She would demand something of him now and Amaury could not wait. "You burned her token," she whispered with undisguised satisfaction.

"I left you a message."

"You could have awakened me."

"I could have, but I knew you had not slept well…"

"You *did* hear me last night!"

"But I do not make promises I cannot keep. I did not know what would happen this day, but I resolved that if I survived, there would be truth between us this night."

She abandoned the cloth and crouched down beside the tub, her gaze level with his. "And what is the truth, sir?"

"That I love you," Amaury said and the words were so right that he wondered at his own ability to hold them back for so long. Now he wanted to say them over and over again.

"You do not believe in love," she insisted, wincing as she removed the blood from the scratches on his shoulder. Her gaze was challenging. "You told me as much yourself."

"It is true that I do not believe love to be sufficient reason for a match."

She fixed him with a look. "And yet, here we are."

"You are most persuasive," Amaury said but she did not smile. He straightened. "But also you taught me that love is more than mere attraction."

"I taught you?" She feigned surprise.

"You are also a woman of good sense. Do you truly believe that I would spend all my coin, change my course and risk my very life for someone I did not hold in high regard?"

"You might do as much for *duty*," she accused but her eyes had begun to twinkle. "And you kept my purse."

He smiled as their gazes locked and held. "I did."

"Let us have this honesty between us, truly. You did not believe love to be sufficient justification for marriage until you saw me in the forest."

"No. That was when I knew I loved you. I did not imagine we would wed."

"Why did you love me? Because you found me alluring?"

"Because you were kind," he said, seeing her surprise. "Because you showed kindness to Persephone when she was lost and afraid, at some risk to yourself."

Elizabeth's eyes narrowed. "And what of Sylvia? Did you love her for her kindness?"

Amaury frowned. "For a long time, I believed Sylvia to be all a woman should be. She was beautiful and sweet in nature. She admired me and she was wealthy beyond all." He shook his head, knowing he had to confess all. "And then I met a lady who did not always do as I suggested, who did not always reply as anticipated, and who did not have any qualms in telling me that I was wrong." He raised his gaze to meet Elizabeth's. "Sylvia would never have called me a wretch, but then, Sylvia never offered to me any favor she did not make available to all. Truth be told, I cannot find it within my own heart to care what happened to Sylvia."

Elizabeth's smile was brilliant. "But still you argued against love and its merit."

"Because if you had guessed that I already loved you, then you might have followed your own impulse and erred mightily."

"By choosing for love?"

"By failing to consider practicalities. I did not wish to be responsible for any hardship that might come to you."

She appeared to find this most satisfactory. "You lied about love to protect me from my impulses and your situation."

"Precisely."

"Yet on this day, you resolved that I should take a man who deliberately deceived me to husband, even though he has only himself to give?"

He nodded agreement. "It is not logical in the least. You see the evidence of your influence upon me."

She placed a fingertip over his lips to silence him. "But the heart speaks true." She smiled. "I say it is more than enough to wed a man of honor and integrity, a man who defends me at his own expense, and a man who I can trust completely."

"Do not forget that I will have to go to France for the lists in the spring," he warned her.

"Do not imagine that you will leave me behind," she said with a familiar ferocity.

"I would not dream of it," he vowed and she nodded satisfaction.

"And we will remain here until Epiphany?"

Amaury winced. "I would leave sooner."

"And surrender your coin to my uncle."

"I have my gain from this day."

"But I would stay until Christmas."

Amaury frowned. "I fear this dispute may not be resolved," he began, but Elizabeth kissed him to silence.

"It is not sentimentality that urges me to stay but duty," she said. "Father Owen always says a mass on Christmas Day for those who are departed. I would honor my mother and father one last time before we go. I may never return to Beaupoint." He wavered before her appeal. "Please, Amaury. It is only a few weeks."

He nodded agreement, unable to refuse her this. "That is the last of it? We are agreed?"

"Upon what?"

"Upon the consummation of this match, loudly and with enthusiasm, that none in the hall can doubt the state of matters."

Elizabeth fought a smile, feigning shock, and lost the battle. "You would not do as much," she protested but he saw in her sparkling gaze how the notion pleased her. "Not while they await us at the board."

She should have known better than to challenge him.

Amaury caught her around the waist and she gasped as he pulled her into the tub. She landed atop him with a splash and a gasp, and he ran his hands beneath her chemise, pushing it over her head so that her skin was bare against his own. She cast the wet garment on the floor then wrapped her arms around his neck, her eyes dancing with merriment.

"Do you prove yourself to be a rogue in the end?" she teased.

"Witnesses, my lady," he murmured as he pulled her closer. "It is always advantageous to have witnesses."

"For there was the flaw in our original tale," she whispered. "You are right again, sir. We must leave no doubt." And then she kissed him with such sweet fervor that Amaury forgot the feast, the company in the hall and every detail save the lady in his arms.

ELIZABETH THOUGHT her heart would burst with joy. Amaury loved her and he had wed her, though she was no heiress and Beaupoint was not part of the bargain. He fought for her and cherished her and kept his vows to her. This match was all she had ever desired and more.

She would love him through eternity.

They would go to France and they would be together. She could readily imagine them riding south with Zephyr and Blanchefleur, the dogs running alongside, Persephone on Amaury's fist. She knew already that she would like his uncle, Raymond, for Amaury admired that man greatly. And though she feared to see Amaury enter the lists, she had to believe he would triumph.

Love would conquer all, just as it did in the tales.

She was cradled atop Amaury in the tub, framing his face with her hands as she kissed him. She did not disguise her relief at his victory, nor did she restrain her response. They were wed and she would ensure he had no cause to regret it. There would be no secrets between them. She knew that life with Amaury would be infinitely better than one without him, and she was determined to convince him of the same.

His hand swept over her and he smiled with a surety that warned her of his intent. She fairly purred when his hand eased between her thighs and she kissed him again as he caressed her. Her blood quickened and her skin flushed, evidence that he had already learned what pleased her most.

"Tell me again," she whispered, kissing his ear.

"I love you," he said, then halted his amorous assault. Elizabeth made a little cry of vexation, though his eyes were twinkling. "But am I alone in this?" he asked softly.

"I love you as well and you know as much," she said.

His satisfaction was evident. "Then we celebrate that mutual affection."

"And our marriage," she had time to say before he eased his fingers inside her. He watched her closely as his thumb moved across her, his other hand around her waist as he held her captive to his touch. When he closed his mouth over hers in a demanding kiss, Elizabeth clutched his shoulders and returned his embrace. Already she trusted in the result she knew to be inevitable.

And when the wave of release came, it was so astonishing in its vigor that she shouted aloud. She thrashed against Amaury so that the water splashed over the sides of the tub.

He cast his head back and laughed, his eyes shining so that she knew he considered this another victory.

She reached down in the water to caress him and his laughter fell silent. He whispered her name, the very sound so filled with delicious agony that she felt her passion rise again. She shifted in the water, straddling him, and he whispered an entreaty.

Then Amaury stood abruptly, sending more water over the sides of the tub. Elizabeth clung to his shoulders and wrapped her legs around him, noting how he glanced down at her, her skin glistening with water, and shook his head in silent admiration. He braced his feet against the bottom of the tub and lifted her against him, moving inside her as if they were meant to be united as one.

This time, it was Elizabeth who whispered his name and she watched, beguiled, as he smiled slowly. She felt him grow taut and rubbed herself against him, liking when he cupped her buttocks in his hands and moved with power. They stared into each other's eyes as the tempest rose between them, each endeavoring to make it last longer and longer, until finally Elizabeth ground her hips against him. The pressure made her cry out in release again and Amaury gripped her more tightly, roaring with satisfaction as he surrendered to his own release.

She leaned her forehead against his shoulder, striving to catch her breath. "They might have heard us in the hall," she whispered, suddenly horrified.

Amaury chuckled, untroubled. "Then there will be no doubt, lady mine. The match is made and no man can put us asunder." He sank back down into the bath with her atop him and gave her another thorough kiss, one so hot it might melt her very bones.

Aye, Elizabeth was satisfied with her situation, indeed.

IN THE HALL BELOW, the sound of the lady's pleasure in the solar above could not be missed. The revelers fell silent to listen as Elizabeth cried out again in apparent ecstasy and more than one endeavored to bite back a grin.

"More ale!" Laurent cried and began a song.

Gavin looked sour as well as bruised, though he drained his cup with a savage gesture.

Overhead, a man roared.

The lady laughed.

The man laughed in his turn and the maidens in the hall blushed.

"There is no doubt of that, then," James said and accepted a cup of ale urged upon him by Laurent, after a moment's hesitation.

"To the happy couple!" Laurent cried, raising his cup. "May they long thrive together!"

"To the happy couple!" the tribute was echoed by all. The health of Elizabeth and Amaury was then saluted with such enthusiasm that the lady's subsequent cry of pleasure was almost—but not quite—obliterated from earshot.

Gavin drank the toast, then rose to his feet and strode from the hall in poor temper. His companions were startled, then quickly followed him.

"Fewer for the meat," James said with satisfaction. "That suits me well enough. There will be sufficient for the morrow this way." He beckoned to Harriet. "Bring me more of this ale. I am paying for it and will enjoy it."

"How long do you intend to remain at Beaupoint?"

Amaury was startled by the question and turned to find Elizabeth's uncle watching him. It was late on the night after the duel of honor. He had gone down to the stables to verify that all was in order and had been leaving the hall when James spoke. The older man sat alone in his small chamber, wrapped in his dark cloak, his eyes bright with curiosity. A candle burned there and the fire in the hall had burned down to ashes. The men would return to sleep in the great hall, but they were playing games of chance in the stables and ensuring the last of the ale did not go to waste. Heloise lingered there with them.

"I am not certain as yet." In truth, Amaury would like to depart soon. He did not trust Gavin to forget that he had been denied his desire and the sooner Elizabeth was far from Beaupoint, the better. He had agreed to stay until Christmas at her request, but the choice made him uneasy.

James beckoned to Amaury, indicating a stool beside him. Amaury crossed the hall and sat down with the older man. James fixed him with a look. "You should know that I guessed the moment I heard it that the tale of your marriage was untrue."

"Ah," Amaury said, not knowing what to say in his own defense.

"She had not the assurance of a woman who knows her allure, not before this day," James said. "I suspected she was yet a maiden as a result. And you, I have no doubt, would not leave your lady wife untouched."

Again, Amaury did not know what to say. He assumed that he was to be chastised and was surprised that the older man was smiling at him.

"You think I know little of such matters, and you are right that I have not enjoyed them myself. I had a brother, though, a brother filled with vigor who savored all the pleasures of this world." He sighed.

"Elizabeth's father," Amaury guessed.

"A man of principle, who did not hesitate to speak his thoughts aloud. A man who upheld justice and defended the weak. A man of honor, integrity and valor." James slanted a glance at Amaury. "You remind me of him, very much."

"I thank you, sir."

"And truth be told, when you rode through the gates of Beaupoint, I thought it was Percival returned from the dead, come to demand a reckoning for my treatment of his daughter. If ever a man could have done as much, it would have been him. Percival did not accept that any obstacle should stand in his path. I have often thought he would not accept death as one." James surveyed Amaury. "He was as broad and tall as you, and his destrier was as impressive. His hair was dark and his eyes brown, but such differences are minor. He would have liked you."

Amaury was glad to hear as much. "What treatment of the lady would he hold against you, sir?"

"That I promised her hand to that deceptive cur." James shook his head. "My instincts were against it, but he had a charm about him and I thought my lack of worldliness was at root. And in the end, I discovered that possessions held a greater allure for me than I had realized. The coin was irresistible, even for me, in such quantity." James grimaced. "But I knew, I knew from the moment it was in my hands, that I had done Elizabeth a disservice. I simply did not know how to repair it. I could not return the coin, for I had made commitments. I could not break my vow to Calum. I did not expect Elizabeth to flee, much less for her to vanish. Percival would have had much to say of my error, to be sure."

Amaury could think of no consolation to give. It seemed he was in agreement with a dead man, but he had made errors as well.

"Beaupoint should have come to Elizabeth, you know," that man continued. "And it would have done so if she had been born a boy. But she was not, and Catherine did not bear a son, and so there was only a daughter. Percival was convinced that it would be folly to leave a holding to a maiden, for he always feared for the safety of those he held in esteem."

"It is a holding of great value," Amaury said. "With its view of the firth. And there are reivers and raiders aplenty in this vicinity. I would agree with his assessment."

"And so he left Beaupoint to me, knowing I wanted only my books and my solitude, my time in prayer. He called it my family duty to take Beaupoint, and so I endeavor to do my best. I take what was surrendered to me, and I make something of merit from it, something I can admire."

Amaury knew he meant the monastery. He nodded, understanding.

He turned a bright eye upon Amaury. "And so I ask of you, how long will you stay?"

"Elizabeth asks that we remain until Christmas Day. She would attend the mass for the deceased in honor of her parents one last time."

James nodded. "She is a good daughter. Will you cede to her?"

Amaury hesitated to pledge as much to another. There was no rush to journey to France, for it would be months before there were tournaments. There was only his uneasiness, which might simply be wrought of his protectiveness toward his lady wife. "Aye, I will," he said finally.

"Pledge it to me," James said with unexpected heat.

"I swear it to you, sir."

"Upon some item holy to you."

"Upon my mother's grave, sir."

"She is dead?"

"In the delivery of me."

James nodded and crossed himself. "Until Christmas Day, then." He flicked his hand, indicating that Amaury should leave and he did so, looking back as James bent closer to another document, his lips moving as he read.

The man had likely forgotten the entire discussion already, but Amaury would keep his pledge.

Christmas Day it would be.

MANY MILES AWAY, to the northwest, and some weeks later, there was a feast at Kilderrick for the solstice. All the village gathered in the newly constructed great hall of the keep, feasting and dancing, celebrating the turn of the year. Oliver enjoyed the festivities, but he could not keep himself from thinking about Amaury and Lady Elizabeth.

The *Loup Argent* came to sit beside him after a merry dance with his wife, Alys. The lady had been spun back into the melée by one of the masons who would depart in the morning, and the laird watched her with a proud gleam in his eyes. "You do not dance," he said to Oliver, slanting a glance at the squire. "Are you not merry this Yule?"

"Aye, my lord. I am most fortunate here at Kilderrick."

"But?" Maximilian invited.

"I wish to know the end of the tale," Oliver confessed, hearing Amaury's own long-ago words echoed in his own.

"Which tale? Some tales are yet unfurling."

The boy frowned. "I wonder if Lady Elizabeth is safely at Beaupoint. I wonder whether she wed again, and better the second time. I wonder if Calum Moffatt's kin sought vengeance for his death and I wonder whether Amaury is in France as yet." Oliver shrugged. "I wonder how he fares, alone with his dogs and his destrier."

Maximilian nodded slowly. "I, too, have wondered. You said he meant to ride for Evroi?"

"To his uncle's abode, where he trained for his spurs."

"It is a good impulse. He would be welcomed there, I am sure."

"The seas, sir, they are rough in winter."

Maximilian smiled. "You became fond of him."

"I did not expect to, but aye, I did." Oliver glanced at Maximilian. "He is more like you than I realized when we rode to hunt here."

"How so?"

"He defends those who are pledged to him. He is honorable and just. He was very determined to defend his principles as a knight."

"He is that," Maximilian said and raised a hand for a cup of ale.

Oliver smiled, remembering. "But the lady thawed him, to be sure."

"This you never mentioned to me," Maximilian said with surprise.

"Oh, aye, they argued aplenty. She said he was vexing and impossible, and I thought he was irked by her, in his turn. But then, he changed his course, repeatedly, always to see her protected. He listened to her, and so...I wonder." Oliver could not speculate beyond that, but he felt his liege lord studying him.

"Do you think he might have stayed at Beaupoint?"

"Perhaps if they had need of a captain-at-arms or a warrior, he might have done."

Maximilian shook his head. "Nay, Amaury was raised to rule a holding. He expected Château Pouissance!"

"Have you seen it, sir?"

"It is a rich holding, indeed." Maximilian nodded. "Lush and pretty. Abundant and so well fortified. A man raised there with the expectation of holding its seal could not be content with less."

"Could he not, sir?" Oliver asked, earning a quick glance for his query. "You were raised at Château de Vries with the expectation of holding its seal, and yet I think you are content at Kilderrick."

Maximilian laughed. "You speak aright, Oliver. I am well content."

"And sir?"

"And I will see what can be learned of my brother's fate, for the sake of your curiosity." Maximilian rose to his feet and Oliver jumped to his own.

"I thank you, sir. And if he is there, might you improve his circumstance somehow?"

Maximilian had been intending to leave the table, but he turned back, ale in hand, to survey his squire. "You do admire him."

Oliver nodded, the back of his neck heating. "I liked his resolve, sir, and I liked his horse and armor. I liked how he treated the lady with such courtesy. 'Twas like a tale." He felt his face heat but continued. "When I was a boy, I yearned to be a knight, though it was not possible. Then I joined your company and learned that war was not so noble as the tales would suggest. But then, I rode with your brother, sir, and I wished to be like him." He fell silent then, certain he had said too much, fearful that his impulsive confession would be interpreted as an insult.

Maximilian surveyed him silently for several moments and Oliver wished he knew what the older man was thinking.

Finally, Maximilian handed him the cup of ale, as yet tasted. His voice was husky when he spoke. "Then I will find out, Oliver, and I will do for Amaury whatsoever I can. I pledge it to you."

"Thank you, sir." Oliver took the cup and bowed, sipping of its contents only after Maximilian had walked away. He had a curious sense of anticipation, though he dared not name its reason.

It could only be because he learned to trust the *Loup Argent* without reservation.

CHAPTER 17

Christmas morning dawned overcast and cold. There was a fierce wind from the west, one that slipped through the shutters and chilled the solar. The firth, when Amaury looked, was silver and its waters rough. Dark clouds were mustering to the west.

Elizabeth stirred as he tucked more fur pelts around her. "It is cold," she said with a playful smile that invited his kiss.

"Linger abed a while. This day will be a long one." Amaury did not mention that it would be their last at Beaupoint.

She nestled deeper beneath the covers. Grise rose and shook, then flung herself against Elizabeth and sighed contentment. By the time Amaury had dressed, they both were sound asleep.

He snapped his fingers and Bête and Noisette darted out of the chamber ahead of him. He could smell the cooking and baking from the kitchens, stews and bread and soups in preparation for the day's feast. James had been persuaded to entertain the villagers on this day, then Amaury and Elizabeth would ride south on the morrow.

He would miss Beaupoint and its people, of that he had no doubt. It was Amaury's intention to walk the perimeter of the holding and secure every detail in his memory. To his thinking, it would be so much less as a monastery, but the choice was not his to make.

Bête reached the hall before him and the wag of that dog's tail revealed that someone was already there. It was James, sitting by the cold hearth, reading some treatise or other. The dogs continued to the kitchen with optimism as Amaury inclined his head to Elizabeth's uncle.

"Good day, sir. Happy Christmas."

"And to you." The older man studied Amaury. "Where will you go when you leave Beaupoint?"

Amaury and Elizabeth had discussed this in detail, planning their course while lying abed. "We will ride south and seek passage from Portsmouth. The journey is shorter and will be easier for the horses. Then, onward to Evroi to visit my uncle."

"And then the lists."

Amaury nodded. At the older man's gesture, Amaury sat down. "The fire should be lit," he said, feeling the chill that radiated from the stone walls. "You will be cold."

"I will not remain here." James rose to his feet with some effort, and Amaury caught the older man's elbow to steady him. "Come with me. I would show you something of interest."

Amaury expected to be led into James' favored chamber to be shown some recently acquired document, but they left the keep and walked together to the west. They made slow progress given that cold wind. Amaury was concerned for the other man's welfare but his suggestions that they return to the hall were dismissed.

"You must see this before you leave," he said. When they were some distance from Beaupoint's tower, James sank down to sit upon one of the stones that would form the wall of his planned monastery. Amaury turned to look back at the imposing tower once more.

"You admire Beaupoint," James said.

"I do." Amaury saw no cause to hide the truth. "It is artfully built and perfectly sited. It is easy to understand why others would covet it."

"Is it your true desire to return to France?"

"It is what I will do."

"Because it is right and honorable," James concluded. "Aye, you even think like Percival. You should know that his notion was always that Elizabeth should be wedded to a suitable man, and when she was, Percival would name that man as his successor. Beaupoint would then pass, not directly to Elizabeth, but to her husband and defender, and thence, with any fortune, to her son. But Percival died before Elizabeth wed, and I promised her hand to a man most unworthy." He nodded. "I have feared for a year that Percival would smite me down, like a wrathful angel, but instead, I believe he was as practical as ever." James smiled at Amaury. "I think he found you and sent you to defend his daughter."

Amaury thought James wished for reassurance before their departure. "I will defend her with my life."

"I know." James nodded, then surveyed the site he had chosen. "I am no warrior but I learned something from my brother. He always complained that the western border of Beaupoint was insufficiently defended."

"Indeed. With the coast beyond to the west and the forest to the south, it is a vulnerability."

"No longer!" James said with satisfaction. "With this foundation here, there will be many eyes watching this flank of the holding, many voices that can be raised in alarm, and many hands to aid in barring the door. There will also be tithes and taxes, to pay for the lord's defense of the foundation and his provision of roads."

Amaury nodded understanding of this, but still he could not see why James had brought him out of the keep. He would have suggested again that they return, but James rose to his feet, again with Amaury's assistance, then shivered mightily before pointing at the rock where he had been seated. "Move that stone."

It was a stone of considerable size and Amaury could not budge it. He called back to the keep and Oscar strode toward them, followed by Bertram. Working together, the three of them managed to tip the stone onto one side.

"'Zounds," Oscar said.

"Do not speak thus here!" James chastised him.

Amaury dropped to one knee. Beneath the stone was a hole, cut square into the earth by design. It was slightly smaller than the stone itself and knee-deep. Two trunks were in the space, one smaller than the other, and a crockery cup.

"It is the beginning of the crypt of the new chapel," James said with excitement. He seized Amaury's arm. "And it has been a fine treasury. Open them!"

As the other men watched, Amaury lifted out the first trunk and placed it upon the rock, followed by the second. James provided him with a pair of keys. Within the first trunk were silver coins in quantity.

Oscar might have repeated his curse, so astounded was he, but James fixed him with a glare.

The smaller one was filled with gold ones, and the combined sum had to be considerable. Amaury looked up at James, seeking an explanation.

"The treasury of Beaupoint. My brother's fortune." James smiled with satisfaction. "I held it in trust for the new lord, whoever he might be. Elizabeth's bride price I have spent on the monastery, but that agreement was made with me. The coin was mine to spend."

"You kept your treasury *here*?" Amaury was incredulous. Oscar and Bertram exchanged glances of wonder.

"Who would find it?" James demanded. "If the keep was attacked and even seized, this humble rock would be overlooked. The reivers did not look here."

"But someone must know," Amaury said. It had taken three of them to move the stone, after all.

"The mason who set the stone for me was pledged to silence. He has seen the plans for the monastery and knew that if this coin was stolen, there would be no labor for him here again. It was a secret, my secret."

It was a secret no longer, Amaury almost observed, his gaze flicking over the two warriors who had witnessed this.

Before his eyes, James removed the signet ring of Beaupoint from his finger. He offered it to Amaury on the palm of his hand.

"Beaupoint is, I believe, your desire."

Amaury wondered whether the older man had lost his wits.

"With respect, sir, I cannot accept this ring."

"Of course, you can. I have watched and I have listened and I have decided that Beaupoint will be yours. I will pass the holding to you, today, as is my right."

Amaury's heart stopped. "But what of you?"

"This foundation will be all I desire. I will retire from the world to live within that establishment, the better to be at one with my studies and my prayers." He sank down to sit on a stone again. "I was not a good judge of men, it is clear," he continued. "And my brother often said as much to me. After I erred with Calum Moffatt, I became more cautious. I have watched you for nigh upon a month and I know this choice is right." James nodded at the chests. "Take the treasury and the ring. I designate you Lord de Beaupoint."

Amaury offered his hand, unable to believe that Fortune smiled thus upon him, and stared in awe as James pushed the ring onto his finger. The older man sighed with satisfaction, clearly glad to be relieved of its burden. When Amaury turned, Oscar and Bertram had dropped to their knees before him to pledge obeisance.

He was Lord de Beaupoint. He looked up at the high window of the solar, knowing that Elizabeth would be delighted with these tidings.

He saw her silhouette at the window and hoped she already knew.

What a gift for Christmas Day!

ELIZABETH LOOKED out the window of Beaupoint's solar, halting there in Amaury's robe when she saw Amaury walking with her uncle. They made their way slowly to the west and stopped at the foundation of the monastery. Her uncle sat upon a stone as if weary.

He should not have walked so far, not when the wind was so cold. And he should not sit upon the cold stone for long. But he appeared to be settled there as well as content. Amaury glanced back at Beaupoint and Elizabeth almost waved to him. He stood beside her uncle, evidently listening.

Then her uncle stood and pointed to the rock where he had been seated. Obviously following his instruction, Amaury endeavored to move the rock aside. He raised a hand and shouted, and Elizabeth saw Oscar and Bertram respond to his summons. The three men moved the stone with considerable effort, then stared into what had to be a hole. James looked markedly pleased with himself, she noticed. Then, upon her uncle's instruction, Amaury lifted two trunks from the space below the rock.

What was this?

Elizabeth fetched her father's reading glass to better see what transpired. The trunks were opened by Amaury, and she caught her breath at the coin within them. Then James offered something to Amaury, something she could not discern, and Amaury extended his left hand. He glanced back at the keep and with the aid of the glass, she could see that he was both surprised and pleased.

James put a ring upon Amaury's hand, the gold glinting in the light.

It could not be!

Elizabeth lowered the glass, then raised it again. He could not have surrendered the signet ring and the lordship to Amaury.

But Oscar and Bertram dropped to their knees before Amaury and Elizabeth knew it was true.

Amaury was Lord de Beaupoint!

It was the most glorious gift ever contrived.

Elizabeth dropped the robe and tugged on her boots, flinging on a kirtle and lacing the sides with haste. She did not trouble with her hair, but left it in one long single braid. Twyla could aid her later. In this moment, she had to see Amaury. She seized his heavy cloak again and opened the door of the solar.

She halted in surprise to find Laurent there, his hand outstretched for the latch. "I have come to fetch you, my lady," he said, his tone prompting her distrust.

"I go only to my husband," she said, disliking that the dagger Amaury had given her was yet on the far side of the chamber. All of Amaury's counsel echoed in her thoughts. This warrior barred the way. Amaury and James and two of the men-at-arms were outside the keep. The kitchens were bustling and noisy. The village was distant. No one would hear her call for aid if she did as much.

"Nay, my lady. In this, you err." Laurent shook his head slowly. "You will come with me. My lord Gavin is most anxious to share your company on this day of days."

Amaury had been right.

"I understand," Elizabeth said. She smiled as if agreeable and made to step out of the solar, as if willing to do as he asked. Grise was fast by his side, and the dog growled when Laurent snatched Elizabeth's hand.

The dog jumped, teeth bared, and Laurent struck Grise hard with his mailed fist. The dog fell whimpering to the ground, then he kicked her.

"Nay!" Elizabeth cried and shoved Laurent hard, planting both hands on his chest. He fell, as she had anticipated, toppling toward the stairs.

But he seized her wrists, his hands locking around hers, and pulled her with him.

As they tumbled noisily, Elizabeth fought with all her might. She kicked at his groin, she bit whatever part of him she could reach, she worked one hand free and scratched at his face. He swore at her when they reached the floor below the solar, and their struggles took them down the stairs to the great hall, fighting all the way.

"If only you were not to be bruised," Laurent said though his teeth when he landed atop her. "I always thought your father indulged you overmuch." He closed his gloved hand over her mouth to silence her, his expression grim.

There was no one in the hall, to Elizabeth's dismay. They must have all gone to Amaury and James.

"And what is this?" Nelwyna demanded, appearing from the kitchens. Laurent had his back to the other woman, so she would not be able to see how he held Elizabeth captive.

"My lady has been injured," Laurent said. "Make haste, Nelwyna, and fetch Erwina from the village."

Lying cur! The older woman gasped and spun around, hurrying back toward the kitchen. It was Elizabeth's last chance. She bit Laurent and he cursed again but did not release her. Indeed, he smiled as she struggled beneath his weight, watching her as he pinched her nostrils shut.

Elizabeth flailed and fought. She could not take a breath. She struggled to dislodge his weight and his hand, but to no avail.

Until suddenly she knew no more.

AMAURY COULD ONLY ASSUME that they had been watched from the bailey, for it seemed all the household streamed out to meet them on their return. Oscar and Bertram had pledged their fealty immediately, and Ealhard and Hugh were quick to follow suit. Simon and Hamish, too, swore to Amaury before he reached the bailey, and he saw Alfred, Twyla and others awaiting him with delight. Bête and Noisette barked and threaded their way through the happy crowd.

"Where is my lady?" Amaury asked, but no one replied. They looked at each other, scanning the company, and his disquiet grew. Amaury strode into the hall to find it empty. He had been certain that he had seen Elizabeth at the window of the solar and had anticipated that she would meet him here, joyously.

Then he heard Grise whimper.

Nay!

He lunged up the stairs and found the dog on the floor of the solar. She tried to get to her feet at the sight of him and her tail wagged feebly, but her leg had been injured and there was blood on her side.

"Oh!" Erwina said behind him. "Nelwyna said the lady was injured, sir."

"When?"

"But moments ago. Laurent bade her fetch us." Behind the healer, Amaury saw her daughter, Audry, who nodded agreement.

Amaury strode across the chamber, noting that Elizabeth's boots and cloak were gone, as well as one of her kirtles. She had not taken a circlet or any other finery and his heart stopped when he found his dagger yet atop the chest where she usually left it for the night. He was aware of Twyla standing in the portal.

"I am sorry, sir. I was bringing her water when I heard the others in the bailey. I thought to bring her merry tidings, sir."

"'Tis not your fault, Twyla."

Elizabeth had been captured and she was unarmed. Amaury seized her father's glass, also left atop a chest, and looked out Beaupoint's high windows. He looked first to the north, for he knew no one had ridden to the west. There was not a hint of disturbance.

But to the east, one lone rider galloped away from Beaupoint.

It was Laurent.

A limp burden was slung across the horse before him.

Elizabeth!

Too late, Amaury knew the name of Gavin de Montgomerie's ally within the walls.

"Tend to the dog," he instructed Erwina and Audry. "She must be healed, or my lady will have my hide."

He raced out of the solar, passing Alfred, bellowing for Oscar as Twyla followed him. "We ride to Clyfford!" he shouted. "My lady has been abducted!"

Bertram, Ealhard and Hugh headed for the stables with purpose. James sank to a seat in the hall, his brow furrowed.

Amaury was in the bailey before he halted to think. Simon was saddling Zephyr with quick hands while the other men saddled their steeds. Heloise was there, against expectation, wringing her hands.

"We will all ride in pursuit, sir," Oscar said. "The lady will be rescued."

But Amaury turned in place, considering what he knew. "That is what is anticipated," he said softly. "There will be a trap laid for me, and perhaps Beaupoint itself will be besieged in my absence."

"But the lady..." Bertram protested.

"Will tell you herself that the objective is always Beaupoint. There are two ways to claim Beaupoint. One is to ensure my demise and take my place. The second is to seize the keep in my absence."

Glances were exchanged and the men nodded agreement.

"Oscar, you have pledged to my service," Amaury said and that man bowed before him. "I leave you in command of Beaupoint. Defend it vigorously in my absence."

"Aye, my lord."

"I will ride after my lady alone."

"Nay, sir," Alfred said. "You cannot ride do as much."

"Where will Laurent go?" Simon asked. "All the way to Clyfford Manor?"

"The baron cannot have endorsed this scheme," Amaury mused.

"Alfred knows where he meets Gavin," Heloise said, nodding at her son. "Tell him."

"The old road to Carlisle runs closer to the firth," Alfred said. "It flooded too often when the tide was high, so the new one was built. It is yet there, but disused, and halfway between Beaupoint and Sutton-by-the-Sands, there is a clearing."

Amaury recalled that Sutton-by-the-Sands was the next village to the east of Beaupoint, a much smaller settlement and one closer to the firth's waters.

"I followed Laurent one night. He met Gavin there, sir."

"When was this?" Amaury demanded.

"When the moon was in its last quarter. I could not hear what they said, sir. I did not know why they met. I did not want to draw closer and reveal myself."

"We did not know, sir, neither of us," Heloise insisted. "We would never see any injury done to the lady."

Amaury was skeptical.

"I thought he had another woman in Sutton-by-the-Sands," Heloise continued. "I sent Alfred after him to find out. But it was only Sir Gavin." She shrugged. "I thought they shared tidings from Laurent's time at Clyfford."

"Laurent did not return there again, sir," Alfred said. "I watched to be certain."

"We thought whatever was between them, it was done," Heloise said. "What can we do to aid the lady and repair our error?"

If Laurent had taken Elizabeth to that clearing to deliver her to Gavin where none might witness his deed, that might be the same place the two intended to attack Amaury.

Amaury turned to Alfred. "Is there another route to this clearing?"

"You can take the main road and ride past it, sir, then return on the lesser road from Sutton-by-the-Sands."

Amaury nodded. "And someone must ride to the baron. We will have need of a justiciar, whatever transpires."

"Send me, sir," Twyla said immediately. "I can ride Blanchefleur, who will be fastest." Aye, the smith's daughter would be a competent rider, and the men sworn to Amaury could remain to defend Beaupoint.

"Go then," Amaury urged. "And Alfred, show me this road. We must make haste!"

~

MEN.

They were wretches, all but one of them.

Elizabeth hid the fact that she had awakened. She would use her wits as Amaury always advised. She needed details of her situation to plan her escape, indeed, to ensure her survival. She was not surprised to be slung over a horse's back again or seized, undoubtedly for the prize of Beaupoint.

But she was furious.

And Laurent! A man her father had trusted beyond all. Even this destrier had been a gift from her father to that warrior, the stallion being the get of her father's own horse. Faithless, disloyal, scoundrel. She could not even think of Grise, lest she weep and reveal that she was conscious.

Elizabeth would avenge them all.

She could see that they had left the main road and the smell of the firth hinted that they traveled the old road, the one that no one used anymore. There would be no chance of witnesses. The tide was coming in, for the ground was wet beneath the horses' hooves, evidence of why the road had been abandoned. She wondered how far they had ridden past Beaupoint village but could not guess.

Elizabeth heard another horse soon enough, but the hoofbeats came from ahead of them. Laurent slowed his destrier to a canter and the other rider turned, his horse cantering alongside. Allies, then. Elizabeth stole a glance through her lashes at the horse, a bay with no caparisons. She could not see the rider but guessed his identity soon enough.

"All proceeded as planned?" that man asked and she recognized Gavin's voice. Amaury had suspected that man had a spy at Beaupoint and he had been right. Yet she had convinced him to set his concerns aside. It was her fault alone that they had lingered at Beaupoint. If Amaury was injured because of her request, Elizabeth would never forgive herself.

She had no doubt that Gavin meant Amaury harm.

"Aye, my lord," Laurent said.

"And he will follow, undoubtedly," Gavin said, proving her suspicion true.

"I ensured that I was slow enough for him to see my departure."

Gavin chuckled. "He will ride out in a fury to defend his lady, alone."

"I expect as much. I ensured that it was clear we had left the main road."

"And he prides himself on his ability to hunt. He will not miss the signs, but he will not return to Beaupoint. This dispute will be solved, today, and in my favor as it always should have been. We will halt here, as planned, and await him."

The fiends. They would lie in wait for Amaury and take him from her.

What could she do?

She recalled Amaury's advice and did not reveal that she was awake. Surprise and subterfuge. There had to be some way she could ensure he survived.

The horses were slowed yet again and they left the road. Elizabeth could discern no more than a track leading away from the firth and the horses climbed slightly uphill. The bare branches of the shrubs were visible on every side. She could hear the water, but was not entirely certain of their location. Hands closed around her waist, lifting her from Laurent's horse, but she remained limp with her eyes closed.

"You were not to injure her!" Gavin said. "There is a bruise rising on her cheek!"

"She tripped me on the stairs. It was inadvertent, my lord."

Inadvertent. Elizabeth could not agree.

Gavin laid Elizabeth gently on ground that was dry and firm. He tucked her cloak more closely around her, and touched her cheek with a gloved fingertip. Any notion that he felt tenderly for her was dismissed by his words. "Fool! My father will never believe she left him willingly with such a bruise."

"Say that he struck her, sir."

"Who will believe as much? You are a cretin to have left a visible mark upon her!"

"With respect, sir, I cannot see how she might have been abducted otherwise."

"With respect, sir," Gavin echoed with frustration. "When men speak thus, what they truly mean is *without* respect, sir." He straightened, undoubtedly to confront the other man, and Elizabeth dared to peek through her lashes at him. He looked to be irked, even petulant, but more importantly, his dagger was on his right side.

Her left as she faced him.

Wherever they were, the soil beneath her fingers was loose and sandy.

"I suppose you wish to be paid now," Gavin said to Laurent, his tone filled with challenge.

"It was our agreement, sir." Laurent's tone was hard. "I was to deliver the lady and I have done so. I have betrayed my host at your request, after all." They faced each other with undisguised hostility. Elizabeth saw the flash of Laurent's eyes and knew he was not so loyal to Gavin as that.

Gavin counted out the coins, then surrendered them to Laurent.

"It is only half of the agreed amount, sir."

"It is only reasonable that I keep part of the payment as a reward for your incompetence." The two glared at each other, then Gavin turned to the path again. "Watch the road. Tell me when there is a hint of his arrival that I might bait the trap."

Laurent hesitated.

"Do the task well if you ever wish to see the balance of that coin," Gavin continued.

The warrior's eyes narrowed, then he strode toward the road, his movements filled with impatience.

Gavin watched until he disappeared, then turned back toward Elizabeth. He sighed mightily at all he had to endure, then crouched down beside her again. "My lady," he whispered, stroking her cheek with his fingertips. "Shall I awaken you with a kiss?"

Vermin, Elizabeth thought. *Blackguard and scoundrel.* Her father had been right about him and she had been wrong.

She did not respond.

She could feel the weight of Gavin's gaze as he studied her. She feared that her racing heart would reveal her feint. She feared that all would be lost...

And then he bent close to claim her with a kiss.

'Twas Elizabeth's opportunity.

She moved like lightning and seized his dagger with her left hand, even as she kicked him in the groin. Gavin choked and sputtered, falling backward in his surprise. He sprawled on his back, astonished, but she was atop him, her knee on his chest and her boot driving into his groin.

His throat was exposed, above his hauberk, a gleaming wedge of flesh that invited a fatal blow, but Elizabeth faltered.

And the fiend saw his chance.

"My lady," he protested with a tight smile. "What is this? It is Gavin before you, not some villain come to waylay you. I come for you, to make matters right between us at last." He reached for the knife, confident that she could not truly injure him. "You know we have always been destined to be together." He spoke with his usual smooth confidence, as if she was a witless child. "Give me the knife and all will be well."

Elizabeth let her expression turn doubtful.

Gavin smiled, reassured.

Then she struck hard. She drove his own dagger into his eye so hard that she was certain the tip touched the back of his skull.

He choked. "What..." he began to ask, but Elizabeth withdrew the knife with a savage gesture, one that left him moaning. Blood spurted from the wound and Gavin grabbed at his face, as if he could close the gap with his hands.

"Wicked bitch!" he cried and snatched for her.

Elizabeth ran. There was a path that led away from the one Laurent had followed. She heard Gavin shout for Laurent and she ran. The path was narrow and choked with briars, giving her hope that she could evade them both. She heard Laurent swear as he crashed through the undergrowth behind her and knew that again, she had only one chance. There was a bend in the path, then another small clearing. She halted on the far side of the clearing, her breath coming quickly as she awaited her prey.

Laurent appeared abruptly, then halted at the sight of her. He raised a hand, walking closer to her. "My lady," he said, his tone cajoling, as if she was a witless fool who could readily be persuaded of her error. "There is no cause for this…"

"No cause?" Elizabeth demanded, keeping the dagger hidden behind her back. "My father trusted you. My husband trusted you." She caught her breath as if overwhelmed and choked back a sob. "What cause have you for this, Laurent? I thought you my ally."

He shook his head and raised his hands, coming toward her as if she was a beast to be soothed. "My lady, all will be well. You have only to come with me…"

"I am not your lady!" Elizabeth cried and flung the knife, just as Amaury had taught her. The blade buried itself in Laurent's thigh below his hauberk and he stumbled. His eyes filled with surprise and he fell to his knees. He tugged the weapon free, his expression incredulous, and his blood flowed vigorously.

Elizabeth found she was fearless in her fury. She picked up a stone and marched toward the injured warrior. She halted a short distance from him, her distrust complete.

"My lady," he whispered as if to appeal for her aid.

"You killed Grise," Elizabeth said. "You treacherous fiend! I hope you die slowly for your wickedness." He lunged for her but she cast the rock. It struck him in the brow and he crumpled to the earth. Fearing a feint, Elizabeth spun away from him for she knew he could not pursue her.

She was immediately seized by Gavin.

There was blood on his face and fury in his remaining eye. "How kind of you to save me the coin," he snarled, then forcibly hauled her toward the road. "'Tis time, my lady, to bait the trap."

"What do you mean?"

"I will offer your life for his," he said, dragging her into the road. Elizabeth stumbled, taking the opportunity to seize a handful of dirt without his awareness. It was sandy and loose, perfect for her intentions.

"It is a lie," she guessed and Gavin laughed.

"It is indeed. I would have let you live, but you have proven your unworthiness to be my bride."

"It is always about Beaupoint," she whispered.

"And why should it not be? A prize is always worth the claiming."

He hauled her forcibly before himself and his gaze bored into hers. "I will have a kiss before you die, my lady, the kiss I have awaited for many years."

Elizabeth struggled, but he seized a fistful of her hair and held her captive in a powerful grip. "You will not thwart me again," he snarled, then Elizabeth heard the first few notes of Persephone's feeding song. The whistle was faint, but she knew it well.

Amaury rode to hunt.

And she obscured his shot. She understood immediately.

"What is that?" Gavin was distracted for the barest moment, but it was enough. "It comes from the wrong direction."

Elizabeth stomped hard on his foot and drove her knee into his groin. His grip loosened slightly and she flung the handful of sand into his face. He staggered backward, cursing, but she dropped to the ground, lying flat on her belly.

She closed her eyes at the whistle of the bolt, and grimaced at the sound of it finding its mark. Then Gavin fell, gasping for breath. Elizabeth crawled quickly away, getting to her feet and backing away as she watched him writhe on the ground. He reached for her, his hand outstretched, his fingers clutching.

"Elizabeth," he whispered. "I only wanted…"

He went limp. Elizabeth retreated another few steps, aware that she was trembling. She heard hoofbeats and knew it was Zephyr, but dared not avert her gaze from the villain, even to see Amaury. He rode from the east, which made no sense, and a palfrey came behind him.

Amaury swept Elizabeth from her feet in one sweeping gesture, slowing the horse only to remove her from harm's way. She was in the saddle before him in a heartbeat, and his arm closed around her as she trembled against him.

He whispered her name and Elizabeth, to her dismay, wept in relief.

THE SIGHT of Elizabeth in Gavin's grasp had filled Amaury with fear that he would reach her too late. It was the terror that had haunted him since her abduction, and he could not bear that he would have to watch that horrific event. There was blood on her kirtle and he feared the worst.

Praise be that Alfred had followed Laurent that night. All proved to be just as the boy had forecast. Amaury had ridden with Alfred and Twyla and when the road forked beyond Beaupoint village, it was clear that someone had recently chosen to ride on the low road. The way was overgrown, but there were tracks and broken branches, one with a tuft of cloth that might have been from Elizabeth's kirtle. The horses raced on to Sutton-by-the-Sands, then he and Alfred returned on the low road while Twyla galloped toward Clyfford Manor.

His crossbow was loaded when Amaury spied Elizabeth and Gavin ahead, but he could not intervene without risking Elizabeth's life. Then he had the idea of using the falcon's feeding song as a signal to Elizabeth. It was distinctive. She knew he used it and Gavin did not.

Gavin glanced up at the song, his expression puzzled. The lady, as clever as ever, seized the opportunity to wrench herself from his grasp. And when she dropped to the ground, giving Amaury a clear target, his heart soared with pride.

His aim was true, and could not have been otherwise, given the stakes.

After Gavin fell, Amaury swept her up and held her close, slinging his bow over his shoulder as he consoled her. She was trembling and he did not wish to think of what she had endured, but she leaned her cheek against his chest and her arms slid around his waist. He realized, to his relief, that it was Gavin's blood upon her garments.

She wept, and he realized he had never seen her weep before. He held her tightly and waited. Amaury doubted that Gavin would move again.

"Laurent," Elizabeth said, then pointed to that man's location. "I struck him with a rock."

Amaury left her with Zephyr as he and Alfred followed her directions, the pair of them dragging Laurent into the road. He was stirring, but Amaury took the warrior's belt and bound his arms to his side. He claimed his weapons, as well, and left Alfred standing guard over him.

Elizabeth was wiping her tears. "I knew you would come. They knew you would come. It was a trap."

"I suspected as much, for you warned me."

"How?"

Amaury reached to touch the bruise rising on her cheek with a gentle fingertip. "If it was about Beaupoint, then my demise had to be the plan." He bent and touched his brow to her hand. "You warned me, though I wanted to do precisely as they anticipated I would."

"Oh, Amaury." Her voice was unsteady again and he lifted her down to hold her close.

"Are you hale?"

She nodded. "You were right that the matter was not done. And Gavin did have a spy at Beaupoint."

"Laurent. He must have aided against the attack of the Moffatts to save Beaupoint for Gavin."

Her voice was filled with disgust. "He was paid his thirty pieces of silver."

"And you struck him with a rock?"

"After he fell."

"Fell?"

"A knife struck him in the thigh."

That would explain the copious blood. "No doubt he deserved as much."

"He killed Grise," Elizabeth said with heat. Her tears rose again and the sight broke Amaury's heart.

"No." He framed her face in his hands and compelled her to meet his gaze, wiping her tears away with his thumbs. "No, Grise is not dead. Her leg is broken and possibly a rib. Erwina and Audry are with her now."

"Healers and bonesetters do not tend dogs," she protested, her tears falling again.

"They do, at my command." He smiled at her, trying to persuade her to believe him. "I knew it would be my lady's desire."

Elizabeth's eyes lit. "She will heal? You do not deceive me?"

"There must always be truth between us, my Elizabeth," he said and she smiled a little. "She will heal." At his insistence, she leaned against his chest again in her relief. "I wager I will be carrying a very large dog up and down the stairs for at least a month, for she will never be parted from you now."

There was a sound of hoofbeats and they turned to look down the road to the east. Twyla rode at the front of a small company, Blanchefleur tossing her head as she ran. Two men rode with her, one on either side, one younger and one older. Both wore the same insignia of a white hart on a green field.

"It is Nigel," Elizabeth said with surprise. "And the baron himself."

"I met them on their way to Beaupoint," Twyla confessed when she reached Amaury. "And urged haste." There were three other men who rode with the baron, knights evidently pledged to his service.

"I feared Gavin's intent when he left Clyfford," Nigel admitted. "He said he meant to end your dispute." At that moment, he evidently spotted his fallen brother in the road, for he pulled his horse up short.

He also extended a hand to block the view of the older man who accompanied him.

'Twas too late for that.

The baron dismounted, his expression inscrutable, and crouched beside his fallen son. He took Gavin's outstretched hand and bent his head in prayer. Nigel crossed himself and bowed his own head.

Long moments later, the baron crossed himself, sighed, then stood. "So many gifts wasted," he said softly. "So many opportunities squandered. He was always like a child." He turned to Elizabeth and Amaury, a frown creasing his brow. "I apologize on behalf of my family, Lady Elizabeth, for the assault against your person. No man of honor attacks a noblewoman, let alone forcibly seizes her from her home."

"I thank you, sir," she said softly.

"I owe you reparation..." the baron began.

"You have lost your oldest son, sir," Amaury said. "The price has already been high."

The baron caught his breath, watching as his men picked up Gavin's body. "I always feared it would come to this," he admitted softly. "He never heeded any directive save his own desire. Such charm. Such cleverness. But always put to the service of himself alone." The baron cleared his throat and fixed Amaury with a look. "You must be Amaury d'Evroi, of whom I have heard so much."

"Aye, sir." Amaury bowed low before the baron.

"Gavin always wished for Beaupoint and never cared at the price. We have argued mightily about my refusal to seize it from James. I had hoped that after your challenge, he would abandon the notion, but yet again, my hope was misplaced." His frown deepened as his gaze brightened. "There is a ring upon your hand, sir, that I recognize well. What has befallen James d'Acron?"

"He is hale, sir, but he surrendered the lordship of Beaupoint to me this very day."

"Took him time enough," the baron said and offered his hand, with its insignia ring. He raised a brow imperiously. "Beaupoint has always sworn to Clyfford."

"Indeed," Elizabeth agreed softly, but Amaury had already dropped to one knee. He kissed that signet ring, then pledged his obeisance.

The baron nodded approval as Laurent stirred. "Strip him of his armor and weapons," he ordered his men. "Take the coin he was paid by my son. I have little patience with disloyalty in any measure."

Laurent opened his mouth, perhaps to argue his cause, but the baron held up a hand to silence him.

"You will have months to compose your defense, if you survive Clyfford's dungeons until the court can hear your case."

"But sir..."

"Silence!" The baron seized the reins of the dapple destrier Laurent had ridden and the stallion tossed his head. "I remember Percival d'Acron giving this fine horse to you," he said to Laurent, then fixed that man with a hard look. "Such a sign of courtesy and esteem, and yet you willingly betrayed his memory and injured his daughter."

"I served your son."

"Yet you were in service to Beaupoint! I think you do not deserve this horse." Laurent paled but the baron raised his voice to instruct his men. "Let him walk and if he cannot walk, let him crawl. If he arrives at Clyfford dead, the courts will have one less case to hear."

Then he led the destrier to Amaury and surrendered the reins to him. "This steed belongs at Beaupoint. I return him to you in the hopes that you will receive him gladly."

"Indeed, sir. He is splendid."

The baron smiled a little and patted the horse's flank. He looked older then and sadder, and Amaury cleared his throat. "Will you celebrate Christmas Day with us, sir?" he invited.

The older man glanced back. "I thank you, but no. There is much to be done at Clyfford and my wife will require my presence on this day." He fixed Amaury with a look. "I will be taking note of your decisions, though, sir, and I may visit Beaupoint at Easter."

Amaury bowed. "You would be most welcome, sir."

The baron turned then and followed his men, reaching for the reins of his horse. Nigel dismounted to aid his father, who leaned upon his younger son. He looked to have aged a decade in mere moments and Amaury felt a wave of compassion for him.

"Nigel was always his brother's opposite," Elizabeth whispered.

"I am glad to hear you say as much. I hope he will make a fine baron when the time comes." Amaury stood beside Zephyr, holding the reins of the destrier Laurent had ridden in one hand and Elizabeth's stirrup in the other. "And you are uninjured?" he asked again and she nodded.

"I want to go home."

He slanted a glance at the dapple, then back to meet her gaze. "Perhaps you should return in splendor, my lady."

Her smile banished all his lingering doubts. She straightened, so regal and magnificent that his chest tightened with pride, and Amaury arranged his cloak around her. He mounted the dapple, leaving her upon Zephyr, and they rode home together, Twyla and Alfred behind.

Home to Beaupoint.

"Will you speak to my father, sir?" Twyla asked Amaury. "He is home for the Yule and be pleased to meet you."

"I hope he can be persuaded to remain at Beaupoint," Amaury said, to the girl's evident delight. "We have more than enough work for a smith now."

Their company were greeted by all the villagers and residents of the keep, who waited in the road for tidings. They rode into the village amidst cheers and applause. Amaury lifted Elizabeth from the saddle to a barrage of questions and congratulations. James shook his hand heartily and the villagers came to swear fealty. Heloise was first to pledge herself to Amaury, her relief that Elizabeth was hale so clear that Amaury knew she had no part in Laurent's scheme.

Finally, Amaury led Elizabeth to the chapel, astonished that this holding should have become his home so quickly.

But then, he knew his home would always be wherever this lady decided it should be, for he would only be content with her at his side.

Elizabeth cast him a smiling glance and his heart thundered with pride that she should be his lady.

Then they knelt together in the chapel and gave heartfelt thanks for all the blessings that were theirs to savor.

IT WAS LATE on Christmas night and the candles in Beaupoint's solar had burned down low when Elizabeth collapsed with pleasure atop Amaury. She laid her cheek upon his chest, smiling at the rapid pace of his heart, and sighed contentment. She closed her eyes and felt him brush her hair back from her temple with his fingertips. She knew he would wind a lock of it around his finger next and smiled when he did.

"Must you always be right?" she asked sleepily.

He chuckled, and she sat up, bracing her elbow upon his chest to look at him. He smiled at her, his gaze so warm that she felt amorous again. She swept her hand across his mouth, liking how much more frequently he smiled. "It could be considered a most irksome habit."

"But I am not always right."

"You were right about Gavin not forgetting that he had been thwarted, and you were right about him having a spy within Beaupoint. You were right about him seeking your demise today…"

"Which I only realized because of your warning."

"And you taught me to fight, undoubtedly because you knew I would need such skill."

Amaury shook his head. "I taught you to fight, lady mine, because that knowledge made you bold. It was the sparkle of your eyes when you succeeded that so compelled me."

"And now you would flatter me," she said, not truly troubled in the least.

"You forget that I was wrong about the most important thing of all."

"What was that? Caerlaverock?"

He winced. "Twice wrong, then."

"What else?"

"When you fled from Kilderrick, I was convinced that I would never have the honor of calling you my wife." He shook his head. "I knew it to be impossible."

She smiled. "And are you discontent to have been mistaken?"

He chuckled. "I am most satisfied to have been wrong."

"You are not so persuasive, sir," she said lightly. "I think I shall have to be convinced."

"I take your challenge, my lady," he said and rolled her to her back so quickly that she gasped aloud. Then she laughed when he leaned over her, his eyes dark with admiration. "I must ensure that my lady wife is satisfied with the situation, as well," he murmured then kissed her thoroughly. Elizabeth kissed him back, secure in the conviction that they were each as happy as each other.

Still, she would prove as much to him, though it might take all the night long.

Nay, it would take a lifetime and even that might not suffice.

EPILOGUE

"Where is Grise?" Elizabeth demanded on Easter morning.

Amaury was dressing for mass. He shrugged as he donned his new surcoat, emblazoned with the insignia of Beaupoint. "You have done a fine piece of work," he said to her, admiring yet again her efforts.

Elizabeth rose from the bed and brushed the surcoat, smoothing it over his hauberk. "You could not wear my father's garb forever." He let her fuss, waiting until she faced him, then caught her close for a kiss.

She smiled up at him, her eyes glowing. "I suppose you intend to walk the walls before we go to chapel."

"You suppose correctly."

"But where is Grise?" she asked again. "Where does she sleep? She has not come to the solar these three nights."

"Perhaps she finds it warmer in the kitchens or the stables. You need not fear for a dog failing to find his or her own comfort."

"But she has gained weight since her leg healed."

"She had lost weight at Kilderrick." Amaury was untroubled.

"Perhaps the stairs are difficult for her."

"I scarce think so, given how she races up them in pursuit of you."

"How old is she?"

"I have no notion. She came to me perhaps two years ago, but was not a pup. She seemed young and vigorous then, but I do not know her age."

Elizabeth was clearly discontent with this reply. "I must find her this morning."

Amaury did not reply. As was his habit, he had gone to the window overlooking the firth with her father's glass. The tide was out this morning and the shallow water on the flats looked like polished silver. There was a party making their way southward and he raised the glass to study them.

"Who are they?" Elizabeth asked from beside him and he handed her the glass.

"They wear the colors of Robert de Maxwell."

Elizabeth sighed mightily. "So they do." She returned the glass to him. "Will this never end?"

"What do you mean?"

"The endless battling of men for Beaupoint." She shook her head. "It continues on and on, as relentless as the tides of the firth."

"Was it so in your father's time?"

"No. We had peace for years."

"And so it will be again. After turmoil and uncertainty, a new balance must be struck," Amaury said. "Perhaps this will be the completion."

Elizabeth turned to look at him as she combed her hair. He knew she awaited an explanation. "Why would that be?"

"'Tis too small a party to be warlike. And today is Easter Sunday, a holy day when there can be no battle."

"Christmas is a holy day and that did not halt Gavin and Laurent."

"Ah, but Gavin was one with no regard for convention. Robert de Maxwell is not of his ilk." Amaury watched the party draw closer.

"Then why do they come?"

"To make détente, I suspect."

"I hope you are right."

"As do I. It will take them some time to reach the gates. I will walk the walls and see what I can learn of Grise while you dress."

~

AMAURY WAS WAITING for Elizabeth in the great hall when she descended and as ever his gaze swept over her with undisguised admiration. Truly, he had thawed since they had met and his passion was undisguised—and not without results. She had kept her secret until she could be certain, but it had been three months since her last bleeding. Their first child, God willing, would be born by the harvest.

"Grise evidently has been sleeping in the stables. Simon said as much."

"I would see her before we go to chapel."

"Of course." Amaury offered his hand and escorted Elizabeth to the stables. Simon looked like a man fairly bursting with a secret, though Elizabeth could not imagine what it might be. He directed them toward the end of the stable that was more quiet. Grise was there, bedded down in the straw, and she was cleaning six puppies.

Elizabeth gave a cry of delight and fell to her knees beside the dog, admiring the tiny creatures. "When were they born?" she asked.

"She began during the night, my lady, and the last came just moments ago. She had been bedding down here of late and I thought this might be why."

"Did you know?" she asked Amaury, who shook his head.

At least there was one secret he had not guessed.

"But two of the pups are black," Amaury said, crouching down beside Elizabeth.

Simon cleared his throat. "That is likely the influence of the father, sir."

Bête sauntered into the stall in that moment and sniffed the puppies, giving each one a cursory lick. He touched noses with Grise, who halted her cleaning for a moment, then laid down beside her in the straw. He surveyed lord, lady and ostler with a look of such supreme satisfaction that his contribution could not be doubted.

"Bête, you are a rogue and a scoundrel," Amaury said with affection and the dog's tail beat against the floor.

They admired the puppies a few moments longer then the bell rang from the chapel. Elizabeth knew it was time to share her secret. "Soon enough I will share Grise's state," she whispered as they walked toward the village and Amaury slanted a glance her way. His gaze was intent and she was sure he had guessed.

"You will sleep in the stables?" he asked and she laughed at him.

"Not that!"

"You will deliver of six puppies?"

"Only one babe, I believe," she said and he caught his breath.

"When?"

"By the harvest."

He counted quickly on his fingers. "And you waited to tell me?"

"I wanted to be certain. I had to consult the midwife…"

"You consulted Erwina," Amaury echoed. "And so, of every soul at Beaupoint, I am the last to know these tidings?"

"Of course not," Elizabeth said but they had come near the village. Heloise smiled at her, her expression knowing. Two of the other women whispered to each other and beamed at Elizabeth. The daughter of one of the farmers brought Elizabeth a spring flower and offered her congratulations.

"Perhaps you are the last to know," Elizabeth ceded. "But I was certain you would have guessed."

"I did," Amaury said with a gleam in his eyes. "You are ever so slightly rounder, my lady. I pay keen attention to such details. But when you said naught of it, I thought perhaps I erred again."

THAT SUNDAY WAS a fine spring day, with early wildflowers abloom in the fields, with warmth in the wind from the firth and birds singing on all sides. The villagers were invited to feast at the hall at midday and James had agreed that his treasured cup could be shown to the villagers this day. Elizabeth hoped it would foster a miracle or two.

They were greeted by Father Owen at the door of the chapel, who had raised his hands to bless them all when there was a canter of hoof-beats in the distance. The priest fell silent as all the company turned to look. It was a party of some size that approached, riding hard on the road from Carlisle.

Amaury's eyes lit and Elizabeth knew he recognized the black destrier in the lead. "It is the *Loup Argent*!" he informed the priest. "My brother comes!" The villagers truly stepped into the road for a glimpse of the mercenary of fearsome repute. Elizabeth craned her neck to see, hoping that Maximilian had not ridden this distance alone.

"Alys!" she cried when she spied her former companion, now Maximilian's lady wife. The women laughed as the horses came to a stamping halt. Maximilian dismounted and shook Amaury's hand, then embraced him with a laugh. Elizabeth was so occupied in kissing Alys' cheeks and exchanging glances over the size of her friend's belly that she did not heed the rest of the party.

Then a man cleared his throat loudly. "All this distance across this rustic land in winter and my nephew does not even greet me," he said, his tone teasing.

"Uncle!" Amaury cried and shook that man's hand heartily. They too embraced once the older knight was on the ground. "My lady, this is my uncle Raymond to whom I owe my training and my spurs."

"And this is the bride you have won," Raymond said, bowing low over Elizabeth's hand. "I could not have made a finer choice for you."

Elizabeth flushed at the older man's attentions. She liked his merry expression and his obvious fondness for Amaury. Amaury introduced his uncle and Maximilian to Oscar, who now was captain-of-arms and the other warriors that defended Beaupoint.

Raymond surveyed the tower of the keep with undisguised approval. "Now, there is a fortification," he said, turning again to Elizabeth. "Was your father's name Percival?"

Elizabeth was startled. "It was, sir."

He shook a finger at her. "I guessed as much. You will not believe but once, oh many years ago, Percival d'Acron and I rode against each other in the lists. We were young and nigh killed each other, so intent were we each upon the triumph. But once bruised a little, we became comrades over ale." He nodded approval. "He was a good man, a noble knight and a strong warrior." He clapped Amaury on the shoulder. "Truly, I could not have made a better match for you than Percival's daughter."

Amaury smiled, his eyes lighting with the heat that still made Elizabeth's heart flutter. "Nay, sir, you could not have done." He claimed her hand and placed it upon his elbow. "You must all join us at church."

"Indeed," Maximilian agreed, gesturing to the rest of his company. Elizabeth realized that the baron was in their company, and recalled his suggestion that he would visit at Easter. He was greeted with enthusiasm and many apologies for their oversight, and shook hands with the men, his manner gruff. There were four squires, along with several palfreys loaded with baggage. Elizabeth was delighted to see that Oliver was amongst the squires and she smiled at him, wishing him welcome. He flushed a little when he thanked her, then remained behind to tether the horses.

To Elizabeth that morning, the miracle of the mass was particularly potent. She knelt at the front of the company at Amaury's left and thought her heart might burst with the weight of all the blessings that came to them both.

When they were bidden to rise, Maximilian stepped forward. "There is another matter for this day," he said with authority and all remained in place. He gestured to the baron. "Our guest, Thomas de Montgomerie, Baron of Clyfford has tidings for the Lord de Beaupoint that you all should hear."

There was a rustle and a whisper in the company of villagers and even Uncle James appeared to be curious. The baron nodded to the priest, who stepped aside, then cleared his throat.

He unfurled a document that was hung with ribbons and seals. Elizabeth had a moment to conclude that this was the source of her uncle's interest, then the man began to read.

"Greetings to the Lord de Beaupoint, the sheriff of Carlisle, the lords of the Scottish marches, the King of Scotland and all others to whom this decree is of import. The post of the Lord of the Western Marches on the English side of the border has been vacant since the demise of Percival d'Acron, Lord de Beaupoint. We hereby decree that the post shall be filled by the new Lord de Beaupoint, Amaury d'Evroi."

Elizabeth was thrilled that Amaury should be granted this honor. Amaury looked to be astounded. Maximilian and Alys smiled with delight. Raymond beamed with such pride that it was clear the three of them had known. Even Uncle James nodded with satisfaction.

The chain of office was unfurled from a box, brought to the man by Oliver, and Amaury dropped to his knees to be granted its burden. He pledged himself to the service of the crown, was given the seal of office, then rose to his feet as the company applauded him with enthusiasm. Elizabeth kissed his cheek, seeing that he was nigh overwhelmed, and knew that not a word would fall from his lips shortly.

"I would ask a favor of you, brother," Maximilian said and Amaury turned to him in silent question. Maximilian gestured and Oliver stepped forward, showing an uncertainty that Elizabeth knew was not in his nature.

There must be something he desired very much from Amaury, Elizabeth thought, and then she guessed what it had to be.

"I propose to you that, though it is unconventional, you might take my squire, Oliver, into your custody and train him as a knight. I believe he would be a most honorable one."

"As do I," Amaury said, offering his hand. "Welcome, Oliver."

And the boy's face lit with his smile. He shook the hands of both Amaury and Maximilian, his delight undisguised.

"I shall grant you a task or six while Amaury is occupied," Raymond threatened playfully.

"And I shall excel at it, sir."

"I have no doubt of that," Amaury said with conviction. He raised a hand. "Come to the hall," he cried, inviting them all. "Our Easter feast is laid. Come to the hall and celebrate these merry tidings with us."

"That is not the only merry tiding," Alys whispered to Elizabeth as they walked together to the keep in the sunshine.

Elizabeth laughed. "It is too soon to speak of it," she said, knowing that many were listening to her words. She dropped her hand to her belly.

"You cannot tease them so, my lady," Amaury said, then raised his voice. "My lady will bear our first child this summer, God willing. I would appreciate all of your prayers."

There was a cheer just as the dogs raced toward them, circling through the company with delight. Amaury had been right that the small party crossing the weth had come from Robert de Maxwell to agree upon peace between them, and Amaury invited them to share the bounty of the midday meal.

"Now this," Raymond said, squinting up at the tower of Beaupoint. "*This* is a keep."

He sounded so much like Amaury when first he had arrived that Elizabeth could not keep from smiling. "I see where you learned to assess a holding," she said, leaning against her husband's arm.

Amaury indicated Maximilian who was craning his neck to survey the drop to the firth. He nodded approval and began to confer with Raymond. "Not just from my uncle,' he said. "I have been taught twice over." He placed the warmth of his hand over hers, his eyes glowing as he looked down at her. "But truly, the marvel of Beaupoint is the lady who has put her hand in mine."

Elizabeth had time to smile before Amaury bent and kissed her soundly, and she was well pleased with that.

ON THE NIGHT of the first new moon after the spring equinox, two women silently entered the circle of the Ninestang Ring near Kilderrick. A raven cried, then swooped low over the women, landing on one of the standing stones with a flutter of feathers.

They did not speak to each other as the blonde one unfastened her braid and set her hair free. She recited the charm she always used on these nights and her companion shivered with dread. The wind was damp with the promise of rain, the sky filled with low scuttling clouds, but that was not what troubled Ceara. She felt a portent of doom, though she was not the seer of they two.

Nyssa raised her hands to the sky in invocation, then lifted the witching stone to her eye to look through it. Ceara watched her with some trepidation, both wanting to know what Nyssa glimpsed in the future and wishing it would stay secret.

"A shadow comes," Nyssa whispered finally, her words husky. "It sweeps from the isles to the mainland, across the moor and thus to Kilderrick to demand its due. It casts darkness before it and leaves a wasteland in its wake." She shuddered and lowered the stone, turning to meet Ceara's gaze. "Your kin come for you."

Ceara had always known it might happen. She had hoped it would not.

"The day of reckoning is upon you," Nyssa whispered.

The raven, Dorcha, cried and took flight, a dark shadow silhouetted against the rushing clouds overhead. Nyssa shook her head, as if to apologize for her vision, then raised the witching stone to her eye again.

Ceara spun away, not wanting to hear more. She strode back toward the hut at Kilderrick with angry steps, her throat tight. Her kin would not find her complacent, that was for certain.

In fact, she might be the one to demand her due.

THE DRAGON & THE DAMSEL

BLOOD BROTHERS #3

A mercenary convinced that each man must see to his own survival first, Rafael has learned to savor the moment and its pleasures. He is interested solely in conquest and coin, not any promise of the future—until an alluring maiden challenges him, defying him to stake a claim. Rafael cannot resist Ceara with her flame-red hair and keen wits, but their cat-and-mouse game takes a dangerous turn when Ceara is stolen by her kin. Rafael cannot stand aside when the damsel's survival is at risk—though if she has stolen his shielded heart, she must never know of his weakness...

Ceara fled an arranged marriage, determined to wed for love or not at all. A horsewoman and huntress herself, she has encountered no man worthy of her affection—until she matches wits with Rafael, with his flashing eyes and seductive touch. She knows the handsome warrior seeks only one prize from her, but hopes to steal his heart. When she is captured and compelled to return to her betrothed, she is thrilled that Rafael lends chase. When he claims her as his own bride, Ceara dares to hope for more than a marriage of convenience.

But Rafael appears to be interested solely in conquest and passion, and their match becomes a battle of wills. Will Ceara be cast aside when her newfound spouse is offered the prize he desires above all else? Warrior and damsel, can these two wounded souls learn to surrender the truth of their hearts—before their union is shattered forever?

The Dragon & the Damsel

Coming September 2022!

Pre-order available at some portals.

~

ABOUT THE AUTHOR

Deborah Cooke sold her first book in 1992, a medieval romance called **Romance of the Rose** published under her pseudonym Claire Delacroix. Since then, she has published over fifty novels in a wide variety of sub-genres, including historical romance, contemporary romance, paranormal romance, fantasy romance, time-travel romance, women's fiction, paranormal young adult and fantasy with romantic elements. She has published under the names Claire Delacroix, Claire Cross and Deborah Cooke. **The Beauty**, part of her successful Bride Quest series of historical romances, was her first title to land on the *New York Times* List of Bestselling Books. Her books routinely appear on other bestseller lists and have won numerous awards. In 2009, she was the writer-in-residence at the Toronto Public Library, the first time the library has hosted a residency focused on the romance genre. In 2012, she was honored to receive the Romance Writers of America's Mentor of the Year Award.

Currently, she writes contemporary romances and paranormal romances under the name Deborah Cooke. She also writes medieval romances as Claire Delacroix. Deborah lives in Canada with her husband and family, as well as far too many unfinished knitting projects.

Visit her websites at:

http://Delacroix.net
http://DeborahCooke.com